the Black C

A No

"Our favorite sleuthing cat is back . . . This series really does have it all: bookstore, cats, likable, relatable characters, and a strong mystery."   —*Cozy Mystery Book Review*

"The story line keeps you guessing and there's even some romance thrown into the mix. The words flow from page to page with ease and make for a delightful way to spend an afternoon. This book is fun, fun, fun! Ali Brandon is a great voice in the cozy mystery world!"   —*Socrates' Book Reviews*

"Fun to read . . . The mystery was very good and the cat really added some interest to the story."   —*Fresh Fiction*

"Cat fanciers will love the role Hamlet plays in the investigation and his strong personality; others will enjoy Darla's investigation as she learns more about her new environ."
—*The Mystery Reader*

Double Booked for Death

"A fun mystery that kept me guessing to the end!"
—Rebecca M. Hale, *New York Times* bestselling author of *How to Tail a Cat*

"Clever . . . Bibliophiles, ailurophiles, and mystery fans will enjoy *Double Booked for Death*."
—*Richmond Times-Dispatch*

continued . . .

"A charming, cozy read, especially if cats are your cup of tea. Make sure the new Black Cat Bookshop series is on your bookshelf."

—Elaine Viets, national bestselling author of the Dead End-Job Mysteries

"Hamlet is a winner, and so is his owner. The literary references in this endearing debut will make readers smile, and the ensemble characters hold promise for fun titles to come."

—*Library Journal*

"An engaging new series . . . Definitely the start of something great."

—Sandra Balzo, award-winning author of the Main Street Mysteries

"[An] outstanding debut to a very promising new series . . . If you enjoy a cozy mystery, a clever cat, a bookstore setting, and smart, realistic characters you are sure to enjoy *Double Booked for Death*."

—MyShelf.com

"This first entry in the Black Cat Bookshop Mystery series is a harbinger of good books to follow." —*Mystery Scene*

"Those who like clever animals but draw the line at talking cats will feel right at home." —*Publishers Weekly*

"The first Black Cat Bookshop Mystery is an entertaining whodunit starring a brilliant feline (who does not speak in human tongues), a beleaguered new store owner and an ex-cop. The story line is fast-paced as Hamlet uncovers the clues that the two females working the case follow up on . . . Fans will enjoy." —*The Mystery Gazette*

WORDS WITH
FIENDS

ALI BRANDON

BERKLEY PRIME CRIME, NEW YORK

THE BERKLEY PUBLISHING GROUP
Published by the Penguin Group
Penguin Group (USA) LLC
375 Hudson Street, New York, New York 10014

USA • Canada • UK • Ireland • Australia • New Zealand • India • South Africa • China

penguin.com

A Penguin Random House Company

WORDS WITH FIENDS

A Berkley Prime Crime Book / published by arrangement with Tekno Books

For information, address: The Berkley Publishing Group,
a division of Penguin Group (USA) LLC,
375 Hudson Street, New York, New York 10014.

ISBN: 978-0-425-25236-9

PUBLISHING HISTORY
Berkley Prime Crime mass-market edition / November 2013

PRINTED IN THE UNITED STATES OF AMERICA

10 9 8 7 6 5 4 3 2 1

Interior text design by Kristin del Rosario.

To John Klingel and Jeffrey Philips,
two of my favorite writing buds.
Thanks for your support, guys.

ACKNOWLEDGMENTS

Thanks, as always, to the great folks at The Berkley Publishing Group and Tekno Books for all they do to make me look good. Hugs to my awesome writing friends who are unstinting in their support, including Patrick, Al, Steve, and Becky. And a special flick of the whiskers to those wonderful bloggers who kindly host me on occasion, especially Yvonne and Melissa and Dru Ann. They do all the hard work; Hamlet and I get all the glory. Finally, thanks to my hubby, Gerry, who doesn't complain too much when I'm squirreled away for hours in my office. Love ya!

ONE

"HEY, I'M NOT AFRAID TO SAY IT. THE IRRITATING BROAD
deserved to die."

The contentious words came from the second level of
Pettistone's Fine Books, drifting down the staircase to the
main floor where owner Darla Pettistone was working
the cash register. Despite being used to overhearing declara-
tions like this, the venom in these particular words made
her pause.

And then the strident nasal voice continued, "I just wish
she'd suffered a bit more at the end, know what I mean? If
I could kill her again, I'd do it in a heartbeat."

"O.M.G!"

The text-speak gasp at this last pronouncement came, not
from upstairs again, but from the twentysomething brunette
whose selection of paperback romances Darla had been in
the process of ringing up. The girl stared in alarm at the
stairway, then whipped her gaze back to Darla and stage
whispered, "Did you hear that? Some guy upstairs just

confessed to murder! Shouldn't you, like, call the cops or something?"

"Don't worry"—Darla paused and looked at the girl's credit card again—"Mandy. He didn't kill anyone."

"Yeah, but, but he said—"

"I promise, no murders," Darla cut her short, giving the girl a reassuring smile. "It's just the book club meeting. And that guy you're hearing tends to get a bit melodramatic at times."

Mandy gave her a sudden look of wide-eyed comprehension. "Oh," she exclaimed, drawing out the single syllable while embarrassed color darkened her already ruddy features. "Someone was killed in a book."

"Yes," another voice broke in, "and I believe this week's someone is Tess Durbeyfield, technically a legal execution by means of the hangman's rope. Are you familiar with the work?"

The explanation and question both came from Professor James T. James, Darla's store manager and retired college-level instructor of nineteenth-century literature. Setting down on the counter the pint-sized HEPA vacuum he'd been using to dust the store's small collection of rare and first edition books, he fixed Mandy with an expectant look.

Apparently realizing a response was required of her, but coming up blank, Mandy shrugged and shook her head.

Darla heard her manager's suppressed sigh—the familiar one that bemoaned the state of today's youth when it came to literature in general, and the classics in particular. Not willing to concede defeat yet, however, he stroked his short gray beard, gave a tug at his vest, and deigned to clarify, "*Tess of the d'Urbervilles.*"

A head shake from Mandy.

"Thomas Hardy's seminal look at sexual mores during the late Victorian era."

Another head shake.

"Made into a tolerably viewable film in the late 1970s."

"Sorry," Mandy admitted in a chipper voice. Then, indicating the stack of slim books she was purchasing, she looked to Darla. "Hey, you should know that all I read are contemporaries. I'm not into historical romance."

Darla suppressed a smile at the sudden mental image the girl's words conjured . . . that of the classic novel's tragic main characters posed half-naked on the cover in a traditional romance clinch. She promptly shook her head to dispel the image, the gesture sending her long auburn braid bouncing between her shoulder blades. She'd probably sell quite a few more copies with cover art like that, instead of the dour illustrations that usually graced the paperback classics she stocked. In fact, she'd recently heard rumors that a publishing company planned to put out X-rated versions of certain well-known novels. Assuming their venture was successful, high school English classes would never be the same!

She only hoped that James was unaware of the pending literary sacrilege. He was clearly in enough pain for the moment, a weary look having crossed his mahogany-hued features at the girl's reply. Still, he hit all the right customer service notes as he replied, "I quite understand. Perhaps next time you are in, however, you might wish to try something a bit out of your usual comfort zone. Unlike much of the prose of that era, *Tess of the d'Urbervilles* is quite accessible to modern readers."

"Yeah, but now I already know that this Tess girl dies," she protested. "Talk about a major spoiler. No way do I want to read it now."

"Ah, good point. *Mea culpa*." When she gave James another confused look, he translated the Latin to a carefully enunciated, "My bad."

"Hey, it's all good." Smiling again, Mandy loaded her purchases into one of the reusable Pettistone's logo bags that Darla had started handing out to her repeat customers, and then struggled into her stylish red wool coat. The color was an unfortunate choice, given her overly rosy complexion, but its practical ankle length was a must for the snowy February weather.

"Thanks, Darla. Bye, Hamlet," Mandy added with a wave at the oversized black cat lounging on the nearby bestseller table. "Maybe you'll be friendlier next time I stop in."

Hamlet opened a single emerald eye at the mention of his name. He was the official cat of Pettistone's Fine Books and had held that role for almost a decade, ever since kittenhood. When Darla had unexpectedly inherited from her late Great-Aunt Dee this converted three-story Brooklyn brownstone—home to both the quirky independent bookstore and two modest apartments, one she lived in herself, and one she rented out—it had come complete with the elderly woman's ornery feline, who ruled the place with a flick of his long black whiskers.

Of the two bequests, Hamlet had definitely been the greater challenge.

Not content to snooze picturesquely in a basket for customers to ooh and aah over, Hamlet instead stalked the shop's maze-like collection of shelving like a scaled-down panther. He considered the shop his personal domain where only Dee—and, to a lesser degree, James—was allowed to be the boss of him. Darla had tried to take on her great-aunt's role, blithely assuming that he'd somehow sense the familial connection. Unfortunately, the only bloodline the stubborn feline recognized was the product of his unsheathed claws. As a result, she and Hamlet had gotten off on the wrong foot—or was it paw?—in the beginning; still, they'd since managed to forge a bond that might almost be termed friendship.

As the departing girl cooed in his direction, Hamlet momentarily raised his inky head from his oversized paws to give the customer a cool green look before subsiding back into regulation nap mode. Darla waited until she heard the string of small bells dangling from the shop door jingle in accompaniment to the girl's exit, then turned a concerned look on James. Her uneasiness, however, had nothing to do with her young customer's blasé approach to literature.

"James, I'm worried about Hamlet. I know it's been a few months since the, er, incident"—she stumbled only slightly over the euphemism for a frightening experience she and Hamlet had survived—"and we all thought he was back to his normal self, but something happened last weekend. I was cleaning out a closet in my apartment, and somehow Hamlet managed to get himself closed inside when I was finished. He couldn't have been in there for more than a couple of minutes, but he was yowling like he was scared to death!"

Darla winced a little at the memory. Actually, the cat had sounded like someone was pulling out clumps of his fur with pliers. She'd done the cat burrito thing with him as the experts recommended, bundling him tight in a towel, and holding him until he had settled down. But it had been an unnerving experience for them both.

"He calmed down pretty quickly," she went on, "but maybe you've noticed that he hasn't been the same the past few days. He hasn't chased a single customer out of the store, or clawed open someone's shopping bag when they weren't looking. I wonder if I should take him back to the veterinarian for another exam."

She deliberately lowered her voice at that last, since Hamlet seemed to understand most words related to bad things like the vet's office. And, to be fair, such visits were not that much more pleasant for Darla. They required her donning oven mitts against his razor-sharp claws, and employing sardines as a bribe in order to cajole the stubborn feline into his carrier . . . a process that usually took a good hour. Still, after all that had happened, she was willing to make the sacrifice any number of times to ensure Hamlet's well-being.

She could hardly do less, given that Hamlet had risked more than one of his feline lives in order to save hers.

James nodded his gray head.

"Perhaps you are right. When you brought him in for a follow-up appointment right before the holidays, you said Dr. Birmingham confirmed that, physically, Hamlet has recovered from all his injuries. Like any other crime victim, he simply needs peace and a bit of time to regain his previous sense of security. But this behavior you mention is a bit worrying. Perhaps you might check with her to see if she can recommend an animal psychologist to treat him."

An animal psychologist? Kitty therapy?

Darla gave the man a sharp look, certain that the pragmatic ex-professor must be indulging his dry sense of humor. But his expression was serious, so she mulled it over. "That might not be a bad idea," she conceded. "Maybe find a cat whisperer who makes house calls."

"And you might consider something similar for yourself," James added, his stern expression sharpening. "Yes, I know that you claim you are just fine after all that happened," he cut her short when she opened her mouth to protest, "what with those self-defense lessons you have been taking, but I would beg to differ. Besides, studies have shown that—"

What those studies proved, Darla was spared learning, as more raised voices and the sound of milling footsteps on the stairs indicated that the book club meeting was breaking up. Darla was finally used to this new routine, given that the club previously was known as the Friday Afternoon Book Club. But with various other extracurricular activities beckoning, the group had voted at the beginning of the year to move their meetings to Thursdays. This had worked out well for Darla, too. She had things to do on Friday nights, and the members were known on occasion to prolong their discussion well after their official 6 p.m. end time.

Today, however, they'd ended on time. Most of the eleven members in attendance had already left behind the Thomas Hardy debate for more interesting current topics, such as the outcome of a popular reality television show. Chatting brightly, they either headed for the door or else remained behind to browse the shop.

Dropping his impromptu counselor role for that of store manager, James followed after the browsers while Hamlet prudently slipped off the table and headed for quieter regions. Darla held down the register. She noted that, unlike the others, the last two club members descending the stairs were apparently still stuck in the nineteenth century.

"Argue all you want; you can't change my mind. Tess was a blithering fool."

The speaker was the same man who, a few minutes before, had wished that literary heroine a repeat of her unpleasant death. *Mark Poole,* Darla thought with a sigh as, with tattered paperback copy of the book in question tucked under one arm, the man clomped down the stairs. Every group had its own version of a Mark, she knew. Unfortunately, this one was more Mark-like than most. And today, he seemed particularly wound up.

"Once the little twit offed Alec," he proclaimed, "she should have hightailed it to America instead of running back to her wimp of a husband, Angel. If she had, she might have lived. But, nooo, she had to be all noble, and all she got for it was—"

He broke off as he reached the bottom of the stairs; then, turning to the woman behind him, he mimed the universal jerking-upward-on-a-rope gesture to indicate hanging. And then, in case no one had gotten the message, he punctuated that bit of pantomime by letting his tongue loll from his mouth.

The woman who was the recipient of these amateur theatrics was Martha Washington, the book club's president and equally ardent participant in the group. A slender, mixed-race woman in her late thirties—*No relation to the late president's wife,* she always assured people upon first meeting—she wore her multihued hair in dreads that dangled past her shoulders.

Today, the cacophony of red, blond, and black locks seemed to fairly bristle with indignation. Her tone, however, was as cool as Hamlet's gaze as she countered in precise British tones, "Mark, I'm telling you this in the nicest way possible . . . you are a bloody idiot."

Darla suppressed a smile at the overheard exchange, reflecting how even the snarkiest comment sounded sophisticated when spoken in a clipped English accent. The woman's enunciation, however, was no affectation. Martha had previously explained to Darla that her father was a career military man from Georgia who had been stationed for a time in Great Britain, where he had met and married Martha's English mother. So while Martha's everyday accent was straight out of a Masterpiece Theatre special, she could occasionally turn on a Good-Ol'-Girl Deep South accent—a honeyed drawl far thicker than Darla's native East Texas twang—when the situation warranted.

But this particular lecture on English literature apparently required the BBC-esque approach. While Mark sputtered, Martha continued, "As a man, you have little understanding of the societal pressures levied upon women throughout the ages. A woman of Tess's class lived in a virtual prison . . . bound by the law, the Church, and society as a whole. Nobly accepting one's fate rather than flailing against it can sometimes seem the better choice, no matter the ultimate outcome."

"Yeah, well, but—"

Martha held up a hand, cutting short whatever argument he had, and then pleasantly asked, "May I finish? Of course, Tess had been wronged most terribly from the very beginning of the story: first by her lover, Alec, and then by her husband, Angel. Remember that at the end, though, she also committed the ultimate crime—she murdered a man in cold blood. Her personal code of honor required that she accept responsibility for her actions and, ultimately, accept punishment. That's where the nobility comes in. Now, you were saying?"

"I was saying, I disagree." Mark used a forefinger to shove his slipping glasses higher on his nose. As he reached the counter, he turned his attention to Darla. As usual, a whiff of stale cigarette smoke clung to his clothing. "You're on my side, aren't you, Darla?" he whined, his pale blue eyes so magnified by the lenses of his glasses that he resembled an anime character. "You don't just sit there and take it. You fight back. You know, like what Master Tomlinson always says."

Master Tom Tomlinson was the martial arts instructor who owned a nearby dojo where Darla had been taking lessons a couple of times a week over the past few months. Founder of a fighting style that blended elements of both judo and karate, Tomlinson had won numerous championships in his multi-decade career and had been a contemporary of Bruce Lee. Now pushing seventy, he'd long since left behind professional fighting to nurture new generations in his small gym. His students ran the gamut from grade schoolers to burly college-aged black belts to people like her . . . adults hoping to gain basic self-defense skills in addition to a physical fitness regimen.

And, unfortunately, they also included Mark.

Now, as Mark stared at her expectantly, Darla obediently echoed the mantra chorused by all of Master Tomlinson's students at the start of every class. *"Run when you can, fight if you must, never give up, and never let injustice go unpunished,"* she said with a smile. "And that's pretty good advice. But I'm not sure that it applies to *Tess of the d'Urbervilles*. Besides, since I'm not a member of your book club, I'll let you and Martha duke this one out yourselves."

"Fine, take her side," was Mark's aggrieved retort as he deliberately overlooked her attempt at neutrality. "You women are all alike, ganging up on men just to do some sort of female solidarity thing. You won't even admit I might possibly be right."

"Mark, you know that great literature—like beauty—is in the eye of the beholder," Darla countered in as mild a tone as she could muster. "I'm not about to tell either of you that you're wrong. Now, do you want to pay for your copy of *To Kill a Mockingbird* before you go, so you can get a jump on the next meeting, or will you come back for it this weekend?"

"I'll pay now."

His thin lips twisted in a sulky line, he snatched one of the copies of *Mockingbird* that Darla had special-ordered for the book club and slapped down a credit card on the counter. Darla took it and swiped it, even as she exchanged glances with Martha. The woman gave her a sympathetic look in return but made no comment beyond a barely audible tsking.

"Here you go," Darla said as she finished the transaction and slipped both book and receipt into the reusable bag Mark proffered. Then, trying to bring back a bit of customer service serenity to the situation, she asked, "So, have you read this one before, or are you coming to it fresh for the book club?"

"I, uh, always meant to read it, but I never seemed to have the time before now," he confessed. His accompanying guilty look was the same she'd seen on numerous customers' faces as they admitted to never having cracked open the cover of a particular classic.

Darla gave him a sympathetic nod.

"I know exactly what you mean. There are so many books out there I know I should have read years ago but didn't, that I always feel a bit guilty coming clean when someone asks. That's why I think it's so great that the Thursday Afternoon Book Club is doing this whole retro thing with reading the classics. And I have a feeling you'll like this one for the very reasons you didn't appreciate our friend Tess."

"Yeah, maybe so," he agreed, brightening a bit as he tucked that maligned paperback into the bag with his brand-new purchase. "Anyhow, see you at the dojo tomorrow night. You and Robert should stay late and watch my sparring class." Robert was Robert Gilmore, an eighteen-year-old goth kid with a love for books who'd been working at the store for the past few months. He and Darla had signed up for the beginner's martial arts class together. Mark was at a more advanced level.

"I'll think about it. You know, just for fun, I think I'm going to reread *Tess* myself and see how it compares to when I read it in school."

She gave Mark a polite smile and then turned to ring up Martha, who had taken her own copy of Harper Lee's novel from the stack and stood with credit card in hand.

Glancing over her shoulder to make sure that Mark was headed toward the door, Martha remarked in a wry tone, "Brava, Darla. You handled our resident complainer like a champ. One minute he's foaming at the mouth, and the next he's wagging his tail like a little puppy. You're not really going to reread *Tess of the d'Urbervilles*, are you?"

"Actually, I might," Darla replied with a grin, taking one of the last copies off the counter and sticking it beneath the register next to her purse. "And as far as diplomacy, I guess James is rubbing off on me. A few months ago, I might have smacked Mark over the head with the darned book."

As Martha chuckled, Darla added, "But you're pretty darned diplomatic, too. We could hear Mark spouting off all the way down here a while ago. I keep wondering why the rest of you book club members just don't tell him to take a hike."

"Ah, we're used to him. In fact, I think the other members are always secretly disappointed if a meeting goes by without Mark launching into one of his silly tirades. It's always so entertaining to watch . . . though I suppose that's very bad of us to enjoy his little temper fits. And the way he acts sometimes does worry me a bit, like he's off his meds or something."

Then, before Darla could query her as to whether she was being literal about medications, Martha added, "Where did James get off to? As soon as his shift is over, we're supposed to meet for an early supper over at Thai Me Up."

Darla stared at her in pleased surprise. "Meet for supper? You mean, as in a date?"

She knew that Martha was unattached. In the few months that she'd known James, she had never heard him mention any sort of personal relationship and so assumed there was no woman currently in his life. To be sure, the ex-professor had to be almost thirty years Martha's senior; still, Darla had no trouble picturing the pair as a couple.

James, however, apparently had overheard her and Martha's exchange and came forward, determined to set the record straight. Stepping out from behind a nearby bookshelf and accompanied by two elderly female book club members who trailed him like groupies, the ex-professor paused at the counter.

"Darla, what I proposed to Ms. Washington was simply a few hours of fellowship between two people with a mutual interest in Asian cuisine and fine literature. Of course, since I put forth the invitation, etiquette dictates that our meal be on my dime, so to speak."

"Uh, huh," was Darla's unconvinced reply while Martha, standing to one side of him now, shook her head and mouthed, *Yeah, right.*

James gave Darla the same quelling look that he had likely turned upon any number of impertinent undergraduates over the years; then, with an apologetic look for the restless ladies queued up behind him, he addressed Martha.

"My shift here ends in another fourteen minutes. If you care to wait, I will be happy to escort you to the restaurant, unless you prefer to meet me there?"

"Oh, I'll wait," was Martha's swift reply.

James responded with a regal nod and then gestured for his entourage to follow him toward the new releases table. Darla exchanged another glance with Martha, who gave her a sly grin and said, "Take my word, it's a date."

Darla chuckled and finished ringing up the woman's purchase. She was already looking forward to the book club's next meeting in two weeks, when she fully intended to pump Martha for a few juicy details. She only hoped that Martha would be a willing participant in the figurative kiss-and-tell. She could guarantee that James wouldn't breathe a word about the evening out, no matter how well—or how poorly— things went.

Exactly fourteen minutes later, James had rung up the remaining book club members' purchases, retrieved his overcoat from the storeroom upstairs, and was looking at his watch.

"My shift is over," he pointed out unnecessarily, "and Robert is not yet here."

Which was a bit unusual, since Robert lived in the garden apartment of the brownstone next door. The place was owned by the Plinskis, an elderly brother and sister who also ran Bygone Days Antiques out of the same building. Darla was surprised and more than a little concerned when James pointed out that the usually dependable youth had not yet arrived for his late afternoon shift. Just as with Hamlet, she and Robert had initially gotten off on the wrong foot, but once hired—and minus his various piercings and goth makeup—Robert had proved himself a dedicated if unconventional employee.

"Go on, James," she told him. "I can handle things myself for a while. And if Robert isn't here in a few minutes, I'll go hunt him down."

"If you are quite certain," James agreed, frowning slightly, "though I am sure Martha will understand if we have to delay our dinner until he shows up."

Darla glanced in the direction of the book club president,

who had settled in one of the small armchairs scattered throughout the store and was touching up her lipstick in preparation for the non-date. Then she shook her head. "I can handle things alone, I promise. Besides, you deserve a fun evening out."

"Very well, if you insist. But telephone me if our young employee does not arrive within a reasonable period of—"

The jangle of bells at the store's front door abruptly interrupted James's words and heralded the arrival of the tardy Robert. Since he lived a mere twenty steps away, the youth never bothered with a coat or gloves, no matter how cold it was out. Slapping his palms together to warm them, he made his usual beeline to Hamlet.

The feline roused himself momentarily—he and Robert had bonded on their first meeting—and lifted a halfhearted paw to do their ritual fist-bump greeting. Robert lightly touched his knuckles to the cat's oversized paw while giving him a concerned look.

"Not feeling good, little buddy?" he asked in a soft tone, adding a gentle chin rub for good measure. He, too, had noticed the change in Hamlet's demeanor over the past few days and had voiced his concern to Darla on several occasions.

Then, noticing two adults staring at him in disapproval, Robert turned his attention to his boss.

"Sorry I'm, like, late, but I was at Ms. Jake's place," he explained in a rush. Eyes wide, he added with a grin, "You're not gonna believe who just hired her as a private investigator!"

‖ **TWO**

"WHOEVER JAKE IS WORKING FOR ISN'T IMPORTANT," DARLA replied, shaking her head in dismay. "The question is, what were you doing in her apartment? You know better than to hang out there during business hours."

Jake was Jacqueline Martelli, ex-cop and now private investigator who rented the garden apartment below the bookstore. Darla had inherited Jake as a tenant from her great-aunt, much like she'd inherited Hamlet. Except Jake paid rent, if at the greatly reduced rate that had been locked in with Great Aunt Dee long ago. But the newly minted PI also served as unofficial security for the building, so Darla considered it a fair trade-off. Besides, she and Jake had become fast friends these past few months.

Robert, meanwhile, assumed a defensive tone.

"Hey, it wasn't my fault. I was about to come to work, and then Ms. Plinski called me. She said she just baked a pumpkin pie and wanted me to take it to Ms. Jake. I was just going to, you know, hand it to her and then head up to the store, but she invited me inside." He brightened and added, "And that's when I saw who her client was."

"Do you intend to reveal that person's identity to the rest of us?" James inquired with a stern look, helping Martha with her coat as she joined them at the register before slipping into his. "Or will you leave us to wildly speculate for the remainder of the evening?"

Robert grinned again, not at all cowed by the man's severe demeanor. Darla found herself suppressing an answering smile as she surveyed her two employees. Despite their many differences—irreverent, teenaged white goth kid versus staid, retirement-aged black former professor—the pair got along surprisingly well.

Not that Robert wasn't above yanking James's chain every so often. The most egregious yank, in Darla's opinion, was Robert's tongue-in-cheek homage to James's unofficial personal uniform. Since James favored sober sweater-vests that hearkened back to his college teaching days, Robert had taken to wearing a vest, too, though his flamboyant choices were less the product of academia and more the spawn of thrift stores. Today's offering had a distinctly mod vibe, with its screaming pattern of oversized paisley that, in most fashion circles, would evoke cries of horror. But worn over Robert's own personal uniform of black jeans and black T-shirts, the vest seemed right at home.

"Any guesses? He's someone you've heard about," Robert offered, still grinning.

Darla gave him another disapproving look, though she had to admit that Robert's deliberate air of mystery had tweaked her own curiosity.

"You know Jake can't reveal her clients' business to anyone else. You really shouldn't be sharing confidential information."

"Yeah, but telling you his name isn't, you know, confidential. He saw me there. Heck, he even talked to me. That's why I'm late."

Which technically voided the whole confidentiality issue, at least as far as his identity, Darla conceded. Feeling vaguely guilty at her interest, she tried to think of people recently in the local news who might have some reason to hire a private investigator. "Okay, I'll bite. What about that local councilman whose father got into a fistfight with him on the street the other day?"

"Nope."

"The newswoman who did the pill mill exposé last week?"

"Nope. I told you, it was a man. Try again."

But when James raised a genteelly menacing brow, Robert threw up his hands in mock surrender and exclaimed, "Fine, you dragged it out of me. Ms. Jake's new client is Alex Putin."

"Alex Putin?"

Darla's curiosity promptly evaporated, replaced by concern. "You mean *the* Alex Putin? As in the czar-father of local construction? The same crook you used to do odd jobs for?"

"Hey, Alex isn't a crook. He's a good guy," the youth protested. "He wanted to know how I was doing. He said if I needed, you know, money or anything, he'd be happy to give me a loan."

"Most likely at a usurious rate of interest," was James's quelling response, earning a nod of agreement from Martha.

Darla couldn't help but agree. She was aware that Robert sometimes made a little extra money by doing grunt labor on various construction sites run by Putin, and she'd always worried that the youth might unwittingly find trouble that way. To be fair, however, all she knew about the Russian immigrant's supposed doings—shady deals, bribery, cutting corners on construction safety—was what was whispered about in the neighborhood. Even so, what was Jake, an ex-cop, thinking, working for someone like that?

Robert, however, continued to defend the man. "Hey, he's

an independent businessperson, just like you, Ms. Pettistone. And he keeps lots of people working. He's even helping sponsor that martial arts tournament that Master Tomlinson is putting on next weekend. You know, giving back to the community, and all that."

"Okay, you win. I'll try not to judge," Darla said with some reluctance, holding up her hands in mock surrender. "You're old enough to choose your own friends, and Jake's clients aren't any of my business."

Then, her earlier curiosity returning, she added, "You know, I've heard all sorts of rumors about the man, but I've never seen him. I've always wondered what a real live Russian gangster looks like."

"He's not a gangster," Robert protested. "But he was wrapping things up with Ms. Jake when I left, so maybe you can see him leaving if you look out the window."

Darla needed no further encouragement.

She rushed to the shop's front door to peer past the gilded lettering that, seen from the outside, read in neat script, *Pettistone's Fine Books*. Her breath on the cold glass momentarily fogged the view of the street, however, so that she had to wipe the window clear again with her sweater sleeve. Now, she had a glimpse of an expensive black wool overcoat as the man wrapped inside it—presumably Alex Putin—stepped into the passenger seat of an oversized midnight blue Mercedes parked illegally at the curb.

As Darla watched in disappointment, he pulled the door closed after him, the vehicle's tinted windows effectively blocking any view of the occupant. Feathery exhaust from the vehicle (a sleeker and far newer version of the ten-year-old Mercedes that Darla's great-aunt had left her) spread in broad white plumes before the car's driver smoothly pulled into traffic.

"Darn it all, I missed him." *Curiosity killed the cat,* she reminded herself with a glance at Hamlet. As if reading her mind, the feline opened one eye again and flicked an ear in what she fancied was a cautionary gesture. She and Hamlet had both had their share of bad guys lately, so it was probably just as well that she remained in the dark about the man.

For his part, James merely snorted.

"I believe the appropriate rejoinder is, better luck next time. Now, excuse us, but Ms. Washington and I are overdue to dinner."

"Yeah, and I'll, like, get to work," Robert added, giving Hamlet another pat before heading upstairs to the stockroom.

Darla, meanwhile, sent James an apologetic look. "Sorry for the delay. But remember, you can stay out late tonight since you'll be coming in late tomorrow. Robert and I will be cutting out early so we can go to the dojo for our Friday night lesson."

"Ah, yes, your weekly excuse to physically pummel similarly inclined adults without fear of legal ramification," was his wry reply, though Darla knew he approved of her self-defense training, so she didn't take offense. He added, "Fear not, I should be quite refreshed by the time I arrive at noon tomorrow, and more than able to handle working until closing time on my own."

"Don't worry, Darla, I'll try not to wear him out tonight," Martha interjected, though the bawdy wink that punctuated that remark was meant strictly for James.

What Darla could only describe as a dumbfounded look flashed across his face before the former professor sternly countered, "I assure you, I am well able to withstand the rigors of dinner and conversation. Now, shall we be on our way?"

Darla managed to keep a straight face until the store door had closed behind the pair with a jangle of bells. Then she burst into giggles loud enough to rouse Hamlet from the nap he'd just resumed.

"Sorry, Hammy," she told him, doing her best to stifle her humor. "I'm just not used to thinking of anyone wearing out"—she gave the last two words finger quotes—"James. You know what I mean?"

The feline obviously did, for he shot her a cold green look that bore an uncanny resemblance to her manager's stern glare. She gave an exaggerated sigh. "Okay, sorry. No more jokes at James's expense. Satisfied?"

Apparently, he was. He settled back to sleep, reminding Darla that she still needed to make that phone call to the veterinarian. She'd do that first, during business hours. And then, as soon as she'd closed the store for the night, she was going to pay a casual visit to Jake and—the heck with confidentiality—find out what was up with Jake's latest client.

"LOOK WHAT I FOUND, A PINT OF VANILLA ICE CREAM," DARLA DECLARED a couple of hours later as she slipped through Jake's front door. She shrugged out of the knee-length, bright yellow parka that she'd tossed on—Texas born and bred that she was, she wasn't enjoying the cold New York weather one bit, even if it was but a thirty-second walk to Jake's place— and proffered the bag that held said frozen confection. "Know anyone with a spare pumpkin pie?"

Jake straightened in her oversized leather chair, the same sort of office chair that some fictional Golden-era detective might have used. Closing her laptop, she shoved back from the 1950s chrome dinette table that served as her work desk and gestured Darla inside the apartment.

"Sorry, I've been putting in a little OT," she said, indicating the pile of documents and photos that surrounded her computer. "I guess it's time to call it a day."

Rising from the chair, she yawned and shrugged the kinks out of her shoulders. Today, the ex-cop wore a robin's-egg blue turtleneck over black jeans, while her mop of curly black hair was pulled back into a fashionably messy bun through which she'd shoved a No. 2 yellow pencil. Darla had noticed too late that her own green sweater, combined with her yellow coat, made her look like something out of a John Deere catalog—but on the bright side, she'd likely be spared a comment from Jake in that vein, since she suspected that her New Jersey-born friend had never seen one of the iconic green-and-yellow-painted tractors.

Not that Jake's look wasn't worthy of a little tweak, Darla thought with an inner grin. Between the bun and the reading glasses, and surrounded as she was by paperwork, Jake resembled nothing so much as a middle-aged schoolteacher. The resemblance, however, was superficial. Darla knew that should the PI whip off the glasses, let down the bun, and toss on her familiar black leather duster, Jake was capable of a kick-butt Diana-Prince-to-Wonder-Woman transformation.

Eyeing Darla's bag with interest, Jake added with a tired smile, "Pumpkin pie, eh? You're either psychic, or you've been talking to Robert."

"The latter. Feel like indulging?"

"I'm considering it. I haven't eaten dinner yet. You?"

Darla shook her head and reached into the sack, pulling out a trifolded piece of paper. "Nope, but I've got a coupon for that new tapas place up the street. How about I order us in a few appetizers, and then we dig into the pie and ice cream for our entrée?"

"Sounds like a plan. You call, and I'll put the pie in the oven to warm up."

"Sure," Darla agreed as she pulled her phone from her pocket. "And then—"

Her reply was interrupted by a series of electronic tones that sounded like a small xylophone. Jake, who had started toward the kitchen, paused and looked back at her. "Cute. New ring tone?"

"No, just means it's my turn to play. Hang on."

Squinting at the screen of her smart phone, Darla thought a moment and then swiped a few letters across the screen. Satisfied, and with a little mental fist pump—*fifty-one points!*—she hit "yes." Another xylophone sound played, and then she frowned. "Crud, now I've got all vowels, except for a stupid L."

"Don't tell me," Jake said with a wry grin. "You're playing that word game, the one like Scrabble that got that Baldwin actor thrown off an airplane."

"No—maybe—okay, so I am. But don't worry, I'm not hooked. *I* can quit anytime."

"Yeah, yeah, I'm sure that's what he said, too." Jake's grin broadened. "But I have to say, I don't get it. Making words sounds like a pretty boring way to kill time."

Darla shook her head.

"If you're just playing one game, then maybe, but not the way most people play. You can have multiple games going simultaneously, so it's always your turn somewhere. And you can accept random invitations from people you don't know, which can be interesting, because you can chat at the same time you're playing." She paused and smiled. "I might even be playing with Mr. Baldwin, himself, and not know it, since you can use a fake name. But the best part is that since it's all one-on-one, if you have a bad round with one person, you can still be kicking butt with someone else."

"I don't know, it sounds like you're hooked to me," Jake replied. Then, assuming a "Mother Confessor" attitude with folded hands and pious tone, she went on, "So, my child, just how many different *friends* are you playing with right now?"

"Eleven," Darla mumbled, realizing she'd momentarily gone into zealot mode over defending the game, and now feeling like she'd just stood up at a twelve-step meeting to confess. Then, rallying, she added, "But that's nothing. Heck, Martha told me she usually has twenty games going at a time. Besides, it's educational, unlike that little jewel game that some people play," she finished with a triumphant glance at her friend.

Jake dropped the abbess routine and shot her a mock-offended look.

"I'll have you know that my little jewel game promotes hand-eye coordination, which is important for someone of my advanced age. And it also helps distract me from smoking, so no apologies here. Now, why don't you see if you can tear yourself away from your game long enough to order us some food."

Half an hour later, the laptop and paperwork had been shoved aside in favor of several small side dishes ranging from calamari to chorizo, all neatly arranged in their to-go containers atop the chrome table. Darla had claimed one of the two small tweed wing chairs that Jake reserved for client seating. In just a few minutes, the pair made significant headway into their impromptu meal, complemented by two frosty mugs of light ale Jake had scavenged from her usually empty refrigerator.

"Ice cream is one thing, but I'm not much on cold beer in the winter," Darla said between sips. "But I have to say I can't think of anything better to wash this all down with."

Then, figuring that this was as good a time as any to pump her friend for info, Darla licked a bit of pepper sauce from her thumb and casually added, "So, I hear that Alex Putin is your latest client."

"That new employee of yours sure has a big yap on him," Jake declared through a bite of paella, though she tempered the criticism with a smile. Darla knew Jake had a soft spot for the goth teen. "Yes, Mr. Putin gave me a retainer. And, no, I can't tell you about the case."

"Are you sure you can't be bribed?" Darla snatched up the last calamari ring and waved it enticingly before her friend.

Jake shook her head. "You know the rules, kid. Confidentiality is the cornerstone of my business."

"Nice saying. Sounds like something you should stick on your business card."

"Actually, it's written on the banner on my website," the older woman replied, her expression pious.

Darla rolled her eyes and popped the would-be bribe into her own mouth. Not that she didn't agree with Jake in principle; it was just frustrating not to be able to tap into that source of gossip. Then she sobered.

"Jake, I understand the whole discretion thing, but I can't help but be worried, all the same. I know it's none of my business, but do you think someone like you—I mean, an ex-police officer—should be associating with a crook like Alex Putin?"

"You're right, kid . . . it's none of your business," Jake shot back, her tone sharp enough that Darla blinked.

Then, apparently realizing that her reaction had been over the top, the PI sat back in her leather chair and sighed.

"Sorry, I didn't mean it to come out like that. I was second-guessing the situation, myself, the whole time I was talking to him. Believe me, I don't want to become one of those cliché private eyes who takes on anyone as a client so long as they can write a check that doesn't bounce. But business has been a little slow the past few weeks, and I've got bills to pay," she said with a meaningful gesture around the apartment.

Darla nodded, glad to brush aside her own momentarily bruised feelings to focus on concern for her friend. "Don't worry, I understand. And if you ever need an extension on the rent, don't hesitate to ask."

"Thanks, kid, but I'll scrape by. Bottom line, though, I'm not about to turn down any halfway decent clients."

She paused and held up a warning hand. "And before you start lecturing again, remember what Reese told you the last time the guy's name came up."

Reese was Detective Fiorello Reese, a former colleague of Jake whose acquaintance Darla had first made when he'd worked security at an afterhours autographing event at her store the previous year. He remained Jake's good friend, though his relationship with Darla was one she was still trying to figure out. It didn't help that Jake subtly continued trying to throw the two of them together, no matter that they weren't exactly a Match.com made in heaven . . . at least, not in Darla's opinion.

"Calling Alex a crook is going too far," Jake went on. "As far as the police are concerned, he's a legitimate businessman. His name may have been mentioned a time or two regarding some questionable deals, but he's never been arrested for anything, let alone been convicted. Bottom line, I don't have any problem letting him hire me."

"Alex?" Darla raised a brow in her best James imitation. "A bit informal, aren't we?"

"Don't push it, kid."

"Okay, okay, but at least tell me why he needs a private detective. Is his wife cheating on him? Or maybe someone's blackmailing him, and he's afraid to go to the police? Or—"

"Enough. You can guess all you like, but I'm not telling you squat. So behave yourself if you want some of Mary Ann's pie. Speaking of which," she added as a small *ding* sounded from the kitchen, "I think it's ready!"

Leaving behind the subject of Jake's new client, they spent another companionable hour eating Mary Ann's tasty creation and speculating instead on how James and Martha's date-that-wasn't might have turned out.

"She's a little young for him—well, a lot young for him—but I've quit worrying about the whole older man–younger woman thing," Darla magnanimously declared. "If it works, it works, and the age difference shouldn't matter. And I think she'll be good for him. I hate to think of him going home to an empty apartment every night."

"Believe me, his apartment is empty only if he wants it that way," Jake assured her.

When Darla gave her a questioning look, she explained, "Besides his work at the bookstore, James is involved in all sorts of organizations. Last I heard, he was part of some sort of wine experts' forum, a 'friends of the orchid' society kind of thing, and I think he sponsors a local animal rescue group. Oh, and he's still a board member on that city arts council. If he wanted female company, he'd have found it. I even went out with him once."

"I'd forgotten about that," Darla admitted. "Another one of those non-dates, right? Though I have to say, it would have been fun if you two had gotten together."

"Fun? It would have been a disaster," Jake said as she cut herself another slice of pie and dolloped on a scoop of melting ice cream. "We're fine as friends, but we have zero in common except for liking Thai food. Martha's more his type with all the reading she does, and that classy accent of hers. That's what he goes for, know what I mean?"

"Actually, I don't." Darla picked a crumb off her now otherwise empty pie plate. "I'm embarrassed to say that I don't really know all that much about James. Except for the board member thing, I didn't know about any of those other extracurricular activities. That's pretty bad, isn't it? I mean, he's worked for me for almost a year. I should know those things."

"Don't beat yourself up, kid. You don't learn everything about a person in the first five minutes you meet them. You and I've been hanging out together ever since you moved in, and there's lots I don't know about you yet."

"Such as?"

"Such as, what made you finally dump your—what do you always call him?—slimeball ex-husband?"

As Darla reflexively curled her lip at the thought—no way was she telling Jake that particular bit of unpleasantness!—her friend gave a satisfied nod. "See, you proved my point. You're no different from anyone else. Not to sound like Forrest Gump, but people are like onions. They've got all sorts of layers to them."

"Yeah, and when you start peeling those layers away, you'd better get ready for some tears," Darla finished for her. "All right, point made. And now I don't feel so bad about not knowing all of James's secrets."

"Yeah, well, sometimes you don't want to know those things," Jake said. "No, I'm not talking about James, in particular," she added when Darla gave her a surprised look. "But if you want to toss around a few more clichés, what was it that Oscar Wilde said about the pure and simple truth rarely being pure and never being simple? You pry around too much into someone's past looking for all the facts, and you're almost guaranteed to dig up something unpleasant. Which works fine if you're a cop, but pretty well stinks if you're not."

"No arguments here," Darla assured her, recalling some of the unpleasant secrets she'd been privy to of late. Then, reaching for the ice cream scoop and waggling it, she added, "This is the only kind of digging I intend to do from here on out."

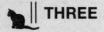 ‖ **THREE**

"I TALKED TO DR. BIRMINGHAM YESTERDAY," DARLA TOLD James the next afternoon when he arrived for his shift. "She recommended a guy to do that whole cat whisperer thing with Hamlet. Apparently, he's the real deal. Of course, he costs a fortune, but he gives a decent discount to her patients."

She glanced again at the note she'd scribbled earlier. "I lucked out in that he has a free slot tomorrow morning. He's supposed to be here about thirty minutes before the store opens for a preliminary consultation."

"And is that consultation to be with you, or with Hamlet?" James wanted to know.

Darla watched for sarcasm in his expression but, seeing nothing other than genuine interest, admitted, "Actually, I'm not sure. I made the appointment with his assistant, and she was pretty vague about the whole thing. If Dr. B hadn't recommended him, I'd think it was a scam. But from what she says, the man gets results."

"Indeed. Will this take place here in the store, or upstairs in your apartment?"

"I'll leave that up to the cat guy. His assistant said, and I quote, 'Brody will feel the vibes and let you know where Hamlet's center is,' unquote. Though as far as I know, Hamlet's only center is somewhere in his belly."

She would have added a few more observations regarding what was sounding more and more like some strange New Age, touchy-feely experiment, except that her worry over the once-cantankerous feline was growing. This morning, he'd merely pawed at his kibble and then had given what had sounded to Darla like a very human sigh before padding his way to the sofa. And it had been only in the last half hour that he'd finally made his way into the shop. He'd taken up residence on the bright green beanbag in the kids' section, much to the consternation of the preschooler who was waiting in that area while his mother browsed the non-fiction shelves nearby.

"I shall keep an open mind," James agreed. "I have watched a few of those animal behaviorist shows on television, and they do seem to accomplish some remarkable results. Perhaps this Brody person will restore Hamlet to his usual cheerful self."

Darla smiled a little at this gentle sarcasm—Hamlet was many things, but never jovial—and replied, "Speaking of cheerful selves, how was your date last night? Yes, I know it wasn't an official date," she hurried to clarify when he gave her a stern look, "but how was it, anyhow?"

"It was . . . edifying," was his only comment before he gave his vest a tug and turned on his heel, marching in the direction of the stairs.

"What does edifying mean?" Robert wanted to know, sidling up beside her.

Darla smiled. "If you want the dictionary definition, it means 'instructive.' If you want the King James version, I *think* it means Martha surprised him, but in a good way."

The youth nodded in approval. "Very awesome. Ms. Washington is a nice lady, and the Big Hoss needs someone to hang with after everything that's happened."

"What do you mean, everything that's happened?"

Robert gave her a quizzical look. "You know, everything. His wife leaving him, his daughter being some kind of radical. All that."

"What? Who told you this?"

"Uh, he did?" Robert replied, looking suddenly chastened. "Uh, maybe it was supposed to be a secret or something?" Then, reaching under the counter for a box cutter, he added, "Guess I should get to work."

He scurried off toward the stack of boxes that had been delivered right after lunch. Darla was tempted to follow after him, but decided against putting the youth on the spot. Still, she couldn't help but silently fume. *Another secret?* Bad enough that she hadn't known about her store manager's various avocations. Now, James was apparently confiding details of his personal life to Robert while leaving her, his employer, totally out of the loop.

Remember what you told Jake. No more digging around in other people's pasts.

She allowed herself to feel noble about that particular resolve. Even so, she was still inwardly grumbling a little when five o'clock came, and it was time for her and Robert to head to the dojo for their Friday night lesson.

"I may stop back in before closing if I don't stay to watch the sparring class," she told James as she and Robert pulled on their coats and shouldered their gym bags. "But don't wait on me if I'm not back by seven."

"Hamlet and I have everything under control," James assured her with a glance at the feline, who had made his way to the main counter and now lay on his back with his rear paws shoved up against the register.

Darla nodded. "All right, then we'll play it by ear. And

if you want to come in early tomorrow to meet Hamlet's, uh, therapist, please do."

"Actually, I have already committed to be out with Ms. Washington again tonight, though I can cancel those plans if you feel I should be here with you."

Darla raised a brow. *James and Martha, two nights in a row?* All she said, however, was, "No, you have a nice night out, and I'll see you when you come in at your usual time."

"Very well, then. You and Robert enjoy your evening, as well, and consider the shop to be in good hands—and paws—until tomorrow."

The walk to the dojo was swift and, by mutual choice, relatively silent. Robert had been avoiding her since his seeming slip regarding James's personal life, likely feeling that she would grill him on it, given the chance. Not that she would ever do such a thing, Darla virtuously reminded herself. She didn't want to put him in the uncomfortable position of worrying about betraying one or the other of his bosses.

Truth was, her only thought for the moment was getting to the dojo, and fast! She was sure she was on the verge of frostbite by the time they reached the Tomlinson Academy of Martial Arts. Compared to Darla's building's elegant entry, with its balustraded steps leading to a glass-windowed door, the street-level storefront that housed the dojo was workman-like, save for a pair of knee-high concrete fu dogs painted red that flanked the doorway. A large window gave a glimpse into the studio, where passersby could see the students practicing their synchronized moves.

And, just in case it wasn't obvious what was taking place inside, the red wooden door was emblazoned with both the dojo's name and the TAMA logo: an anime-styled, oversized punching fist with the letters *T*, *A*, *M*, and *A* tattooed on its respective knuckles. Cliché and macho as it might be, the logo made for a cool-looking T-shirt. She and Robert had each bought one after their first class.

Inside the dojo was a wide vestibule leading directly to the sensei's office. Darla privately called that hallway *Master Tomlinson's Hall of Fame*. Interrupted only by the broad archway midway down, which opened to the training area, the walls were a veritable scrapbook of the man's long martial arts career. In one large glass case, ribbons and medals covered four decades of championship wins, while another case held rows of trophies. The rest of the wall space was covered with photographs of Master Tomlinson over the years.

He'd worn his dark brown hair tied back in a short ponytail in some pictures, while in others he'd had the long hair and bangs look straight out of Woodstock. He'd been rugged-looking rather than movie star handsome in his prime, his six-foot-tall frame straight and well-muscled, but what Darla found most attractive about him was his grin, which was toothy, and filled with welcoming good humor.

Some snapshots were of him alone, and others taken with martial arts pioneers whose names she'd looked up in a reference book she had at the shop. Probably her favorite memorabilia were a dozen framed martial arts magazine covers that featured Tomlinson as the cover model kicking and jumping and punching along with such corny headlines as, *Learn to Knock Out Bad Sparring Habits*.

Of course, these days the sixty-something sensei didn't look much like the virile man in the photos. He'd packed on a good fifty pounds over the years, primarily to his belly. His once dark hair was mostly gray now, and thinning, cut shorter though combed back rakishly and held in place with a strip of black cloth. The toothy grin was a bit yellowed with age, combining with the rest to give him an unremarkable appearance. But anyone doubting his rank had only to look at the faded black belt, embroidered with five red stripes and a tiny red dragon, that tied his black gi jacket.

"Do you think Roma will be here tonight?" Robert asked as they slipped past the archway. "I wanted to, you know, see her for a few minutes before class started."

Darla gave him an indulgent smile. "She's usually here on Fridays. If she is, she's probably at the front of the class with Master Tomlinson. Come on, let's get dressed while the kids' class is finishing up, and then you can go look for her."

They swiftly changed into their uniforms and then joined the parents watching from behind the windowed panel, rather like a section of office cubicle wall, which ran along one side of the training area. On the other side, the entire floor was covered by a series of thick red mats, while both front and back walls were covered by mirrors. At first glance, the room reminded Darla of a gymnasium or dance studio, but a closer look revealed American and Japanese flags gracing one side wall, the dojo's traditional altar with its reclining Buddha and a single flower in the front corner, and in the rear corner, a trio of man-shaped kicking dummies—upper torso only—awaiting their nightly punishment.

At that moment, twenty miniature would-be warriors—both boys and girls—were punching and kicking their way through a kata, which Darla had learned at her first class was the Japanese term for the choreographed forms they performed. Most of the kids already had moved up the ranks to yellow, orange, or even green or blue belt.

Darla self-consciously tightened the knot on her beginner's white belt. Made of heavy cotton material that had been parallel stitched to hold its shape, the belt was long enough to wrap twice about her waist and still leave long floppy ends hanging even after it had been knotted. Here was one place where being an adult didn't automatically confer status, she wryly reminded herself. And she hadn't yet gotten used to the idea of bowing to someone twenty years her junior just because they were a black belt.

Robert, however, had something other than rank on his mind. As the kids' class finished the drill and settled on the floor in a kneeling position for a moment of silence, he gave Darla a nudge with his elbow and stage whispered, "You were right. Look, she's here."

Darla smiled as she followed his glance through the glass to see Roma sitting daintily at the front of the class next to Master Tomlinson. Seeing Robert, she cocked her head in their direction and flashed bright brown eyes at him. Apparently, the admiration was mutual.

"She's like, so sick," Robert whispered, a bit of teen-speak that Darla mentally translated as *really cool*. "I wish I could take her home with me." Then, at Darla's stern look, he sighed and shook his head. "Don't worry, I won't do it."

"Good, because Hamlet would be pretty ticked off if he thought you were two-timing him—and with a dog, no less." She added a smile, "Besides, you know Master Tomlinson would never give up Roma without a fight. He might be older than James, but you'd last about two seconds with him in a ring!"

But even the prospect of losing a theoretical battle to his sensei wasn't enough to dampen Robert's enthusiasm. He'd been smitten by the tiny gray and white Italian greyhound—not a miniature whippet, as Darla had first assumed—the first night he and Darla had shown up for class. Darla had always preferred large dogs, the sort one could trip over with no resulting injury to said beast; still, she had to admit that Roma was a cute little thing. Like her larger greyhound cousins, she appeared to be all legs and whip-thin tail, her sleek fur softer even than Hamlet's. Her delicate ears usually were folded back into neat rosettes against her narrow head, but they could fly up at a moment's notice when something caught her attention, making her look like a goofy, long-nosed fruit bat.

Just as Hamlet ruled the roost at Pettistone's Fine Books, Roma was the mascot of the martial arts studio. And to all the students' delight, her owner had taught her dojo etiquette. That meant that she made a doggie bow when entering and leaving the mat area, and sat quietly at full length with her dainty paws crossed before her whenever the students assumed a kneeling position. But what never failed to make Darla laugh was the way Roma would give a little howling bark whenever the students uttered their kiais—a quick exhalation that sounded like a yell—while practicing their punches.

By now, Master Tomlinson was dismissing his junior students, who promptly made beelines to where their parents waited.

"Good job, everyone," he called, sounding sincere despite the gravel in his voice that portended an incipient cold. "Don't forget to turn in your tournament registrations. And remember to bow before you leave the mat."

The prompt caused several students who'd been remiss to rush back to make a quick obeisance. Roma the dog, meanwhile, lightly padded her way across the mat, high-stepping like a dressage horse. Once she reached the mat's edge, she turned and gave what Darla knew in the dog training lingo was called a play bow. Then, with a happy if surprisingly deep bark for such a small dog, she waited for Robert to walk around the panel before bounding toward him, her whiplike tail creating a small breeze with its wagging.

While Robert gently wrestled with Roma, the rest of the adult class filed in. As Darla joined her fellow students, she heard a vehement female voice from behind the windowed wall. "You can't ban my son from the tournament! I pay good money for his lessons, and he's gonna be there. That first-place trophy is his!"

Darla covertly glanced over to see which parent was taking out her frustration on the sensei. She'd quickly learned that martial arts, like any other sport that catered to children, had more than its share of "karate moms." These mothers—though a few fathers also fit that bill—spent class time on the sidelines alternately cheering on their kids and attempting to countermand the sensei's instruction.

To his credit, Master Tomlinson was not one to tolerate that sort of interference for any extended period, so it wasn't as disruptive as it could have been. And, to be fair, those same involved parents were the first to volunteer to take tickets and run the food concession at the local events.

Tonight, the mom currently venting was one whom Darla had seen most class nights.

Of course, Grace Valentine was hard to miss.

With her "mob wife" wardrobe that leaned heavily toward tight leopard prints, short hemlines, and dominatrix boots, Grace stood out from the other, more conservative moms. In her mid-thirties, and with black hair that had been straightened into a submissive long bob, she'd also been Botoxed and enhanced to the point that she resembled a living Barbie doll. Even with the windowed panel serving as a barrier, her strident "New Yawk" accent was always noticeable as she offered nonstop correction and encouragement to her son, Chris, during the course of every class.

But the other thing that distinguished her was the fact that she, too, was a student. A few other parents took beginner classes with their kids, but most never progressed beyond a couple of belt ranks. Grace, however, was working toward her black belt. From what Darla had heard, the woman mainly took private lessons with the sensei, apparently not wanting to mix with the other students. Every so often, however, she joined in the sparring class with her son. According to Robert, who'd seen her in action, the woman was a pretty competent fighter.

Not surprisingly under her self-important tutelage, her high school freshman son Chris had an overdeveloped ego regarding his own skill on the mat. While the other students routinely went through a basic aerobic warm-up prior to class, Chris could never resist showing off. He tirelessly performed spinning and leaping kicks straight out of a Jackie Chan movie, his Bieber-inspired blond do swirling with equal vigor.

Most of Robert and Darla's class was male, though tonight there were two other women, both red belts. And the age span amongst students was large—the adult class was open to any student over fifteen years old. Darla always dreaded being partnered up with Chris during drills. This was partly because, though only a high school freshman, he was already several inches taller than her five feet four inches, with a reach to match, and partly because of his obnoxious attitude. He always seemed to conveniently "forget" the dojo rule against higher-ranking students making actual physical contact with the newbies. More than once, she'd come home from class with bruises because of him. If she wasn't careful, she'd end up with ten crooked toes just like Master Tomlinson, who, from the sorry look of his swollen feet, had obviously broken every single digit at least once.

And Master Tomlinson had grown tired of the junior black belt's attitude, too. A week ago, he'd warned the boy in front of the entire class that one more breach of dojo rules would leave him sitting on the sidelines at the next tournament. From the current argument Darla was overhearing, it seemed that Chris had not taken the warning seriously. He must have transgressed in some way, and Tomlinson had enforced his threat, banning Chris from participating in the event. Much to his mother's vocal displeasure.

Darla could hear the rumble of the sensei's calm voice explaining the situation to Grace, but she could only make out a word or two . . . *self-control* and *opportunity* being among them. A wave of sympathy for the sensei swept her. Retail could be challenging enough, but at least it wasn't usually personal. She didn't envy Master Tomlinson's ongoing balancing act between parents and students.

Apparently, the sensei won this particular match. Darla saw Chris's mom throw up her hands in disgusted surrender and flop into one of the hard plastic chairs, her bright red lips pressed into a hard line. Master Tomlinson, looking equally disgusted, reappeared around the divider and signaled to the two black belts lounging in the far corner.

"Hal, Hank, line them up and warm them up," he ordered between coughs, waving in the direction of Darla and the rest. "I'm going to grab another lozenge, and I'll be back in a few minutes."

Trailed by Roma, Tomlinson limped off in the direction of his office—apparently his gout, as well as a head cold, was kicking in—leaving the class to the tender mercies of his two stepsons.

"Great, the Steroid Twins," Robert murmured as the pair sauntered to the front of the room. "Hope you ate your Wheaties this morning."

Darla gave a commiserating nod. Hal and Hank seemed to delight in tormenting the students. Their favorite pastime was piling on the warm-up exercises, whether it was running laps around the mat or doing sit-ups and push-ups. By mutual agreement, however, the class had found a way to undermine the twins' petty tyranny. After the first dozen or so of each set, they'd begin "accidentally" accelerating the shouted count by skipping a number every so often, which ended up knocking down the total by a significant number of reps. So far, Hank and Hal did not appear to have caught on to the subterfuge.

Darla snarkily attributed the plot's ongoing success to the fact that the men simply didn't know how to count past ten.

If someone in the class hadn't told her, Darla never would have guessed that the brothers were fraternal twins, for they looked about as much alike as she and Robert did. Hal was close to six feet tall and rocked the bald head, tattooed neck look. In flagrant violation of dojo rules, he'd lopped off the sleeves of his black gi jacket to better display an impressive set of tattooed biceps. Hank was shorter and stockier than his brother, and had chosen to let his black hair grow long enough to wear in a ponytail, rather like his stepfather had worn in his younger days. Hank, too, went in for the sleeve-less look, with arms even bigger than his brother's, but minus the tattoo ink.

Though now in their early twenties, the pair apparently

had been part of the dojo since their grade school days. A good portion of the trophies and ribbons on display in the front case belonged to them.

"All right, people, line up," Hal called, despite the fact that the students had already arranged themselves into two lines in order of rank, meaning that Robert and Darla were in the back.

Hank chimed in, "Now, bow to the flag, bow to the instructors, bow to each other. Oh, yeah," he added in a bored tone when the bows were completed, "don't forget to repeat the creed."

"Run when you can, fight if you must, never give up, and never let injustice go unpunished," Darla obediently chorused, preparing herself for a dose of Hal and Hank boot camp.

The twins must have been in a better mood than usual, however, for the warm-up was relatively short and comparatively painless. By then Master Tomlinson, accompanied by Roma, had returned to his usual spot in front of the class.

"Let's run through a couple of katas, and then I have some new self-defense techniques to show you," he began.

The hour-long class flew by, the students rotating partners as they moved through the various drills under the sensei's direction. Darla suffered a momentary bit of angst when she found herself paired up with Chris during one technique, but apparently the lesson of being banned from the tournament had sunk in, for the teen was remarkably subdued. As the drill commenced, he was careful to pull his punches and even offered Darla a grudging compliment on her progress. She was so shocked by his unexpected praise, however, she forgot to block his next attack—and for that momentary inattention, promptly found herself on her rump on the mat.

Unfortunately for her ego, Master Tomlinson had turned his attention to her just in time to witness her ungainly landing. But barely had she hit the ground when a panicking Chris was grabbing her hand and dragging her upright again.

"Sorry, Master Tomlinson, it was an accident. I thought

she was blocking me, honest," he sputtered, blue eyes wide beneath his curtain of bangs as he shot Darla a frantic look that said, *Dude, back me up here!*

Though fleetingly tempted to indulge in a bit of payback, Darla's sense of fair play kicked in. "It was my fault, Sensei," she agreed. "I let myself be distracted and forgot to block him."

"That doesn't matter," was his stern reply. Turning to the teen, he went on, "Chris, you're the senior-ranking student. You should have been able to avoid hitting her. Now, go to the back of the room and do push-ups until the rest of the students finish the drill."

"Yes, Master Tomlinson."

His tone sullen, the youth made his bow to the sensei. Then, with a resentful glare in Darla's direction, he stomped off to the far corner. Feeling guilty now, Darla opened her mouth to protest what she considered to be an unfair punishment. Just in time, however, she glimpsed Robert standing behind the instructor and anxiously pantomiming lips being zipped. She prudently shut her mouth again. She might be boss of her bookstore, she reminded herself, but the sensei was boss of his dojo. How he ran it was his business.

Tomlinson's stern visage relaxed into amusement, and Darla realized in embarrassment that the man had probably seen Robert's performance reflected in the mirror behind her. All he said, however, was, "Since you lost your partner, you can finish the drill with me."

For the next few minutes, she practiced blocking techniques with him, silently marveling at the difference between working with him and working with Chris. She'd often heard her father quote the old saw about old age and treachery overcoming youth and skill. Here was an actual example of the concept . . . at least, the old age part of it. Compared with Chris's flashy if uncontrolled athleticism, the aging sensei seemed slow and out of shape. But Darla swiftly found that appearances were deceiving.

Despite his gouty legs and arthritic hands, Tomlinson was able to move effortlessly from her path at every attack and defend against her fledgling efforts with a silent economy of motion that came only from a lifetime of dedicated practice. Forget the wild flying through the air and punching through boards, Darla thought in awe. This was the real deal. In fact, she suspected that even his stepsons would be hard-pressed to best him in a fair fight . . . six-pack abs and impressive guns notwithstanding.

With a final "good job" for Darla, Tomlinson called a halt to the drill. Hank and Hal, who'd been assisting some of the other students, sauntered back up to the front of the training area.

"All right, people, line up," Hal called again.

Chris, who'd been gamely carrying out his punishment in the corner, rushed to claim his spot at the front of the class. Sweat now drenched the Bieber bangs, but from the sour look he shot in her direction, Darla could see that enforced exercise had done nothing to quench his resentment. A glance toward the sidelines convinced her that, unless someone had installed twin lasers in the waiting area, Grace Valentine was equally peeved at her.

Maybe she'd take a rain check on watching the sparring class, after all. The last thing she wanted to do was sit beside Chris's mother for the next hour while the woman chewed off her red lipstick and stared holes in her.

After a quick cool down and a moment of meditation, Hal dismissed the class. Darla and Robert bowed their way off the mat to find Master Tomlinson waiting for them.

"So, are you two looking forward to your belt test?" the sensei asked with a smile.

Robert's nod was eager. "I practice, like, every night at home. I know I can ace the test. I just wish we didn't have to wait until next month."

"Maybe you don't have to wait." When Darla and Robert gave him a quizzical look, the man said, "I have to be here at the dojo on Sunday morning. If you two want, you can come in and I'll give you your own private belt test."

"If you're sure it's not too much trouble," Darla began, only to have Robert cut her off.

"Sweet! We'll be here," he agreed, his grin as broad as Darla had ever seen it. "What time?"

"How about eleven?"

Robert hesitated, his enthusiasm obviously dimming as he looked at Darla for confirmation. Both of them were scheduled to open the store at noon on Sunday, which would be cutting it pretty darn close. But seeing how much this meant to Robert—and looking forward herself to trading her beginner's white belt for a yellow one—Darla gave him an answering smile and then turned to Tomlinson.

"Eleven would be fine . . . and if the store opens a few minutes late, I'm sure everyone will survive it."

"Sweet," Robert happily repeated. He gave a few air punches to punctuate the sentiment, while Roma enthusiastically bounded up and down at his feet. "Thanks, Master Tomlinson."

"Thank *you*. Nothing is better than finding students who truly want to learn. So come ready to show me your best."

"We will," Darla promised.

"We will," Robert echoed, and then bent to tussle a moment with Roma, who promptly grabbed hold of his gi sleeve with tiny sharp teeth and began play growling as she tugged at it.

Tomlinson smiled a little even as he assumed a stern tone. "Leave it, Roma. You know better than that."

The small canine obediently let go of Robert's sleeve, but her bright brown eyes still flashed with mischief as she sat beside the instructor. Hank, meanwhile, strolled past them on his way to the equipment area, pausing a moment to give Roma a disapproving look.

"We're about to start the sparring class," he announced.

"That rat's gonna get stepped on. Why don't you stick it in its cage?"

By way of answer, Tomlinson abruptly clapped his beefy hands. With a graceful vertical leap, Roma landed in the older man's arms. From the safety of her owner's arms, she gave Hank what Darla could only interpret as a smug look before snuggling with her long snout tucked beneath the lapel of his gi.

Tomlinson, meanwhile, gave his stepson a cold look. "Roma knows how to behave in the dojo, which is more than I can say for some other people."

"Well," Darla brightly broke in, "I think it's time for Robert and me to head out so we're not in the way of the next group. We'll see you Sunday morning, Sensei."

She made her quick bow to Tomlinson and Hank; then, grabbing Robert by his gi sleeve, she dragged him toward the changing area.

"But I wanted to watch the sparring class," he complained as he stumbled after her.

She halted and let go of his sleeve. "Sorry, I just wanted to get us out of fist range in case something happened. This isn't the first night I've seen those two do a little verbal sparring, and it always makes me nervous."

She glanced over her shoulder and saw in relief that the two men had apparently parted with nothing worse than the few harsh words already exchanged. Even so, she wasn't going to hang around. "Stay if you want," she told the teen, "but I'm going to leave before—"

Before Mark shows up, was what she intended to say. But she made it only halfway through her sentence when she caught a whiff of stale cigarette smoke, and a familiar nasal voice chimed in behind her, "Hi, Darla."

Too late.

Wincing a little, Darla turned back around to see Mark Poole and his overstuffed gear bag wandering in from the training area. "Long time, no see," he trotted out the old cliché, and then grinned in appreciation of his perceived wit. "You staying to watch me spar tonight, maybe give me a little encouragement?" He dropped his gear bag at his feet and opened his skinny arms in what was a blatant invitation to a hug.

Appalled, Darla took a reflexive step back. Nothing set off her redhead's temper like some guy trying to coerce a woman into a "harmless" embrace. Maybe she should demonstrate on him the little stomp-and-shove technique they'd learned tonight.

Just in time, however, she recalled that the man was a customer, and so she managed a tight smile instead.

"Hi, Mark. Actually, I'm going to change and then run back to the store before it closes so I can help out James. But good luck with class tonight."

"Uh, sure."

Taking the hint, he awkwardly let his arms fall to his sides again, looking so downcast that Darla almost felt sorry for him. *Almost*. Then he gave Robert a quizzical look. "You're the kid who works for Darla at the bookstore, right? You gonna watch tonight?"

"Only if there's, you know, blood," was Robert's exaggeratedly cheerful reply. Only Darla noticed that he followed that declaration with the silently mouthed word, *creepoid*.

Buoyed by her employee's reaction, Darla now suppressed a grin. Out of the mouth of babes . . . or, rather Gen Y-ers. Robert would probably spend the class cheering on every opponent Mark sparred against. She only hoped that he wouldn't be too blatant about it.

Mark looked as though he was struggling to reply with something clever, and not having much success. He was saved from total humiliation, however, when his cell phone abruptly rang from the recesses of his gym bag. He gave a guilty look around—dojo rules said all cell phones off in the training area—and quickly dug the phone out from under his sparring gloves. Then, with a glance at the caller ID, he pressed the "Talk" button.

"Gotta take this," he told Darla. "Don't say anything to Sensei."

Darla gave a silent sigh of relief. "Don't worry, I won't tattle." To Robert, she added, "I'll see you later," before heading off to the changing room.

This had not been the best of evenings, despite the sensei's offer to give them their belt test early. First there had been that secondhand stress from witnessing the altercations between Master Tomlinson and Mrs. Valentine, and then Master Tomlinson and his stepsons. Then there had been that incident with Chris. And Mark's unalluring presence was the cherry on a not-so-tasty sundae. All in all, she wasn't in the mood tonight to hang around the dojo. She'd check in with James at the store, and then spend some quality time with Hamlet in advance of the cat whisperer guy's arrival Saturday morning.

A few minutes later, she slipped out the front door, leaving behind the faint echoes of shouting fighters and the inevitable whiff of gym sweat. Unfortunately, she found Grace Valentine outside, leaning against the building a short distance from the door, her short blond mink jacket leaving her fishnet-clad legs exposed to the cold night air.

She seemed not to notice the chill, however, for she had her cell phone pressed to her ear and appeared to be intently listening to someone on the other end. In her free hand, she dangled one of those long, skinny cigarettes that gave off a surprising amount of toxic smoke for all its dainty size. Grace's red lips were bright beneath the light from the studio window and still twisted into an angry line. Whether that emotion was directed at the person on the phone, or was simply a holdover from her earlier verbal fisticuffs with Master Tomlinson, Darla couldn't guess.

As for Chris, he stood on the sidewalk a few steps from her, hunched so low into his blue, down-filled coat that Darla could see only his sweat-darkened bangs as he fumbled with his own cell phone. Apparently, he still was in trouble with the sensei since he wasn't inside sparring with the rest of the advanced students.

She didn't know if Chris noticed her, but his mother certainly did. Catching Darla's eye, Grace shot her a look that made Darla hope the woman's mob connections were limited to her wardrobe.

"Yeah, hold on, wouldja?" she abruptly barked into her cell. Then, pressing the phone against her surgically enhanced bust, she turned her attention to Darla.

"Hey! Yeah, Cherry Top, I'm talking to you," she called, pointing in Darla's direction with her cigarette. "Don't think I didn't see what happened tonight. If you'd have been paying attention, you wouldn't have walked into Chris's fist, and then Tom wouldn't have banned him from sparring tonight."

"I know . . . sorry," was the safest response that came to Darla's mind. She'd long ago learned not to engage the crazy, and Mama Valentine definitely fell into that camp. Defending herself would only make matters worse.

Grace, however, was not appeased by her apology.

"I know your type," she persisted, cigarette waving wildly. "Ladies like you come to class, thinking it'll be fun, or maybe you'll find a guy. Well, let me tell you, it ain't like that. It's hard work. You *ladies*"—she made the word sound like an insult—"you never last. So just don't screw things up any worse for my kid before you get bored and quit. I don't care what Tom says, Chris is gonna be in that tournament, or else."

Definitely a "run when you can" moment, Darla swiftly decided as the woman took a threatening step in her direction. She was pretty sure that Grace could take her in a fight, even wearing leopard print pumps and a mini skirt. The sooner she beat it, the better.

Determined not to let Grace have the last word, however, Darla managed a bright smile in return. "Well, nice chatting with you. 'Bye, Chris," she added in the youth's direction and gave him a friendly wave. "See you next class."

Chris glanced up from his phone, appearing startled before promptly returning his attention to his phone. Grace looked a bit surprised, too, Darla saw in satisfaction. With a final sneer in Darla's direction, the woman stuck her phone back up to her ear and resumed her conversation.

Darla gave a mental shrug. *I tried,* she reassured herself as she started back in the direction of the store. True, she might have given up a bit easily in the face of Grace's outrage, but that didn't mean she was intimidated. It simply was that she had plenty on her plate to contend with without worrying about being on a high schooler's mom's bad list. Hamlet was her priority for the moment. She could only hope that this so-called cat whisperer she'd hired would find a way into the clever feline's psyche and discover what it would take to return Hamlet to his ornery self once more.

Darla pulled out her phone—her usual safety precaution when walking alone in the evening—and the now-familiar xylophone sound chimed, indicating an opponent had just played a word in one of her dozen open games. Swiftly, she pulled up the screen for a look.

This player was an anonymous competitor with the user name *fightingwords* (Darla's was *pettibooks123*). And he— she?—had lived up to that moniker, Darla thought with a smile. This was their eighth or ninth game, and the wins had been pretty evenly split thus far. Both of them usually scored high, with only a handful of points determining the victor.

Actually, *fightingwords* was the only random user that Darla played anymore. She had been burned too many times by unknown, casual players who flitted from game to game, quitting halfway through whenever they were behind on points. Worse, however, were the cheaters. These were the ones who had installed a sneaky little app to their game that allowed them to play all seven letters at once for an outrageous score, no matter that the word formed was nothing but a jumble. The minute someone slapped up a word like *ypeortn* and gained a cool seventy or eighty points because they were on triple word and triple letter spots—plus a bonus for using all their letters at once—it was Darla who swiftly resigned!

Before scanning her own letters for a suitable word, Darla checked out her opponent's latest offering. *Twenty-four points* . . . decent enough score, courtesy of a "double word" square. As for the word played, she decided with a rueful smile that it was oddly appropriate for the situation at hand. For, glowing up at her from the backlit screen was the word *sucker.*

FOUR

DARLA FROWNED AS SHE REVIEWED HER NOTES FOR Hamlet's appointment with the cat whisperer. *Nine thirty,* she confirmed, checking her watch to see that it was already a quarter to ten. She'd actually been down in the store since nine, keeping a close eye on Hamlet in case he decided to try his occasional disappearing act. But, as he'd done the past few weeks, the feline had barely budged from the spot where he was lounging, in this case on one of the more inaccessible shelves in the food and cooking section. He was lying on his belly and stretched to full length, paws dangling like small black pompoms from the shelf's edge.

Darla had all but given up on the cat whisperer guy when, just a few minutes before ten, she heard a sharp rapping on the front door glass.

"Finally! Don't go anywhere, Hammy," she warned the cat as she hurried to unlock the door. "This visitor is for you, not me."

And we want to get our money's worth, she mentally

added, recalling again just how much this little bit of cat psychoanalysis was going to set her back. With what this guy charged, she could keep Hamlet in kibble for a year. But if his techniques worked, she wouldn't begrudge him a penny.

Eagerly, she unlocked the door to find a gently smiling young man standing before her on the stoop, fists crammed into his jacket pockets. Her first disappointed thought was that the cat guy had stood her up, since this person didn't look like someone who charged beaucoup bucks for a consultation. Obviously, her visitor was some homeless man who had wandered to her door wanting to get out of the cold, or else was looking for a handout.

Darla gave him a sympathetic look-over. The fellow wore a patched denim coat, the sleeves of which rode a good three inches short on his skinny arms and was far too thin for the weather. Though scrupulously clean, his battered jeans suggested not so much fashionable distressing as real-life wear and tear. She was about to send him on his way with a couple of dollars and directions to the nearest shelter, when she noticed the red ball cap with the blue embroidered words, *Have You Hugged Your Cat Today?*, that he wore over his stringy blond hair.

So much for first impressions!

"Hi, I'm Darla Pettistone," she finally managed, smiling and sticking out her hand. "You must be Brody Raywinkle, the cat whisperer."

"If you don't mind, I prefer the term feline behavioral empath." Easing one fist from his pocket, he bypassed the handshake to gingerly pass her a creased business card with that same title beneath his name. "That whole cat whisperer thing sounds a little *woo-woo*, if you know what I mean."

"Sorry," she replied . . . though, to her mind, *feline behavioral empath* flirted with woo-woo territory, too. Tucking the card away, she added, "Please, come inside."

She gestured Brody in and locked the door behind him

again, covertly studying him as she did so. He seemed to be something of a germaphobe, given the way he'd avoided her handshake. And obviously, his exorbitant consulting fees went to something other than his wardrobe.

Hopefully a good sign? she thought. On the bright side, unlike that cat guy on the animal cable channel, he didn't cart around a blinged-out guitar case filled with cat toys—something told her that Hamlet would not have approved. Though, when it came down to it, she suspected he wasn't going to think much of Brody, either.

"So, where's our client?" he asked with a glance about the store.

Darla pointed to where Hamlet still reclined on an upper shelf. "There. You probably should know that—"

"Wait!"

He raised one shoulder in lieu of raising a hand, stopping her short. "I don't want to crowd my mind with any preconceived notions. All I need to know is his name, how old he is, how long he has been here, and how long ago his problems started."

Gamely, Darla filled in those blanks, earning a nod when she was finished. "Perfect," he replied. "Now, if you can bring me a chair—preferably wood, no cushions, please—I'll find out why Hamlet is not functioning at his highest level."

Darla hurried to find an appropriate seat. By the time she had wrestled a vintage ladder-back chair from its spot in the social sciences section, Brody had made his way over to the shelf where Hamlet lay. Now, the pair eyed each other, Hamlet's green eyes suspicious emerald slits, and Brody's wide brown eyes reflecting calm watchfulness. Darla quizzically studied them both as she set the chair next to the man.

"I'll be opening the store in another minute," she reminded him. "Are you sure we shouldn't take Hamlet upstairs to the lounge where you won't be disturbed?"

"We're fine here. Give us half an hour or so."

He took the chair Darla had brought for him and arranged it a couple of feet from the shelf, sitting with his elbows propped on his knees, and his chin propped on his fists. At this intrusion into his personal space, Hamlet opened his eyes wider and pulled his paws under him, as if preparing to haul tail. Then, apparently deciding flight was too much effort, he relaxed and settled in a similar position to Brody, chin on paws and cool green eyes unblinking.

The first influx of Saturday morning customers did not disturb them. In fact, the two were still staring down each other thirty minutes later when Jake came strolling in, her black leather duster billowing from a gust of cold air before she shut the door behind her. A faint whiff of cigarette smoke accompanied her as well, and Darla wrinkled her nose. Apparently, Jake's attempts to ditch the smoking habit still hadn't fully taken, though she was proud of her friend for having cut down to just a couple of cigarettes a day.

"Hey, kid, my printer just croaked," the PI said by way of greeting. "Mind if I borrow yours? I've got a photo here I really need to get printed," she explained, waving a shiny silver flash drive which Darla assumed held said files.

"No problem," she agreed. "Any special kind of paper?"

"No, I . . ."

Jake trailed off, having caught sight of the man-feline stare-down the next aisle over. Joining Darla at the counter, she lowered her voice and asked, "What the heck is going on between that guy and Hamlet?"

"Remember I told you the other day that he seems to have some kind of PTSD thing going on? Well, Brody's here to figure out how to help him. He's Hamlet's feline behavioral empath," Darla softly told her, proud that she'd managed the unwieldy title without stumbling over her words.

Jake opened her eyes wide. "Feline behavioral who? No, never mind. So, is he doing a Vulcan mind meld or something?"

"I guess," was Darla's doubtful reply as she glanced at her watch. "Whatever it is, I don't think either one of them has blinked for a half hour. I just hope I'm not paying overtime here. Now, what about your document?".

Jake handed over the thumb drive. "It's the one tagged Putin101. Give me five . . . no, ten copies, and that should be enough."

Nodding, Darla booted up her computer and turned on the printer; then, casually, she said, "I guess this has something to do with your case for our gangster friend?"

"If you mean *Alex*, then yes." The older woman hesitated, and then added, "I guess it doesn't hurt to tell you, since I'm going to be showing her photo around town. His mother has gone missing, and I'm trying to track her down."

"Oh, no, how awful."

Regretting her previous flip attitude, Darla tried not to feel guilty now as she pictured some tiny old lady in a babushka wandering the streets of Brooklyn. Gangster or not, surely the man was frantic with worry.

"Shouldn't he call the police, too?" Darla asked as she plugged the tiny drive in a free USB slot. "I mean, it's a good thing he has you on the case, but if poor old Mrs. Putin is suffering from Alzheimer's or something, then maybe the authorities should be notified."

"Believe me, this isn't a case for the cops."

Something in Jake's dry tone made Darla glance up from the computer. The PI was shaking her head, while a smile played about her generous mouth. "Go ahead, look at her picture, and you'll see what I mean."

Puzzled, Darla quickly opened the file. An image popped up on screen, and she blinked. After a moment of stunned silence, she said, "Wow. Seriously?"

"Seriously," Jake replied "Yeah, kid, that's poor old Mrs. Putin . . . aka the Russian Bombshell, as I like to call her."

Russian Bombshell.

That pretty well nailed it, Darla thought as she stared at

the exotic beauty whose image filled her screen. The woman looked Jake's age, maybe a couple of years older. Her hair had been cropped into a fashionably short do and hennaed to the blazing shade of red favored by Eastern European women of a certain age. Her gray eyes had an exotic Slavic tilt to them that was exaggerated by the heavy black liner she wore. Her full lips had no need of any artificial plumper and appeared even larger with the application of red lipstick a shade darker than her spiky tresses. Staring at the screen, Darla was seized by a momentary urge to rush to the salon down the street and demand that her own auburn hair be chopped off into something that chic.

"But I was expecting . . . I mean, she's so—"

"Young? Hot?" Jake supplied, the smile broadening into a grin.

While Darla began printing the photos, her friend continued, "I have to admit, I was pretty shocked myself when Alex showed me the picture. Seems she married his father back in Russia when she was sixteen, so that only puts her in her mid-fifties now. Old Mr. Putin—and he really *was* old, almost thirty years older than his wife—died last year. Apparently Mrs. Putin is making up for lost time and lost youth. Alex thinks she's run off with a younger man."

"Well, good for her," Darla replied with an approving nod, handing over the finished prints and unplugging the thumb drive. "Can you imagine being sixteen and married to someone middle-aged like that?"

Jake snorted. "Even worse, can you imagine being forty and stuck with some guy who probably is too old to—"

She broke off as Darla gave a frantic wave and gestured in the direction of Brody, who was well within earshot.

"Well, you know what I mean," she finished with a wink. "Anyway, Mama Putin took off one day last week while Alex was at work. Packed up all her clothes, all the tchotchkes. All she left behind was a note that pretty well translated to *See you later, Sonny.*"

"But what's wrong with that?" Darla wanted to know. "She's over twenty-one. If she wants to run away with some totally inappropriate guy, he can't stop her."

"I know, but Alex insists that this particular inappropriate guy"—she gave the phrase finger quotes—"is only interested in her money. She doesn't speak much English, and he's worried the guy might coerce her into getting married and signing over all her assets. But don't worry, Alex understands that all I'm going to do is find her and let her know that he's worried and wants to be sure she's okay."

Privately, Darla suspected that the man's true motivation was finding his mother's supposed boyfriend and kneecapping him, but all she said was, "Sounds like a straightforward enough case. Feel free to stop back by if you need to print up any more pictures."

"I will. Say, why don't we grab a bite tonight over at the Thai place after you get off work? I'm dying to know what Mr. Cat Whisperer has to say about Hamlet."

"Uh, *feline behavioral empath*, if you don't mind," a gentle voice behind them corrected.

They both turned to see that Brody had left his chair and had wandered up to the register. A glance at the bookshelf showed that Hamlet had vacated his post and was nowhere in sight. Darla wondered if he had finally tired of the staredown and stalked off, or if the two had parted by mutual agreement.

"Oops, sorry," Jake said, not sounding terribly sorry at all. Turning to Darla, she added, "Okay, gotta fly. I've got pictures of Russian bombshells to show around town."

The PI departed in a swirl of leather, leaving Darla alone with Brody. Her earlier anxiety returning, she asked, "So, what's the diagnosis? Did you figure out why Hamlet's so depressed?"

"He suffered a terrible trauma a few months ago," the man began, his expression dismayed. "Not only was he hurt physically, but he was damaged spiritually. He faced the biggest challenge of his many lives, and he fell short. Now, his body has since healed, but his psyche has not. And I believe there was something more recent that distressed him, too."

Darla nodded, first recapping the original incident that had traumatized them both, and then relating the closet scare.

"I think being locked in like that brought back all the bad memories, kind of like a flashback," she told Brody. "He's definitely been moping ever since."

"And with good cause. Hamlet feels like a failure and unworthy to remain here as mascot."

"What? He told you all that?" Darla asked in wary disbelief, trying to recall just how much detail she had given the man's assistant when she'd made the appointment. As best she could remember, all she had mentioned was the vet's recommendation. But maybe Dr. Birmingham had given him Hamlet's medical history . . . no breach of confidentiality there, since HIPAA didn't apply to pets.

If Dr. B hadn't said anything, however, then that whole man-cat mind-meld thing must actually have worked!

Brody, meanwhile, was nodding. "He's most upset over the fact he failed you, since you are his human family. He's been trying to atone for it ever since."

"But I don't understand. Hamlet was a hero. He risked his life for me!"

"From your point of view, perhaps. But from his, things are far murkier. Cats have their own code of honor, you know."

Darla hesitated. The situation was rapidly leaving woo-woo land and careening straight into Crazyville. But if Brody knew a way to snap Hamlet out of his funk, then off to Crazyville she'd go with him. "So, how do I help Hamlet, uh, atone?"

"I'm not sure, and he wasn't able—or willing—to tell me. That's something you and Hamlet will have to figure out for yourselves. And if that doesn't work . . . well, I've found that the Universe has a way of shaking things up for you when you need shaking up."

Then, when Darla stared at him, he added, "I always include a free follow-up visit on any consultation, so I'll pop back in sometime in the next week or so to see if there's any progress. And you have my card, so feel free to call me if you need to chat before then."

With another guileless smile, he made his way to the door, his hand carefully wrapped in his coat as he turned the knob and wandered out into the crisp morning air.

"Well, that was special," Darla announced to the empty store, unable to contain her disappointment. She wasn't certain what she'd expected to happen from this visit, but what she did know was that she could have left Hamlet to his own devices without benefit of Brody's consultation and accompanying exorbitant fee!

On the other hand, maybe Mr. Feline Behavioral Empath had communicated something of value that would put Hamlet's cat brain in motion and jog him from his apathy.

She repeated the same sentiment to James and Robert a couple of hours later when they arrived for their shifts.

"My main worry," she finished, while both Robert and James listened intently, "is that he's not eating like he should, and he's not getting any exercise."

"I hardly think he is going to shrivel up from hunger," James replied. "Cats do have a strong sense of self-preservation. But perhaps there is something to Mr. Raywinkle's theory about allowing him to perform a service. Suppose that we stage an event that would require Hamlet's intervention?"

"I could, like, pretend to hurt myself so he could run get help," Robert suggested, and promptly performed a dramatic pratfall worthy of a professional comedian.

Impressed, Darla reached a hand to help him up again. "That would make a great YouTube video," she conceded, "but Hamlet is too smart to be taken in by something that obvious."

"Okay, then, what about a shoplifter?" the youth countered with equal enthusiasm as he dusted himself off. "I can get a friend to, you know, pretend to steal a book in front of him. Hamlet can pounce on him and save the day."

"Not altruistic enough," Darla declared, while James nodded his agreement. "I hate to say it, but if Brody is right, the only way Hamlet will recover is if he overcomes a situation similar to the one that sent him into this tailspin in the first place."

Which meant that the doughty cat would have to face down another killer. And not only was that something that Darla would never allow, it wasn't like she had any desire to conjure up a murderer strictly for therapeutic purposes!

Discouraged now, she exchanged looks with Robert and James, who both appeared equally discouraged. Then the latter shook his head.

"I am certain we will find some way to perk him up again. Maybe Jake will have a suggestion."

But Jake, too, proved of little help when they met that evening at Thai Me Up. After they'd settled in their favorite window spot at the restaurant, Darla gave her friend a blow-by-blow account of her conversation with Brody.

"I really don't know what to do with Hamlet now," she finished and took a miserable stab at the last curry puff on their appetizer platter. "If Brody is right, and Hamlet really is trying to atone, this might never get resolved. Any brilliant suggestions?"

"'Fraid not, kid. I could use a few brilliant suggestions, myself. I haven't had much luck tracking down Alex's mother."

"Mrs. Putin," Darla exclaimed. "Sorry, I forgot about her, worrying about Hamlet all day. What happened?"

"I made the rounds of all her usual places . . . the greengrocer, the beauty parlor, a couple of other places. Heck, I even bit the bullet and got my nails done at her favorite salon," Jake said, waving one hand to display a French manicure before reaching for her soup spoon. "But either no one knew where she was, or no one was saying."

"Talk about sacrificing all for your work," Darla murmured, momentarily distracted by the sight of her friend's white-tipped nails. While Jake had been known to indulge in a dramatic slash of red lipstick when a night out demanded it, Darla had never actually seen the woman sporting fingernail polish before. Then, recalling herself to the subject at hand, she added, "Do you think Mrs. Putin left the city?"

"That's a strong possibility. I've got a couple more leads to follow up on tomorrow. If they don't pan out, I'll rent a heap and head out of town."

She paused to take a sip of coconut soup, and then added with a grin, "Hey, maybe I can recruit Hamlet to help. He's pretty good at unraveling mysteries. I can stick him in a harness, give him one of Mrs. Putin's old babushkas to sniff, and let him do the bloodhound thing around the city."

"Cute," Darla deadpanned. "You supply the harness, and I'll run out and get him a meerschaum pipe and a magnifying glass."

"Aw, c'mon, kid, I'm just trying to cheer you up."

"I guess I'd be in a cheerier mood if I knew for sure what was ailing him. I mean, when you think about it, the idea of a cat seeking atonement is pretty crazy."

"Yeah, well, not as crazy as getting one of those live fish pedicures."

"What? You don't mean . . ."

Jake gave a rueful nod, and Darla stared at her in horrified amusement. She'd heard about spas that offered exotic services like a foot soak in water teeming with tiny carp whose job was to nibble away at your dead skin. Surely Jake hadn't gone the extra mile in her investigation and had a fish pedicure, too!

"You actually let minnows chew on your feet? But I thought that kind of thing was illegal in New York City."

"Technically, yes, but people like Mrs. Putin don't care about that. Kind of like Cinderella's stepsisters . . . they'll do anything if someone says it's the latest beauty fad." She shrugged, her smile broadening. "If you've got the cash and know who to ask, let's just say that you, too, can have baby-smooth tootsies like me."

"Ugh, I'll live with the calluses. So other than getting your feet munched on, I guess that spa was a bust, too?"

"With a capital B. Those girls who work these salons are tough cookies. Bribes, pleas, threats . . . none of that works on them. This one is going to take good old legwork to solve."

Darla gave her a commiserating smile. "You'll find her. But whatever you do, don't come back with hennaed hair tomorrow."

"Not a chance," the older woman retorted and shook her curly black mane. "But some gal in leopard-print heels slipped me a card for a Botox party at her house. That, I might check out."

"A Botox party?" Darla echoed. "Now you're really out of my league. What in the heck is that?"

"Pretty much what it sounds like. A bunch of middle-aged women, a lot of wine and cheese, and a doctor—or someone who plays a doctor on television—who drops in to inject everyone's wrinkly foreheads with Botox."

"No thanks," Darla said with a shudder. "A woman at my old job invited me to a microdermabrasion party once, but I had a night class and couldn't go. Talk about dodging a bullet. I think the esthetician was slugging down the wine with the rest of them, because my friend came to work the next day looking like hamburger."

"Hmm, good point on the wine. If I decide to get Botoxed, I'll give the doc a breathalyzer test first. Now, let's get back to Hamlet. Have you thought about getting a kitten for him to buddy up with?"

"A kitten?" Darla gave a doubtful frown. "I'm sure Brody would have suggested that already if he'd thought it would work. And you know Hamlet. It's hard enough to get him to play nice with the customers. I can't see him sharing the place with another cat."

"Maybe a change of scenery, then. Find a pet-friendly place down the shore. It's off-season, so you could get something cheap for a long weekend."

"Hey, now that's not a bad idea," Darla eagerly agreed. "I know that the farthest Hamlet has ever traveled has been to the vet's office. Forget that whole atonement thing. A whiff of salt air might just snap him out of his funk."

She paused while the waitress served their steaming plates of pad Thai and then added, "I'll talk to Brody about it when he stops in next week for the follow-up visit. If he thinks it's worth a shot, I'll start looking for a weekend rental. And if you find Mrs. Putin in time, maybe you can take off work and come along with us."

"Sure, it might be fun," the older woman agreed. "Not that we'll get in any swimming this time of year, but we could do the big-pot-of-clam-chowder and bonfire-on-the-beach thing at night. And during the day, Hamlet can lounge inside on the windowsill and watch the little birdies skittering around on the beach."

"It's a plan," Darla agreed, feeling far more cheerful now than when she'd first walked into the restaurant. In fact, both she and Hamlet would likely benefit from a little getaway. She hadn't had a vacation since she'd moved up to New York, and life had been more than a little crazy—not to mention terrifying, at times—in the interim.

And if Jake's idea didn't work? Then she'd just have to wait around for the whole shaking Universe thing that Brody had talked about . . . and hope that he didn't mean a literal earthquake.

FIVE

"YELLOW BELT, HERE I COME," ROBERT DECLARED, PUNC-
tuating those words with a *"hi-yaa"* and a leaping front kick
that drew a halfhearted smile from Darla.

She and Robert were on their way to the dojo, gear bags
bouncing against their hips as they hurried to make their
eleven o'clock appointment. They weren't the only ones out
and about. The sun was shining on this crisp Sunday morning, and locals bundled in scarves and light jackets wandered the sidewalks in search of coffee or brunch. Darla was
dressed even more casually than the people they passed,
having donned a well-worn green velour track suit and a
white down vest for the short walk. Normally, she would
have opted for something that didn't make her look like a
1980s throwback, but this morning fashion was the least of
her worries.

Noting Darla's lack of enthusiasm, the teen slowed and
asked, "Are you, like, nervous about the test or something?"

"No, not a bit," Darla promptly lied.

Robert nodded. "I'm not either," he agreed, only to con-fess in the next breath, "Well, maybe, you know, a little.

Darla definitely felt his pain. It wasn't that she didn't know the katas they'd be tested on, she reminded herself. She had those kicking and punching routines down pat. Rather, she was suffering from the same stage fright that, years earlier, had left her frozen on the splintered stage of the Sam Houston elementary school, unable to remember the words to the prelude of *Evangeline*.

Darla grimaced at the decades-old memory. With a proud smile for her teacher, Mrs. Morgan, she had skipped onto the stage that day prepared to recite her poem as her part of the annual grade school talent show. Mindful of her poem's setting, she had dressed in a flowered dress that was her best attempt at evoking nature. Then, as she smoothed her bright red pigtails and squared her shoulders, she had glimpsed the audience seated beyond the blinding spotlight.

That had been her undoing.

She had managed to choke out the opening lines about the forest primeval and its murmuring pines and hemlocks, but then her eight-year-old mind had gone totally blank. She'd never forgotten the snickering from the audience, or the dis-appointed look on Mrs. Morgan's face. Ever afterward, she'd been dogged by a fear of public performance that even a stint in Toastmasters hadn't totally erased. And how much more public could you get than wearing what basically was white pj's while performing stylized punches and kicks? To be sure, she'd dodged the "public" portion of that bullet today, since it would be just the three of them; still, she couldn't help feeling nervous about her upcoming performance.

Robert, meanwhile, was trying to cheer them both up with a similar rationale. "Hey, at least we won't have the whole class watching today. Just think, when we move up higher in the ranks, we'll have to do this in front of a whole committee of black belts . . . Master Tomlinson, and the Steroid Twins, and probably even that punk Chris."

"Great," Darla muttered. "Maybe I'll stick with yellow belt for a while."

"Yeah, I know what you mean. Master Tomlinson is fair and stuff, but those other dudes—"

Robert broke off in mid-sentence and halted, his gear bag almost smacking Darla. Reflexively, she brushed aside his swinging bag with the same defensive technique she'd learned at the last class. Then, concerned he was about to talk himself out of the challenge, she gave the teen an encouraging smile.

"Take a deep breath and don't think about that now. Remember, today it's just going to be the sensei who—"

He cut her short and pointed. "Look, over by the door."

They were less than half a block from the dojo now, close enough to see the pair of red fu dogs that flanked its entry. But today the concrete beasts did not guard the studio alone. Following Robert's gaze, Darla could just make out a small gray and white muzzle poking from behind one of the statues.

"It's Roma!" Robert cried. "What's she doing outside in the cold?"

Together, they sprinted the remaining distance to the dojo, where they were greeted by the tiny hound. Bolting from behind her stone sibling, she gave a sharp bark in Darla and Robert's direction, and then began pawing at the dojo door.

"She must have slipped outside, and Master Tomlinson didn't realize it," Darla exclaimed as she tried the knob. The dojo entry was unlocked, and she had barely pushed open the door a few inches when Roma dashed in.

"Poor thing, she must have been freezing out there," Darla added as she and Robert entered, too. Then, smiling a little as she closed the door after them, she added, "Listen to her still barking. She's telling her daddy he'd better never let that happen again."

Their footsteps echoed as they made their way through

the shadowed vestibule area, its gallery of darkened photos reminding Darla of some ill-lit museum. In contrast, fluorescent light streamed from the training area, where in the next few minutes she and Robert would be showing their martial arts mettle. They made their way around the divider to see a long table that held stacks of paper, no doubt registrations for the upcoming tournament.

"Master Tomlinson!" Darla called as they reached the mat. "It's Darla and Robert, here for our belt test."

She expected the man to step out from the dressing area, for Roma was barking and bounding before those doors like a hound on springs. No one answered her greeting, and she exchanged an uncertain look with Robert. "I don't understand. He knew we were coming, and the front door was unlocked. Where did he go?"

"He must be out looking for Roma," the teen exclaimed. Dropping to one knee, he set down his gym bag and clapped his hands, trying to entice the dog to him. "He must have, you know, figured that she snuck out, and he doesn't know she's back."

"You're right, that makes sense. He's probably worried sick about her."

Roma, meanwhile, had rushed over to Robert and was anxiously pawing him with one delicate foot. He reached out to scoop her in his arms, but she wriggled away and began barking again. Watching the hound's antics, Darla shook her head.

"Hush, Roma, bad girl," she lightly scolded the pup. To Robert, she added, "Why don't you go ahead and get changed into your gi. I'm going to take a look outside for Master Tomlinson. With any luck, he's somewhere right here on the block, and I can let him know that Roma's just fine."

"Okay, sure," Robert agreed, getting to his feet again, and grabbing his bag. "Roma, c'mon with me."

Roma bounded after him. Darla dropped her bag at the mat's edge and headed back toward the reception area.

Having once lost Hamlet, she could readily imagine the man's concern. It was obvious to anyone who'd ever seen man and dog together how much he doted on the little canine. With luck, he was searching in the immediate neighborhood; and, even better, perhaps he'd realize that the wayward hound had made her way back to the dojo.

Passing by the front reception desk, she saw posted on the wall a list of cell phone numbers, two of which belonged to Hank and Hal. If Master Tomlinson didn't return soon, maybe she should try to call—

A shriek from the vicinity of the training area momentarily froze Darla in her tracks.

"Robert! Is that you?" she shouted back, forgetting her errand and rushing back toward the main studio. "Are you hurt? What happened?"

"Hurry! Help!" came a frantic, sobbing scream that she barely recognized as belonging to the teen.

Darla rushed across the mat. The door to the dressing room was closed, but she could hear Robert's wordless shouts within, as well as Roma's frantic barking. She yanked open the door . . . and then gave a reflexive scream of her own, unable to believe what she was seeing.

Her first impression was of a large man in a bulky white gi sagging in a seated position against the dressing room wall. She didn't recognize him at first, for his face was suffused with blood. But the swollen feet with their crooked toes were unmistakable. The black belt that hung in a loose loop around his neck was less so, as it lacked the five red stripes and the tiny red embroidered dragon. But even without that identification, she knew with a sinking heart just who it was. *Master Tomlinson!*

"Quick, he's still alive!" Robert sobbed out, trying to lift the man's bulk. "But he's too heavy. I can't get him out of here on my own!"

Heart attack? The thought flashed through Darla's mind as she promptly wrapped her arms around the sensei's legs.

"Hurry, bring him out onto the mat," she cried.

Even as she struggled to lift him, however, she noticed something odd. Not only was a black belt draped around the sensei's neck, but a heavy iron hook that was partially embedded into a broken chunk of particleboard lay beside him. She glanced up above to where two rows of iron coat hooks were installed on the back wall. One of those hooks was missing, as was a section of wall the same size as the piece attached to the hook at the fallen man's side.

Roma had prudently cowered in one corner of the tiny area during all this. Now, she rushed out onto the mat and began barking again while, between them, Darla and Robert began dragging the man through the narrow doorway. The teen's breath was coming from him in panting sobs as they struggled with the man's bulk. Darla was gasping, too, pulling with all her might, even as she realized that Tomlinson's hairy flesh beneath her sweating palms felt unnaturally cool. She'd stumbled across a dead man once, and she had a terrible feeling she had just found another. Or was it simply her frantic imagination working overtime?

"I'll call 9-1-1," she gasped out, as soon as they had tugged the sensei out of the dressing room and well out onto the heavy red mat. Now the man sprawled on his back like a fighter who had not been able to avoid his opponent's final winning punch. The black belt hung loosely from around his neck, like an oversized bow tie gone askew. He still wasn't moving . . . and Darla could see no rise and fall of the pale hairy chest exposed by the gaping lapels of his gi jacket.

As she dug in her gear bag for her phone, Robert cried, "Shouldn't we do mouth-to-mouth or something?"

Darla paused and stared over at the still form on the mat, trying to tamp down a rising sense of horror. "Robert," she began in a halting voice, "I don't think—" She broke off at the despairing look on the teen's face, not wanting to shatter any last hope he had. "That is, I don't think they do mouth-to-mouth anymore," she hurriedly improvised, "just chest compressions. Why don't you try that while I call?"

"Yeah, okay, they taught us that in gym class."

He gave a vigorous nod and dropped to his knees beside the man. Darla finally found her phone and, moving a few feet farther away from Robert, she placed the call.

"Yes, it's an emergency!" was her swift if somewhat tremulous reply once the dispatcher came on the line. She gave a quick rundown of the patient and the situation, and then waited while her call was transferred yet again.

"The ambulance is on its way," she assured Robert a few moments later. The teen grunted his acknowledgment, his attention fixed on the still form before him. He was performing the resuscitation routine like a pro, Darla thought, impressed. The gym class instruction had obviously taken.

Roma, meanwhile, had settled nervously alongside her master's feet, uttering little howls that sounded unsettlingly like a child's cries. Realizing that the tiny hound would be in the way once the paramedics arrived, Darla rushed again toward the front of the building. Roma's leash would likely be in Tomlinson's office. Best to make certain that the pup wouldn't be able to slip from the building again in the midst of the commotion . . . though now she found herself suddenly wondering just how Roma had gotten outside the first time, after all.

Darla didn't have time to follow that train of thought, however. She grabbed Roma's bright purple lead from atop Master Tomlinson's desk, alongside his key ring, then hurried back to snap it onto the dog's matching collar. She touched Robert on the shoulder.

"The ambulance should be here any moment," she told him. "Why don't you let me do this for a minute, while you hang on to Roma. I took a class once, too. I remember how to do it."

"I'm fine," he gasped out, though she could see drops of sweat—or maybe they were tears—slipping down his check and spattering onto the sensei's white jacket. He was clearly avoiding looking directly at the man's slack face lest he have to admit that his efforts were making no difference, that Master Tomlinson likely was past saving. Darla didn't bother arguing. She could hear the faint scream of sirens; soon the paramedics would be taking over.

"Okay, you stay here. I'll grab Roma and go let the emergency people in." Darla scooped up the tiny greyhound, who obediently submitted to her grasp. By the time she reached the dojo's front door again, the sirens' pulsing cries were almost deafening.

The next few moments were a blur of action. Not only had the ambulance service responded, but the police and fire department, as well. The studio entry was overwhelmed now with large uniformed men hauling all manner of rescue gear, a gurney clattering as they rushed behind Darla through the maze-like path to the training area. While the responders gathered around the collapsed man, a shaken Darla pulled Robert a safe distance back to give them room.

The teen was manfully trying to hold it together, though Darla caught him rubbing his eyes with one sleeve. Roma whined, and Darla promptly handed the dog over to Robert.

"Here," she said softly, managing a tremulous smile as the little dog burrowed into Robert's arms. "She needs her friend right now."

It seemed Robert needed the little dog even more, for he promptly settled cross-legged on the floor and buried his face in the velvet softness of her small body, his shoulders silently shaking.

And then the chaos before them was punctuated by one word that sent a frisson of hope through Darla.

"Pulse!"

On a quick count, several of the men lifted Tomlinson's bulky frame onto the gurney. She glimpsed an oxygen bottle and an IV drip, and what she guessed was some sort of heart monitor all attached to, or piled atop, the motionless form.

And then, radios squawking, the paramedics rushed the gurney back in the direction from which they'd come, followed more slowly by the firefighters. One of the police officers, a stocky young Asian with a large shaved head, remained behind with Robert and Darla in the training area.

He pulled a business card from his shirt pocket and handed it to Darla.

"I know this has been a shock to you, ma'am, but you guys have done a great job so far," he said and then jerked a thumb in Robert's direction. "You two related, or you just both happened to be here at the same time?"

"Robert works for me. I own Pettistone's Fine Books a few blocks from here. We take classes together, and we came in special for our belt test this morning."

The cop—Officer Tommy Wing, Darla saw from the name on his business card—nodded, jotting down a few words in the small notebook he'd pulled from his belt. "If you're up for it, I need to ask you both a few questions. Let me get the victim's name, first, and then yours, and then you can show me where you found the gentleman."

Darla spelled out the names for him, shakily recounted how they'd found Roma outside the dojo, and then how Robert had found Master Tomlinson slumped unconscious in the dressing room. "I-I thought it could have been a heart attack," she told him, "but then I saw that—" She paused and pointed to the fallen hook. "And now I'm not so sure."

"That black belt lying out there on the mat—was that the one you saw around his neck?" the officer wanted to know.

Darla nodded, and he wandered back out of the dressing room again. He stopped to kneel beside the black length of heavy fabric which the paramedics had removed as they'd attempted their resuscitation. "You're sure it belongs to him?"

"I-I guess so. But the one he always wears is fancier—it has five red stripes and an embroidered red dragon. That one doesn't."

The cop studied the rank belt for a moment and then unsnapped a pouch on his own belt, pulling out an evidence bag.

"He probably put the other belt away for safekeeping," Wing guessed as he carefully slid the length of heavy black fabric into the evidence bag. The officer rose again and moved over to Robert. The teen had composed himself now, though he still clung to Roma like a child with a stuffed toy. They went over the same questions, and when he was finished, Robert demanded, "Where did the ambulance take him? Will Master Tomlinson be okay?"

Wing gave them the name of the hospital before adding, "I know this is going to sound harsh, but don't get your hopes up. The docs will do everything they can for him, but the guy is in pretty bad shape."

"But he had a pulse," Robert protested, his tone angry now.

"Yeah, I saw you doing chest compressions. If your sensei has any sort of chance of pulling through, it's because of you." Then, glancing around the mat, the young cop shook his shaved head. "A real shame, too. He was a pretty big name back in the old days."

"Yeah," Robert glumly agreed. "There's, you know, pictures on the wall."

The cop, meanwhile, was warming to the topic.

"When I was a kid, I trained at Tiger Lee's dojo across town. We had a pretty big rivalry going with the TAMA guys in those days, and I don't think my sensei liked Master Tomlinson much. I never figured out why, because from what I saw of him at some of the tournaments, he was an okay guy. Maybe it was because he was an American kicking Asian butt," Wing added with a hint of a smile.

Then, recalling his duty, the cop spared another look at his notes. "I know you two are just students here, but you know anyone connected with the dojo . . . partner, spouse, kids . . . that we should notify?"

"Actually, Master Tomlinson's stepsons work here at the

dojo," Darla ventured. "And he's got a wife . . . Maybe she's an ex, I don't know. But there's a phone list hanging in his office with their names on it."

"Great, lead the way."

Darla escorted the cop to the sensei's office. Wing scribbled down the names from the list into his notebook, and then frowned. "Hank and Hal Tomlinson," he mused. "Those are his stepsons, right? I still remember those guys from the tournaments. Both of them were real—" He broke off and looked faintly embarrassed.

"Real jerks?" Darla helpfully supplied, drawing a wry smile from the man.

"Yeah, that about covers it." He paused and scanned the desk top, and then caught Darla's questioning gaze.

"I didn't want to say anything in front of the kid out there, but from what I've seen so far, it doesn't look like the old guy had a heart attack."

"He tried to commit suicide, didn't he?" Darla asked, feeling her chest clench a little as she finally gave voice to her suspicions.

The cop nodded. "That's my opinion, yeah. And it's pretty cliché, but in cases like that we always like to look around for a note. There's usually not one, but you never know. I don't suppose you and Mr. Gilmore found anything you forgot to tell me about?"

"You mean, like some kind of good-bye to his family? No, we didn't find anything like that," Darla assured him in a shaky voice.

The cop nodded. "Well, let's wait and see if he pulls through. If the worst happens"—he shot a sidelong look at Robert outside the office door, and lowered his voice—"we'll dig a little deeper."

Flipping closed his notebook, he gestured Darla back to the vestibule and added, "Now, why don't you grab your stuff, and let's get out of here. I'll check in with the hospital and let you know how Master Tomlinson is doing."

Leaving Robert with the officer, Darla hurried back to the training area and retrieved her bag. Then, steeling herself, she went back to the dressing room to retrieve Robert's gear. Already the dojo had taken on an air of angry tragedy that seemed almost palpable, while the dressing room itself—usually such an innocuous spot—felt heavy with inescapable oppression.

"Stop it," she whispered to herself. "He may still be alive."

A bag over either shoulder, she made her swift way to the vestibule again, in time to hear Robert passionately protesting, "But I can't leave her. Hank and Hal hate her. They'll send her to the pound, and she'll die there! She'll be safe with me. I swear it!"

Teen and cop were facing off, Wing looking weary and Robert clutching Roma protectively to his chest, his expression stubborn. The small hound did her part by giving Robert's chin a quick lick with her long pink tongue.

The cop sighed. "Officially, I should have animal control pick her up and hold her until a family member claims her. But if the dog vanishes before I can do that"—he paused and deliberately turned his back on Robert—"I guess it is what it is."

The teen needed no further encouragement to dash for the door, Roma barking excitedly all the way. Wing, meanwhile, was succumbing to what sounded like a suspiciously fake bout of coughing. When he turned around again, Robert and Roma both were long gone.

"Coulda sworn there was a dog here," he said with a shake of his head. "Guess not."

"Guess not," Darla echoed, managing a smile. "But if Robert happens to find her, I can guarantee he'll keep her safe until we know what happens with her owner."

While the officer locked the dojo with the keys that Master Tomlinson had left on his desk, Darla blinked against the midday sun, barely noticing the chill in the air. A glance at her watch showed that it was just after twelve, though the nightmare in the dojo had seemingly gone on for hours. She didn't know if the sensei had survived his trip to the ER . . . didn't want to know yet, until she'd thought of a way to break the news to Robert should the worst happen.

"Ms. Pettistone, can I give you a ride?" Officer Wing asked as he headed toward his squad car.

Darla followed his glance to the gear bags at her feet and then shook her head. "They're light, and I need the walk to clear my head. But thanks."

"Suit yourself," he said with a professional nod. "And I'll ring you as soon as I hear anything about Mr. Tomlinson's condition."

Darla watched him pull out into traffic; then, shifting the bags onto her shoulders again, she started down the sidewalk in the direction of the bookstore. Little more than an hour ago, her biggest worry had been succumbing to stage fright and forgetting the moves to her katas. But now . . .

She swiped away a sudden tear and concentrated her thoughts on Robert, instead. Hopefully the teen was almost back to the store now, Roma in tow. What Mary Ann would say about her young tenant bringing home a dog, Darla wasn't certain, but surely the kind old woman would make a temporary exception to the "no pets" rule, given the circumstances. And if not, then Hamlet would find himself with a canine roommate . . . at least until they learned Master Tomlinson's fate.

SIX

"JEEZE, KID, THAT'S AWFUL," JAKE REPLIED ONCE DARLA
finished giving her an account of how she and Robert had
found Master Tomlinson in the dojo dressing room that
morning. The PI leaned against the register counter—Darla
had gone ahead and opened the store as usual—and absently
rearranged the stack of giveaway papers. "So, have you told
him yet?"

Darla shook her head, not trusting herself to speak.

By the time she'd made it back to the store, Robert was
already hunkered down in his apartment, with Roma settled
on a stack of pillows on his sofa. His door was double-locked
against anyone—that was, any Hal or Hank—who might be
inclined to come after the little Italian greyhound. And he'd
only let Darla in once she had assured him she was alone.

Darla had told him to take the day off work and given
him a few dollars to have the local grocer deliver dog food,
promising to speak to Mary Ann as well about this technical
breach of his lease. She'd then hurriedly checked on Hamlet,

who'd been asleep in the apartment. After putting in a couple of minutes of official chin-scratching time—which Hamlet reluctantly tolerated, but which made Darla feel much better—she rushed downstairs again to open the store a good hour late. Luckily, no angry customers were waiting at the locked door, and only two people so far had wandered in after that.

Which meant that Darla had been alone in the store when the call had come from Officer Wing a few minutes earlier. Sounding regretful, he'd let her know that, despite Robert's valiant efforts, the sensei had been pronounced dead once he reached the hospital. Darla had thanked him in a shaky voice and then dialed Jake, desperate for advice as to how to break the news to Robert. Jake had promptly come up to the store to lend a sympathetic ear.

"I need to go down and do it, but I just don't know how," Darla said now with a helpless shrug. "Robert will be heartbroken when I tell him, especially under the circumstances. I mean, from the look of things, Tomlinson deliberately ended it all."

"Suicides are the worst," Jake agreed with a grim expression that made Darla realize that the ex-cop had likely seen more than her share. "Far be it from me to judge—God knows someone would have to be in horrible pain to do something like that—but my sympathies are always with the people left behind. You don't know how many times I sat on a cold stoop holding someone's hand while they cried their hearts out."

She paused and gave Darla an apologetic look.

"Sorry, I don't mean to lecture, but that kind of thing sticks with you. You've got the family and friends all wanting to know, *why* . . . and no one but the dead person can ever answer that. It doesn't matter if the victim leaves behind a note or not. Usually they don't. But either way, there are always questions, and anger, and guilt. The dead guy is neatly out of it, and everyone else gets to spend the rest of their lives picking up the pieces."

Darla nodded in understanding. And then a surge of anger welled inside her as it occurred to her that she and Robert were part of Master Tomlinson's *everyone else*. He had told them to be at the dojo at that time. Why not call them and cancel the test, or wait until afterward to carry out his plan? How could he have been so cruel as to deliberately have let them find his body like that? And to leave Roma out in the street, where she might have been hit by a car and killed!

Trying to keep her voice steady, she said as much to Jake.

The older woman gave a sympathetic nod. "I know, it sounds pretty damn selfish, but there's always a logic to these things. He probably thought it was better for you and Robert to find him right away, rather than have his family come looking for him a day or two later. Obviously, it hadn't occurred to him that the hook might not hold his weight. He figured he'd be dead already. And if for some reason you two didn't show, maybe the dog pawing at the door would have raised someone's suspicions."

"I guess that does make sense, but it's still pretty horrible for Robert." Darla took a deep breath, deliberately tamping down her anger. Then an even worse thought occurred to her. "Do you think"—she hesitated over the next words—"I mean, was he already too far gone when Robert and I found him? I mean, if we'd gotten there a few minutes earlier, could we have saved him?"

Jake shook her curly head and pointed her finger at Darla.

"Don't even go there, kid. The fact that the hook gave way before he quit breathing permanently probably just prolonged things by a few minutes."

Darla sighed. "I can't put it off any longer, I suppose. I need to go tell him."

"Go tell him what?"

The bleak words made Darla jump. So intent had she been on her conversation with Jake that she hadn't heard the bells jingle at the front door. Now, the teen was standing beside the register, a subdued Roma cradled in his arms.

"Robert, I told you that you could take the day off," she scolded him. "What are you doing here?"

"I wanted to find out how Master Tomlinson is doing. I called the hospital, but they wouldn't tell me anything, even when I lied and said I was Hank." Then, blue eyes dark with grief, he added, "He didn't make it, did he?"

"No, I'm so sorry, he didn't," Darla replied, her tone gentle now. "I got the call from Officer Wing a few minutes ago. He died on the way to the hospital. I was trying to figure out how to tell you."

"So, who needs him, anyhow?"

The teen's tone had taken on a sudden angry edge, his expression belligerent. At Darla's startled look, he added, "I'm not dumb. I know what happened. That hook on the wall, and the belt around his neck. He didn't have a heart attack. He killed himself."

Robert's grip on Roma tightened, so that she gave a little yelp. "All that stuff he said about never giving up, that was just bull. He didn't believe it. I don't care if he's dead!"

"Robert, I know you don't mean that," Darla countered. "He didn't do this to hurt you, or anyone else. You have to understand that something must have been terribly wrong for him to take his own life."

"Yeah, like what?"

"Maybe he was sick, or maybe he had money problems and didn't know how to get out from under them." Then, recalling the brief but contentious words between the sensei and his stepson, she added, "Or maybe he had family issues that drove him over the edge."

"Whatever. All I know is—"

"Hey, Robert," Jake broke in. She had listened to the

exchange in silence, her expression sympathetic. Now, briskly, she said, "I have a file cabinet downstairs I need to move, but I can't do it myself. Since Darla gave you a little time off, maybe you can come down for a couple of minutes and help me with that. And your little dog, too."

She gave him a friendly wink at that last, but either the Oz reference went over the teen's head, or else he simply wasn't prepared to be cheered up yet. Instead, with a sullen nod, he said, "Sure."

Turning, he headed with Roma toward the door, Jake following after. The older woman glanced back at Darla and gave her a nod that said, *I've got this.*

Darla gave a grateful nod back and mouthed, *Thanks.* Young as Robert was, he still saw the world in black and white, and in his eyes the sensei's death was nothing less than a betrayal. Jake would know far better how to handle the teen who obviously was succumbing to the anger the ex-cop had just described.

It was slow for a Sunday afternoon. Between waiting on the handful of customers—browsers, every one—that wandered in, Darla spent the next hour puttering about the store straightening merchandise and trying to forget the ghastly image of Master Tomlinson sagging half-dead against the dressing room wall. She briefly contemplated giving herself the day off, just as she'd done for Robert, but then decided against it. She knew from past experience that the only way to get past a trauma like this was to talk it out, until the narrative became rote. Even better would be talking it out with someone who would understand what she was going through.

And so, on impulse, she did something she'd been putting off for almost two weeks. She picked up her phone and dialed Reese.

Her reluctance to call stemmed from the uncomfortable memory of the so-called date with him that she'd impulsively gone on a couple of weeks earlier. She had been of two minds about accepting his invitation in the first place. On the one hand, there had been a feeling of anticipation at possibly taking their relationship to the next level. On the other, she'd had a vague sense of dread over basically forcing a friendship into a romance. And, unfortunately, her forebodings had proved correct.

While the food had been outstanding, the evening's conversation had been stilted, and mostly regarding the virtues of said superb meal . . . but there was a definite spark. The problem was, how best to fan it, assuming she wanted to create an actual blaze.

Personality-wise, Reese was what Darla had begun to categorize as the typical Brooklyn "guy" . . . blunt, sarcastic, and definitely appreciative of the ladies. Like most of the "guys" she'd met thus far in her new city, beneath the tough image he had the stereotypical big heart. Not her usual type, to be sure, but she was open to variety at this point in her life.

Not that Reese lacked anything in the looks department. He had what Darla always thought of as corn-fed Midwestern good looks, despite an Italian mother who contributed little to his physical gene pool but saddled him with the Christian name of Fiorello, an appellation his fellow cops used at their peril. Tall and blond, he had a bodybuilder's physique and a broken nose that had never been reset, which kept him from being dismissed as another pretty boy. And he'd proved himself to be both loyal and resourceful, two major traits she required in any potential love interest. His main flaw, to her mind, was that while street-smart and blessed with a cop's intuition, he wasn't a book kind of person. Which was something of an issue, given that she owned a bookstore!

As to what Reese saw in her, Darla wasn't certain. She was a year, maybe two, older than he, and her Southern outlook on life was a definite one-eighty from his. She'd been unable to figure out what to do during the meal, and the walk back to her apartment had proved equally uncomfortable. Obviously sensing her ambivalence, Reese had stopped short of any overly familiar gesture such as taking her arm, settling instead on the chummier alternate of hand on shoulder that was less an embrace than a steering gesture. But the truly awkward part had come at her front door, when she'd been faced with the ultimate question.

Handshake? Kiss? Run for the door and avoid either?

In the end, he'd given her a peck on the cheek and a "let's do this again sometime" farewell that had left her relieved and vaguely insulted all at the same time.

And the truth was that Reese and Hamlet shared a love-hate relationship that was decidedly skewed toward hate. Which didn't bode well.

But she was willing to move past all that awkwardness in the wake of the day's events.

The detective answered on the first ring.

"Hey, Red," he greeted her with the nickname she detested, but which she'd finally allowed from him. At least it was better than Cherry Top. "I, uh, was wondering if I'd hear from you . . ."

"Sorry, I really did mean to call," she temporized, "but I've been kind of busy at the store. And then I've been worried about Hamlet. He's still not the same after everything that happened."

Hearing his name, Hamlet lifted his chin from his oversized black paws and stared at her from his lounging spot at the end of the counter. Half an hour earlier, he had wandered his way down to the store to grace her with his company. Fortunately, that had been well after Robert had left with Roma, but the way Hamlet had sniffed about the store told her that he suspected some other animal had set foot in his territory.

To Reese, she said, "But Hamlet's not the problem . . . at least, not at the moment. I just need someone to talk to besides Jake. Since today is Sunday, I'll be closing the store in a couple of hours. Maybe I can meet you somewhere for an early supper?"

"Hang on."

She heard another voice—female?—in the background, and then heard Reese mutter something about residue before he came back on. "Sorry, work's getting in the way of my afternoon, too. Anyhow, I can do seven. How about the Italian place we went to last time?"

"Sure. I-I really do need to talk to you."

She was dismayed to hear the catch in her voice. Reese must have heard it, as well, for his own tone sharpened.

"What's wrong? If it's an emergency, I'll see if I can break free in a few."

Darn right, it's an emergency, she wanted to say. *Our sensei practically committed suicide in front of me and Robert a couple of hours ago.*

But she didn't want Reese to feel obligated to come play nursemaid to her during working hours. After all, they technically were just friends. And so, she replied, "No, it's not like that. I'll explain when I see you."

She rang off, feeling somewhat better knowing that by suppertime she'd be able to dump her concerns on him. That part of it, she didn't feel guilty about. After all, it had been Reese who had pushed her to seek therapy after that same incident that was responsible for Hamlet's funk. He had even offered the name of a counselor, and though she'd not yet dialed that number, given today's events, maybe she'd dig it out. In the meantime, she'd press Hamlet into service as her confidante.

"Hey, Hammy," she addressed him. "You weren't here when Jake stopped in, so you're not up-to-date on everything that's happened. You got a minute?"

While the cat comfortably slumbered, Darla related again the circumstances surrounding finding Master Tomlinson's all-but-lifeless body. "Robert pretends like he doesn't care, but that's just because he's angry. So we need to help him deal with this. Got any words of advice you want to pass on?"

By way of answer, the cat gave a small snore and rolled onto his side. He kicked a paperback that had been left on the counter by a previous browser who'd seen the signs asking customers not to reshelf books they'd decided against buying, but to instead bring them to the front. It was a new policy she'd recently instituted after determining that she and her staff spent far too many unproductive hours returning errant books to their proper places after a busy day.

Not that she didn't suspect that many of those wayward volumes had been misshelved deliberately. How else to explain the *Field Guide to Body Art* she'd found squirreled away in the kids' section, or the copy of *365 Decadent Desserts* tucked in among the diet books?

The book hit the ground with a resounding splat.

"Don't bother getting up, I'll handle this," Darla muttered in Hamlet's direction. She went around the counter to retrieve the fallen volume, the latest release in a popular fantasy series. She scanned the beefy anime-inspired warrior on its cover and then reflexively read the title aloud: *"Nothing is What It Seems."*

Darla frowned in Hamlet's direction. In the time since Darla had assumed ownership of the bookstore, she'd had more than a couple of odd situations occur, all of which Hamlet had seemingly had some feline insight into. Lacking opposable thumbs—the sole reason, Darla often joked to Jake, that Hamlet was not already dictator of some small country— the wily cat found other ways to communicate. Often it was by means of pulling various book titles from the store's shelves; "book snagging," as Darla liked to call it.

To anyone else not privy to the circumstances, this sort of behavior from a bored cat might be nothing more than mischief. Darla was certain by now, however, that Hamlet's choices in literature were anything but random. In retrospect, the various snagged titles had had a definite connection to circumstances, and had even yielded valuable clues.

So maybe Hamlet was at it again? *"Nothing is What It Seems,"* Darla repeated as she again studied the garish cover. Given that the character depicted in the artwork was obviously of Asian influence, Hamlet might well be trying to give her a heads up about Master Tomlinson's suicide.

Did he know something she didn't about Master Tomlinson's death?

Her frown deepening, she demanded, "All right, Hamlet, spill. Are you trying to tell me that his suicide wasn't suicide? Should I be talking to Reese about this?"

Hamlet did not deign to answer but simply let loose another snore before settling into a more comfortable position.

But how did one inadvertently hang oneself?

The first explanation that came to mind promptly made her wish she hadn't decided to explore that train of thought. Hadn't there been a cult actor known for his martial arts roles who had accidentally strangled himself while engaging in some kinky solitary play? Darla shuddered, hoping Master Tomlinson had not gone down that same path—yet on the other hand, a fatal accident of any sort was marginally less devastating than a death deliberately planned.

Wishful thinking, kid. Darla could practically hear Jake's voice in her ear, swiftly dispelling the unlikely scenario she'd been trying to conjure. Even if the sensei had been standing on the bench reinstalling a hook, how could a knotted belt have managed to accidentally wrap around both that hardware and his neck?

"Try again, Hammy. Reese will laugh in my face if I bring this up," she muttered as she carried the book back to its proper spot on the shelves. She should accept what happened and move on. After all, sometimes things actually *were* just what they appeared to be.

Splat!

Darla jumped at the unexpected sound. Could that have been another fallen book, courtesy of Hamlet? She glanced back and spied the feline still sprawled on the counter where she'd left him. Surely he couldn't have jumped down, snagged a book, and leaped back onto the counter to feign sleep so quickly.

Or could he?

Shaking her head, Darla marched back in the direction of the register, eyes peeled for a book lying on the floor where it shouldn't be. Nothing. After a few moments' searching, however, she found a book in the section of the store that used to be the brownstone's back parlor. Now, the refurbished room housed the old standbys of her stock . . . history, travel, crafts, biographies, politics. Warily, she picked up the heavy volume from the floor and read the title.

"Trust Me."

The book itself was a recent autobiography of a well-known political commentator. Whether or not the author could indeed be believed, Darla had no idea. But if Hamlet had chosen this title to bolster his previous unspoken commentary, then she likely would do well to keep her eyes and ears open. Because maybe the clever cat was right.

Maybe nothing really *was* what it seemed.

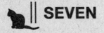 || **SEVEN**

"OH, MY. I'M REALLY NOT SURE ABOUT THIS, DARLA."

Mary Ann Plinski stood behind the counter of her antiques shop with her wrinkled hands clasping and unclasping before her, her pursed lips reflecting her uncertainty. "As I told you before, I've never cared much for dogs."

Which was just as well, Darla briefly reflected, because a dog let loose in the woman's shop would have spelled disaster for the merchandise. Bygone Days Antiques specialized in eighteenth- and nineteenth-century Americana, though Darla had noticed a steady trend in the past few months to collectibles dating from the early twentieth century, too.

Budget, Mary Ann had confided to her, explaining that the market for cheaper collectibles was growing, while the demand for true antiques was slipping.

In fact, according to Mary Ann, her brother had recently sent a good number of their more pricey pieces to a local auction to clear room for the more modern merchandise.

Even so, the faintly musty scents of old wooden furniture and vintage clothing and linens made Darla feel at home in the crowded shop, which never looked the same from visit to visit.

Now, she nodded in understanding of the old woman's protest.

"I know you don't normally allow pets in the apartment, but Roma is very friendly with strangers, and she has perfect manners. And this is an exceptional situation."

"Yes, so it seems," Mary Ann said with a sigh.

Darla nodded again. She'd stopped by the Plinskis' shop the night before to explain to Mary Ann what had happened at the dojo, confiding as well how deeply Robert had been affected by the tragedy. Mary Ann had agreed that, under the circumstances, the dog could stay the night. But she had politely dug in her heels at the prospect of adding Roma to the lease.

"It's not just me, you know," the old woman had explained. "Brother is frail, and he's sensitive to unpleasant noises like barking and howling."

Brother, of course, being Mary Ann's older sibling who owned the building and store with her. Darla still had yet to meet the elderly gentleman in person, although she'd seen him in passing—and not long ago, had witnessed him being loaded into an ambulance following a heart attack scare. She understood why Mary Ann was so protective of her brother but she also knew how much Roma meant to Robert, particularly at this moment.

Now, she gave Mary Ann an encouraging smile and gestured to Robert, who'd been huddling with the tiny dog near the shop's front door. "Robert, why don't you introduce Roma to Ms. Plinski?"

Darla had stopped in to see Robert first thing that morning, to check on his welfare. She'd had a text from Jake the previous night, saying that the teen was coping as well as could be expected but needed a little alone time to process everything that had happened. Darla was sure that having the little hound at his side would no doubt make things easier for him.

Whether it had been the heart-to-heart with Jake or simply the resiliency of youth, Robert had seemed pretty much back to normal that morning . . . that was, normal for a kid who favored all black in his wardrobe and wore rings and studs in various appendages. Now, Robert gave Mary Ann a tentative smile and set Roma on the ground at his feet, careful to keep hold of the purple lead. Roma, looking uncharacteristically subdued, quivered slightly where she stood, her ears tightly folded back against her narrow head and her long whip of a tail tucked between her legs. Mary Ann walked around the counter, halting a prudent distance away and giving the little dog a doubtful look.

"Well, she is very pretty, I will admit, and much tinier than I'd expected. Is she a miniature greyhound?"

"No, ma'am, she's an Italian greyhound. That's a whole different breed. But Iggies—that's what people who own them call them—are sighthounds just like regular greyhounds. That means they, you know, hunt by sight instead of scent," he explained with an expert air.

Darla suppressed a smile. No doubt Robert had spent the prior evening on his smart phone searching the Internet for information about the breed.

As Mary Ann leaned forward for a closer look, the teen went on, "Iggies have been around for almost two thousand years, but they were especially popular during the Renaissance in Italy. That's why, you know, they're called *Italian* greyhounds. If you look at old paintings, you'll see them hunting or lying around on pillows. And they always wore those big fancy collars with lots of jewels and stuff."

"That's very interesting, Robert," the old woman agreed. "Why, the Borgias or Machiavelli or even Leonardo da Vinci might have owned one of these dogs."

"Right. And they're smart, too. Watch this."

Unsnapping Roma's collar, Robert took a few steps away from her and then gave a swift hand signal. "Roma, sit."

The dog promptly planted her thin haunches on the floor. With another series of signals that Darla recalled seeing Master Tomlinson use with her, Robert said, "Roma, shake. Roma, lie down. Roma, roll over."

The small hound quickly performed each trick in sequence and then returned to her seated position. Her pink tongue lolled from her mouth in a wide doggie grin, matching Robert's proud smile. "All right, this is, like, the best trick of all. Roma, up," he commanded and clapped his hands.

Just as she'd done with Master Tomlinson, the little dog gave a gazelle-like leap and landed in Robert's open arms.

Now, it was Mary Ann who was clapping. "My, how clever she is," the old woman exclaimed. Taking a tentative step forward, she added, "Do you think I might pet her?"

"Sure," Robert agreed, offering up the dog now snuggly settled in his arms.

Mary Ann reached a wrinkled hand toward Roma's narrow brow and gave her a gentle stroke. "Why, she feels just like velvet," she marveled, smiling when Roma gave her fingers a quick lick of approval.

Darla smiled, too. "So, what do you think, Mary Ann? Maybe we could try it for a week, just until other arrangements can be made?"

Not that Darla expected that any other arrangements were going to be made. She hadn't heard from Officer Wing since he'd called her yesterday to confirm Master Tomlinson's death. And while the cop had turned a blind eye at Robert taking Roma away, he surely would have tracked him down if someone had been looking for the little dog. But Darla suspected from the sensei's stepsons' attitudes that Roma was not high on the priority list for the man's surviving family, even though the tiny hound had been his beloved pet. Since no one had tried to locate her by now, chances were that no one would.

Mary Ann, meanwhile, was nodding.

"Robert, she can stay in your apartment temporarily so long as you promise she won't chew up the furniture or disturb Brother. And I expect you to walk her regularly and pick up after her, and make sure she always has fresh food and water. Agreed?"

"Agreed," he exclaimed, happily hugging the dog to him. "Thanks, Ms. P. You're, like, the best!" Then, to Darla, he added, "Uh, Ms. Pettistone, could I maybe have an advance on my next check? With it getting so cold out, I want to buy Roma sweaters and stuff to wear."

"I've got a better idea," Darla replied. "There's a pet boutique a few blocks away. Since we're closed today, how about after lunch we head over there to go shopping? I'll charge it on my card, and you can pay me back a little at a time."

"Sick! You're the best, too, Ms. Pettistone."

"Well, I was planning on going anyway. I'm thinking I should buy Hamlet one of those fancy interactive toys and see if that perks him up a little."

"Speaking of perking him up," Mary Ann ventured, "why don't you introduce him to Roma?"

Hamlet and Roma?

Darla stared at her elderly friend in horror, visions of a howling dog and long, bloody claw marks crisscrossing velvet fur flashing through her mind. "I really don't think—"

"Yeah, that's a great idea," Robert broke in. "That'll, you know, shake Hammy up a little."

"I said perk, not shake," Darla reminded him, even as she recalled what Brody the cat guy had told her . . . something about the Universe shaking up things when you least expect it? Though she suspected Roma the Italian greyhound didn't exactly fall into the category of Universe shaker.

"You know how Hamlet is," she continued. "He's always been an only cat. Once, a woman came into the store with a puppy zipped inside one of those dog carrier purses. She put the purse on the counter, and Hamlet deliberately knocked the poor thing right off."

Darla shuddered at the memory, grateful that she'd been within arm's length of the tumbling puppy on that particular day and had caught the purse before any harm was done.

Robert shrugged. "Well, I still think it's a good idea. Besides, Roma is a tough karate hound. She can take care of herself."

"Maybe, but let's not put that to the test just yet. Let me get a few things done at home, and I'll meet you outside the store at one o'clock, okay?"

"Okay."

Pausing to give Mary Ann a peck on the cheek, the youth tucked Roma's muzzle under his vest against the cold and hurried out the front door of the shop. Darla stared fondly after him before turning the same pleased look on the elderly woman.

"Thanks, Mary Ann. That was kind of you to let him keep Roma. Poor kid, having a dog to love really means a lot to him."

She didn't have to explain to Mary Ann that Robert had no family of his own to speak of. The old woman already knew from Darla that the youth's parents were long divorced, with his mother living in California and his father having kicked Robert out of the house when the latter had turned eighteen. While Robert had plenty of friends his own age, Darla, James, Jake, and the Plinskis had pretty well become his surrogate family.

"I suppose it's true, that every boy should have a dog," Mary Ann declared. Then, tapping a finger to her chin, she added, "You know, I think I have something here in the store that he might appreciate. I'll surprise him with it this afternoon."

With a final promise to help Robert with the dog should he need assistance, Darla made her good-byes to the old woman and headed back to her apartment. More than anything, she wanted to spend a little quality time with Hamlet. If Brody the cat whisperer—scratch that, the feline behavioral empath—was right about Hamlet feeling the need to atone, the least she could do was hang out with him and give him a chance to do so.

The cat was where she'd left him earlier that morning, lounging on the back of the horsehair couch. "Hey, Hammy, how's tricks?" she greeted him in a breezy tone. "Anything interesting happen while I was gone?"

Hamlet opened one emerald eye just long enough for her to pick up on the definite *you lookin' at me?* vibe coming off him. Then, flexing one front paw, so that his claws made a brief but unmistakable appearance, he shut his eye again.

So much for the atonement theory, Darla told herself with a small grimace. Brody must have gotten some wires crossed somewhere.

"Fine, be that way," she told the cat and plopped onto the far end of the couch. "But you're stuck with my company for a while . . . at least until I meet up with your buddy Robert after lunch."

At the mention of Robert's name, Hamlet opened the other eye. This time, she sensed slightly less disdain on his part. "You know that Robert is pretty upset about what happened yesterday. So when he comes in to work tomorrow, be extra nice to him, okay?"

Hamlet closed his eye again and settled himself more comfortably on his perch. Marginally encouraged, Darla continued, "I know I act like I'm always in control, but finding Master Tomlinson like that was pretty darn awful. Every time I think about it, I feel sick to my stomach. He was such a nice man, and he really cared about us students. I know I told Robert that we shouldn't judge, that he must have felt overwhelmed by life to do such a thing, but that's just talk. It's really hard not to be angry on top of being so sad."

She paused and brushed away a tear that threatened. Hamlet, meanwhile, opened both eyes now and stared at her.

"I know Jake understands," she said, "but she's seen a whole lot worse, so I hate to dump on her with my problems. That's why I called Reese. He's the one who told me last time that you have to talk about this kind of thing, and not keep it all in. And he's right."

For Reese had served as a literal shoulder for her to cry on. Thinking back on the previous night at the restaurant, Darla was torn between embarrassment and gratitude. In between courses, he'd let her rant, rave, and basically carry on like a five-year-old, all the while assuring her that everything she was feeling was what anyone in her place would feel.

Smiling a little, she went on, "I really do feel a little better today. You know, if he ever decided to quit being a cop, I think Reese would make a great priest. Uh, minus that whole celibacy thing, of course."

She gave Hamlet an encouraging look, waiting for the feline version of an eye roll at her small attempt at humor. Instead, and much to her surprise, Hamlet stretched out a paw again. This time, however, his claws were sheathed, and he momentarily touched her shoulder in a gesture that, had it been made by a human, would have been the equivalent of a *there, there*.

"Thanks, Hamlet," she told him, genuinely touched. Then, with a shake of her head, she said, "I really do need to do a few chores before I head out. I hope the vacuum won't bother you too much."

Hamlet blinked once and shut his eyes again, which Darla took to mean she was free to proceed. She spent the next couple of hours giving the place an overdue cleaning, stopping only when her cell rang.

"Hey, kid," Jake's sharp New Jersey tones greeted her. "I could use a little feedback from a divorced woman. You want to come down to share some leftover ziti for lunch and let me pick your brain?"

"Sure, so long as I'm out by one. Robert and I have a date for the pet store."

"Cradle robber," Jake promptly shot back, though her tone indicated that she knew full well what Darla meant. "Okay, see you in five."

Darla hung up and collected her purse, and then pulled on a coat and scarf for the brief walk down to Jake's apartment. Not that she'd freeze to death in the thirty seconds it would take to go from door to door, but she'd need some warm outer clothing for the walk later.

"Hey, Hammy, any requests?" she asked the feline, pausing with her hand on the front knob. "I'm going to grab a bite with Jake, and then Robert and I are off to the pet shop."

Hamlet gave her a slanted look but made no reply. And thank goodness for that, Darla told herself with a grin. If he started actually talking to her, she'd be asking Brody for a refund . . . that was, once she awakened from her faint!

She walked into Jake's apartment to find that the usual paperwork had been shoved aside to restore the chrome table that served as her desk to its original dining function. Two places had been set atop woven kitchen towels doubling as placemats on its bright red Formica top. A partially filled glass casserole dish rested upon a pair of ceramic trivets, the spicy aroma of tomato, meat, and cheese filling the room. Darla's stomach immediately began to growl in anticipation.

"Grab a plate and dig in," came Jake's voice from the kitchen alcove. All that was visible of her, however, was a pair of tight black jeans. The rest of her was hidden within the vintage fridge, from whose depths she emerged a moment later, bearing two chilled bottles of sparkling water.

"Too early for wine or beer," she explained with a grin as she set the bottles down on the table and gestured for Darla to sit. "If you're a good girl and eat all your lunch, there might be a bit of tiramisu left over from my bakery run the other day."

"I swear, I don't know how you stay so fit," Darla good-naturedly complained as she took her seat and served herself a sizeable portion of the pasta. "The way you eat, you should be at least three hundred pounds, but you look great."

"Daily visits to the gym, kid. You should try it."

Since Darla's previous attempts at gym membership had ended badly—she'd never forgotten the time she'd been bodily moved from a territorial woman's self-declared permanent spot in Pilates class—Darla concentrated on the food, instead. Besides, between her martial arts classes and all the hoofing around town she'd done since she had moved to Brooklyn, she figured she got her share of exercise.

Instead, she asked, "You said you needed some feedback. Does this have anything to do with the Russian Bombshell case?"

"Yeah, I'm still trying to track her down, and I think Alex is way off base with this whole 'younger man' thing," Jake mumbled through her own mouthful of ziti. Washing it down with a sip of bottled water, she added in a clearer voice, "I mean, if you just got out of a lousy marriage, would you hook up with a new guy right away . . . assuming you and the guy weren't already doing the horizontal mambo beforehand?"

"Not a chance!" Darla set down her fork with a clank and vigorously shook her head. Once her own divorce had been finalized, her initial emotions had been a combination of relief, elation, and a bit of trepidation over what she would do going forward. There'd even been some sorrow over the fact that she and the man she'd once sworn to love forever now barely tolerated each other's existence. Horniness, however, had not entered into the equation . . . at least, not for some time.

"Not a chance," she repeated more calmly. "The night my divorce was final, I went to a couple of clubs with some friends to celebrate. After that, I took in a foreign film at the midnight movie—the kind my ex always hated, with subtitles. Then I drove to the lake and sat there watching the stars until the sun started to come up. The finale was going to one of those twenty-four-hour places to eat chocolate chip pancakes and drink a strawberry milkshake . . . extra large."

She grinned a little at the memory and grabbed up her fork again. "But don't worry, I paid for my sins. I went home and slept the rest of the day, and I woke up that night with a sugar hangover you wouldn't believe."

"I've had those before. Almost as bad as the real kind," Jake agreed with a matching grin. "So your prime motivation wasn't finding a new squeeze, huh? Kind of what I figured. I don't think she's gone underground with some man, but I do need to figure out where she's living now."

"You said she had money. Do you think she left town, maybe went on a cruise?"

"That's a possibility, especially if she doesn't want Alex to find her. No way she can keep her whereabouts a secret if she sticks around the Russian immigrant community. The question is, what did she do with all the stuff Alex said she took with her?"

"Maybe she rented a storage locker to stash it?" Darla suggested.

Jake shrugged. "Maybe. Or maybe she found a cheap apartment in the suburbs to stash herself. Except I'm not finding any record of new utilities in her name. And I haven't found cell phone service for her, either. Either she's smart enough to keep her name out of the public records, or she's been so sheltered she doesn't know how to do the basics on her own."

"Yeah, well, even when you know how to do it, it's still a lot of work setting up house somewhere new," Darla reminded her, vividly recalling the hassles she'd recently gone through several months earlier when taking over her great-aunt's property. There was no such thing as a free lunch . . . or a free bookstore.

"So maybe Mrs. Putin found a place that paid utilities for her," she suggested, "and maybe she uses one of those prepaid phones."

Jake gave her a pleased look. "Sharp thinking, kid. You must be taking sleuth lessons from Hamlet. So now what?"

After a couple more bites of ziti, Jake answered her own question.

"Call it a hunch, but I'm still liking the Atlantic City idea. All our bombshell would have to do is hop one of those gambling shuttles, and she's there. She's got the cash to find herself a nice hotel there and hole up. Even if she already found herself an apartment around here, it would be a smart move. You know, let her new place sit unoccupied for a while, just to make sure her devoted son doesn't track her to it. Then, when things cool down, or sonny agrees to back off, she can go home."

"I've always heard that a tourist town is the best place to hide," Darla agreed, dabbing at some stray tomato sauce on her chin. "And no one will think twice about her accent and the fact she doesn't speak much English."

"So, you feel like leaving the store to James's tender mercies and taking a little field trip to the big AC?" Jake asked, shoving aside her now-empty plate with a satisfied sigh.

Darla finished off the last bite of her own meal and gave her head a regretful shake.

"I'd like to, but with the whole Hamlet situation and Master Tomlinson's death, and now Robert hiding out with the dog, things are kind of unsettled here. I'd better stick around here until everything is worked out."

"Yeah, I forgot. Since you're a prime witness, the cops are probably going to need to question you again, so you might as well make it easy on them and not go gallivanting off," Jake told her, slicing two generous slabs of the promised tiramisu.

"But Robert and I already told Officer Wing what we knew," Darla reminded her after absently accepting her portion and taking an automatic bite. The term *prime witness* was more than a little disconcerting. "Why would he need to talk to us again?"

"You mean Reese didn't say anything last night?"

"About what?"

Jake waved a forkful of her tiramisu in a "never mind" gesture. "Forget it, drop the subject. I shouldn't have said anything."

"You *haven't* said anything, that's the problem. What happened that Reese didn't bother to mention?"

For a moment, Darla thought Jake would refuse to answer. Instead, the PI finished off the bite of dessert and then settled back in her chair with a frown.

"You'll know soon enough, so I guess there's no harm in giving you a heads-up. Reese told me he heard that the attending physician in the emergency room had some suspicions about the cause of your sensei's death. Nothing's formal until the ME finishes up, but talk is that it wasn't a suicide."

"You mean his death was an accident, after all?" Darla demanded.

"No, not an accident."

Darla stared at her friend in dismay, not wanting to put her thoughts into words, but knowing she had no other choice. "If Master Tomlinson didn't kill himself, and his death wasn't an accident, then that means . . ."

"Yeah, kid, that means he was murdered."

EIGHT

MURDERED?

Of course, that was the only logical scenario left. Even so, Darla caught her breath at the word and dropped a forkful of tiramisu back onto her plate. Jake, meanwhile, was saying, "From what I hear, it was a pretty poor attempt to stage a suicide scene. Whoever did it didn't stop to think that the man weighed too much for that hook to hold him. Besides, there's an obvious difference in the marks you find on the neck of a hanging victim versus someone who's been strangled. And there are other signs, too. Someone wraps a rope around someone else's neck, you get burst capillaries in the eyes, skin under the fingernails where they struggled—"

At Darla's gasp of horror, Jake broke off and added, "Sorry, kid, didn't mean to get graphic there. But it's Forensics 101. Even the greenest street cop knows what to look for in these situations."

Jake, who was well-versed in that sort of unsavory

business, returned her attention to her dessert plate. Darla, however, had lost her appetite. But why would someone kill Master Tomlinson . . . and, more important, who?

Abruptly, she recalled the argument between the sensei and Grace Valentine, whose son had been excluded from an important tournament. But surely that wasn't a motive for murder. Just as swiftly, she recalled the few chill words exchanged between Tomlinson and his stepsons just two days before the man's death. Could the enmity between them have run far deeper than anyone suspected?

Then she frowned. "But the man was a martial arts expert. No way would someone have gotten the jump on him. He'd have fought off any attacker who tried it."

"Maybe they took him by surprise, or maybe he was sleeping or drugged," Jake said with a shrug. "Just because you're the second coming of Chuck Norris doesn't mean someone can't take you out. So don't let your imagination run away with you."

"What do I tell Robert about all this?"

"Don't tell him anything yet," Jake advised. "Like I said, none of this is official yet. Let the kid have a little fun buying that dog some cute stuff without worrying about a murder investigation, okay?"

Darla considered that for a moment and then nodded. "Okay. Time enough for him to find out when the cops come around asking questions."

Then she looked down at her barely touched dessert, and her practical side kicked in. "Mind if I wrap this up and take it with me?"

A FEW MINUTES BEFORE ONE, DARLA MET ROBERT AND A BUNDLED UP Roma outside the bookstore for the trek to Fluffy Faces Pet Boutique. The day was sunny despite the chill in the air, and Darla felt her spirits rise a bit. As Jake had said, nothing about Master Tomlinson's supposed murder was official yet. She'd enjoy assuming ignorance for a couple more hours.

A couple of blocks into their journey, however, Darla realized that they would be passing the dojo on their way to the pet store. That reminder was something that Robert didn't need right now. And surely it would be confusing for little Roma to be taken past what had been her second home now that her master was gone.

The same thing must have occurred to Robert, for he halted momentarily and said in a subdued voice, "Can we, you know, take the long way?"

"Of course," she assured him and made a quick turn at the next corner. Robert made no other comment, though she saw him surreptitiously swipe at his eyes with his free hand, Roma tightly cradled in the other.

Quickly, Darla started a conversation about a shipment of books due later that week, and her ideas for some Easter promotions. By the time they reached the pet shop, Robert was almost smiling again, and his attitude was eager as he reached for the door.

"She'll need two sweaters in case one gets dirty," he determined, "and maybe I should get her some of those doggie boots for when it snows."

"Don't go too crazy in there," Darla reminded him. "Technically, you're only fostering her until we know that no one else wants her."

"Yeah, I know," he agreed as he hurried in, Darla following after.

The pet boutique lived up to its descriptor. Rather than items being tossed in bins, as in the pet supermarkets she'd seen back home, the merchandise in this shop was beautifully presented on heavy glass shelves. Rhinestone leashes and collars mingled with vases of exotic blooms and vintage pottery, while designer canine couture was artfully arranged upon antique children's tables and chairs. On one wall, a variety of dog bowls had been mounted to form a mosaic that, at a distance, resembled the shop's poodle face logo. The staff all wore smart bib aprons with that same logo embroidered on the chest.

Definitely not a pet supermarket.

Darla wandered to the cat toy section (which the sleek hand-painted sign above that aisle branded *feline diversions*), and found a toy she thought would appeal to Hamlet's hunter instincts: a flexible wand with a mass of feathers and small leather strings bundled on its end like some captive steampunk bird.

Perfect, she thought, and then did a double take when she checked the price tag and saw the item cost more than the last pair of shoes she'd purchased for herself. Well, maybe not so perfect, after all.

Sorry, Hamlet, she silently told the cat in absentia. *Looks like it's the old toilet paper cardboard core and piece of string for you.*

Robert, meanwhile, seemed unfazed by the prices. He was walking Roma up and down the dog aisle, accompanied by a gushing young woman who seemed as impressed with him as with Roma. Suppressing a bit of indulgent amusement, Darla watched as Robert tried various colors and styles of sweaters on the little hound, who wiggled a bit but was surprisingly agreeable to the process. She expected the teen to settle on one of the doggie goth looks in black that were displayed alongside a somewhat frightening arrangement of spiked collars. To her surprise, however, he chose a more sedate mauve that complemented Roma's gray and white coat. Its slouch-style neckline allowed the fabric to be pulled high enough up so that it covered her delicate ears like the canine version of a hoodie.

"Let's get the yellow one, too," Robert told the salesgirl. "Oh, yeah, and the red one, just in case she wants to look, you know, festive for Valentine's Day. And we need a harness—the stretchy kind, so the straps don't scrape her—and a matching leash. And maybe some toys."

A few minutes later, he had completed his selections and was proudly carrying Roma, wearing her new mauve sweater, up to the register to check out. The salesgirl—Tina, according to the embroidered name on her apron—followed behind carrying the rest of his purchases. But halfway to the counter, he halted in front of a small display from which hung perhaps two dozen wide collars crafted from richly embroidered fabrics in jewel tones that looked straight out of a European history book.

"Sick," the teen exclaimed, and held up Roma so she could better see the collars. "If you wore one of these, you'd be a real Renaissance dog. Check it out, Ms. Pettistone," he added in Darla's direction. "Wouldn't Roma look epic in one of these?"

While Darla nodded her assent, Tina declared in a strong Brooklyn accent, "They're called martingale collars. They're for dogs like yours with delicate necks, so they don't squish their tracheas when they pull on their leads. Seriously, you should buy one for her."

Robert set Roma down and handed the salesgirl his other purchases. After a moment's consideration, he reached for the tag hanging from a particularly handsome collar threaded with the same shade of mauve as Roma's new sweater. Darla saw his eyes widen in disbelief as he read the price; then, reluctantly, he shook his head.

"Sorry, Roma, maybe later."

"Wait," Darla impulsively declared. "How about I buy that collar for her as my own little present?"

"Really? That would be, like, awesome!"

He grabbed the collar he'd admired and put it on Roma. While the salesgirl removed the tag and handed it to Darla—more expensive than the cat wand, but cheaper than a car payment, she told herself—Robert walked Roma over to the full-length mirror where she could presumably admire her reflection.

Darla, meanwhile, took herself over to the cash register, trying not to wince when Tina finished totaling up Robert's purchases. The teen was going to be putting in a lot of OT the next few weeks if he hoped to repay Darla for Roma's new wardrobe before the end of the year, she told herself as she signed the charge slip. Then, feeling guilty over her splurge on the collar for the dog, she told Tina to wait a minute and then headed back to the *feline diversions* aisle.

Grabbing the fluffiest of the cat wands, she returned to the register. "This one, too," she said, hesitating only a little as she handed over her credit card again.

A few minutes later and many dollars lighter, she and Robert were headed back in the direction of the brownstone. Snug in her new sweater and wearing her fancy collar, Roma pranced her way down the sidewalk like a tiny dressage horse.

"Thanks again, Ms. Pettistone," Robert told her, looking far happier than he had since the previous day's tragedy. "I'm going to take great care of Roma. You'll see."

Then, as they approached a grocer on the next corner, Robert halted and thrust the little hound's leash and his bag of purchases in her direction. "Can you, like, hold her for a minute while I get something?"

She had barely grabbed hold of the lead before he had vanished into the small store. Darla gave Roma a quick scratch and then took the opportunity to whip out her phone and pull up her word game. Before she and Robert had left for the pet store, she'd hurriedly responded to a couple of the in-process matches. *Fightingwords* had made a counter play to that last for a modest seventeen points.

Grinning, Darla slid the *Q* on her virtual rack to the spot on the playing screen where two I's now were kittycorner to each other. The move formed the same word, *Qi,* both ways. Since the Q tile was worth ten points, and the open slot was a triple letter, that meant she had just scored over sixty points. *Take that!*

While she basked in this momentary triumph, Robert reappeared bearing a paper-wrapped bouquet of seasonal blooms. For a confused moment, Darla thought the flowers were meant for her. But when he took the leash back from her and casually asked, "Do you mind if we, you know, go home the regular way?" the light dawned and she realized he meant to leave them as a tribute in front of the martial arts studio.

"Sure, if you want," she replied, keeping hold of the bag for him since he was now juggling both dog and flowers.

For both their sakes, she prayed that no official word had yet come from the medical examiner's office. The last thing she wanted was for Robert to find crime scene tape blocking the dojo door and police swarming the place.

Which was pretty much what she and Robert saw when they turned the next corner.

Even from a distance, they could readily spy the yellow-and-black tape stretching from one of the red concrete fu dogs to the other to form a visual barricade across the studio's entry.

"What the—what's that?" the teen demanded, halting and scooping up Roma in his arms. Holding the dog protectively to his chest while awkwardly juggling the flowers, he exclaimed, "There's, like, cops and stuff at the dojo. Why are they back?"

Darla had stopped in her tracks, too. For a moment, she contemplated feigning ignorance. If she confessed that she already knew what the police were looking for, Robert might wonder why she hadn't said anything before. She was hard-pressed to come up with an explanation that didn't sound vaguely patronizing, like he was a child and she was protecting him. Better to treat him like an adult and lay it on the line now.

"I was going to wait to tell you until I found out if it was official," she admitted, "but I guess it must be now. You see,

I heard from Jake that there was some question about how Master Tomlinson died."

"What do you mean, question?" Robert's blue eyes darkened. Roma, sensing his change in attitude, wriggled in his arms and gave a small whine. For her part, Darla raised a warning hand.

"Nothing's written in stone yet," she told him . . . though given the two squad cars parked along the curb and a van marked *Crime Scene Investigations*, it was starting to look pretty darn official. "But Jake said the police think it's possible that he"—she paused, struggling a moment for the words—"that he was murdered, instead."

"Murdered?"

Robert's disbelieving tone echoed the same incredulity that Darla had expressed to Jake a bit earlier. Then the teen shook his head.

"No way," he declared, his smooth features knitting into a frown. "Who would do that to him? Everyone loved Sensei." In the next breath, however, he added, "Well, maybe not everyone. Those jerks, Hank and Hal . . . they were always, like, in his face about stuff."

The teen's voice began to rise, and he shifted into a defensive posture reminiscent of one of their class drills. Looking as menacing as he could, given that he was cradling both a small, sweatered dog and a bouquet of flowers in his arms, he went on, "I swear, if I find out that—"

"Don't start accusing anyone," Darla broke in, putting a restraining hand on his shoulder. "The police will probably want to talk to us again, and you can't go around pointing fingers at people just because you don't like them. It could have been some crazy person off the street looking for something to steal, and Master Tomlinson had the bad luck to catch them in the act."

"Yeah, but then why would they do what they did? I mean, that was like, all psycho and stuff, hanging him up by his belt. And no way some random dude could've killed him," he said. "Sensei trained with Bruce Lee and Chuck Norris. He wouldn't let himself get gotten by some, you know, street punk." Robert shook her hand off and strode down the sidewalk toward the dojo.

Shouldering the bag of pet gear, Darla hurried after him. At the moment, all of the police seemed to be elsewhere— with luck, she could convince Robert to pay his respects with the flowers and move on before that changed. But as they drew closer, the dojo's front door opened and Officer Wing, accompanied by Reese, wandered out.

Darla muttered a few bad words under her breath but managed to regain her composure by the time the men spied the teen bearing down on them.

"What are you two doing here?" Reese bluntly greeted them, his tone belying the fact that he'd played the part of confidante to Darla's weepy role of witness the evening before.

So much for good old Father Fiorelli, she told herself, more than a little stung.

Officer Wing's reaction was more formal. "Ms. Pettistone, Mr. Gilmore, I'm afraid this is a crime scene. We may need some further witness statements from you later, but for now we have to ask you to leave."

"Good to see you again, too, Officer Wing," Darla coolly replied. She pointed to the modest mound of cards and flowers that had accumulated beside one of the fu dogs. "We just stopped by to pay our respects. I'm sure you understand."

Robert, meanwhile, had ignored the officer's warning and slid past the yellow tape to squat beside the small memorial that the sensei's students had raised. Watching him, Darla felt an answering tug on her emotions. While not as impressive as other displays she'd seen, this tribute to the departed martial artist was more personal . . . more poignant. Among the random stems and cards, Darla spied a tiny stuffed bear wearing a gi, and a pair of white china fu dogs, miniature siblings to those who guarded the dojo door.

One of the younger students had even left his small yellow rank belt—doubtless one of his prized possessions—curled among the bouquets.

Soberly, Robert added his flowers to the lot. Darla saw Reese and Wing exchange glances, but neither man made a move to roust him. Apparently, they agreed that the teen's presence on the other side of the tape, so long as he didn't actually go inside the building, wouldn't be enough to taint the investigation.

Darla, however, wasn't getting off that lightly. Taking her by the arm, Reese walked her several feet down the sidewalk and then muttered, "All right, Red, what gives? I talked to Jake, and she said she already gave you the heads-up on what happened. So you'd better not have come here looking for clues on your own. This is an official investigation."

"I'm well aware of that," Darla clipped out and yanked her arm from his grasp, giving him a slanted look that she was sure Hamlet would have approved. "Not that it's any of your business, but Robert and I were out shopping at the pet boutique a few blocks away."

She reached into the bag and pulled out Hamlet's cat wand by way of demonstration, letting the feathers dangle perilously close to Reese's nose for a moment before shoving it back into the bag again. "And on the way back, Robert said he wanted to leave a little tribute at the dojo, and I said okay. That's all that 'gives.'"

Reese suppressed a sneeze—apparently, he was sensitive to feathers, Darla noted in satisfaction—and then grudgingly nodded.

"Fine, sorry for jumping on you like that. But we don't need anyone else tromping around on our crime scene."

Before Darla could question just what this halfhearted apology meant, the dojo door opened. A second uniformed officer ushered out a trio of civilians. From their mutually outraged expressions, Darla guessed that they weren't leaving the premises voluntarily. That impression was deepened when the female member of the group angrily shook off the cop's hand and stopped to reach into her handbag for a ciga-rette. The officer, meanwhile, sourly confirmed that the three had apparently gone afoul of police procedure with a quick, "The scene's secure again, and everyone's out now," to Reese and Wing.

It took her a few seconds to recognize two of the crime scene crashers as brothers Hank and Hal, used to as she was seeing them with their bulging biceps bared. Today, how-ever, they were both wearing heavy down jackets, and Hal's bald head was covered with a knit cap. They seemed to have had no trouble recognizing her, however, for they gave her similar perturbed looks, as if resenting her presence. Not that she necessarily blamed them. Had it been a relative of hers that was murdered, she'd probably not appreciate any gawkers.

But Darla's attention was for the impeccably dressed bottle blonde who had taken a couple of puffs on her ciga-rette before tossing it down and grinding it out beneath a designer heel. The woman appeared to be no older than her mid-forties, though Darla assumed that she had to be a decade older than that. For surely from the solicitous way Hank and Hal were escorting her, this was Dr. Jan Tomlin-son, the Steroid Twins' mother . . . and, more to the point, the late sensei's wife.

Some grieving widow, was Darla's first reflexive if admit-tedly unworthy thought, noting that the woman appeared more outraged at the police than distraught over losing her husband. Despite herself, Darla couldn't help a stir of indig-nation on the sensei's part. Why, she and Robert had known the man only a few months, and as best she could tell, the two of them were more distressed over the situation than Tomlinson's own family!

But even while that thought crossed Darla's mind, the woman leveled an assessing look in Robert's direction. She wore fashionable dark glasses on her perfect nose, but they had slipped enough to reveal the pale eyes—what shade, exactly, Darla wasn't close enough to distinguish—that unblinkingly took in his every detail.

The sound of the dojo door opening had roused the teen from his reverie. Now, he scrambled to his feet, Roma clutched to his chest as he tried to shrink backward into the flowers and look inconspicuous. Dr. Tomlinson raised one perfectly penciled brow . . . an impressive feat, Darla thought, given her obvious level of Botox. And with a sudden sense of resignation, Darla knew what would happen next.

She wasn't wrong.

Pursing lips made larger by artfully applied red lipstick, Dr. Tomlinson turned to the cop beside her.

"Officer, arrest that boy. He's stolen my late husband's dog."

‖ **NINE**

"I DIDN'T STEAL HER!"

Eyes wide, Robert gripped Roma more tightly and backed away from the second cop, bumping into the raised paw of the concrete fu dog beside him. That officer, meanwhile, exchanged quick looks with Reese and Wing. The latter gave a quick shake of his shaved head. Darla saw the second officer relax just a bit, though she could sense Reese beside her snapping to full alert.

For his part, Robert seemed on the verge of panic. With a frantic glance at Officer Wing, he insisted, "I was, you know, just fostering her so she didn't have to go to the pound."

"Nonsense," was the doctor's clipped reply. "None of us gave you permission to take the dog. Why, we've been worried sick about little, uh, little . . ."

"Roma," Hal supplied while giving Robert a sharp look.

His reaction made Darla frown. No doubt the man had seen Robert playing with the hound at the dojo in the past. Would that cause him to doubt the teen's claim?

His tone suspicious now, Hal added, "We figured the little rat ran off. How'd you get hold of her?"

"Sorry, sir, I forgot to mention it," Officer Wing smoothly broke in. "Mr. Gilmore and Ms. Pettistone were the witnesses we told you about, the ones who found Mr. Tomlinson and called 9-1-1. The dog was here when we found the . . . that is, when we came on scene . . . and she was acting pretty crazy. I was worried what might happen if I sent her off to Animal Control, and I didn't know how long it would take to locate the family to come get her."

When the family in question merely stared at him, Wing explained, "You know how it is, a little dog yapping like crazy." He paused and used one hand to pantomime barking. "It goes from barking to biting, and then Animal Control has no choice but to put the dog down. And I didn't want that to happen on top of everything else. So I asked Mr. Gilmore if he could help out and keep Mr. Tomlinson's dog until a relative was ready to reclaim her. I've got that in my report, if you'd like to see."

Reese gave the faintest approving nod, and Darla relaxed just a little. At least the detective seemingly was on their side and wasn't going to allow anyone to slap cuffs on anyone yet.

Robert had bristled a little at Wing's exaggerated characterization of Roma as frenzied; still, he prudently kept quiet until the cop finished his fictionalized version of events. Then he nodded vigorously.

"I was just trying to help," he spoke up. "She's, like, way too small to get put in a cage with a pit bull or something, so I figured she'd be safer with me."

"Really, Officer, that was quite presumptuous of you, removing our property from the studio," Dr. Tomlinson replied, her tone unconvinced. To Robert, she added, "You may return the dog now."

"Are you sure? I can, you know, keep her at my place awhile longer if you want."

"That won't be necessary." With a cool look at Hank, she added, "Take it."

"Hell, Ma, why don't you let the kid keep the little rat?" Hank replied with a shrug. "It was Tom's dog. None of us want it, and I'm sure not going to feed it or take it on walks."

"Me either," Hal agreed, folding burly arms over his chest. "I want a rat, I'll get one outta the basement."

The two brothers exchanged grins at their little joke while Roma, apparently getting the gist of their comments, responded with a small growl. Their mother, however, did not appear amused.

"You may not want the dog, but it hardly qualifies as a rat," was her frosty reply. "It's a registered show animal and worth money. You can't just give away a dog like that."

"I'll buy her from you," Robert offered in an eager tone.

The woman pursed her red lips again and then shrugged. "That might be a solution. Very well, I believe that three thousand dollars would be a fair price for her."

"Three thousand?"

"Dollars. Cash," she clarified with a small smile. Then, when Robert visibly gulped, she added, "Why, that's a bargain. I'm certain I could sell her to a breeder for more than that."

"I-I don't have that kind of money," he admitted in a small voice, his gaze dropping to the dog he cradled.

The woman's smile broadened, and Darla felt her temper flare. She wasn't sure which was worse, the doctor's smug attitude toward Robert, or her threat to sell the small dog to a breeder. Thanks to an animal activist friend back in Dallas, Darla knew that some pet breeders were compassionate and ethical, but that a great many more were in the business simply for the money. In the hands of an uncaring businessperson, a dog's future was almost guaranteed to be bleak and short-lived, indeed.

"Let it go, Red," Reese murmured, sensing her outrage. "It stinks, but she's one hundred percent within her rights."

Officer Wing shifted uncomfortably where he stood, his sympathies obviously with Robert, but both his and the other cops' expressions remained impassive.

"Wait," Darla broke in and quickly fumbled for her wallet. "Maybe we could do a payment plan. I've got some money on me, and—"

"I don't do payment plans. Cash only, up front. No takers?" The smile vanished, and the woman shot Hank a meaningful look. "Get the dog. Oh, and remove that tacky clothing from her while you're at it."

Hank shrugged and rolled his eyes, but obediently walked over to where Robert stood.

"Sorry, kid," he muttered and took the dog from him.

Roma did not go willingly. Delicate legs flailing, she tried and failed to evade the larger man's grasp. Tucked under one of his bulky arms, she whined and gave a small bark that was quickly muffled in the folds of Hank's jacket as he efficiently stripped the mauve sweater from her and tossed it back to Robert.

As for the teen, he clutched the empty sweater and bit his lip, gaze fixed on the sidewalk. Darla wasn't certain if he was holding back tears or anger. Probably both, she decided. She certainly was.

Reese, meanwhile, took a casual step forward. "We're finished with our questions for now," he said to Dr. Tomlinson and the twins, "but like we told you earlier, we're still investigating the scene. We'll let you know as soon as we can release the dojo back to you."

"Yeah, well, it better be soon," Hal retorted. "We still got a tournament to put on this weekend, and our students need a place to practice."

"You're not canceling the tournament?" Darla asked in surprise.

Hank gave her a sour look. "We got sponsors, we already paid for the venue across town, and people already paid their registrations. We cancel now, and we lose lots of money.

Not to mention we got a lot of ticked-off students from all the major dojos in the state who were counting on a sanctioned tournament. So that would be a no."

"Tom would want us to carry on," Dr. Tomlinson said with a pious nod. "Nothing was more important to him than his studio and his students."

"You can say that again," Hal muttered, the bitterness in his tone taking Darla aback.

Reese nodded. "We'll get you running again as soon as we can. Right now, our priority is finding out what happened to Mr. Tomlinson."

Dismissed by the police, the three headed to a sporty yellow two-door parked a short distance down the curb. Darla was mollified a bit to see that Dr. Tomlinson, at least, glanced back a final time at the impromptu tribute that the sensei's students had left. Her expression was unreadable, however, and Darla wondered if maybe the woman simply was deciding how long she was obliged to leave the memorial intact.

Hank, still holding Roma, squeezed his bulk into the backseat. Hal helped his mother into the front passenger spot and then folded his own muscular figure into the driver's seat. Obviously, their training had come in handy, Darla thought in grim amusement as she watched Hal hit the gas and speed off. Anyone else their size would have had a heck of a time contorting into that tiny vehicle.

Robert, meanwhile, had slipped back from behind the crime scene tape. Tonelessly, he asked, "So, can I go, too?"

"Actually, I think they want both of us out of here. Right, Detective Reese?" Darla answered before the man could speak up. Giving Reese a look that held just a bit of challenge, she finished, "If you need to ask me or Robert any more questions, you can stop by the shop during business hours."

"Sure thing, Ms. Pettistone," he replied, the formality making it equally clear to Darla that he was just as peeved with her.

Not that he had any right to be, she thought in righteous indignation as she and Robert hurried off. It wasn't her fault that the Steroid Twins and their Mommy Dearest apparently had wandered inside the dojo without the detective's consent and had to be escorted out again. All Robert had wanted to do was pay his respects to the murdered sensei, and for his trouble he'd been forced to give Roma back to a woman who didn't want her, except as a possible investment.

She stole a glance over at the teen striding silently beside her. She'd warned him that keeping the little greyhound might be a temporary proposition, but she'd truly believed that none of Master Tomlinson's family would actually want her back. Still, she should have known better than to encourage him to take Roma home and buy her so much gear.

"Here," the youth suddenly said and thrust the small mauve sweater in her direction. "She won't be needing this, not if she's going to be sold into dog slavery." With that, he crammed his hands into his jacket pockets and began running.

Darla stuffed the sweater into the bag with the rest of the pet gear, wondering about the boutique's return policy, and rushed after him, though following at a respectable distance. No doubt he wanted to be alone, but she wanted to keep an eye on where he was going.

A moment later he made a turn at the next corner, and she saw in relief that he was headed back home. She watched as he reached the stoop at Mary Ann's brownstone, a mirror image of Darla's building, where a short stairwell led beneath the stoop to his apartment door.

To her surprise, she saw Mary Ann was standing there, holding what appeared from a distance to be a rectangular package the size and shape of a coffee table book. She and Robert exchanged a few words, though Darla couldn't hear what was said from her vantage point. And then the teen abruptly disappeared down the stairwell into his apartment, leaving Mary Ann staring after him, the object still clutched in her arms.

As the old woman turned back to the steps leading to her shop, Darla quickened her pace and waved in her direction to stop her. "Mary Ann, wait, what's wrong?"

The woman halted; then, as Darla joined her, she gave Darla a troubled look before shaking her head.

"I'm not quite sure. Remember that I told you I had something in the store that I thought Robert would enjoy? Well, I was bringing it downstairs to hang in his apartment before you two got back, and there he was. Of course, that spoiled my little surprise, so I showed it to him."

She pulled back the brown paper, revealing the elaborate gilded wood of a small picture frame. "I thought he'd be pleased, but he told me he didn't want it, and then he ran into the apartment. I don't understand. Why, I thought it would be perfect."

Mary Ann turned the picture so that Darla could see the hand-tinted print, likely once part of a vintage art text. The subject matter was traditional: a young Renaissance courtier walking in an elaborate garden. But what made the scene special was the fact that trailing the youth was a small, whip-thin hound in a broad embroidered collar that looked remarkably like Roma.

The image of that hound apparently reminded the old woman that something else was wrong, too. Glancing about, she asked, "Why, where is the little greyhound? I thought you two took her to the pet shop."

"We did. And the picture is wonderful, Mary Ann . . . very thoughtful," Darla agreed with a smile that rose and then quickly faded. "But I'm afraid Robert has a good reason not to want it."

Darla walked the woman back to the antiques shop while explaining how Roma had been unexpectedly reclaimed by Master Tomlinson's family. When she had finished, Mary

Ann tsked and replied, "My gracious, that's too bad. Though, keep in mind, the poor woman just suffered a terrible shock, losing her husband, and in such a fashion. I wonder if it's a tiny bit uncharitable to blame her for being snappish right now."

Mary Ann was right, Darla realized, feeling guilty as charged in the face of the woman's gentle lecture. So caught up had she been in Robert's drama that it hadn't occurred to her that the doctor's anger might simply be her way of coping with what had to be a devastating loss. At any other time, Dr. Tomlinson might be a lovely person. Darla would have to remind Robert of this later . . . though she doubted even that explanation would do much to comfort him right now.

Aloud, she ruefully acknowledged, "You're entirely correct, and thanks for the reminder. I need to give her the benefit of the doubt right now. Maybe she'll change her mind about Roma later."

"Oh, I do hope so. But if not, do you think she really will sell the poor dog to someone? Maybe Officer Reese could convince her otherwise."

"Detective Reese," Darla automatically corrected. Then, recalling that she still was ticked at the man, she added, "And I doubt he'll be much help. He's pretty busy investigating Master Tomlinson's murder."

Her statement brought a gasp from the old woman and led to another explanation from Darla that left Mary Ann shaking her gray head.

"Oh, my gracious, what is this world coming to?" she asked with a sigh as she settled onto the stool behind her register. "I hate to say this, Darla, but things have gone downhill in this neighborhood ever since Dee passed away."

Which is a polite way of saying that people are dropping like flies ever since I took over the bookstore, Darla thought, trying as she did so to dismiss the sudden, unsettling image of herself as some red-haired, bookselling Angel of Death.

But Mary Ann surprised her by reaching across the

counter and giving her hand a comforting pat. "Now, dear, remember that we're in a large metropolitan area, much as we like to think of ourselves as a cozy neighborhood," she said in a reassuring voice. "And things tend to go in cycles, good and bad. This is just one of those bad cycles. But I think it would be prudent to keep our eyes open and our doors locked until your Officer Reese finds out who killed poor Mr. Tomlinson."

"Agreed," Darla said with a vigorous nod.

Because she wasn't sure what would be worse, finding out that the murder was some random, crazy person that Master Tomlinson had never seen before . . . or finding out it was someone that he—and maybe the rest of them—knew.

"SO WHAT DO YOU THINK, HAMLET? PRETTY SNAZZY, ISN'T IT?"

Darla sat on the floor in front of her horsehair couch waving the feathered cat wand she'd bought earlier that afternoon in what she fancied was an enticing pattern back and forth across the rug. Hamlet, who was stretched in his familiar position along the sofa back, stared down at her from that lofty height like a small furry potentate surveying his subjects.

And it seemed that His Highness was not amused.

Instead, Hamlet watched the proceedings with cool green eyes, with nary a flick of a tail tip to indicate that the bundle of fluttering feathers had stirred his hunter's instincts. Darla, however, was not about to give up. Not when that particular feline plaything had cost her a few months' worth of kitty kibble.

"Oh, come on, this is the toy that all the really cool cats play with," she coaxed him, shaking the wand so that it danced even more frantically. "Why, I bet that your friend Brody has a whole flock of these things for his favorite clients."

Hamlet was not swayed by this argument, either. Instead,

he stretched out his back legs and yawned, revealing an expanse of soft pink mouth and a formidable set of sharp white teeth. And then, quite deliberately, he closed both eyes.

"Why, you—"

Darla glared at him; then, recalling that she was supposed to be helping him resolve his trauma, she let it go. If the new toy didn't appeal to him, then she wouldn't hold that against him. Maybe he'd play with it later. And if he kept ignoring the toy, she would simply return it along with the rest of the items she and Robert had bought at the pet boutique. Tossing the wand onto the sofa, she got to her feet and headed to the dining table, where she'd left the logo bag filled with Roma's little sweaters and leashes. Shaking her head, she took out the items one by one for another look.

Poor Robert, he'd been so thrilled to pick out all these things. If the sensei's family had been equally happy to have the little dog back, she—and, likely, Robert—would have accepted their decision with good grace. But it was obvious that Dr. Tomlinson cared only about the possible profit she could make from her late husband's cherished pet. What really bugged Darla, though, was how the woman seemed almost to enjoy Robert's misery at giving up the little dog.

The thought made Darla want to track her down and shame the good doctor into surrendering the small greyhound back to Robert. Not that she'd had any illusions she would have any influence on the supposedly grieving widow. But maybe Reese would. At the very least, the fact that he was a cop vouching for Robert might make the woman more open to negotiation. Darla nodded to herself. If Reese did stop by to question her as he'd promised, she'd take that opportunity to convince him to have a word with the woman.

And if that didn't work?

Darla considered the question for a moment. Maybe Robert would be willing to adopt another dog . . . a rescue, perhaps, who needed a home even more desperately than Roma did. She'd have to get Mary Ann's thoughts on the situation, however, since the old woman had waived the *no pets* rule specifically for Roma. But if she agreed, maybe Darla would suggest it to Robert when he came into work in the morning. In the meantime, she'd hold on to all his purchases awhile longer before returning them to the boutique. Just in case.

The sound of a soft smack from the direction of the sofa abruptly distracted her from thoughts of Robert. She looked in that direction, and then did a literal double take.

In the few moments that she'd been occupied with Roma's things, Hamlet had slid from the back of the sofa onto the seat cushion, captured the abandoned cat wand between his front paws, and was gnawing away on the feathered bundle at its end.

"Ha, I knew it," Darla muttered with a satisfied smile as he roughhoused with the toy. Maybe later, the finicky cat would even let her play with him.

A sudden buzzing sound made her jump. Hamlet jumped, too, dropping the wand and leaping back upon his sofa perch. Despite their startled reactions, however, they both knew that buzzing meant someone was at her downstairs door.

As always, it took a moment for Darla's heartbeat to get back to normal after hearing that sound . . . and, as always, she vowed to replace that buzzer with a chime. In the meantime, however, someone was waiting on the stoop in the cold for her to ring them up. Jake, perhaps? Except she usually called first. A customer who didn't understand closed meant closed, and was hoping she'd come down and open the store for them?

Or maybe Robert was ready to talk about what had happened a couple of hours earlier, Darla thought as she punched the intercom button.

"Who is it?"

"Hi, Red. Wanna buzz me on up?"

The voice, though made tinny by the intercom, was still

more than familiar. She exchanged looks with Hamlet, whose expression reflected her own pique. Maybe it was some sort of macho male, territorial thing, but Hamlet and Reese had never gotten along well. Sparks—and claws—tended to fly when the two of them got together. Hamlet would have her back if she elected not to let the man in.

"Detective Reese, is this an official police visit?" was her frosty reply.

The tinny voice sharpened.

"Yeah, it's official. But I'd rather do it here than drag you down to the precinct." A pause, and then he added in a more conciliatory tone, "Look, Darla, I'm sorry if I was short with you earlier, but there's some stuff going on behind the scenes that you don't know about. I really could use your help, and given that you knew the dead guy, I'd think you'd be more than happy to volunteer."

He was right, of course. Still, she hesitated, floundering for the right combination of snark and dignity. In the end, however, recalling her final, sad view of Master Tomlinson's unresponsive body being bundled into an ambulance, she decided that finding the truth far outweighed her own ego. And she couldn't forget what the sensei always had said:

Run when you can, fight if you must, never give up, and never let injustice go unpunished.

What had happened to the sensei was the greatest injustice she could imagine. She wouldn't let it go unpunished if she could help it.

"Come on up, Reese," was her resigned response as she hit the buzzer.

|| **TEN**

BY THE TIME DARLA HAD UNHOOKED THE CHAIN AND unlocked both the dead bolt and thumb lock on her front door, Reese had already made it up two flights of stairs and was waiting on the landing. And he wasn't even breathing heavily, she noted in some annoyance. Of course, like Jake, he hit the gym daily, which probably had something to do with it. Maybe she *should* add a gym workout to her modest fitness regimen, since even after all these months she still puffed a bit if she took the stairs at any pace faster than a sedate climb.

"Thanks for not holding this afternoon against me," he said as he peeled off his long wool overcoat—black, like the leather bomber jacket he'd worn when the weather was warmer—and strode past her. He was still dressed for work in dark gray slacks and a tweed sport coat over a surprisingly cheery yellow shirt. He tossed the overcoat on the back of the sofa. Then, pulling a notebook and pen from his jacket, he took a spot on that couch as far from where Hamlet lounged as he could manage.

"I think we might be due for some snow by morning," he observed as he crossed an ankle atop a knee, and flipped open the notebook. "It's getting cold enough, that's for sure. So, how about a cup of coffee to warm up the old bones?"

As always, his expectation that the women around him didn't mind playing waitress grated; still, Darla knew that refusing a simple request like that would only make her look churlish. And if she was going to take the opportunity to see if he could intervene on Robert's behalf with Dr. Tomlinson, she'd do well to get on his good side.

Plus, she always got her petty revenge by serving his coffee to him in some hideously inappropriate mug.

"Sure, Grandpa. Cuppa joe, coming right up," she brightly agreed, resisting the temptation to suggest a lap rug to go with the coffee. "You can chat with Hamlet while I'm in the kitchen."

But when she came back into the living room a couple of minutes later, the coffeemaker primed and beginning its cycle, she immediately saw that both males—human as well as cat—were still studiously ignoring each other. Reese was flipping through his notebook as Hamlet lay atop the couch back, one long furry front leg dangling so that he could idly bat the feathers on the cat wand.

Darla took a seat on a small wingback chair that she'd recently had reupholstered in a whimsical Puss in Boots toile. She didn't mind answering a few questions, but first things first.

"What about Robert?" she wanted to know. "Have you talked to him yet?"

"I knocked on his door first, but I didn't get an answer. Don't worry, he's on my list, since he's the one who found the body . . . er, Mr. Tomlinson."

"I'm sure he'll be glad to help with the investigation all he can," Darla assured him, "but last I saw he was still pretty

upset over losing Roma. I just wanted to warn you in case
he goes all moody on you."

"Don't worry, Red, I've actually done this questioning
thing a time or two," was Reese's deadpan response. "I think
I can handle an unresponsive witness."

Darla felt herself blush. "You're right, sorry. Go on."

"If you're sure . . ."

When she shook her head, he flashed a grin; then, lapsing
back into formal detective mode, he sobered and said, "All
right, here's the scoop. We cops have what we call the twenty-
four-hour rule . . . if we don't have a viable suspect within
the first twenty-four hours after the crime, there's a good
chance we may not solve it. So that's why we have as many
people as we can working the case getting witness statements and talking to people who knew the victim. Since
you and Robert were both first on the scene, plus you have
knowledge of the victim and some of the people who knew
him, your input is pretty critical."

Darla nodded. She understood how critical it was to narrow the suspect field right away. But having Reese spell it
out like this brought it home to her in a way she hadn't considered it before.

"I'll tell you what I can," she assured him. "Just ask."

"Then let's take it from the top. You already know from
Jake that we suspect Mr. Tomlinson didn't kill himself.
Luckily, the ME found a few things that should help narrow
down our list of persons who might have taken him out. But
my problem is that the officer on the scene—"

"Officer Wing?"

"—didn't shut things down right away like I would have
yesterday," he continued, acknowledging her interruption
with a small nod. "So your sensei's family managed to wander around inside the dojo for a while this morning before
we taped it off. You and Robert showed up right around the
time we were hustling them out of there before they con-
taminated every potential bit of evidence in the place. And

I have a bad feeling that they got rid of some stuff before we put a halt to it. We found what looked to be some newly shredded papers in the wastebasket."

"I don't understand. What could they be getting rid of?"

"Computer printouts, canceled checks, love letters, enemies list, whatever." Reese shrugged. "You'd be surprised what sort of incriminating paperwork people leave around."

"Right, but Master Tomlinson ran a dojo, not a law office or an investment firm."

"Some of the slickest illegal operations I've ever run across took place in pretty mundane storefronts. My favorite was the money laundering outfit that worked out of a literal laundry. Some of these guys have really bent senses of humor, know what I mean?"

"Not Master Tomlinson," she stoutly defended the dead man. "He was the kind of guy that my dad would say was honest as the day is long. Why, before every class, he had us repeat this mantra thing about never giving up and fighting injustice."

"Yeah, and that tower sniper guy down in Texas was an eagle scout. Don't worry, Red, I'm not saying that your guy was involved in anything bad. But he may have known someone who was. This wasn't some impulse killing. Someone walked in there with a plan."

Darla shuddered to think that she and Robert could just as easily have walked in on that plan, themselves. Once before, she'd battled for her life against an attacker; in fact, that was the whole reason she had begun her self-defense training. The idea that she might have wandered unknowingly into another such situation was enough to make her want to huddle inside the bookstore with Hamlet and never venture out again!

"Speaking of plans," Reese added while she tried not to let that last thought consume her, "I planned to have a cup of coffee. Any idea what happened to that?"

His question was enough to drag her back to the present.

Suppressing the urge to tell him what he could do with his plan, Darla rose.

"Let me check on that." She plastered a smile on her face as she headed again to the kitchen. Her smile grew genuine, however, when she remembered the Tinker Bell coffee mug her nephews had sent Auntie Darla as a souvenir from their recent trip to the land of the Mouse.

Perfect.

A couple of minutes later, she handed Reese a steaming mug of black coffee. Embroiled again in his notes, he gave her a cursory thank-you and took a tentative sip before setting the drink on the coffee table to cool. It was only then that he apparently got a good look at the mug itself. He shot her a look that said *what the heck?*—a look she answered with innocent raised brows that said *what, is something wrong?*—before he obviously decided it wasn't a battle worth fighting.

Darla took her seat again, glancing over at Hamlet as she did so. He was still on his side of the sofa back, tail end deliberately facing the detective. But then the green eyes flicked Darla's way before taking in the Tinker Bell mug, and Darla could have sworn that the cat winked. Heartened, she settled back to wait on Reese's questions.

Taking another sip from the girlie cup, the detective flipped to a fresh page in his notebook. "All right, let's take this from the top, starting with what Mr. Tomlinson said to you and Robert about meeting him at the dojo."

For the next several minutes, Reese took her painstakingly through each detail, from that final class until the sensei's unresponsive body was loaded into the ambulance. Darla answered as best she could, struggling to remain businesslike about the whole situation even as the occasional tear threatened.

"Let's get back to your original statement to Officer Wing," the detective said once they'd seemingly exhausted the time line. "You told him that Mr. Tomlinson told you to come on a Sunday morning, a time that the dojo normally wasn't open, because he was going to be there, anyway. Are you sure he didn't say anything about why he was going to be there? As in, was he meeting someone else prior to eleven o'clock?"

"All he said was that he had to be there. I figured he was getting ready for the tournament."

"But that doesn't mean he *wasn't* expecting someone," Reese countered, making yet another note. "So how about we put together a list of people. Anyone—students, teachers, parents—who you know from the dojo, just start naming names."

The instructors were easy enough, given that the dojo's staff consisted only of the sensei and his two stepsons. Many of the students in her class Darla knew only by sight, while others she knew only by first name . . . not to mention that at least half were teenagers and, in her opinion, not very likely suspects. Still, she gave it her best effort, listing off as many as she could while Reese took notes.

"Oh, and there's Mark Poole," she added. "He's in the upper rank class, but he's also one of my customers. I found out about the dojo from him in the first place."

Reese scribbled a bit more and then asked, "Any of these people seem to have a beef with Mr. Tomlinson?"

"Well, the Steroid Twins—I mean, Hank and Hal, his stepsons—sure seemed to be at odds with him."

"What do you mean?"

Darla shook her head. "It wasn't anything specific, just their attitudes. But I did hear Master Tomlinson pretty much tell Hank that he didn't know how to act in a dojo. Oh, and I almost forgot," she exclaimed. "Chris's mom—her name is Grace Valentine—was pretty ticked off at Sensei for banning Chris from the tournament this Saturday, the one that Hank mentioned to you."

Reese grinned a little. "Yeah, those sports moms are pretty brutal, no matter what game it is. You shoulda seen my ma on the sidelines when I was playing high school football." Then, reaching for his Tink mug and finding it now empty, he held it out to her, saying, "We're not quite done yet, so I've got time for a refill."

Darla rolled her eyes but carted the mug off to the kitchen again. As she poured the coffee, she called from the kitchen to him, "Okay, Reese, you've been asking all the questions. Now I have one."

"Yeah? Shoot," came his absent reply.

Mug refilled, she set the pot down again and pulled a tea towel from a drawer to mop up a couple of spilled drops. "All right, here it is. A little while ago, you said something about it not being an impulse murder. But the door to the dojo was unlocked when Robert and I got there. Anyone could have walked in on him. I know you're a detective and all, but how can you be so sure Master Tomlinson wasn't murdered by someone off the street?"

"Because I've never seen your run-of-the-mill street punk wandering around town with a vial of Botox stuck in the pocket of his baggy pants."

By now, Darla was carrying the mug back into the living room. Reese's reply made her halt in mid-step so abruptly that she sloshed a bit of the steaming beverage.

"Ouch! Hot! What do you mean, Botox?" she shot back in quick succession, blowing on her burnt hand in between exclamations.

Reese dropped the notebook to hop up from the sofa and take the cup from her. Then he headed into the kitchen, returning a moment later with the tea towel she'd been using wrapped around a few cubes of ice.

"Botox," he repeated as he handed her the makeshift icepack. "You know, the stuff all the rich people get injected into their faces to make themselves look younger, but all that really happens is that their foreheads freeze up."

"I know *what* Botox is," she retorted, sighing a little in relief as she applied the chilly bundle to her reddened flesh and sat down again. "But what does that have to do with how he died? If someone strangled him before they tried to make it look like he killed himself . . ."

She trailed off momentarily at the noncommittal expression on his face.

"Now I'm really confused," she finally went on. "Jake was talking about marks on necks and bloodshot eyes being signs that what looks like a suicide isn't. You're talking about wrinkle treatments. Are you trying to say he died of Botox?"

"Let's just say that Jake didn't have her psychic hat on when she started her Monday morning quarterbacking about the case."

Darla stared at him a moment, ignoring the damp stain on her leg from the melting icepack. Then she shook her head. "That's crazy. How can you die of Botox, anyhow?"

"Easy. Remember that the full name for that stuff is *Botulinum Toxin Type A*." The words rolled off his tongue so smoothly that Darla knew he must have practiced. "Bottom line, it's poison. You know how you can get botulism and die from eating bad canned food? Well, Botox is the same toxin, except it's injected instead of swallowed."

Then, as Darla listened in growing dismay, he said, "According to our ME, it's not just used for cosmetic purposes. There are other medical applications—migraines, muscle spasms, overactive sweat glands—but all of them require only a minuscule amount of the toxin. In the hands of a doctor who knows what he's doing, the stuff is safe enough even for kids. But if someone, say, injects a whole syringe of Botox into your neck, that's a whole other ballgame."

Darla shuddered. "That's a horrible way to go. But I can't believe someone could just walk up and inject him with the stuff. He might have been old, but I bet he could have taken you in a fight."

"Yeah, I know the guy was a karate master," Reese

agreed, "but if the killer was someone he knew, he'd have no reason to suspect anything. His guard would be down; he might even have been working at the table and had his back to the person. The killer could have snuck up on him with the syringe and pumped him full of the toxin before he knew what hit him."

"And that's what you think happened?"

"That's the doc's theory. As for what it does, the toxin itself will eventually kill you, but most people die a lot faster from the side effects." He took on a lecturing tone that reminded her of James. "An overdose of Botox weakens your muscles, and can paralyze your throat and chest enough that you can't breathe. And if you already have some sort of respiratory problems, the effects are magnified. You're basically going to suffocate if you don't get treatment ASAP."

"So that's why he was hanged without a struggle," Darla murmured, recalling how the sensei had been suffering a head cold that night in class. No doubt that congestion had added to the drug's effects. But who had Botox just sitting around in their medicine chest, to use as a handy murder weapon?

Then realization hit, and she looked at Reese in dismay. "Master Tomlinson's wife . . . she's a doctor. Any idea what kind?"

"Yeah, that's where it gets interesting." Reese paused for another gulp of coffee; then, absently cradling Tink in both hands, he added, "Our grieving widow just happens to be a plastic surgeon."

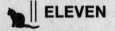 **ELEVEN**

MASTER TOMLINSON'S WIFE WAS A PLASTIC SURGEON!

At Reese's words, Darla felt her stomach clench into a cold little knot. As a plastic surgeon, chances were Dr. Tomlinson had access to as much Botox as she could want. On the other hand, while the Tomlinson family wasn't exactly the Brady Bunch, Darla wasn't aware of any motive for his wife to kill him. Just because the woman was not what one would call warm and cuddly—heck, she made Cruella de Vil look like an animal rights activist—that didn't make her a killer. But on the third hand (she was going to need to borrow Hamlet's paws to finish her mental argument!), according to what Jake and Reese both had explained to her in the past, half of all murder victims were killed by people they knew. And spouses were always high on the initial suspect list.

Which made good old Dr. Tomlinson look like a pretty viable suspect, after all.

But since it was obvious that the petite doctor couldn't

have lifted a man the sensei's size, let alone try to hang him from a hook high upon a wall, that would probably mean involving one or both of the twins as well. Somehow, she just couldn't see Master Tomlinson living among such treachery . . . not when he espoused never giving up and fighting injustice.

Then another thought occurred to her that seemed to put the kibosh on Reese's theory.

"Wait, isn't the whole point of Botox treatments that they last awhile?" she pointed out. "Months, even. Dr. Tomlinson would have to know that the Botox would be discovered in his body during the autopsy."

"I'm not saying it's the missus," Reese replied, snapping shut his notebook. "But you can bet she and her boys are at the top of my list. Of course, the full tox report won't be in for a while. Who knows what else might turn up?"

Then he gave a quizzical look in the direction of Darla's kitchen. "What in the heck is your cat doing now?"

Surprised by the question, she glanced over to where Hamlet had been sitting on the back of the couch. He was no longer there. Following Reese's gaze, she saw that the wily feline had made his way to her dining area and was perched atop the table amid the dog paraphernalia that Robert had purchased for Roma. More surprising was the fact that he had slipped his head into the stretchy harness, so that it dangled from his neck like a bright red undershirt.

"Hamlet, do you want to go for a walk?" Darla asked with a smile. "Or are you just trying to cheer me up by acting silly?"

Hamlet ignored the question as he pawed at the harness's armhole, seemingly attempting to put on the gear. Reese, meanwhile, was grinning as he watched Hamlet's efforts.

"Hey, Red, you need to take a movie of this with your phone and put it up on YouTube. A cat dressing itself. It'll go viral, I guarantee you. And it would be a great plug for the store."

"Ignore him, Hamlet," Darla advised with a brief frown

for the detective, and a reassuring look for the cat. Not that Pettistone's couldn't use a million hits of free publicity, but she couldn't do it at the expense of the dignified feline. "Don't worry, I wouldn't embarrass you like that. But if you want your own harness, I'll get you one. Roma's is way too small for you."

Hamlet apparently agreed, for he quit struggling and shook off the harness. Darla went over to the table and, after giving him a reassuring pat, scooped everything back into the bag.

"I'll be taking the rest of these things back to the pet boutique tomorrow," she told Reese. "Poor Robert, he was devastated over giving up Roma. I swear that woman took her back just out of spite. You saw that none of them wanted her as a pet. Roma is simply"—Darla paused and gave the shopping bag a shake—"merchandise to them."

"Yeah, it was a raw deal for the kid, but like I told you, that's their right."

"Well, just because it's a *right* doesn't make it right."

With that pronouncement, Darla set the bag down again and gave him a considering look. *Time to cash in on the coffee service.* It was a long shot that he'd be able to do anything, but she owed it to Robert to ask.

"Look, Reese, do you think you could mention something to the family about Roma when you talk to them again? Hank seemed like he was willing to be pretty reasonable about the whole thing. Maybe he could get his mother to see the light. We'll even buy Roma from them, if she'll let Robert do some sort of payment plan. But we can't let her be sold off to a puppy mill."

"Darla, you know better than that." The detective stood and reached for his overcoat. "I feel for the kid, just like you do, but in case you forgot, I'm in the middle of a murder investigation. The last thing I need is for the victim's family to accuse me of official repression. And that goes double since they're all on my suspect list."

She had expected as much; still, she couldn't help feeling discouraged that this avenue to rescue Roma was being shut down before they could even travel it.

"I suppose you're right. And I can see how it would look bad if you said anything. But I'm not going to give up. I'll try talking to Hank and Hal as soon as you let them open up the dojo for business again."

"You'll have a chance to do that first thing tomorrow," Reese assured her. He paused, his coat half on now, and then added, "I don't suppose that you and Robert are registered for that martial arts competition the dojo is putting on, are you?"

"Robert is. I don't know if he's still planning to go, but if he does, I thought I'd go cheer him on if I can get James to hold down the fort alone for a few hours. Why?"

"Just asking. See you later, Red."

Before she could press him for more, or even say good-bye, he was out the door again. A moment later, she heard the front door downstairs close behind him.

"Well, Hamlet," she addressed the feline still sitting on the dining table, "on the bright side, at least you and I aren't on the suspect list."

Darla wandered over to the coffee table and picked up the empty Tink mug, giving the green-garbed fairy a gloomy look. "And on the not-so-bright side, this whole situation just keeps on getting more convoluted. Poor Master Tomlinson. He didn't deserve for things to end like this."

The tears she'd managed to hold back earlier began to sting her eyes. Angry all at once, she swiped them away. *Never let injustice go unpunished,* the sensei had drilled into them. And injustice was exactly what had happened there. For she was sure that, no matter what sort of trouble he'd landed in—even if accidentally—Master Tomlinson had been an honorable man to his final breath. And for him to have left this world in such an ignominious manner . . .

"Meow!"

The demanding cry momentarily distracted her from darker thoughts. Hamlet, still on the table, was pawing in the bag that Darla had repacked, seemingly in search of something.

"Hamlet, what is it? What are you doing?"

She rushed back to the table and grabbed the bag away from him. "You're acting like there's a mouse or something in there," she lightly scolded him, dumping the bag's contents back out again.

The same familiar items spilled onto the table, but this time a bright red half sheet of paper she hadn't noticed before slid from the bag's interior. Hamlet reached out a paw and batted the small paper so that it landed face up on the pile.

"What's this, a cat food ad?" she asked with a smile as she picked it up for a closer look.

It was an ad, all right, but not quite what she'd expected. In bold letters, it read, *Don't Leave Your Dog out in the Cold.* Beneath that headline was a second, far smaller line that said, *Bring This Ad in for 50% off Selected Dog Coats.* But what kept Darla from tossing the ad back into the bag was the accompanying illustration . . . a stylized rendering of an Italian greyhound.

"Hamlet, what are you trying to say?" she demanded, only to realize that the feline in question had slipped away while she was distracted. She glimpsed the tip of a sleek black tail sliding around the corner leading back to her bedroom. Obviously, what he was trying to say was, *my work here is done.*

Or was it more? Maybe Hamlet was urging her and Robert to fight harder for Roma . . . not that the cagey feline had ever even met the dog in question. Darla shook her head in amusement. Surely she was giving Hamlet a bit too much credit. He was smart, but last she knew he didn't have a 1-800 psychic hotline. Still, it did seem that he was showing more interest in life this past day than he had in a while, which could only be a positive. Maybe he was finally starting to pull out of that funk he'd been mired in. She could only hope that Robert would be equally resilient when it came to dealing with the loss of both the sensei and little Roma.

She reached for her phone and started to dial the teen's number, only to change her mind before she pressed the last digit.

"He's not a child, and you're not his mommy," she reminded herself, setting down the phone again. At almost nineteen, the youth was surely old enough to deal with heartache. After all, he'd survived being kicked out of his father's house and, showing great enterprise, had managed to keep employed most of that time, even if he'd not always had a roof over his head. Definitely a tough young man. And no matter how distraught he was, he'd likely resent being treated like a little kid, particularly by his boss.

But it never hurts to have a shoulder to cry on.

With that in mind, she thought for a moment and then settled on a quick if non-threatening text—*hope ur doing ok*—and then went to clean up in the kitchen for a few minutes. When she finished there and then checked her phone again, she was disappointed but not surprised to see that no return message had popped up.

Let him deal in his own way, kid, was the advice she knew Jake would give her, so she didn't bother to check in with her friend. Besides, she knew Jake must be busy with her Russian Bombshell investigation. She contemplated phoning James, but didn't want to interrupt him on his day off; besides, she suspected he'd likely tell her the same thing Jake would. But that reminded her to give James a heads-up when he came in the next morning, so that the manager would be prepared to handle the youth should there be any sort of crisis.

Darla decided that the best thing she could do was let Robert have some time to himself to regroup from what had been an undeniably traumatic weekend. Then she brightened.

Maybe this was what Hamlet had meant by the ad that he'd made sure she had noticed. Was supporting Robert the task he'd chosen to redeem himself? It might be a humble mission in the scheme of things, but an important one, nonetheless. She would let James know her theory tomorrow, and then between them they could make sure that the feline spent as much time as possible in the store while Robert was there.

And maybe both cat and youth would find a bit of emotional healing as a result.

THE NEXT MORNING, DARLA HAD JUST FINISHED HER OPENING routine—flipping on the lights and powering up the register, making a run through the shelves looking for anything out of whack, rearranging the front floor displays for the greatest impact—when from the corner of her eye she saw movement through the wavy glass of the front door.

She glanced at the clock. Quarter to ten. Either someone was impatient for the store to open, or someone was looking for *her*.

For some reason, this last notion sent a small shiver through her. Tamping it down again, she set down the stack of paperbacks she was carrying and strode toward the door. *Can't leave a customer waiting on the stoop, even if they're here early,* she told herself. Still, even though the glass was difficult to see through, she made a point of peeking first before unlocking the door.

The distorted image, best as she could tell, was male, and something about his posture rang a bell with her. She turned the deadbolt knob and opened the door to a chill breeze.

She'd been right. There on the stoop stood a raggedy looking young man in a familiar patched denim jacket, his features all but hidden by the garish striped knit scarf wrapped around the lower portion of his face.

"Brody Raywinkle? What are you doing standing out

there in the cold?" she demanded, hurriedly ushering him inside and shutting the door after him. "You should have knocked. Why, it's got to be thirty degrees out."

"Probably," he cheerfully agreed. "But you weren't open yet, and I didn't want to disturb you," he added, unwrapping the scarf to release a multihued sprinkle of cat hair upon the wooden floor.

Biting back a comment at the fur invasion, Darla instead replied, "I'd rather be disturbed than find your frozen body on my stoop. But what are you doing here? I thought you weren't due back for at least a week."

"Normally, yes, but I had a communication from Hamlet that made it necessary for me to return sooner than usual."

"Communication?" Darla smiled a little. "Surely he didn't pick up the phone and call you, did he?"

Brody gave her a mildly rebuking look. "Actually, there have been several documented cases of cats dialing 9-1-1 in an emergency. Most times, the authorities later determined that the number was already programmed on speed dial, and they speculated that the cats in question knocked over the phone in a panic and hit the emergency key randomly. But in a few instances, the speed dial wasn't programmed, and yet 9-1-1 was called anyhow."

Then, while Darla digested that interesting bit of information, the young man's frown became a smile. "As far as Hamlet, his communication with me was this way," he said, and lightly tapped his forehead.

Darla smiled back. "I'll take your word for that. But what did Hamlet say he wanted?"

"This."

Brody reached into the pocket of his denim jacket and pulled out a tangle of thin black straps. It wasn't until he'd shaken them out and held up the resulting object for Darla to admire that she realized in surprise just what it was.

"He—he asked you to bring him a cat harness?"

"Hamlet thought it might be a good idea if he

accompanied you when you go out," Brody said with a nod. "I have a matching leash here, as well. Shall we see if he approves?"

Darla managed a nod. Only the night before, the cat had wrestled with Roma's harness, and now his official feline behavioral empath had brought him one of his own, seemingly out of the blue. Coincidence, or . . .

She reflexively put her fingers to her own forehead, and then yanked them away. Hamlet might be smarter than the average cat, but no way was he sending telepathic messages to Brody the Cat Whisperer.

Hamlet, meanwhile, apparently had determined—telepathically or otherwise—that Brody had arrived with the requested harness, for he appeared all at once atop the register counter. From that vantage point, he surveyed the man with a seemingly expectant look.

"Hi, Hamlet," Brody greeted him. "I think this size should fit you, and I took the liberty of choosing a harness that coordinates with your fur, so that it's not as obvious that you're wearing a restraint. Don't want to give the local toms the wrong impression, you know."

As he conducted this one-sided bantering with the cat, Brody was unbuckling a strap on the harness. Then, while Darla watched in amazement, he slipped the contraption around an uncomplaining Hamlet's muscular frame and fastened it securely onto him. The final step was clipping on the matching lead.

"Now, let's take you for a test drive," the man said with another smile and a guiding tug on the leash.

Hamlet hesitated; then he gave a graceful leap off the counter onto the wood floor. There, he paused again to sit and scratch with one rear foot at the strap wrapping around his belly. Apparently deciding it was there for the duration, he rose again and gave Brody a questioning *meowrmph*.

"It's easy, just one paw in front of the other," the man prompted him.

Hamlet took a tentative step, and then another, until he was striding toward the shop's front door, Brody walking alongside him with leash loosely in hand. For the next couple of minutes, the pair executed figure eights and quick turns up and down the aisles, Hamlet performing like a circus big cat. Luckily, no customers came in during the demonstration, so that man and cat had the store to themselves.

Then Brody halted before Darla and handed the leash to her. "Your turn."

"Are you sure?" she asked, tightly gripping the loop. "I've never walked a cat before, only dogs."

"It's pretty much the same thing, except he won't be sniffing every tree and post," Brody assured her. "Give it a try."

Nodding, she took a step, and then another. Hamlet kept pace with her, tugging only a little when he wanted to go in a direction different from her.

"I think he likes it," Darla finally declared with a delighted little laugh after they'd made a circuit up and back along one aisle. "Are you sure it's safe to take him outside in this harness?"

"As long as it's securely fastened so he can't slip out of it. And don't just hold the leash; be sure you keep the loop hooked over your wrist, too. There's nothing more dangerous than a dog or cat that's gotten away from its owner and is dragging a leash behind it. But I have a feeling Hamlet is going to enjoy walking with you."

He reached down to unsnap the leash, and then unbuckled the harness. Hamlet endured all the activity with surprising patience, though he did succumb to the urge to bat at the harness as Brody slipped it off him.

His expression satisfied, the man handed the gear to Darla, making very certain as he did so that their hands did not touch. Darla suppressed a smile but did her part to keep her fingers at a safe distance from his. She'd have thought that the fur of the average cat probably was a lot germier than human flesh, but maybe not.

"Practice with him inside a couple more times to make sure you're both comfortable before you go out," he recommended. "Any problems, call me. Either way, I'll come back in a few days to see how you two are getting along."

"Thanks," she replied, feeling the sentiment was somewhat inadequate for what he'd accomplished. She suspected if she'd gone with her original plan to buy the harness on her own, Hamlet would have been quite a bit less cooperative.

"Oh, I almost forgot," she added as he started for the door. "Remember the whole atonement thing you talked about the first time you were here? Well, I think I know what Hamlet's mission is."

"Do you?"

He paused, hand on knob—with, of course, the end of his scarf serving as a germ buffer—and turned back to her with another of his gentle smiles.

"I've learned not to make those sorts of pronouncements until everything has come full circle," he said. "Atonement can be a tricky thing, especially from a cat's point of view."

With that cryptic pronouncement, he opened the door and slipped out into the cold, leaving Darla to stare after him. She didn't have much time to ponder the statement, however, for James arrived a few moments later for his shift.

"Good morning," he greeted her, a thermos of his personal coffee blend safely tucked beneath one overcoated arm. "And may I ask the identity of that young man in the horrific scarf whom I just saw leaving the store?"

"Good morning. That was Brody Raywinkle. Remember, Hamlet's feline behavioral empath?" she added when he gave her a quizzical look. "He had an emergency communication from Hamlet and stopped in."

"Ah, yes. The, ahem, cat whisperer," he confirmed, setting down the thermos to peel off his classic camel-colored coat. "And dare I ask the nature of this urgent situation?"

"Apparently, Hamlet wants his own harness and leash. He and Brody mind-melded, or whatever it is they do, and

Brody brought these over for him," Darla explained, holding up said items by way of explanation.

James raised a brow.

"Indeed? I must say, I wish that I shared your Mr. Raywinkle's powers. If I did, perhaps I would not have had to read about the passing of a certain Mr. Tomlinson in the newspapers, instead of hearing about it from you."

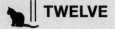 **TWELVE**

DARLA WINCED A LITTLE AT JAMES'S POLITELY PHRASED
rebuke. Truth be told, she'd deliberately avoided the local
news these past couple of days, not wanting to see or hear
a recap of what she'd experienced in real time.

But it should have occurred to her that James—news
junkie that he was—would have stumbled across the story
at some point over the weekend. While she likely hadn't
been listed by name in the piece in question, chances were
that "a local bookseller" was mentioned somewhere in one
of the later paragraphs as a witness.

"Sorry, James," she told him. "I really didn't mean to
keep you in the dark. It's just that so much happened so fast,
I wasn't up to rehashing it right away. But I did plan to tell
you everything today, honest."

To her surprise, he gave her an understanding nod.

"Your point is well taken. I can understand not wanting
to treat such an event like so much fodder for gossip. And I
would suspect that young Robert is equally upset by what

occurred." At Darla's nod, he said, "But when one undergoes a harrowing experience, it does sometimes help to discuss things with a friend."

"You're right, James. It does."

And so, between customers, she spent the next couple of hours telling him everything. He listened with well-bred astonishment to it all. For her part, Darla found that with this telling the original sharp emotions were finally beginning to dull. And she found, too, that with each repetition she was looking more carefully at every detail.

"The whole part about hanging him by his black belt, that's the oddest thing about this whole situation," she confided to James between their lunch hour customers. "Whoever killed him had to know that the autopsy would show the Botox, so what was the point of setting up his murder to look like suicide?"

"Perhaps the killer was trying to send a message of some sort. From what I know of the martial arts, one's belt is something of a revered object. To hang a man from it seems a great insult, indeed."

"I get that," Darla replied. "But although he was hanged with a black belt, it wasn't the fancy one he always wore, the one with the red stripes and the dragon. This was just a plain black rank belt. He probably had a bunch of them in that box under his desk." She paused, then mused, "I wonder what happened to his real one. Surely he'd be wearing it, since he was planning to do our belt test."

"A souvenir for the killer, perhaps?"

James's suggestion made her shiver. Somehow, that possibility made the whole situation seem even more grisly than it already was. She'd need to check with Reese and see if maybe the missing belt had been found somewhere in the sensei's office. But if not, that likely meant it had been taken by someone who knew just what that belt represented. A student, or maybe a fellow instructor? She frowned, considering. The sensei's wall of fame had pictures of him with some of the world's finest competitors, past and present. Perhaps among them was someone who held a grudge.

Then she recalled Reese asking her if she planned to attend the tournament that weekend. Maybe one or more of the participants were on the detective's suspect list, and he was looking for a subtle way to scope out that field without tipping his hand.

"James, if you can handle the store on your own this Saturday afternoon, I think I need to go to the martial arts tournament," she told him.

James momentarily turned his attention from her to nod a greeting at the middle-aged brunette woman who'd just walked in. Then, giving Darla what she could only interpret as a faintly sheepish look, he replied, "Actually, I already took the liberty of asking Martha if she would care to lend some assistance should both you and Robert be gone that afternoon. She said she would be glad to help out . . . assuming, of course, that you approved my suggestion."

"I think that's a marvelous idea. She knows books from a reader's standpoint, and she's been in this store almost as much as me. Besides," she added with an arch smile, "that will give the two of you more time together."

"Really, Darla, I do not require you to play Cupid for me," was his swift response, but she heard a smile in his voice as he said it. "So let us consider that settled. I shall tell Martha we will prevail upon her services, and you go have a good time on Saturday with Robert."

"With me?" a downcast voice spoke up. "Where are we, you know, going?"

"Robert!" Darla exclaimed in relief, turning to see the youth standing behind her. Apparently, he'd slipped into the store behind the customer James had greeted, for she didn't recall hearing the bells on the door ring yet again.

She gave him a considering look. A few stray snowflakes clung to his black hair—Reese's prediction of the night before had been accurate—though, as was his habit, he'd not bothered with a coat for the quick walk up from his apartment. But something about his black wardrobe lent him an even more subdued air than normal. She realized after a moment it was because he hadn't worn his usual tongue-in-cheek vest, which added a punch of color to the regular black shirt and jeans backdrop.

"I didn't get a text back from you yesterday," she explained, "so I was a bit worried. I'm glad you made it in."

In fact, she'd been tempted to knock on his door that morning, just to make sure all was well. She'd decided on further consideration to give him his space, as well as the benefit of the doubt. He was an adult, and the decision to wallow in disappointment or take it in stride would be his alone. She was glad to see that he'd followed the latter path.

Robert, meanwhile, had ducked his head. "Sorry I didn't text you back yesterday. I was, you know, busy the rest of the day. I didn't see it until a little bit ago."

"No problem," she assured him. "James was talking about the karate tournament this weekend. You still want to compete, don't you?"

He shrugged. "I'm not sure, not after . . . well, you know. Besides, I need more practice."

"I talked to Detective Reese again yesterday. He said they'd be releasing the dojo back to Hal and Hank today, so we can go to class tonight if you want."

"Maybe," he agreed, his tone still noncommittal. Then his expression darkened, and he added in a baleful tone, "But not if *she* is going to be there."

"Don't worry, Dr. Tomlinson never hung out at the studio before, and I doubt she'll start now," Darla assured him. "And I really think you should compete. If nothing else, do it as a tribute to Master Tomlinson."

The notion must have appealed to him, for he gave a thoughtful nod as he absently petted Hamlet, who had returned to the counter. Seeing the cat reminded Darla of that morning's lesson with Brody.

"James, if you don't mind taking care of the lady who just came in, Hamlet and I have something to show Robert."

Reaching for the harness and leash she'd stowed beneath the register after Brody's departure, she showed them to Hamlet. "Wanna go for a stroll?"

Hamlet gave a little chirp that she took as an affirmative. While Robert watched in bemusement, she struggled a bit with arranging the straps properly around the feline. Fortunately, he was still inclined to be cooperative, although the look he shot her over his shoulder spoke volumes . . . none of it complimentary.

"I think I have it," Darla finally said, fastening the main buckle. Then, clipping on the lead, she finished, "C'mon, Hamlet. Let's show Robert that you really are smarter than the average cat."

The feline needed no further urging but gave a graceful leap to the floor. Then, with Darla following behind, he made a loop around the register and padded down the romance novel aisle. Robert trotted after them, grinning.

"That's like, you know . . ." Apparently the latest teen slang failed him, for he shook his head and simply followed after them. As they reached the travel section, however, he pleaded, "Can I try?"

"Sure."

Darla handed off the lead and watched in satisfaction as teen and cat paraded through the store with the precision of a high school drill team. The sight drew an appreciative smile from James's customer, and a nod of approval from the manager. As for Darla, she gave a small smile of relief. Perhaps giving Robert the task of walking Hamlet outside once a day—weather permitting!—would distract him from thoughts of Roma.

"Wait," Robert said, pulling out his phone. "I want to get a picture of this and post it on our social network. Go ahead, Ms. Pettistone."

Feeling a bit silly—but well aware of the promotional

power of the Internet—Darla obediently took the leash again. She posed with Hamlet alongside the bestseller table while Robert snapped a few shots.

"Be sure you use the one where Hamlet and I look thinnest," she playfully warned him as he started scrolling through the pictures. Going over to peer past his shoulder, she exclaimed, "No, not that one! My smile looks goofy. Nope, Hamlet has his eyes closed in that one. There, that one, it's perfect."

By the time Robert finished cropping and uploading the approved picture to the various Internet sites, James had finished checking out his customer and excused himself to take a break upstairs, leaving the store momentarily empty save for her and Robert. Darla took the opportunity to tell Robert what Brody had said about taking Hamlet for a regular walk.

"It'll make him feel like he's doing something important, watching over the neighborhood. And it might help with his wanderlust. Do you think you'd be able to take him out for me during your shift if things are slow?"

"Sure," he agreed with a smile. "And he, you know, seems like he's perked up already. You look happier now . . . don't you, little goth bro?" he addressed Hamlet, who was sitting beside Darla, tail wrapped neatly around him.

Robert leaned toward the cat with fist extended to do their little fist-paw bump ritual. It was something that had fallen by the wayside during Hamlet's funk, and so Darla was pleased to see the cat raise his paw to respond. But barely had they "bumped" when Hamlet leaped to his feet again and, with a single strong tug, abruptly broke free of Darla's grasp. Before she realized what was happening, he went bounding toward the front of the store, black leash chasing like a whip snake after him.

"Oh, no, that's exactly what Brody warned me about," Darla exclaimed over her shoulder as she rushed to stop his flight. "Thank goodness we're not outside on the street."

Fast as Hamlet was, she didn't catch up to him until he halted at the shop's door. There, he sat back on his haunches and then proceeded to climb his front paws up the wooden door as if he were trying to look out its window.

"That's weird," Robert observed as he joined Darla at the door. "I've never, like, seen him do something like that before."

"Me, either," Darla replied, bending down to take a firm grasp of the leash again. "Hamlet, what's wrong? Is something out there?"

By way of answer, the cat gave a low growl. Darla peered through the blurry glass but saw nothing other than the misty image of the street below.

"Maybe it's the snow?" she suggested.

Robert shook his head. "No, look at him. It's like he's hearing something."

And, indeed, Hamlet had tilted his head as if listening, his green eyes wide and fixed somewhere beyond the door. Darla frowned, remembering how Brody had given her a momentary start that first day they'd met, when she'd mistaken him for some homeless person looking for shelter inside the bookstore. If the weather was getting worse, perhaps someone *was* out there, maybe shivering on the steps leading down to Jake's garden apartment.

"Here," she said, and once again passed the leash to Robert. "You keep a tight hold on him. I'm going to take a peek outside."

Assuring herself that Robert had the leash looped in approved fashion over his wrist, she opened the door and peered out. A whirl of fine snow, like a gust of confectioner's sugar, greeted her. Other than a couple of passing cars and a single well-bundled passerby strolling along, she saw no one, or nothing, that might have triggered the cat's response. A glance back at Robert and Hamlet, however, showed the cat still at full alert, ears flicking like tiny satellite dishes.

Curious now, she stepped onto the stoop and, shivering, peered over the balustrade to the steps leading down to Jake's apartment. "Someone there?" she called. "It's cold. Come on out."

When she got no answer, she shrugged and turned back to Robert in the doorway.

"Nothing," she told him, hugging her sweater tighter around her. "Maybe he's just getting more telepathic messages from Brody. I'll tell you about that later," she added when Robert gave her a quizzical look. "But it's too darned cold out here to go chasing ghosts that only Hamlet can see. Come on, let's go back—"

She broke off as she heard a faint sound from the direction of Mary Ann's building. "What's that? Why, it sounds like—"

"Barking!" Robert cried, rushing with Hamlet to join her on the stoop. "Quick, hold Hamlet. I need to look."

All but shoving the leash into her hand, Robert rushed down the concrete steps to the sidewalk and hurried the few feet to the steps leading down to his apartment, quickly vanishing from Darla's view.

Tightly clutching Hamlet's lead, Darla anxiously peered after her employee. Hamlet, she noticed, seemed to have forgotten his earlier distress that had brought them outside in the first place. Instead, he was sniffing at the gentle drift of snowflakes while fastidiously avoiding the small puddles of melting snow that were accumulating atop the stoop.

"Robert, what is it? Is something down there?" Darla called through chattering teeth, concerned when the youth didn't make an immediate reappearance. "I can't stay out here much longer. It's freezing, and I need to take Hamlet back inside."

When she heard no response, she turned, prepared to head back into the store again. Just then she saw Robert's dark head and then the rest of him reappear as he walked up the stairs from his apartment. Now, however, he moved huddled over, his attention seemingly fixed on whatever it was that he carried. Darla's puzzlement grew.

"Robert, what is it?" she repeated as he drew closer.

The youth looked up as he started up the steps, moving carefully now so that he didn't slip. One corner of her mind was reminding Darla that she'd need to break out the salt pretty soon, so that the steps were safe for customers. But the greatest portion of her attention was fixed on the white bundle cradled in Robert's arms.

Before he could answer her, a sharp little bark and the glimpse of a broad tapestry collar confirmed her suspicions.

"Look," Robert exclaimed, his expression reflecting both uncertainty and joy as he joined her on the stoop. "It's Roma!"

|| **THIRTEEN**

"QUICK, GET HER INSIDE," DARLA URGED HIM. SHE PULLED the door open wider and ushered Robert and Roma in, and then followed after with Hamlet. Once the door was safely closed, she unbuckled the cat before joining them at the register.

"She must have escaped and come to me for help," Robert was saying in an excited tone as he hugged the small gray and white dog to him. "But, look, she's shivering."

And, indeed, the tiny greyhound shook as if she were being bounced about in an old-style washing machine. Alarmed, Darla hurried around the counter and reached for the bag from the pet boutique that she'd stashed there.

"I was going to return all these things today," she exclaimed as she pulled out one of the dog sweaters. "Here, set her up on the counter so we can put this on her."

While Robert held the dog as still as he could, Darla managed to get the sweater on her, pulling up the broad neckline so that Roma was now snuggled in fleece from tail to nose. "Go ahead and sit down over there," she told Robert, pointing him toward the beanbag chair in the kids' section. "I'll get some warm water for her to drink. That'll help take off some of the chill."

While Robert trotted over to the beanbag, Darla headed upstairs toward the lounge, where she found James finishing his own warm drink—and told him what had just happened.

"An interesting turn of events," he observed as Darla pulled a bowl from the cabinet in the kitchenette area and began filling it from the hot water tap. "It would seem the dog has made its choice of owner."

"Well, I wouldn't put it past Dr. Tomlinson to track her down to here," Darla observed in a dark tone as she took the now-filled bowl and started toward the stairs again. "Let's get the poor thing thawed out first, and then we can figure out what to do with her."

"Indeed. I may have a few ideas on that score."

Darla gave him a questioning look at that last comment but decided it could wait until she'd taken care of Roma. By the time she made it back downstairs again to where Robert sat cuddling the dog, Roma's shivering had subsided to the occasional shake. Still, she lapped eagerly at the warm water that Darla offered her, looking expectantly up at her when she'd finished.

"I bet she's, you know, hungry, too," Robert said in an accusing tone. "I bet that lady didn't even feed her."

"Let's decide what to do with her, first," Darla told him, "and then you can take her down to your place to eat. James," she added as he joined them, "this is Roma, the Italian grey-hound that used to belong to Master Tomlinson."

"A handsome animal, at least from what little I can see of her. She is obviously quite resourceful to have made it here safely from several blocks away . . . or maybe even farther, if she came from somewhere other than the dojo.

And weather like this is hardly conducive to creatures of her size."

"Yeah, Hamlet is a real hero," Robert declared, giving the cat a grateful look. "Roma would have, like, frozen if Hamlet hadn't told us she was out there."

Hearing his name, the hero in question padded over to where the youth sat. He leaned in for a quick sniff at the swaddled dog. For her part, Roma squirmed in Robert's arms and stuck her narrow muzzle out from the fleece coat so that cat and dog were nose-to-nose. Then Roma gave an excited yap.

Her small bark was promptly answered by a hiss from Hamlet. The feline raised a paw for a swipe, and Darla opened her mouth to call a warning. But before she could intervene, Roma stuck out her own delicate paw and tapped Hamlet's fuzzy foot.

"Hey, fist bump!" Robert exclaimed in delight. Hamlet, obviously taken aback by the dog's response, dropped the threatening paw and gave another, slightly more half-hearted hiss. Then, green eyes blazing, he turned and stalked away.

While James joined Robert in amusement over Hamlet's antics, Darla was considering the manager's earlier statement. Had Roma fled the dojo? Or had she leaped from a car, or maybe even escaped from the Tomlinsons' home, wherever that might be? Or, more disturbing, had the good doctor simply turned Roma loose to fend for herself?

That last idea set Darla's temper aflame, though she swiftly reminded herself she had no idea how Roma actually came to be on the street. Hank and Hal might be out in the cold looking for Roma this very minute. The important thing was that the little dog had found Robert, and that she was safely out of the weather. But how could they assure her well-being for the future?

"I don't know what to do, Professor James," Robert was telling the man, his tone sober now. "Hal and Hank—they're

Master Tomlinson's stepsons—seemed, you know, okay with me keeping her. It was Master Tomlinson's wife that said no. And that's only because she wanted to sell Roma to a breeder where she'd live in a cage forever."

"Ah, yes, and allow some commerce-minded incompetent to make a few dollars by unnecessarily adding to the domestic animal population in this country." His tone was sharper than usual, and Darla suddenly recalled Jake mentioning that the man was involved in a pet rescue of some sort. Maybe that would be a solution.

"James, Jake once told me that you had some connection to an animal welfare group. Do you think they could figure out a way that Robert could keep Roma for good?"

"I was about to suggest that very thing," he replied. "But it will take a leap of faith on Robert's part. He will have to give Roma over to the rescue people. Wait," he added when the teen started to protest. "This would be only for a short time, until they determine that no owner will step up to claim her. It would be at that point that he could legitimately adopt her. I would, of course, be happy to cover all the fees involved."

"Are you, like, sure about these rescue dudes? What if they stick her in a cage somewhere?" the youth asked, eyes wide. He hugged the little dog still closer, and a long pink tongue flicked out from the folds of fleece to lick his cheek. "And what if Dr. Tomlinson says she does want her, what then?"

"I agree there is a risk involved, but it is the best way to assure that dog stays safe, and that your claim to her cannot be contested."

"It sounds like the right thing to do," Darla spoke up, "but won't the rescue group just phone Dr. Tomlinson right off the bat and tell her someone found her dog? And then Roma will be back in the same bad situation."

James shook his head.

"Let me explain in more detail. When I make the call to

our contact, I will dissemble somewhat and merely state that the dog has been found. The rescue group will pick her up and bring her to their veterinarian for a check-up. At that point, she will be scanned for a microchip implant so that they can retrieve her owner's information. If both the original breeder and Mr. Tomlinson neglected to take that step, then with no information on her owner, they will upload Roma's particulars to various lost pet sites to see if anyone claims her."

"And if no one does, then Robert gets to keep her?"

James held up a restraining hand. "It is not quite that simple a process. I will suggest—and, believe me, I have a certain influence with that group—that Robert be approved to foster her in the meantime. If, after a certain amount of time has passed, the owner still has not responded to these advertisements, Roma will then be put up for adoption. With my recommendation, Robert should be approved immediately as her new owner."

Darla considered this for a moment. Technically, James's plan seemed a bit underhanded. With the possibility of Roma being shipped off to a puppy mill to end her days, however, she was willing to squelch her conscience's nagging reminders of same.

"And if they do find a chip," she asked, "what then?"

"They are obliged to make that call to the number on file with the registry, and I fear that Roma and Robert are back in the same situation where we started."

"Then I won't tell anyone," was the youth's stubborn response. "I'll just keep her."

Darla gave him a sympathetic look. "I know where you're coming from, Robert, but she *is* a valuable dog. You could be charged with theft if Hank or Hal learns you have her. And if Reese ever finds out, he'll be obliged to do something about it. Really, I think James's plan makes a lot of sense."

She could see the emotions—anger, dismay, hope—play across his young features. Then Robert struggled out of the beanbag chair and got to his feet, his expression determined.

"Okay, I'll do it, but only if you'll wait until tomorrow to have someone get her. She came all the way here to find me, and I don't want her to think I'm trying to get rid of her like Dr. Tomlinson is."

"Agreed," James said with a small smile. "I will make the call but explain we will hold her until tomorrow."

"Robert, why don't you take your break now and carry Roma down to your apartment and get her fed?" Darla suggested and handed him the bag of dog gear. "James and I can take care of things until you're back."

"You hear that, Roma?" he whispered into her neatly folded ear. "You're safe with me, at least for tonight." To James and Darla, he added, "I'll get her settled and then I'll be back to work."

Robert hurried out the front door, Roma yapping happily in his arms. Darla waited until boy and dog had disappeared into the frosty swirl on the stoop before turning to James. "Do you think you'll be able to keep your promise to Robert that he'll get to keep Roma?"

"I made no such promise," James countered in a stern tone. "I merely laid out the most favorable path and assured him I would do my part to help."

"Yes, but you know Robert is taking what you said as gospel. If this doesn't work out with Roma, he'll be devastated."

"Then we simply must hope for the best. Now, if you will excuse me, we have a customer needing assistance."

Darla took the hint and said no more about the situation, even after Robert returned half an hour later to continue his shift. It was enough that the youth seemed cheerier than he had the past few days. As her mother always told her, no sense borrowing trouble. She'd put her faith in James's ability to get things done.

After a final check on Roma a few hours later, she and

Robert—both bundled up from ears to toes—set off on foot through the cold night toward the dojo. Earlier that afternoon, Robert had almost backed out of going, afraid that Hank and Hal would somehow guess that he was harboring the fugitive greyhound.

"Don't worry," Darla had assured him. "Chances are that Dr. Tomlinson hasn't even bothered telling them that Roma is missing."

"Yeah, but what if the Steroid Twins have that martial arts psychic thing going? I've seen those movies where the karate masters could read minds and stuff."

"Movies, Robert, not real life," Darla reminded him.

After considering that advice for a few minutes, the teen had agreed. Then, recalling the class mantra and the sensei's admonition to fight injustice, he'd been spurred to a new mission.

"We should look for clues at the dojo," he had told her as he unpacked the new shipment of cozy mysteries. Holding up a popular author's latest release—the cover of which featured a dog and a plate of cookies and a knife—he had said, "In the books, there's always something the cops miss that regular people notice. Maybe we can discover something to help Detective Reese track down Master Tomlinson's murderer."

"Books, Robert, not real life," Darla had answered with a small sigh, wondering if this was how Reese felt whenever she offered him advice. "Just act natural tonight and concentrate on the lesson."

But that was easier said than done—not just for her and Robert, but for the entire class. The first thing she noticed as they reached the studio was that the small tribute alongside the fu dog had grown significantly since the day before. Someone had tied an Asian-style parasol to the statue's raised paw to shelter the collection of cards, flowers, and other offerings from the earlier dusting of snow.

Inside, the atmosphere was equally reverential, even

though the number gathered was far larger than on most class nights. Darla had feared that some people would be there simply to gawk at the spot where the sensei had met his tragic end. Instead, the students and parents milled about in respectful silence, most of the conversation limited to murmured questions and answers at the table where one parent was helping finish up the tournament paperwork. Even the young grade-schoolers going through their drills seemed more focused than usual, snapping to attention immediately each time Hal barked another order.

Darla and Robert drew curious looks as they settled behind the divider panel with the others to watch the junior class. Apparently, word had gotten out that they were the ones who had discovered Master Tomlinson's body there at the dojo. On the way to class, she had discussed with Robert how to reply to any questions about the tragedy. Their agreed-upon response was likely not dojo-approved. She was relieved, therefore, that no one had the poor taste to try to pump them for information as they sat there.

No one, that was, except for Mark Poole.

A few minutes before the junior class was to end, he slipped into the seat behind Darla and tapped her on the shoulder hard enough to leave a bruise.

"Hey, Darla," he greeted her in a stage whisper. Leaning forward to breathe a reminder of his earlier garlic-laced supper on her cheek, he pushed up his glasses on his nose and added, "I hear you were the one who found Sensei's dead body. How weird was that?"

"Ouch," was Darla's reflexive reply as, rubbing her shoulder, she turned to give him a quelling look. Her first impulse was to ignore the man, but she'd been around Mark often enough to know that he wouldn't give up until she answered him. Better to apply the non-dojo-approved response and get this over with.

Jumping up from her seat, she grabbed Mark by his gi

sleeve. Ignoring the stares of the students around her, she started dragging him toward the lobby.

"Hey, what are you doing?" the man protested as he stumbled after her.

Darla made no reply until they were safely out of earshot of the others; then, letting go of his sleeve, she gave him another outraged look. No matter that the man was a customer of hers, it was time to put him in his place.

"First, don't ever poke me again like that," she gritted out. "And, second, why in the world would you think it was appropriate to ask me about finding the sensei, especially here?"

"What? I thought we were friends," he whined. "And friends tell friends stuff. I didn't mean anything by it. I just wanted to know."

Darla took a deep breath, debating whether or not to correct him regarding that whole "friends" assumption. Finally, she said, "Let's get one thing straight. I'm not gossiping about this with you, or anyone else at the dojo, and neither will Robert. So show a little respect, will you?"

"All right, sorry."

The man sounded chastened, although his blue eyes behind the glasses shimmered with an emotion that she could only interpret as resentment. *Too bad,* was Darla's own annoyed response. He had no right to play the injured innocent when he'd shown no similar consideration toward the late sensei and his family. And if she'd lost a customer by telling him off, then so be it.

Then, to her surprise, Mark began to sob.

"I know, I was being a jackass, but I just can't believe he's dead," he said between gulps. "I mean, one minute he's alive, and the next minute he's gone."

"It was quite a shock," Darla agreed, taken aback by this sudden show of emotion. She'd had no idea that the man was so attached to their instructor. Maybe, like Martha had suggested a few days earlier, he *was* off his meds and, as a result, overly emotional. When the sobs continued, she sighed and gave him an awkward pat on the shoulder.

"Don't worry, it's okay to be upset," she reluctantly assured him. "But the best thing we can do is keep Sensei's memory alive by being good students and following his mantra. Now, I'm going back to watch the rest of the junior class. See if you can pull yourself together, then come sit with us."

He nodded, snuffling into his sleeve, and then made as if to give her a hug. Darla had been watching for such a move, however, and so she was able to sidestep the attempt. *Why does he always try to hug me?* she thought, hurrying back to the training area. As she retook her seat, Robert shot her a sidelong sympathetic glance and gave his head a disgusted shake.

"What a loser," he muttered in a voice just loud enough for her to hear.

She was tempted to agree; still, she couldn't help feel a bit sorry for the man. Awkward and socially inept as he was around other people, especially women, it probably was easy for him to read something that wasn't there into even the most casual relationship. But that didn't mean she intended to encourage his touchy-feely shtick.

By now, the junior class was ending. As the twenty or so small warriors made their final bows and soberly broke ranks, Hal made his way to the waiting area. Looking sober himself, he began conferring with the gathered parents, simultaneously discussing the upcoming tournament and accepting condolences.

Darla and Robert, meanwhile, made their way to the mat area along with their fellow students to prepare for their session. It was the moment that Darla had been dreading, returning to the scene of the tragedy. How could they casually gear up in the same place that such a heinous crime had occurred?

She knew Robert felt the same apprehension as well. She

felt his sudden grip on her sleeve, rather like a shy child hanging on to his mom, and gave him an encouraging smile. "We can do it," she softly assured him.

But as they stepped around the divider and onto the mat, she noted in surprised relief that the two dressing rooms were no longer accessible. Instead, the American and Japanese flags that once had graced the opposite wall now hung there, one over each door. Anyone unfamiliar with the studio would not guess that anything but a wall lay beneath. The dojo's altar with its reclining Buddha had been moved as well, now positioned directly in front of the flags and effectively blocking any access to the small rooms beyond. To complete the impromptu remodel, two folding screens had been set up in the far corner to serve as replacement dressing areas.

"All right," she heard Robert say in similar relief beside her, his grip on her sleeve easing as the breath he'd been holding whooshed from him.

Slightly more at ease now, Darla changed quickly into her uniform and then rejoined her classmates for their usual few minutes of informal warm-up. She saw in surprise— because she'd not spied his mother among the other parents—that Chris Valentine was among the night's students. The teen caught her gaze and walked over toward her.

"Uh, hi," he greeted her, his expression uncomfortable. "It's okay, you know, about last week. Hal said I could fight in the tournament, after all."

"That's great. I hope you win your division," Darla told him, sincere in her congratulations. Showboating and attitude aside, he seemed like a good enough kid who had learned his lesson.

Chris nodded. "Yeah, but it doesn't mean that much now, know what I mean?"

He shrugged, and trotted off to practice the previous week's technique. Knowing that any show of sympathy she might make would be brushed aside, Darla let him go.

Instead, she found one of the other adult female students and paired up with her to review the previous week's holds.

"Line up," Hank called a few minutes later, striding to the front of the class.

As he stood waiting for the students to take their places, Darla frowned. Something about the man looked different, but she couldn't quite put her finger on it. Black gi, check. Hair tied back in a ponytail, check. Ticked off expression in place, check. And then it hit her. For the first time since she'd known him, Hank's black gi jacket actually had long sleeves.

A new mark of respect toward his late stepfather? Or, far more disturbing, perhaps the convenient camouflaging of the marks of a struggle?

The last possibility sent a shiver through her, but she had no time to mull that over, for he called out, "Let's begin. Bow to the flag, bow to the instructor, bow to each other." Then, those obeisances made, he added, "Now, repeat your student creed."

"Run when you can, fight if you must, never give up, and never let injustice go unpunished," the group obediently chorused.

Darla knew that most of the adult students had always considered the words an eye-rolling exercise in feel-good, better suited to the junior class. But for her and Robert, the rote recitation had become a rallying cry, especially now. She exchanged a glance with the teen beside her. Maybe he was right, she told herself, and they *should* poke around the dojo for clues that Reese and his men might have missed.

With that in mind, she did her best to blend into the background during the night's lesson, but it soon became obvious that Hank had his eye on both her and Robert. The realization made her nervous, so that the routines she thought she had down pat seemed a greater challenge than usual.

Robert felt the scrutiny, too. At one point during a

practice drill, he sidled up to her and murmured, "I think he, you know, knows about the d-o-g."

"I don't think that's it," Darla reassured him in a low tone, "but you're right, something's up. Maybe he's just uncomfortable with us here, since we were the ones who found his stepfather's body."

Robert shook his head, seemingly unconvinced, but returned to his spot. Darla focused as best she could on the series of blocks and punches, even as she continued to be awkwardly aware of Hank's scrutiny. She couldn't help but wonder if he realized she had her own suspicions about him.

She managed to get through the class, however, and after the final bows, she quickly pulled Robert aside. "Are you going to stay for the sparring class?" she asked him.

At his nod, she went on, "Good. Keep your ears open in case any of the senior students say something incriminating. I'm going to hang out at the registration table and talk up the karate moms. Maybe there's an old friend of Sensei's from out of town that we should know about."

"Yeah, maybe Norris or Seagal will be there," he said in excitement, "except I doubt they, you know, had a grudge against him."

"Probably not," Darla agreed. "I had in mind someone more like a rival, or another dojo owner," she added, recalling how Officer Wing had mentioned how his old sensei had kept a rivalry going with TAMA and Master Tomlinson. "Just keep your eyes and ears open for anything that doesn't seem right. Now, go get changed and I'll meet you up front." But barely had she said that when a familiar voice called their names.

"Pettistone, Gilmore . . . front and center!"

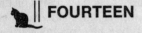 **FOURTEEN**

HANK.

Darla and Robert exchanged wide-eyed glances and then turned as one to face the black belt. Bulky arms crossed over his chest, he gave them a sharp look from across the training area. "You two, come to the front office with me."

"We don't have to, do we?" Robert whispered. "I mean, he can't make us."

"Don't worry, it's probably no big deal, maybe something to do with the tournament," she softly assured the youth while giving Hank what she hoped was a disarming smile. Taking Robert by the sleeve, she urged him forward, murmuring, "It will look suspicious if we run out. And if this has to do with you-know-who, we'll call his bluff. He can't know that you have her."

They followed Hank off the mat and past the registration table with its knot of students waiting for the intermediate class. Mark was among them. He gave Darla a curious look but prudently refrained from touching or calling out to her.

Once they reached Master Tomlinson's office—which now, of course, was Hal and Hank's domain—the latter ushered them in and shut the door behind then. "No, don't sit," he barked when Robert made as if to slip into one of the wooden folding chairs set before the desk. "I want you two on your feet."

When Robert and Darla both snapped to attention, the man gave them a steely look. "Do you know why I called you here?"

Darla shook her head. "No, Sensei."

"No, Sensei," Robert muttered, gazing down at his feet.

Hank leaned against the desk and gave them both another considering look. "I know why you were here at the dojo on Sunday morning. Tom—Master Tomlinson—was going to test you for your yellow belts, right?"

Now, both Robert and Darla gave a cautious nod.

"Bad luck how things worked out . . . for everyone," he darkly observed. "But that shouldn't mean you two get cheated out of what you earned. Take off your belts."

The two of them exchanged confused looks but complied. Hank, meanwhile, straightened and reached behind the desk. Then, giving them what Darla realized was an actual smile, he held up two folded gold-colored cloth belts.

"I've watched you in class, and you've earned the rank. You are both now officially yellow belts." Before they could say anything in reply to this pronouncement, he swooped down on them and swiftly knotted the new belts around their waists.

"Uh, thanks, Sensei," Robert choked out, grinning as he made his bow.

Smiling, Darla followed suit. "Thank you, Sensei."

Hank made them a formal bow back and replied, "Now, don't get big heads or nothing. You've still got a long way to go. But now that you've moved up to a colored belt, I want to see both of you competing in this weekend's tournament. Robert is already registered for the beginning sparring division. I'd like to see you there, too, Darla."

"Me?" Darla squeaked. "I-I haven't registered. I don't think I'm good enough to spar with anyone yet."

"You can compete in beginning forms and do your katas," Hank assured her. "Your technique is nice and crisp. Besides, competition in your age bracket is pretty sparse, so you've got a good chance at a trophy."

"Really?" she exclaimed, choosing to ignore the age reference as visions of a shiny silver cup abruptly flashed through her mind. She'd never been much for athletics in high school, and her only sports award of any sort had been a fourth place ribbon one year in the running broad jump. But a trophy! Why, she might even display it in the bookstore!

"Sure, I'll go sign up now," she impulsively agreed.

The decision earned her a congratulatory fist bump from Robert. Then, turning back to Hank, he eagerly asked, "Hey, can I go show Chris my belt?"

The black belt nodded. "Go ahead. And we'll see you Saturday at the tournament," he reminded Darla while Robert took off like a shot.

The smile Hank gave her was friendlier than she'd seen before, and as she started out the office door, her cynical side abruptly wondered if he was playing them. Maybe he simply was trying to follow in his stepfather's footsteps and encourage his students . . . or maybe the whole belt and tournament thing was a distraction to keep her mind off Master Tomlinson's murder.

That last thought made her pause. Turning again, she said, "I didn't really get to tell you this before, but we're all terribly sorry about Master Tomlinson. He was a great guy, and a wonderful teacher."

"Yeah, he was." Hank's smile faded, and his expression turned momentarily bleak. "We may have had our differences, but Tom was my stepfather for almost twenty years. Believe me, I'm going to make sure the cops find out who murdered him."

"I know Detective Reese personally," Darla hastened to assure him, "and I can tell you he's doing everything he can to solve the case."

"Yeah?" Hank crossed beefy arms over his chest again, his stance menacing. "Well, if I find Tom's killer first, it ain't gonna be pretty. Let's just say that person is gonna wish he surrendered to the cops."

And Darla believed him, she realized as she left the office. His reaction seemed too visceral to be an act. Which meant that, Botox or not, Dr. Tomlinson likely didn't have anything to do with her husband's murder. *No*, she corrected herself. It only meant that if Dr. Tomlinson was guilty, then Hank was unaware of it. But if she *was* the killer, and Hank learned the truth, could he turn on his own mother?

That thought niggled at her as she returned to the studio area to fill out her last-minute registration. Several of her fellow students immediately noticed the new belt she sported and came up to offer their congratulations. Robert, she saw in amusement, was already preening about the area, doing a fair imitation of Chris with a spinning kick that nearly clipped the latter.

"Hey, a little control there," she heard Chris scold him, sounding suspiciously like one of the adult students. Then, apparently realizing they were going to be late for the sparring class, the two teens hurried in the direction of the mat.

"Don't wait for me if you don't want to," Robert called over his shoulder. "I can walk home by myself."

"I'll stick around a couple of minutes and then I'll see you tomorrow," she agreed, waving him on.

Not that she wouldn't mind watching the full class—particularly if Robert landed a lucky punch on Mark!—but the karate moms handling the registration were closing up shop now. In a few minutes, the only ones left in the dojo other than Hank and Hal would be the students sparring. While everyone else was concentrating on punching and kicking, she'd take a casual glance at the tournament roster, which was sitting out in plain view.

Unfortunately, since the sparring class had started, it was too late to return to the dressing area to change. Darla did the next best thing and slipped off her new yellow belt and gi jacket, folding them into her gear bag. Now, she was wearing just her gi pants and the tank top that she'd had on under her jacket. Hurriedly, she pulled on the oversized sweatshirt that she'd worn for the walk to the dojo. The combination of baggy white gi trousers topped by a University of Texas fleece wasn't the most fashionable look, but it was better than sitting around in her practice uniform. Besides, once she threw her long coat back on, said fashion faux pas would be virtually covered.

Waving good-bye to the last of the departing moms, she settled into her chosen seat behind the viewing panel. She knew, based on her usual vantage point from the opposite side, that anyone sitting in this chair could not be seen from the main mat area unless they pressed up against the glass for a look. Just as no one in the sparring class would notice her sitting there, neither would anyone notice when she slipped away after a few minutes to surreptitiously check out the tournament paperwork.

Once she was certain that the sparring students were well into their drills under Hank and Hal's direction, Darla shouldered her gear bag and casually sidled up to the now-empty registration table. The tournament registration list was neatly attached to a black clipboard alongside an alphabetized expandable file. Checking again to be sure she wasn't being watched, she flipped through the pages on the clipboard.

The top page was a list of the TAMA students taking part in the tournament . . . almost fifty of various ranks and ages. Subsequent pages had names of registered students from various other dojos, as well as a number of participants listed as unaffiliated with any studio. Many of the latter were from out of town, a few even from other states. At a quick estimate, perhaps two hundred participants were already registered. Obviously this tournament was a much bigger event than Darla had realized.

Keeping one ear open to the shouts and cheers from the training area, she scanned the list more closely. Not that she was certain what she was looking for, she told herself, it was just that she had a feeling there might be something of importance to be found. And then she spied a name that rang a bell.

Tiger Lee's Fighting Academy.

Darla frowned. Hadn't that been the dojo where Officer Wing said he'd trained as a youth? She counted sixteen names from that dojo, more than half listed as junior competitors under the age of twelve, and the rest adult students at red belt level and higher. Turning to the final page, she found the list of tournament officials—among them Tiger Lee himself.

Her frown deepened. Would Master Tomlinson have recruited a man who held a grudge against him to take part in such an event? Or had the cop's recollection been a boy's faulty memory, and the supposed rivalry was nothing more than a healthy competition between martial arts schools?

Then she shook her head. Even in the unlikely event that the two men had been bitter enemies, nothing about Lee's name on the list was at all suspicious. She was fishing for clues, and not successfully. It was only coincidence that Officer Wing had happened to mention his old sensei, and even greater coincidence that the man happened to be officiating at the upcoming tournament.

On impulse, Darla left the waiting area and made her way to the vestibule. At this hour, the outer door was locked against anyone wandering in off the street, and the "hallway of fame" with its collection of photos was but dimly lit by a single fixture at the front. Squinting and wishing she dared flip on the overhead lights, Darla searched the hand-printed names on each picture frame.

She'd passed that wall many times these past weeks but had paid scant attention to any save the famous names: the pictures of Master Tomlinson sharing moments with Lee and Norris and Wallace and Burleson. Looking closer now, she saw other, even more personal photos. Here was the sensei caught in mid-jump, legs extended to land an in-air kick. Another one was taken as he accepted a trophy fully as tall as he. Several were snapped as he landed a blow on an opponent in some tournament or another. She even found one of the sensei and several other men posing in full ninja garb and wielding swords.

Finally, she discovered near the beginning of the photo time line a black-and-white snapshot of two youthful men, one American and one Asian. This was the one, she told herself in satisfaction. The label on the snapshot read, *Tom Tomlinson and Tiger Lee*.

She studied the photo more closely, smiling a bit sadly at the vibrant, sixties-era image of a ponytailed man in his twenties that had been Master Tomlinson. He was grinning, as was the slim, shaggy-haired Asian whose arm was around his shoulder. Small as the picture was, she could still readily make out the men's expressions . . . that of two kindred spirits sharing a good joke. No matter their relationship later in life, at that point the two men obviously had been fast friends.

Darla shook her head again. It had been a long shot anyhow, but finding the photo in a place of honor sealed it. Friends like that didn't murder each other. She'd have to look to someone other than Tiger Lee for the sensei's murderer. Barely had she made that determination, however, when she heard the scrape of chair legs against a wooden floor from the direction of Master Tomlinson's office.

She froze, feeling momentarily guilty at the possibility

of being found there in the vestibule, yet knowing she could readily claim simply to be leaving the dojo after her lesson. Then she frowned. The office itself was even darker than the hall; still, through the open blinds of the office's broad window, she could see a dark shape moving about inside that room.

Hal or Hank?

Or neither?

For she had seen both men coaching the students in the training area before she left her seat, and neither had left the mat area while she was still perusing the registration papers. In the short time she'd been there in the vestibule, she hadn't heard footsteps behind her or a door opening to indicate someone's approach. Whoever was in the office must have entered it while she was still watching the sparring. Which meant that it wasn't one of the twins poking about in the shadows.

Heart pounding a little faster now, Darla stealthily moved through the dim hallway toward the window's far edge. Her white gi pants would surely reflect any ambient light, and she found herself wishing that she had on a ninja outfit like she'd seen in the sensei's photos. Failing that, all she could do was shift her gear bag so that it concealed as much of her lower body as possible. Besides, she sensed that the office intruder was more intent on searching than being seen.

As she drew closer to the window, she saw a pinpoint of light flicker on behind the glass. The intruder had turned on a penlight, its narrow beam slicing lines along the dark surface of the sensei's desk. Then the beam swooped over to the file cabinet in the corner, and Darla saw a drawer slide open.

What was this person looking for?

Crouching so that she was just peeking over the windowsill, Darla pressed closer to the glass. By now, her eyes were adjusted enough to the low light for her to make out a few details of the searcher. He—she?—appeared of medium height and an oddly shapeless build, until she realized that the person was simply wearing a long winter coat that disguised his—her?—actual figure. Worse, a stocking cap pulled low and a scarf wrapped around the lower half of the person's face made any identification—young, old, male, female—all but impossible. If Reese were to later ask her to ID the intruder, she'd have nothing.

Run when you can . . .

Darla clutched her gear bag more tightly, fervently wishing she was more than just a newly minted yellow belt. She could confront the person on her own, but then she would be gambling that the intruder wasn't armed or, worse, better trained than she. Or, she could find Hal and Hank to let them know someone was poking about their late stepfather's office. But by then, the intruder might already have slipped out, perhaps taking away some incriminating evidence that might have pointed to the sensei's killer.

Of course, she might be seeing conspiracy where none existed. For all she knew, the person might have permission from the twins to be there and was using a flashlight simply because the office bulb had unexpectedly burned out. And raising a stink about it would only make her look foolish when her mistake was revealed.

But then the memory of the sensei's lifeless body flashed through her mind, and her resolve stiffened. A crime of some sort was being committed, and she was the only one there to stop it.

Fight if you must . . .

Setting down her gear bag, she duckwalked the few steps to the office's closed door and eased into a standing position as she reached for the knob. At least she'd have the element of surprise on her side . . . that, and a room full of trained martial artists to back her up if she yelled loudly enough for help. Taking a steadying breath, she slowly turned the knob, wincing as she heard the small click that was the bolting mechanism releasing. This was how Jake would do it, she told herself. Burst in, and take the intruder unawares.

Slowly, she released the breath, shoulder against the door ready to shove inward as she mentally counted down, *three, two*—

"Whaddaya think you're doing?" an angry voice behind her demanded.

🐈 ‖ FIFTEEN

DARLA GAVE A LITTLE SHRIEK OF SURPRISE. HAND DROPPING
from the knob, she swung about, her heart beating wildly.
Hal was staring back at her, black brows knitted and bulging
tattooed arms—he'd not followed Hank's example by
returning to the sleeved look—crossed over his chest. Before
she could answer, however, she glimpsed another flash of
light from behind the office window. And then she heard
another quick scrape of chair against wooden floor.

Hal saw and heard it, too, for he exclaimed, "Hey, who's
in there?"

Shouldering past her, he grabbed the door handle and
twisted, only to be stopped short. Someone had locked the
office from the inside. Through the window, meanwhile,
Darla could see the flashlight beam swing wildly and then
flick off, leaving the small room in darkness.

In the next instant, Hal gave a swift, powerful front kick.
With a crack of shattering wood, the door popped inward.
He shoved his way into the office, his entry momentarily

impeded by the chairs that had been backed up against the door as a temporary barricade. Darla prudently remained several feet back while, with an economy of movement, Hal shoved the furniture out of his path.

The overhead light flashed on, and she squinted against the sudden illumination. Hal stood there in the cluttered office, his hand on the light switch and glancing wildly about. Save for him, the room was empty.

Darla gasped, abruptly recalling the photo of the ninjas she'd seen on the vestibule wall. Had Master Tomlinson's office been breached by a martial artist trained in the more esoteric fighting arts?

"The emergency exit," Hal shouted, slapping himself in the forehead.

He squeezed behind the desk, and Darla saw an exterior door she hadn't noticed previously, partially covered as it was by another TAMA banner of a giant punching fist, painted on canvas. Hal yanked the banner from its hooks and tossed it aside, and then shoved against the door's crash bar. Cold air whipped in through the open door, sending paperwork on the desk swirling as the man rushed out into the night.

The sudden breeze kicked up something else . . . the lingering scent of cigarette smoke which dissipated almost as quickly as it had risen. Darla barely had time to wonder about this when she heard the sound of a car engine revving from somewhere in the alley, and the squeal of tires before the door closed with a thud after Hal.

A few moments later, she heard the loud pounding of fist on metal. Darla rushed over to open the exit door again, letting in another blast of winter air and a very angry man.

"The SOB got away," he clipped out, throwing himself into the overstuffed leather desk chair and glaring up at Darla. "He had a car waiting in the alley. Now, you wanna tell me what *you* were doing in the hall, skulking about?"

"Me?" she squeaked for a second time that night, all too

aware she was alone in a small room with a guy who could beat her to a pulp without breaking a sweat. Better she tell him the truth . . . or, at least, the parts that wouldn't reveal that *she* had her suspicions about *him*.

"I-I was on my way out"—which was pretty much true, she reminded herself—"and I saw someone moving around in here. I wanted to catch them in the act of, well, whatever they were doing. And then I was going to call the police," she hurriedly added when he gave her a suspicious squint.

"Why didn't you call me or Hank first?" he demanded, apparently not mollified by the explanation. "How do I know you're not teamed up with whoever it was poking around in here? Maybe you were playing lookout so they could get away with stealing something. You and that kid Robert were the ones who found Tom. For all I know, maybe you two had something to do with his death."

Darla stared at him in disbelief. Could *he* actually suspect *them*? Then her redhead's temper flared.

"Robert and I are the ones who tried to save your step-father," she declared in a heated voice. "We got him out of that dressing room, and Robert did chest compressions while I called for an ambulance. We did everything we possibly could . . . just ask Officer Wing. And we're not the ones who could lift up a man that size, or who have access to all the Botox anyone would want."

"Botox?"

Hal's irate expression swiftly smoothed into one of cool curiosity, and he got up from the chair. "Who told you about that?"

"I-I read it in the paper," she hedged, worried all at once that she had repeated something that Reese meant to be kept confidential. But surely the detective wouldn't have told her about evidence that the police were holding back.

Hal, meanwhile, was shaking his bald head as he neatly circled around her, so that now he was blocking the battered doorway.

"We just found out about the whole Botox thing today," he said, his tone still casual. "Ma had to turn over all her records on the vials she had to that detective. There wasn't anything in the papers yet about it. Pretty much the only ones who know about it are us and the doctors and the cops . . . oh, and whoever murdered Tom."

Abruptly, the conversation had shifted into a whole different gear. Darla felt a chill far worse than the winter evening's wind rush over her. She'd dismissed Hank as his stepfather's killer, but that didn't mean that his twin brother Hal was innocent. And what better way to cover his tracks than to accuse her of the crime? Maybe he even had staged the whole office break-in to throw off suspicion from him and his family.

Darla nervously swallowed, hands behind her clutching the desk edge for support. She glanced at the Zen clock with its kanji face that sat on the sensei's desk. The sparring class wouldn't be over for at least another quarter hour . . . far too long a time for her to try to keep Hal talking until someone wandered by and noticed them. Still, she had to give it a try. If not, the black belt might decide to deal with her as efficiently as he might have done his stepfather.

"Look, even the police understand that accidents happen," she spoke up, striving for a reasonable tone while trying to keep her voice from trembling. "I'm sure things just got out of hand and everyone panicked. If you explain what happened to Detective Reese, he's sure to—"

"What are you talking about?" Hal interrupted her, the brightly inked Asian tiger on his neck bulging alarmingly. "You're the one who needs to start explaining, and I mean now. Who was in this office, and what do you know about Tom's death?"

At his accusing tone, she promptly forgot reasonable.

"I have no clue who was in here," she shot back, "Maybe if you'd been a bit faster, he wouldn't have escaped. And all I know about Sensei's murder is what the police told me."

Then, when he continued to scowl at her, realization dawned.

"You really didn't kill him, did you?" she asked in surprise.

The tiger bulged again as Hal favored her with a few of Jake's favorite expressions, ones that Master Tomlinson undoubtedly would have disapproved of. When he'd gotten that out of his system, he growled, "Are you crazy? He was my dad. If I find the lowlife who did this before the cops do, let's just say there won't be much of a body left to stand trial."

Darla let out a slow breath. Despite the seeming lack of concern she'd seen from him the day before, this reaction to his stepfather's death had been identical to Hank's. Reese and Jake had cautioned her in the past that murder victims often knew their killers; still, instinct told her that neither twin was involved. But the fact that someone had been searching for something in the sensei's office couldn't be overlooked.

"Hal, believe me, I had absolutely nothing to do with Master Tomlinson's death," she told him, raising her hands in a conciliatory gesture. "In fact, Detective Reese is a good friend of mine, which is why I knew about the Botox."

"So, you spyin' around here for him or something?"

"No. In fact, he'd be pretty ticked if he knew I was even here discussing the case with you. But since I'm one of the people who found him, I feel responsible. I'm just keeping my eyes and ears open, in case I run across a clue the police might have missed. That's why I was trying to stop the person we saw in your stepfather's office."

Then, when the black belt still looked unconvinced, she added, "I know I only knew him for a few months, but Master Tomlinson made a real impression on me. I believe in that creed he always made us recite. And I can't think of any injustice worse than murder."

Hal considered this a few moments and then gave her a

small smile, the tattooed tiger subsiding a bit. "Me, neither. Well, guess I need to get back to the sparring class. You want I should call the cops about this break-in, or you want to?"

"I think it would be better coming from you. I mean, I was the one who saw the intruder first, but you're the one who did all the heavy lifting," she said with a meaningful look at the broken door and disarrayed chairs.

Hal shrugged. "Yeah, well, I'll give your detective friend a shout after class. I probably messed up any evidence already, anyhow." Then, smile brightening uncharacteristically, he added, "I see you and Robert managed to jump from white belt to yellow sometime during the night. I guess my brother did the honors?"

She nodded.

"Yeah, well, you two earned it. Congratulations. See you Saturday." Then, before Darla could thank him, he slipped out the broken door as silently as he'd come in.

Darla waited until she was sure she was alone before sagging in relief. They might not be the best of friends, but apparently she and Hal were on the same page when it came to his father. And from Hal's last words, she was relieved to know he'd basically absolved her of being complicit in his stepfather's murder . . . at least, in his mind. That settled, she went to gather her gear bag, and then reflexively turned back for a last look at the desk.

From the methodical way that the intruder had been searching, it was apparent the person had not been intent on simple burglary, but instead was looking for something specific. And Darla suspected that he—or she—had been run off by Hal's arrival before they'd found the item in question. Maybe with the lights on, Darla would have an easier time finding whatever the intruder had sought.

With one eye on the splintered door, she surveyed the desktop. Whatever his strong points, Master Tomlinson apparently had not been an effective manager of paperwork. On his desk lay piles of papers that likely had been accumulating for some time. Some were fliers for various martial arts events; others, circulars for sparring gear and uniforms and such. On one corner of the desk was a wooden tray stacked with what appeared to be bills. The top one from the electric company was due in the next couple of days. Hopefully Hal or Hank would take charge and handle the bookkeeping for the dojo now; otherwise, the next class might be held in the dark!

But nothing among the paperwork stood out as worth breaking in to steal. Of course, doubtless Reese or one of the other officers had already given the room a thorough look, maybe even had already seized some documents that could've had a bearing on the case. She remembered Reese mentioning shredded paperwork, though whether that had turned out to be evidence, she had no idea. But perhaps what the police would find interesting to their investigation and what the intruder wanted were two totally different things.

She glanced over at the file cabinet that the intruder had been perusing. One drawer still hung open a couple of inches, and Darla moved over to it.

The papers crammed in this file drawer were more personal than anything on the desk . . . letters, certificates, and a folder of still more photos. Setting down the gear bag again, she pulled that folder from the file and began flipping through the snapshots.

These photos had nothing to do with Master Tomlinson's professional life. Instead, they were pictures of what appeared to be his family. Some were of a pretty, smiling woman who looked like a young version of Dr. Tomlinson, long before the Botox had taken hold. Several others were of two dark-haired, grade-school-aged boys who had to be Hal and Hank from a good twenty years earlier. Even back then, the twins had favored scowls over smiles, she thought with no little amusement. Still more photos had captured other people: an older couple she guessed were his parents,

and several younger men and women who might have been
siblings or in-laws.

Halfway through the stack, she saw that one photo was
turned on edge so that it stuck up from the others. It was flipped
over, as well, so that the first thing she noted was the penciled date on the back: June 1998. Assuming the year was
correct, it had been taken several years later than the other
pictures in the folder, and she wondered at its inclusion.
Curious, she turned it over for a look and then frowned.

The man in the picture was Master Tomlinson, no doubt
about it. She'd seen enough photos of him in his younger
days to be certain. The shot had been taken at a short distance from the subjects, an informal portrait snapped near
what appeared to be a mountain rental cabin. The Poconos,
perhaps? The sensei was smiling proudly, one arm casually
wrapped around the shoulders of a dark-haired, overly
made-up female who appeared barely out of her teens.

Definitely *not* Dr. Tomlinson.

Even so, the woman looked strangely familiar, so that
Darla ignored her fear of discovery to study the photo for a
few moments longer. And then, with a gasp, she recognized
the woman.

Grace Valentine.

A closer look left her with no doubt the photo was Chris's
mother, the woman whom Darla had dubbed the mob wife.
And the young Grace was gazing up at Tomlinson with a
look that Darla could only describe as adoring. But what
held Darla transfixed was the fact that the unknown pho-
tographer had snapped the couple at an angle. She stared a
moment longer at the picture, studying the woman's pose,
her hands cupped low around her bulging belly. No doubt
about it. Grace had been a good six or seven months pregnant when the picture was taken.

And from the protective way that Tomlinson's free hand
was splayed atop the obvious baby bump, Darla would almost
guarantee that the sensei was the unborn child's father.

▎ SIXTEEN

"AND SO, I FIGURE IT HAD TO BE GRACE VALENTINE WHO broke into the sensei's office," Darla declared to Jake the next afternoon over her half-eaten turkey Reuben. "She must have been trying to find that photo so no one would learn that Master Tomlinson was Chris's father."

"That, or grab herself a little proof that he was," Jake mumbled through a mouthful of chips.

Darla and the PI were having lunch at the deli while Robert and James held down the fort at the store, it being Darla's half-day off. She had texted Jake the previous night as soon as she'd gotten home from the dojo, anxious to share her discovery of the incriminating photograph.

And so, to the surrounding rhythm of their fellow diners' conversation, she had spent the past few minutes giving Jake a detailed account of everything that had happened the previous night at the dojo. As backup to her theory that Grace was the culprit, she explained about the smell of cigarette smoke that had lingered in the sensei's office once the intruder had left. Not that Grace was the only smoker to hang out at the dojo. During her short tenure there, Darla had caught any number of parents and adult students, including Mark, sneaking a cigarette between classes. But who else other than Grace would have wanted that picture of her and the sensei?

More important, Darla needed Jake's opinion as to what, if anything, she should tell Reese about what she had found in the file cabinet. Technically, she might be accused of interfering with a police investigation by rummaging through those photos . . . a fact that hadn't occurred to her until the wee hours of the morning when she was still trying to get to sleep. And so she waited anxiously for Jake's take on it all.

As soon as Darla finished, the PI put down her own half-eaten sandwich, settled back in her chair, and sighed. "All right, kid, first things first. Please tell me you left the picture exactly where you found it."

"I did. I even turned it backwards like it was originally."

"Good." Jake shook her curly head and then, leaning forward again, gave Darla a stern look. "Now, not to point out the obvious, but haven't you been hanging out with me and Reese long enough to know not to stick your nose into a police investigation? And don't give me any of that crap about good intentions and all that," she added when Darla opened her mouth to defend herself. "Reese's job—and he's actually pretty darned good at it—is to figure out who killed the guy. Your job is to stay the hell out of the way so he can do his job. Got it?"

"Got it," Darla muttered, feeling chastened. Jake was right, of course, but that didn't make the lecture any easier to take. Picking up her cell phone from the table, she asked in a humble tone, "So, should I give him a call now and tell him what an idiot I am?"

"I have a feeling he already knows about the idiot part," Jake replied, though she tempered the insult with a small smile. "And, yeah, give him a call once we're done here. Just make sure you put on your fireproof undies, first."

"I was thinking more on the lines of a whole fireproof jumpsuit," was Darla's ironic reply. "I expect Reese to stop by, anyhow, since Hal said he'd call in to report the break-in. So if you hear any yelling coming from my place later, you'll know why."

"Yeah, he'll yell a little . . . okay, probably a lot," Jake corrected herself, her smile broadening, "but between you and me, your buddy Hal probably destroyed more evidence than you did when he went all Bruce Lee on the place. Not that Reese and the boys didn't already take any papers out of that office that they figured were pertinent to the case, but they wouldn't necessarily know the significance of that picture."

"That's what I figured," Darla said. Then she added, "So do you think I'm right? Do you think this photo is what Grace was looking for?"

Jake held up a forefinger.

"First, we don't know for sure that she was the one who broke in. You said yourself that you couldn't make out much in the way of description. I don't suppose you stuck around to see if this Valentine woman picked up her kid after class?"

"I couldn't really justify hanging around at that point, so no, I didn't wait around. But I smelled cigarette smoke, and Hank and Hal don't smoke. Grace does."

"Yeah, and so do about fifty million other people in this country." Jake flashed a second finger, looking like a Boy Scout making his oath. "Now, second, we don't know that your burglar necessarily broke in to steal something. Maybe he/she/them broke in to *leave* something for someone to find . . . something like that lovely baby bump picture that just happened to prove that your sensei wasn't the fine upstanding guy everyone thought he was."

Darla had reached for her sandwich again and taken another bite. As the import of Jake's last words occurred to her, however, she almost choked. She chased that bite down her throat with several gulps of ice water and then managed, "Wait, you're saying Grace—or whoever—might have *wanted* the police to find the picture?"

"Makes sense," was Jake's response as she tackled her meal again. "I kinda doubt your Master Tomlinson would keep an incriminating photo like that in his file drawer for anyone to stumble across. Besides," she added, "it was pretty convenient that it just happened to be turned backwards and on end in the pile, so that someone would be bound to turn it over for a look."

"You're right. There were so many pictures that I might have flipped right past it if it hadn't been put in there wrong. Do you think that's why someone murdered him, because he knocked up Grace Valentine sixteen years ago?"

Darla frowned. Her first impulse was to chalk it up to Grace's husband . . . though, come to think of it, she really didn't know for sure if the woman was actually married, or if she ever had been. Maybe there wasn't any Mr. Valentine out there who'd suddenly learned the truth about his supposed son Chris's parentage and then wanted revenge. On the other hand, maybe Chris himself had discovered the truth and had gone to confront his father, and then things got out of hand. Where the Botox came in, however, she couldn't guess.

Jake, meanwhile, gave her a considering look and then shrugged.

"That's as good a motive as any. Or maybe someone is just taking advantage of the situation to do a little postmortem blackmailing. Or maybe your sensei's killer is trying to pin the murder on someone else, like this Valentine woman." Jake paused and shook her head. "I mean, seriously, if this whole secret baby thing was hush-hush for what, fifteen or sixteen years, then it's kind of odd that it becomes a big deal right this minute."

"Yes, I suppose you're right."

Yet even as Darla agreed with her friend, her own disappointment in the sensei abruptly hit her like a roundhouse kick to the head. No matter how good a teacher he was, what it boiled down to was that Master Tomlinson had not only cheated on his wife, but had gotten a teenaged girl pregnant. On top of that, he'd betrayed his own stepsons, as well as the boy he had fathered. It was a hard offense to understand, let alone forgive, particularly when the man had spent years preaching to impressionable youths about core values like staying out of trouble and defending others.

Jake, meanwhile, pushed back from the table and stood. "Sorry to run, but I've got to go pack a bag and take a little trip out to Atlantic City this afternoon."

"The Russian Bombshell?"

"Got it in one," Jake said with a grin as she gathered up her plate and glass. "My client is getting impatient, and I've exhausted all my leads here, so I'm going with my gut. I'll be gone for a couple of days, probably, so do me a favor and grab the mail and water my African violet if it starts looking puny?"

Darla managed a smile at that last as she, too, rose.

"Sure. And if you're home by Saturday, come see me compete in the big martial arts tournament. Hal gave me and Robert our yellow belts last night, and he wanted me to compete in beginners forms, so I signed up."

"Congratulations, kid. I'll do my best to make it. And who knows," she added with a wink, "I might even bring a date."

Jake wouldn't elaborate further on that last comment, however, despite Darla's good-natured badgering on the chilly walk home again. Once back at the brownstone, they said their good-byes, and then Darla hurried upstairs to change from sloppy gray sweats to brown wool slacks and a mint green sweater set that contrasted nicely with her neatly French braided auburn hair. She'd almost forgotten that the rescue people were supposed to stop by that afternoon to collect little Roma. She wanted to be there for moral support for Robert when they did, and also to serve as a character witness, if needed.

But the scene when she finally made her way down to the store was not the bucolic farewell gathering for the little hound that she had anticipated. She'd given Robert permission to bring Roma to work with him, as long as he kept her in the small pet kennel that James had brought in, or else kept her on a lead the whole time. Unfortunately, Darla had neglected to inform Hamlet of same. Now, as she made her way from her private hallway into the shop, she could hear the feline vocally protesting this intrusion into his personal domain.

"James, Robert, what in the heck is going on here?" she exclaimed over the sound of Hamlet's hissing and Roma's excited yapping. "It sounds like World War Three, animal version. James, any customers in the vicinity?" Darla asked.

The man shook his head. "Actually, I fear that the most recent vocal altercation ran off everyone who was still here."

"Great."

"Hamlet and Roma do not appear to be getting along well," the manager explained unnecessarily, looking more frazzled than Darla could ever recall seeing him. "We tried separating them into different rooms, but Hamlet persists in finding her and then looming over the carrier to hiss at her in a most threatening manner. And that, in turn, causes the dog to bark."

"Yeah, I don't know what to do," Robert chimed in, looking equally distraught. "I thought the other day they were, you know, gonna be friends, but Hamlet is all mad and stuff. And I hate to leave her alone in the apartment if she's going away in a couple of hours."

"Well, we need to do something," Darla insisted, already feeling a bit frazzled by the situation, herself. "I'd take Hamlet up to the apartment—assuming he'd let me pick him up in this state—but he'd probably march right back downstairs again. If you and James think it's safe, why don't you let Roma out of the kennel, and let the two of them duke it out? Put her coat on her so she doesn't get scratched if Hamlet takes a swipe at her, and let's see how it goes."

Robert shot a glance at James, who gave a helpless shrug. "Okay, if you're sure," the youth replied, his tone doubtful as he dug under the counter for her gear.

Pulling out the mauve sweater, he hurried over to the kennel that, for the moment, was tucked away beside the restrooms. Hamlet, sprawled atop the plastic and wire cage, gave him the evil green eye as he approached.

Robert caught the look and stopped in his tracks.

"Whoa, he seems pretty p.o.'d," he exclaimed. "C'mon, little bro. Let me let Roma out for a minute."

Darla feared, at first, that Hamlet wasn't going to relinquish his post. But to her relief, the feline slid down the kennel's side and stalked a short distance away, where he dropped to the ground and flung a hind leg over one shoulder to lick his hindquarters in what was his official cat version of flipping the bird.

"Yep, p.o.'d," Darla agreed as Robert knelt beside the carrier and opened the door. Taking the wriggling little dog into his lap, he slipped the sweater over her and pulled the hood up over her ear tips. A moment later, Roma was fully protected against flailing cat claws everywhere but paws and tail and long narrow snout.

"Let's get this experiment over with, then, before those two put us out of business. Robert," she addressed the youth, "go ahead and let Roma go, but be ready to grab her if things get out of hand."

"Right, boss."

Gingerly, he let the little greyhound loose, and then got to his feet. As the three of them anxiously watched, Roma gave herself a big shake. Then, making her little play bow, she pranced in the direction where Hamlet still studiously groomed himself, her tiny nails clicking against the wooden floor.

Hamlet flicked a black ear in her direction and halted in mid-lick. Then, in a single fluid move, he untangled himself so that he was standing on all four paws again facing her, green eyes watchful.

This, apparently, was encouragement to the little dog. Roma gave a tiny, commanding bark and waved a paw in his direction. When Hamlet made no move, she pranced forward a few more steps, until cat and dog were almost nose-to-nose.

"Hamlet, be nice to the puppy," Darla said in an encouraging tone, wincing a little as Roma gave another yap right in the cat's face.

Hamlet's green eyes widened, and he hissed like a cobra on steroids. Darla tensed, ready to fling herself into the fray if needed. And then, to her astonishment, Hamlet gave a small *meowrmph* before turning and casually trotting back toward the register.

Roma gave another little yip and pranced after him, keeping a polite distance between them. As Hamlet reached the counter, he gave a graceful bound and landed near the register. There he stretched and then, kicking aside the karate tournament fliers Darla had piled there, settled into a neat inky ball. Roma reached the counter and sat, her long nose pointing curiously at the cat above her. Apparently satisfied, she stood again and spun in a few quick circles. Then she plopped into a similar neat mauve huddle on the floor, directly beneath where Hamlet lay, and proceeded to go to sleep.

"Epic," Robert decreed, all smiles now. "Maybe Hamlet, you know, just didn't like seeing her in the kennel."

"That is a possibility," James agreed. "There are many recorded instances of animals protesting the caging of other animals by means of some drastic behavior. And, as a cat, he does not understand the den concept that allows dogs to be comfortable in a kennel when a cat would find such a situation intolerable."

"Just as long as they're not fighting, I'm happy," was Darla's smiling take on it. Then, drawing James aside, she softly asked, "When will the rescue group be here?"

"In approximately twenty minutes," he replied, consulting his watch. "I have already forewarned Robert that they will want to see his apartment as part of the fostering approval process, so perhaps you will allow him a short break to give them a brief tour."

"Certainly. And, James, thanks for doing this."

"It is my pleasure. I have no doubt that young Robert will make an exemplary pet guardian for Roma."

Soon, the bells on the front door jingled. Along with another sharp blast of winter air came two women bundled against the cold. Unwrapping matching red scarves from around their faces, they revealed themselves to be similar enough in appearance but different enough in age that Darla guessed them to be mother and daughter.

"Hi, James," the older of the two cheerily called, waving in the manager's direction. She was perhaps Jake's age, but her straight black hair was cropped short as a boy's and liberally shot through with gray. Pink-cheeked tending toward plump, she was the same height but a few dress sizes larger than the slim girl next to her.

Turning in Darla's direction, she stuck out her hand and added, "You must be Ms. Pettistone. I'm Bonnie Greenwood, and this is my daughter, Sylvie. We're from the Furry Berets Pet Rescue." Sylvie had the same black hair as her mother, though her locks were shoulder-length and untouched by gray. Darla guessed her to be around the same age as Robert.

"Please, call me Darla," she politely protested as she shook both women's hands. "And we're very happy you were able to help us."

"Yes, James gave us the lowdown. So, where's our little dog, and who's the young man who wants to foster her?"

"Uh, that would be me," Robert said, coming out from the back room where he'd been restocking the science fiction and fantasy shelves. "I'm Robert, uh, Gilmore. And that's Roma."

Ducking his head nervously, he hurried past them to the counter and scooped up the small dog from where she'd been snoozing on the floor. She gave a wide yawn, her long pink tongue lolling, and then snuggled into his arms, bright eyes blinking at the newcomers.

"Ah, she's sweet," Sylvie exclaimed as she went over to where Robert stood. Reaching a hand toward the little hound, she asked, "May I?"

"Uh, sure."

Robert grinned proudly as the girl gently scratched Roma behind the ears and then proceeded to ooh and aah over her, which no doubt helped put the youth at ease, for he said, "Here, want to hold her?"

While the pair bonded over the little dog, Bonnie briskly got down to business with Darla and James.

"First thing, we'll take her by the vet for a checkup and scan," she said, proceeding to outline the process much as James had previously explained it to Darla. "Of course, we need to take a quick look at Robert's place, just to make sure it's set up for a dog. And we'll need a signed statement from his landlord allowing him to keep a pet."

"That would be Mary Ann Plinski next door," Darla explained. "I'm sure she would be happy to sign. And she'll give Robert a sterling reference, too."

"As will I and Ms. Pettistone," James interjected.

His pronouncement drew a smile from Bonnie. "Don't worry, James, if you say the kid is good for it, I believe you. Now, let's go look at his place and then visit with his landlady."

Thirty minutes later, Sylvie and Bonnie walked out with Roma. Robert stood with his nose pressed to the door glass for several moments watching them drive off before turning back to James and Darla.

"Are you sure, you know, that they'll take good care of her?"

"The Fuzzy Berets are one of the finest rescue organizations in the city," James assured him. "And do not worry, I will let you know the moment they call me with the results from the veterinarian. Now, those chapter books will not stock themselves, will they?"

Nodding, Robert wandered dejectedly back toward the children's section where a cart was piled with boxes of books.

"Poor guy, it's got to be tough waiting," Darla said, shaking her head in commiseration. "I just hope that Bonnie and Sylvie aren't able to get hold of Dr. Tomlinson. Which reminds me . . ."

She sighed and reached into her trousers pocket for her cell phone. "I've got to run upstairs and call Reese about something I found out about last night at the dojo. I'll be back in a few minutes."

But she'd barely made her way up the steps and reached her front door when her phone began ringing. She glanced at the caller ID and then shook her head.

Too late for fireproof undies now.

◣ ‖ SEVENTEEN

THE CONVERSATION WITH REESE WAS SHORT AND WENT pretty much as Darla had expected . . . meaning the detective had remained relatively calm until she brought up how she'd found the photo of Master Tomlinson with Grace Valentine. At that point, holding the phone at arm's length from her ear, she'd decided that a whole fireproof apartment might be a worthwhile investment.

Eventually, however, Reese piped down enough to tell her that he was getting a warrant for a more thorough search of Master Tomlinson's files. "And unless I tell you different, I don't want you going back there anytime soon."

"Actually, I have to," she replied, bristling a little at his commanding air. "Hal gave me my yellow belt last night, and I signed up to compete in beginner forms at the tournament Saturday, so I have to get in some more practice before then. Who knows, I might even bring home a trophy."

"Hey, Red, that's great," he answered, warm approval now in his tone. "Okay, change of plans—I'm going to go with you to the tournament. Don't worry, it's not a date," he clarified as, in a fair imitation of Brody's mind-meld routine, he apparently picked up on her reflexive rejection of the suggestion. "I'll carry your gear, and I'll be out there in the crowd cheering you on. But in between I'll do a little unofficial poking around to see what sort of bad blood there might be between your sensei and anyone else."

"I suppose that's all right. But you pay your own way into the tournament."

"Deal. And in the meantime, keep on practicing at the dojo, but stay out of file cabinets and desk drawers and any other place you might be tempted to snoop in."

"I'll try to control myself," was her sardonic response.

He either didn't catch the tone or chose to ignore it. "Oh, and by the way, good find on that photo. It'll probably be a dead end," he cautioned as she perked up at the unexpected *atta girl*, "but it's definitely worth checking out."

He hung up before she could make any response, leaving Darla to stare in amazement at the phone before pressing the "End" button and setting it down on the couch beside her. Hamlet had wandered his way back to the apartment following Roma's departure, and he now lay in his usual spot sprawled along the sofa back. Darla gave him a fond smile and put out her fist.

"How about a little fist bump love?" she asked the cat. "Reese actually complimented me. Twice. In the same conversation."

Hamlet looked at her clenched fingers and then turned his head.

"Right, you only do that with Robert and Roma," she said with a pretend huff, dropping her fist again. "That's fine, don't mind me. I'm only the one who keeps you in kibble and fresh litter. Oh, and I'm only the one who bought you this," she added, grabbing up the kitty wand and waving it enticingly before him.

This, Hamlet deigned to acknowledge. They played

companionably for several minutes, until Darla reluctantly reminded herself that she really needed to get back to the store.

"James's shift is almost up," she apologized to the feline. "But if you want, we can go on a practice walk outside tomorrow. How would that be?"

Hamlet gave her another blink that she interpreted as a *sure, why not?* She checked first to make sure he had plenty of food and fresh water; then, with a guilty look back at him, she paused a moment at her desk to check her computer.

It was open, as had been usual these past weeks, to her favorite online word game. Preoccupied as she'd been with what had happened to Master Tomlinson and, now, the Roma situation, she'd let most of her in-progress matches sit for a good day. A few of her virtual friends had already "nudged" her—an instant message reminder that it was her turn.

Swiftly, she shuffled her letters for each game and played them, on the virtual board. *Fetid, acids, heaven, chaw . . .* all combined with existing words for decent scores. But her best this round was the game with her virtual buddy, *Fightingwords*. Darla smirked a little as she played *chart* on the existing word *ale* which turned it into *tale*. With the help of a triple word tile, her turn netted her a cool fifty-nine points. Not too shabby! And the score, which had just been at a virtual tie, now tipped way in her favor.

Even as she was savoring this little victory, a "ting" sounded, telling her that *Fightingwords* had just sent her a message. She pressed the word bubble icon to go to the chat function, which this particular gaming pal used quite often. His/her latest missive said in text-speak, *i'll get u my pretty.*

"And your little dog, too," Darla replied, typing out that same sentiment while her smile broadened. Whoever it was on the other end had a dry sense of humor that added an extra bit of fun to the game. Then, reminding herself she was supposed to be working and not playing, she hurried back downstairs to finish out the shift.

Right before closing, Robert announced he was going to grab his gear and head to the dojo for the sparring class as soon as Darla gave the okay. "I want to, like, get in some more practice before Saturday. You wanna go, too, Ms. P?"

Darla raised her hands in mock horror.

"No way. I'm competing in forms, remember? I don't need some black belt using me for a punching bag until after I come home with my trophy. I'll practice on my own upstairs tonight, thank you very much."

"Okay, but you're missing all the fun," he told her. "I'll practice with Chris. He said he'd teach me a few tricks to use in the competition. Not anything bad," he hurriedly clarified when Darla shot him a disapproving look. "He was talking about ways to, you know, psych out your opponents."

"So long as he's not teaching you to fight dirty, I won't say a word. But ask Hank or Hal if you need any real help."

"Yeah, I guess they're not that bad, after all. But I'm still not telling them about Roma."

"Our secret," she agreed, uncomfortably aware that more than one secret was drifting around that dojo. Glancing at the clock, she added, "I'll finish up here. Why don't you run home and grab your gear so you can get to class early."

"All right, thanks!" he said, shooting her a grin as he headed for the door.

A few minutes later, she rang up a last-minute customer who'd only just remembered as he'd passed her store that it was his partner's birthday. Feeling generous, Darla grabbed a fancy sheet of paw-print wrapping paper from under the counter and expertly wrapped the book for him, earning herself some good karma and a couple of air kisses as the man hurried out with his purchase. Smiling, she locked the door after him and made quick work of her shutdown routine. After the uproar of the past few days, all she wanted to do tonight was head back to the apartment, have a big bowl of veggie soup for supper, and watch an old movie with Hamlet before bedtime.

Oh, and practice her forms, she reminded herself, mentally picking out a spot in the store for the trophy she expected to win.

Once back upstairs, she put the soup on the stove to simmer and changed back into sweat pants and a T-shirt. Then, returning to the living room, she addressed the cat. "All right, Hamlet. Check out my form and let me know what you think."

She made her bow to a panel of invisible judges. Then, assuming her beginning stance, she moved through the stylized series of punches, blocks, and kicks that represented defense and attack against an unseen opponent. She finished the first kata. Then, with another bow, she moved on to the second kata, and then the third. Each was a slightly more complicated routine than the one before it, and a couple of times she needed to stop and regroup when she accidentally left out a move. Only when she'd made it through all three katas, one after the other, without error, was she satisfied.

"All right, break time," she declared a bit breathlessly to Hamlet, dabbing away the sweat from her forehead. "Let's have a little soup, and then—"

The abrupt, insistent drone of the downstairs door buzzer cut her musings short and made her jump.

"I have *got* to get that thing changed," she muttered, rushing over to the door to hit the intercom button before whoever it was buzzed her again. With Jake out of town, and Robert still at sparring practice, she wasn't expecting anyone.

"Yes, who is it?" she cautiously greeted whoever was downstairs on her stoop.

"It's me, Reese," a familiar voice shot back. "I need to talk to you."

Again? she thought with a sigh. She really needed to broaden her circle of friends. Aloud, she said, "About what?"

"We'll talk about that when I get up there," was the clipped reply. "Look, Red, it's freezing out here. Be a pal and buzz me in now before I turn into an icicle. I've even got a bag of buffalo wings I'll share with you if you're nice."

"Deal," Darla agreed, unlocking the door. "Come on up."

She didn't wait for him to knock at her apartment but already had the door opened by the time he'd made both flights of stairs.

"You're my new best friend," she said as she surveyed his sauce-stained bag in approval.

She gave *him* an approving look, too. He'd changed from his work clothes into the more familiar jeans and black leather bomber jacket, paired with a wool hat and thick scarf. She always did like a man in leather, she reminded herself.

Gesturing him in, she said, "Let me get a platter to put those on. I've got some homemade soup ready to go, too. There's just enough to split. You want some?"

"Sure," he agreed, following her to the kitchen. Then, taking in her outfit and sweat-dampened face, he added, "What, you've been working out?"

Darla pretended not to hear the surprise in his voice. "Actually, I'm practicing my katas for the tournament. Hal says he thinks I've got a pretty good chance to win."

"Yeah, there's usually not a lot of competition in your age group for beginners," Reese observed with a shrug. Then, when Darla shot him an annoyed look—why did everyone seem to think the only way she could win was if she were the only one in the category?—he quickly backpedaled.

"What I mean is, you won't have kids in your group, so you have to be pretty good. You want to show me, and I'll give you a little coaching? "

At her doubtful look, he added, "Hey, I got a closet full of trophies from when I took karate lessons as a kid. I know my stuff."

"All right, but I really want to win this thing, so I'll be trusting that you do."

She pulled down a platter from the cabinet and handed it off to Reese. Then she stacked bowls, plates, and cutlery on the table before heading back for the soup pot, leaving Reese to arrange the wings and celery sticks and blue cheese dip. She winced a little when she returned to find that his version of "arrange" was simply dumping the bag's contents onto the platter she'd provided.

Men, she thought with a roll of her eyes, fighting the urge to separate celery from chicken into two neat piles. Instead, she ladled out the soup. That accomplished, she set the pot down on one of Great-Aunt Dee's antique trivets and reached for a wing.

"Uh, uh," Reese interjected, stopping her with a wag of his forefinger as he took his chair. "You're in training. Katas first. You do a good job, you get to eat."

Who died and made you sensei?

It was on the tip of her tongue to ask that aloud. But given the fact that someone *had* died and left a sensei opening, she bit back the retort and contented herself with another eye roll.

"Fine," she told him, setting down the wing and licking the buffalo sauce from her fingers. "But constructive criticism only. No jokes."

At his nod, she took up position in the living area, feeling a bit self-conscious as she made her bow and began the form. When she'd finished, she made her bow again and gave him a questioning look. "Well?"

"Not bad," was his assessment through a mouthful of chicken. "You've learned not to bob up and down when you move, which is what gets most beginners. But watch your arm and hand position. You don't want to break your wrists."

Setting down his wing, he demonstrated by holding out one muscular arm as if he'd just thrown a punch. Then, keeping his arm still, he momentarily raised his clenched fist so that his knuckles pointed upward rather than forward before returning his hand to its original position. He repeated that a couple of times before grabbing up the wing again.

"See, that's breaking your wrist. You want to keep everything in a straight line down your arm through your hand when you're punching. You do one of these in competition"—he demonstrated again, wing flapping—"the judges will knock off points. Plus you do that in an actual fight, you really will break a wrist. Worst of all, it makes you look like a sissy girl."

"Well, I am a girl," she grumbled, but she carefully adjusted her position anyway. "Okay, got it. Anything else?"

"Don't run through the kata too slow, or the judges will think you can't remember the next move. And don't go crazy fast, or the judges will think you're trying to look too cool for the mat and penalize you, too. Swift and steady, clean and crisp."

She nodded and ran through the same kata again. When he gestured her to keep on, she did the next two katas in succession, and then repeated the entire set. When she had finished, she was sweating again but feeling pretty good about her progress.

For his part, Reese gave her a grin and an approving nod. "Do that on Saturday, and you've got yourself a trophy, Red. Now, grab some of these wings before they're all gone."

She didn't wait for a second invitation, particularly since the pile of wings had diminished appreciably while she'd been practicing. At least there was plenty of soup. She made a pretty good veggie medley version, if she said so herself.

But she'd only made it through the first wing and a couple of mouthfuls of soup when Reese's cell phone rang. He pulled it out of his jacket pocket and stared at the caller ID, frowning as he hit the "Talk" button.

"Reese."

Darla watched the brief, one-sided conversation, which mainly consisted of the detective frowning, nodding, and repeating "uh, huh" a few times. Finally, he said, "I'm two minutes away. Keep everyone there and don't do anything else until I get there."

"What's going on?" Darla asked as he hung up the phone and got to his feet.

Reese shook his blond head as he headed for the door. "Trouble down at the TAMA dojo. Wing was the responding officer. I'm going to give him a hand sorting things out."

"Wait!" Darla called after him. "Robert is there practicing. I'm going with you."

"No way," he shot back as he paused in the doorway. "We're talking police business. Last thing we need is an extra civilian hanging around."

"Fine."

As he trotted down the stairs, not bothering to close the door, she grabbed the wing platter and shoved it into the fridge. Snatching her coat and purse off the door hook, she threw on the first, shouldered the second, and then grabbed up her boots from where they sat beside the entry and stuck them under her arm.

"Don't worry," she called down the stairwell, "I'll run. I'll probably beat you there, anyhow."

She heard the click of the front doorknob echoing in the silence, followed by the sound of an unmistakable sigh. "You've got two seconds to get your butt down here. One, two!"

But she'd already started down the stairs, and so by the time he called two, she was at the front door with him.

"Put those on first," he demanded, pointing to the boots she still carried. Hopping on one foot and then the other, she pulled on the boots and then, locking the door behind her, followed him out to his car. As usual, it was another drab, department-issued beater.

"Stay in the background, keep your mouth shut, and don't talk to anyone when we get there," were his instructions as they accelerated down the street, colored lights flashing.

Darla clung to the armrest for balance and nodded. "Can you tell me what happened?"

"All I know right now is that a couple of the students in the sparring class got into it for real, and someone pulled a weapon."

Weapon? Robert! Was he okay?

"Don't worry, no one's hurt," he added as he heard her gasp. "Hank and Hal disarmed the guy and held him while one of the students called us. Tommy—Officer Wing—and a couple of other guys showed up, and they've got the perp in handcuffs. As soon as I get there, we'll get statements from everyone."

Reese said nothing more during the brief ride to the dojo, save to call into dispatch on his radio and mutter some cop jargon she couldn't make out. Darla paid him little heed, however, heart pounding as she wondered what had gone wrong. She pretty well knew—at least, by sight—all the students who attended the sparring class. She'd never witnessed any genuine altercations before, not even when Chris tried to pull rank and attitude on the others. And the idea that someone had brought a weapon into the same studio where little kids practiced was nothing short of appalling!

Reese, meanwhile, screeched his car to a stop outside the dojo, pulling halfway onto the walk alongside the two marked police cars already there.

"Remember, out of the way," he said as he strode into the building.

Darla nodded as she followed him past the vestibule and the office with the broken door. As they wound through the waiting area, she could see the sparring students through the partition window. Adults as well as teens stood silently near one of the new folding screens that served as a make-shift dressing room. Hank and Hal had taken up position on either side of the group. With their crossed arms and grim expressions, they fleetingly reminded Darla of the fierce fu dog statues that stood protectively outside the studio.

Robert and Chris were among the others, both youths looking troubled. Indeed, Chris appeared on the verge of tears; Darla wondered if he was the student who'd been attacked. As she and Reese entered the mat area, Darla broke away from the detective and hurried over to where Robert stood.

"Are you okay?" she murmured.

He nodded, apparently distraught enough over what had happened that he forgot to be embarrassed by the way she'd just swooped down on him like his mom.

"Everything's, like, under control," he whispered back. "Hal and Hank, they took care of stuff."

"Was it a gun?"

He shook head.

"Knife," he softly replied, pantomiming a gang-like slicing gesture. "Hank did some kind of fancy arm grab thing. Don't worry, no one got hurt," he added, attention fixed on the group across the room.

Officer Wing and the two other cops were gathered at the front. While Reese joined them, Darla noticed another student seated on the mat a short distance away. His back was pressed to the mirrored wall, and his head was buried in the crook of his folded arms that rested atop his upraised knees. Then, as if feeling her gaze on him, he raised his head and stared directly at her.

Mark Poole!

Then one of the cops shifted position, and Darla saw yet another student kneeling within the semicircle that the four men had formed. The seated pose was the same that the dojo's students assumed during class meditation . . . and also the same pose temporarily taken by the victor when a sparring opponent went down. Unlike the others in the dojo, who were all dressed in white or black, the kneeling student wore a red gi the same blood-bright color as the mats.

This, then, was the person who'd pulled the knife, Darla realized. And maybe the reason Mark was separated from the rest of the class was because he had been the one who'd been attacked. But who—

Abruptly, the two other uniformed cops reached down and pulled the kneeling student into a standing position. The student made no struggle, doubtless because both arms were cuffed securely behind his back. At first, all Darla could make out was a slim form and long black hair obscuring any facial features. Then Officer Wing, in a considerate gesture, brushed aside the captive's hair from his face.

Her face!

Darla choked back a gasp, her gaze whipping from the handcuffed woman to Chris standing nearby. Another look at the teen's miserable expression confirmed it.

The student who'd pulled the knife was none other than Chris's mother, Grace Valentine.

▲ ‖ EIGHTEEN

"IT WAS, YOU KNOW, PRETTY WEIRD," ROBERT WHISPERED to Darla in what she privately determined was a gross understatement.

They were seated along the mirrored wall of the training area, patiently waiting for Robert's turn to give his statement to the police. Reese had allowed Darla to stay with the youth, as long as they refrained from chatting with any other of the witnesses regarding the incident. And, of course, that same admonition applied to the other students, too. That meant that the twenty or so in the sparring class were now scattered along all four corners of the room while the officers took statements in the waiting area behind the partition.

"You know how it goes," Robert now told her in an undertone. "We, like, spar for a little bit, and then everyone on one side moves over one spot so you can spar with someone new. That's what we did tonight. It was all going fine until Grace and Mark got paired up."

He gave his head a disgusted shake. "You know what a

creepoid that Mark is. Grace kept scoring points on him, and he was getting all mad, getting beat by a girl. Then he said something to her that really ticked her off, I guess."

"And she pulled a knife on him?"

"Not right that second," Robert replied. "But I could tell she was mad. When the round was over, she ran over to her gear bag and got something out of it. And then she told Mark she wanted, you know, a rematch. She made him swap places with her new partner so they could fight again. I guess Hal and Hank were busy, 'cause they didn't seem to notice. But I was right next to them, so I saw everything."

Dropping his voice even lower, he continued, "I think she was, like, messing with him, because he started scoring points on her. So he got all loud about how good he is. And then, *pow*, she knocked him right on his butt," the teen said, pantomiming the winning blow.

"Then what?"

He shrugged. "Everyone started laughing at him. Then he got all mad, calling Grace, like, bad names. I mean, real bad names. And then suddenly she had this, you know, knife. And she goes, *Say it again and I'll cut you.*"

His expression disgusted again, he went on, "So Mark, I can tell he's all scared, but he still calls her names again. By then, Hal sees what's going on, and he goes all badass on Grace. He does some kind of cool thing and grabs the knife out of her hand, and then pins her on the mat. And then he tells me to phone the cops."

So Robert had been the one to put in the call. She gave him a proud smile.

"I guess you really kept your head, didn't you? Sometimes that's more important than being the best fighter in the room."

"Yeah, well."

He ducked said head and then glanced over to where Chris now sat in the far corner, his youthful features frighteningly blank. "I was thinking I might ask Chris if he wants to stay at my place tonight until, you know, his mom gets home."

Darla followed his gaze to give the younger teen a sympathetic look. To her mind, the worst part of the whole night so far had been when the uniformed officers, each gripping one of her arms, began escorting Grace out of the training area. Chris, who had shrunk down into his bulky gi jacket like a lanky blond turtle, had abruptly straightened.

"Mom? Mom?"

The plaintive cry as he'd rushed toward the handcuffed woman had brought tears to Darla's eyes. Grace, however, apparently had felt no similar rush of motherly concern. Instead, she had shot her son a sour look and snapped, *"For Chrissakes, quit whining and call Jerry to come bail me out already."*

Darla turned her attention back to Robert, while wondering again just who this Jerry person was, and why he was supposed to do the bailing out. Of course, with a temper like hers, the woman probably had a lawyer on retainer just for such situations.

"You can ask Chris to stay," Darla agreed, "but don't be surprised if he'd rather wait at home for his mother to make bond."

It was another good thirty minutes before it was Robert's turn to give his statement to Officer Wing. By then, most of the other remaining students had already somberly filed out of the dojo. Darla waited out in the vestibule for Robert to finish, absently studying the collection of photos that were now becoming as familiar to her as her own family album. Finally, she heard a step behind her and turned.

"Uh, hey, Darla," Mark Poole ventured, clutching his gear bag to his chest like he was afraid someone was going to steal it. "I guess we had some excitement tonight. It's a good thing I was able to kick that knife out of Grace's hand, or I might have ended up . . ."

He trailed off and gave a wordless squeak while slashing a forefinger across his throat.

Darla raised her brows and favored him with a frosty look. "Really? Story I heard was that Sensei Hal was the one who disarmed her and saved your sorry butt."

Mark's face flamed an ugly red. "Yeah, well, maybe he got there before me, but I had the situation under control. A tramp like Grace, I'm not letting her show me up."

"I'm sure you're not," she agreed and deliberately turned away.

Though Grace's actions were indefensible, Mark certainly didn't come out of the situation smelling like a rose. *More like stinkweed,* she told herself. He'd deliberately goaded a volatile woman with his taunts. Darla found that she had very little sympathy for the man, no matter that he'd almost become Grace Valentine's personal pincushion.

She studiously kept her attention on the gallery until, from the corner of her eye, she saw Mark slink past her and go out the door. With luck, this might be the last time she'd have to see him at the dojo, assuming Hank and Hal decided to ban him . . . presumably along with Grace. Of course, he'd probably still show up at the bookstore, but at least she'd be getting paid for enduring his presence. "Hey, Ms. P," Robert spoke up behind her a moment later. "I gave my statement. Can we, like, go now?"

"Sure. Did you talk to Chris?"

He nodded. "You were right. He wants to go home and wait for his mom. I guess I understand."

"All right, let me tell Reese we're out of here. Oh, and I have a few leftover wings at the house if you want some."

Leaving Robert there for a moment, she made her way back into the training area. Now, it was just Reese, Officer Wing, and the two black belts remaining. Spying her, Reese abruptly broke away from the group and walked over to her.

"I don't know what's going on around here," he muttered, taking her by the arm and walking her toward the vestibule, "but I don't like it. It's, like, bad karma or something is hanging over the place."

"Bad feng shui," Darla automatically corrected him. "Karma is an Indian concept. Feng shui is Chinese."

"Karma, feng shui, whatever. You know what I mean," he replied, sounding annoyed. "And the Tomlinsons agree. They just told me they're going to shut down the dojo, at least until after the tournament."

"I wonder if Dr. Tomlinson will agree to that. Isn't the dojo hers now?"

"That's not my problem. My concern is with this Valentine woman."

They'd reached the vestibule where Robert still waited. Bag at his feet, he had his phone out and was frantically typing away with both thumbs. *Forget the eleven o'clock news,* Darla wryly thought. These days, the only things necessary to spread the word were a smartphone and a Twitter account!

Dropping her voice so that Robert wouldn't overhear, she replied, "Do you think Grace is the one who murdered Master Tomlinson?"

"Let's just say she's moved herself to the top of the suspect list with tonight's little stunt. And, by the way, we got into your sensei's office this afternoon and took a few things with us, including that photo you told me about. Her personal connection to Mr. Tomlinson via that picture sure paints a possible motive, and she's proved she'll strike out when provoked."

Like a bad-tempered leopard, Darla thought, recalling the woman's penchant for animal print.

Then, following her cue and glancing Robert's way, Reese added, "But unless we get a written confession out of her, I still plan to be at that tournament with you on Saturday. The more people I talk to, the more reasons I'm finding for someone to have had a good reason for offing him."

"Wait, what?"

Darla stared at him in confusion. Who else besides Grace Valentine and the Tomlinsons—whom Darla had pretty well crossed off her own private list—could there be?

Reese, meanwhile, was shaking his head. "Sorry, Red. Can't tell you any more. You'll have to read about it in the papers like everyone else." Then, ignoring her look, he added, "So, pick you up at, say, ten o'clock on Saturday?"

"Make it eight thirty. We have to be registered and ready to go on the floor by ten or else risk being disqualified. And why don't we take Maybelle, instead?"

Maybelle was the decade-old Mercedes sedan that Darla had inherited from her great-aunt. It had been a welcome gift for a Texas girl who got itchy feet if she couldn't hit the open road every so often. Sleek midnight blue on the outside, incredibly cushy on the inside, and with an engine that purred even more quietly than Hamlet, it was very much the coolest car that Darla had ever owned. And, fortunately for her in this city of limited parking, Great-Aunt Dee had pre-paid a year's rental space in a nearby parking garage, so that the trusty Mercedes was always available for expeditions such as this.

She suppressed a grin as she saw Reese's eyes light up. The detective, she knew, had a weakness for luxury cars . . . probably because all he ever drove were junkers. And so, sweetening the pot, she casually added, "I'll even let you drive."

"Eight thirty, it is," was his prompt response. "Bring her around early, so we don't have to schlep all your gear to the garage, and I'll make sure you don't get any parking tickets."

Darla left him studying the wall of photos and made her way to Robert, still madly texting away. "Let's go. Hamlet will be worried."

He nodded his agreement, his attention fixed on his phone. Then, as they headed out into the chilly night, he held out the phone to her. "Look, Sylvie sent me a picture of Roma."

Darla glanced at the tiny screen and smiled. The small hound had shed her mauve sweater but still had on her fancy martingale collar. She was squeezed between two equally small pups, a black teacup poodle, and what looked like a mottled dachshund. All three were grinning at the camera, mouths wide open and pink tongues lolling.

"She's got some new friends," Darla said approvingly.

Robert nodded. "Yeah, maybe she won't be too lonely while she's in rescue."

Darla heard the plaintive tone in his voice and gave him an encouraging pat on the shoulder. "It hasn't even been a day yet. Let Bonnie and Sylvie do their thing, and I'm sure Roma will be back to you soon enough."

He nodded, but Darla could see he wasn't convinced. And when they reached the brownstone a few minutes later, he took a pass on the leftover wings. "I'm not really, you know, hungry," he explained. "I'll see you tomorrow, okay?"

Darla waited until she was sure the teen had made it safely into his apartment before unlocking her door and heading upstairs. A few moments later, she was opening the door to her apartment, which was ablaze with light. Feeling a bit guilty at how she'd rushed out earlier, she hurriedly snapped off some of the more egregious offenders, leaving on only a few low-wattage fixtures. She'd just have to recycle a few more plastic bottles to help offset that little lapse, she wryly told herself.

Jake, of course, would have genially sneered at her eco-guilt had she been there. *As long as I can afford the bill, I'll burn as much light as I want,* the older woman had proclaimed more than once. As Darla tossed her purse and coat back onto the hook and pulled off her boots again, she briefly considered giving Jake a call to discuss things over a glass of wine or maybe a decadent dessert. But Jake was away in Atlantic City on a client's dime now, and no way would Darla bother her friend while she was on the job.

As if on cue, her cell phone—which she'd just plugged

in to recharge—abruptly chimed, indicating an incoming text message. She pulled up the app and grinned.

Hot on Bombshell trail, ETA looks good 4 Sat.

A second text followed a few moments later.

PS won $573 at slots. Ka-ching.

Darla typed back a quick *congrats*, but just as swiftly she found her grin fading. As Jake's clientele base continued to increase, the PI would probably be gallivanting off to Atlantic City and other places on a regular basis. Which meant that she, Darla, was going to be at a loss for a BFF on occasion. Maybe it was time to broaden her friendship horizon a little, now that she was well and truly settled into job and home.

She considered the idea as she cleaned up the soup dishes and pot. She and Martha had hit it off pretty well and seemed to have several interests in common. Maybe she should suggest lunch one day—assuming that the woman was not spending all her free time now with James. In the interim, though, she always had . . .

"Hamlet," she called belatedly, looking around the living room for the feline. "I'm back."

Hamlet did not deign to reply, nor was he lounging in any of his usual spots, as she discovered when she made a walk-through of the apartment. Maybe he'd felt neglected by the way she'd dashed out, and he had wandered down to the bookstore in her absence. With all the secret cat passages that existed in the brownstone, the feline pretty well had access to the store anytime he pleased.

While she waited for him to reappear, Darla opened the kitchen cabinet drawer where she'd stowed away Hamlet's new harness and lead, and set them on the dining table. Tomorrow morning, weather permitting, she and Hamlet would definitely go for a walk before the store opened. But tonight, she'd indulge in that movie that she'd promised herself earlier in the day. Especially after the debacle at the dojo—a great title for a film, she told herself—she deserved a bit of mindless fluff before going to sleep.

But when she flipped on the television, it seemed that every movie she clicked on was an angst-filled drama. With a groan, she turned off the set again and wandered over to her computer. She was halfway through a word game match with Martha that she was eager to end, mostly because the woman was already 157 points ahead of her.

"Luck of the draw," Darla reassured herself, conveniently ignoring the fact that of the twenty or so matches they'd previously played, Martha had beat her all but twice. Unfortunately, this turn she was once again stuck with a rack of low-point letters, so the best she managed was *s-n-a-g*. She pressed play, and then sat back with a thoughtful frown.

The word reminded her of Hamlet. It occurred to her that, save for the one time, the wily feline hadn't indulged in any of his usual book snagging activities since she'd learned that Master Tomlinson's death had actually been murder. Maybe now that he had Brody the feline behavioral empath to mind-meld with, he didn't need to resort to such crude methods of communication.

Or maybe for once even Hamlet was stymied and had no idea who the killer was.

Splat!

The unexpected sound came from the vicinity of the kitchen. Darla gave a reflexive shriek, only to laugh at her edginess when she saw Hamlet stalking his way into the living room.

"Speak of the furry little devil!" she exclaimed. "Where have you been, and what kind of trouble are you getting into there in the kitchen?"

She jumped up from the couch and headed in the direction from which the cat had come. Sure enough, she could already see that a small volume lay sprawled on the tile floor of the unlit kitchen. So much for taking a break from knocking books off of tables! Hands on hips, she turned again to face the cat, who had settled on the sofa back once more, panther-like tail languidly waving.

"Have you been digging through my cookbooks?" she demanded in mock outrage. "I thought you liked my cooking. Fine, what will it be, Mexican or Caribbean cuisine? Oh, wait, I think I have a copy of *Mastering the Art of French Cooking*, if you prefer."

When Hamlet merely gave her a cool green stare, she relented and added, "Okay, so I've never actually cooked out of that one. So sue me."

Smiling a little, she shook her head and went into the kitchen to retrieve the wayward book. But as soon as she turned on the overhead light, she realized that the fallen volume was not one of her cookbooks, after all. Instead, it was the copy of *Tess of the d'Urbervilles* that she'd meant to reread.

But how in the heck had it ended up in her kitchen for Hamlet to kick off the counter?

She picked up the book and stared thoughtfully at its bleak cover for a few moments before shutting off the light switch again. Hamlet was still lounging on the sofa back, but this time his green eyes were tightly shut. *Sleeping . . . or else, pretending to?*

She snorted and set the book down on her coffee table.

"Maybe I'll just go to bed early," she announced to no one in particular. No way was she going to finish off the day with a grim read like Hardy's classic. Then, on impulse, she picked up the book again anyhow.

"Might as well remind myself how it ends," she told the sleeping feline. "It's been, what, almost twenty years since I read the darn thing."

She settled on the sofa beside Hamlet and scanned the pages, racing through the account of country girl Tess being seduced by the local rich cad, Alec, and having an out-of-wedlock child who dies in infancy, then going on to marry a nice young man—appropriately named Angel—who leaves her when he finds out about her past. Darla slowed her reading a little as it got interesting again, with Tess hooking up once more with the cad, whom she then murders right before Angel returns to tell her that all is forgiven. Then came the slowest pursuit scene in the history of literature, and an anticlimactic capture, followed by more platitudes.

"Ugh, there's a reason I read this just once," she said with a groan as she plowed through the final pages. The entire book, she determined, was a sanctimonious exercise in angst and intolerance, topped by a generous dollop of misogyny.

And then she reached the novel's final paragraph, which stopped her cold. She read it again, and then she spoke its first line aloud.

"Justice" was done, and the President of the Immortals, in Aeschylean phrase, had ended his sport with Tess.

Slowly, she closed the book again. Classical allusions notwithstanding (best as she recalled, Aeschylus was one of the grimmer Greek tragedians . . . something about Prometheus and that liver-eating eagle) the words were more than a melodramatic conclusion. On impulse, she flipped the book back to its cover again, nodding as she reread the novel's subtitle, *A Pure Woman Faithfully Presented*. Now, a few pieces of the dark puzzle that was Master Tomlinson's murder slowly began rearranging themselves in her mind.

Then, as Hamlet opened one emerald eye just a slit, she slowly shook her head. "'Justice' was done," she repeated, and gave the feline a considering look. "In the book, maybe . . . but in real life, I don't think it was."

NINETEEN

BUT SUSPICIONS WERE NOT FACTS, AND GUESSING WASN'T knowing.

Darla found herself silently repeating that sentiment like a mantra the next morning as she showered and got dressed. The subtitle of *Tess* was *A Pure Woman* . . . and there were two women involved in this particular scenario of betrayal: Grace Valentine and Jan Tomlinson. Swiftly, Darla did the mental math again just to be certain that she hadn't jumped to conclusions on the betrayal part of her scenario. Given Chris's age, the picture of Grace had to have been taken about sixteen years earlier. And she recalled Hank saying after the break-in of the dojo office that Master Tomlinson had been his stepfather for almost twenty years. So the sensei and Dr. Tomlinson had been married at the time that he apparently had cheated on her with Grace!

But, motive aside, was either woman physically capable of killing him?

Grace, she knew, was a trained martial artist. She wasn't

sure about Dr. Tomlinson, but considering that she'd been married to an expert and her sons were also professionals in the field, chances were that she had at least a passing knowledge of the techniques. So despite Master Tomlinson's size and expertise, and assuming Reese's argument that the man simply had been taken unawares because he knew his killer, it was possible that either one of them could have done it.

And then there was the matter of the Botox. The doctor obviously would have access to such a drug. Grace, with her "mob wife" connections, probably attended the sort of wrinkle-erasing parties that Jake had told her about. Get enough wine flowing, and maybe she could sneak out with a syringe of the drug. Besides, wasn't poison considered a woman's weapon? Intimate, clean, easy.

Then she moved on down her mental checklist of evidence . . . or, at least, interesting observations. The sensei's office after the break-in had smelled of smoke for a few critical moments. Grace was a smoker. As for Jan Tomlinson, Darla had seen her taking a couple of quick puffs that day outside the dojo; still, the way she'd hurriedly discarded the cigarette made Darla guess that she was in the final throes of quitting. Or maybe an ex-smoker, who lapsed in times of stress. Given the fact that the woman was an MD, Darla guessed that she'd probably witnessed an aberration.

Then Darla frowned. Of course, that didn't explain why Dr. Tomlinson would have had to break into her own late husband's office. Moreover, just because Hamlet had pointed his paw at a classic novel filled with murder and betrayal didn't mean that she was interpreting his cat logic with any accuracy. Heck, since he'd left the book in the kitchen for her, maybe he'd simply been hinting that he wanted a nice kidney pie for supper one night.

"You're slacking off, Hamlet. Guess your crime-solving days are behind you," Darla observed with a resigned shake of her head. "But I sure wish you could tell me who Master Tomlinson's real killer is."

A sharp *meow* cut short her musings. Hamlet—apparently immune to her criticism—was reminding her that breakfast was what was foremost in *his* thoughts at the moment. Turning her attention to the insistent feline, she filled his food and water bowls. Then she grabbed herself a yogurt from the fridge before starting the coffeemaker.

While Hamlet crunched away at his kibble, she took her breakfast over to her computer and pulled up her game screen. Martha was the sole "friend" who had taken a turn since last night. Unfortunately, Darla still had a big point gap to make up, but at least this time she had a decent rack of letters to play with.

"Finally," she said in satisfaction, shuffling the *R*, *J*, *D*, *O*, *S*, *N*, and *W* for the best word to set down.

SWORD. DROWNS. JOWS. Not huge points on their own, but tagging onto the right existing word, and landing a triple tile or two, could net her a big score this turn. She was contemplating the most advantageous layout when the coffeemaker ended its cycle. Feeling triumphant, she went to retrieve her caffeine fix. But when she returned to the living room a minute later, coffee cup in hand, what she saw sent her into true warrior mode.

"Hamlet, get down from there!"

During her brief absence from her computer, the cat had abandoned his food bowl and uncharacteristically jumped up onto her desk. He turned and shot an innocent green gaze her way as if to say, *What, I'm not allowed up here?* Then, before she could stop him, he deliberately wandered across her laptop before hopping down again.

"Darn it, cat!" she exclaimed, rushing over to see what havoc he'd wrought. Hamlet wasn't exactly a featherweight, and his oversized paws could have damaged the keyboard. If nothing else, he had to have messed up her game.

She set down her coffee cup and settled back into her chair to assess the damage. The keyboard appeared none the worse for wear, she saw in relief. As for the game, he'd managed to step on a combination of keys that had sent a couple of random letters onto the screen, leaving only five of them remaining on the rack. An easy enough fix . . . no harm, no foul. Had she not seen his lapse into mischief, she'd probably have passed it off as a bit of caffeine deficiency amnesia and assumed she had done it herself.

"Well, Hamlet, you're not a bad player," she conceded, addressing him where he now sat atop the sofa back. The remaining letters on the rack had been shuffled by his paw work, as well, and now spelled out—most appropriately, Darla thought with a smile—WORDS. And, even better, she saw the perfect spot for this arrangement where she could get a good fifty points.

Before she played, however, she hit the recall key to bring the two errant letters home again. As she watched, the *J* and the *N* came sliding back to the rack from where Hamlet's paw work had sent them.

"What the—"

Heart beating more quickly, Darla dragged the two letters back to where they'd been on the screen, tagged vertically onto the first letter of the horizontal word ACRID. Now, the word going downward read JAN.

"Jan," she repeated, slowly turning in her chair again to face Hamlet. "Are you trying to tell me that Jan Tomlinson is the one who killed the sensei?"

Hamlet blinked once and then shut his emerald eyes. Darla gave herself a mental shake. "Will you listen to yourself?" she exclaimed. "No way is Hamlet writing messages about killers' identities."

She pictured herself telling Reese that she knew who killed Master Tomlinson because Hamlet had typed it out on her keyboard. The detective would laugh himself sick . . . and then probably have her bundled off to a nice padded cell somewhere. No, this was way too much of a stretch.

Besides, she reminded herself, Reese was the detective. He'd already implied that he had a few ideas of his own as to who'd murdered Master Tomlinson. And it wasn't like Reese didn't have years of professional training along with the considerable resources of the NYPD behind him. All she had on her side was a wily feline whose track record in crime solving, despite her recent doubts in ability, was pretty darn good. Maybe if she ran her—or rather, Hamlet's— theory past Jake . . . ?

"Not your job, Nancy Drew," she said in imitation of what she knew her friend's response would be to *that*. From day one, despite the PI's grudging acknowledgment of Hamlet's seeming ability to intuit bad guys, Jake had persisted in encouraging Darla to butt out of police business.

And she would . . . at least, for the moment, Darla virtuously decided. Today, she had other things to worry about, like getting Hamlet used to walking on a lead in the great outdoors.

And so, after shutting down her game, she carried him and his gear down to the bookstore a bit earlier than usual so she could spend a few minutes of quality time prowling the neighborhood with the feline. If all worked out well, she'd follow Brody's advice and make this a regular routine for them.

"All right, Hammy," she said once she'd buckled him into the harness and snapped on the leash, "we're going to make a test run outside. I know it's cold, but you've got that warm fur coat. And we haven't had any more nasty snow flurries in the past couple of days, so your paws will stay nice and dry. You up for this?"

By way of response, Hamlet leaped from the counter and, leash snaking behind him, padded toward the front door.

Smiling, Darla picked up her keys and flipped up her coat collar so that it covered her ears, rather like Roma's little mauve sweater. The comparison made her smile slip a little. She fervently hoped for Robert's sake that everything with the dog would work out. With luck, Bonnie the rescue lady would soon ring James to let him know that the teen had been approved as a doggie foster dad.

Steeling herself for the blast of arctic chill, Darla looped Hamlet's lead over her wrist in Brody-approved fashion and opened the front door. It was cold, just as she'd feared, but the sun was shining as brightly as it could be for a late winter morning. Maybe a few minutes of this would be bearable.

"They're only steps, Hamlet," she warned him as he walked over and sniffed at the edge of the stoop. "Don't worry, you've gone up and down steps a million times."

They made it down the stone stairs without incident, and after a few halting stops and tugs, the two of them settled into a brisk pace down the sidewalk. Despite the cold, Darla found herself grinning broadly at the sight of the large black cat padding gracefully before her. She felt rather dramatic and more than a bit dangerous. It was like she'd stepped from one of those high-end magazine ads, the kind where a gorgeous woman in a slinky gown walks a sleek panther down the street while marveling passersby stare after her. To be sure, she was dressed in boots and a puffy down coat, but close enough.

Her fellow morning walkers seemingly agreed . . . at least, with the sleek panther part. From the smiles and comments that came their way, it seemed that she was dismissed as just a crazy cat lady. Hamlet, however, was a feline star!

"Time to go back," she told him a few minutes later. "We've got a business to run. But don't worry, I'll let Robert take you for a stroll tomorrow, too."

Feeling invigorated by the walk, she decided to put aside the worst of the past days' events from her mind and concentrate on selling books. Unfortunately, that vow lasted only until James arrived right at ten to start his shift. Between customers, she related what she knew of Grace Valentine's meltdown at the dojo the previous night, and the fact that Chris had seen his mother being hauled off in hand-cuffs in front of everyone.

"Poor kid. How is he ever going to show his face there again?" she mused as James shook his gray head over the unfortunate event. "And it's funny that even Reese seems to think there's some bad juju or something going on with that dojo. And he's not a woo-woo kind of guy."

"Actually, juju is a term of West African origin," the professor dryly observed. "Perhaps you are referring to feng shui, which is an East Asian concept regarding the optimal orientation of—"

"Juju, feng shui, whatever," Darla said with a wave of her hand, cutting short the lecture. "But I wonder if it really is possible for bad luck to be attached to a place like that."

"I hesitate to speculate on such matters, although it is inter-esting nourishment for contemplation. Will you continue to attend classes there?"

"I'm not sure," Darla replied after a moment's hesitation. "Let's see what happens after the tournament. Maybe by then Reese will have finally made an arrest, and we can all feel comfortable going back there again."

By mutual consent, they let the subject drop for the remain-der of the morning. Darla also kept quiet about her own newly formed theory as to Master Tomlinson's probable killer: none other than his grieving widow, Jan. If she was wrong, then she risked destroying the woman's reputation, which would be murder of a different sort. "Because Hamlet says so" *wasn't* a valid enough reason to accuse someone of so serious a crime.

Robert came in around two, freeing James for lunch and Darla to catch up with paperwork. After she'd paid a few bills, she rejoined him on the floor—ostensibly to help him with restocking, but more to gauge his mental state. To her relief, while he seemed a bit more subdued than usual, he gave off a more optimistic vibe than he had since the first time Roma had been taken from him.

While they stocked, they chatted about inconsequential

things, like how Operation Walk the Kitty had been a rousing success, at least the first time out.

"You should have seen Hamlet," she said with a proud smile in the feline's direction. "He looked like he'd been walking in harness for years. All the people passing by probably thought he was one of those trained movie cats."

"Yeah?" Robert gave Hamlet an approving look of his own. "Maybe we should take a video of him and send it in to one of those, you know, funniest animal shows."

"Not a bad idea. It's about time Hamlet started earning his keep," Darla replied with a smile. "Just be sure you get a good shot of the store's name on the front door. Free publicity, you know."

The rest of the afternoon progressed at a brisk pace, though Darla noticed that the later the hour, the quieter Robert grew. No doubt he was anxiously awaiting word on Roma's fate. She was equally concerned, and it was only with an effort that she refrained from prompting James to call the rescue people for a status update. Even so, she still wasn't prepared when she finally heard a few notes of a Beethoven symphony that was James's cell phone ring tone.

He pulled the phone from his trousers pocket and frowned at the caller ID.

"If you do not object, I believe that I should take this call," he said to Darla as he pressed the "Talk" button. Giving her a little signaling nod in response to her questioning look, he spoke into the phone, "Professor James T. James, here."

"Robert, why don't you help that lady who just walked in," Darla quickly suggested, pointing him in said elderly woman's direction.

The youth shot James an uncertain look, obviously aware that this might be *the call*. Then, with a nod, he went off to assist the customer while Darla tried to discreetly listen in on James's half of the call. The store manager had anticipated her interest, for he just as discreetly took himself off to the upstairs lounge to finish the conversation.

He returned a few minutes later, giving away nothing by his expression. Robert hurriedly checked out his customer and even carried her purchase to the exit for her. Then, bells jingling as the door shut after the woman, he rushed back to the counter.

"Was that the rescue lady?" the teen anxiously demanded, all but wringing his hands. "What did she say about Roma?"

James inclined his head. "Yes, that was she, and I believe that we have a conclusion to the Roma situation."

"A good conclusion?" Darla asked in a hopeful tone, drawing closer to the counter where he stood.

Now the manager gave an unmistakable sigh.

"I fear not. The women took Roma to the veterinarian's office per protocol and had her scanned for a chip. Unfortunately for Robert, her previous owner had done the right thing, and so Bonnie was able to put in a call to Dr. Tomlinson letting her know that Roma had been found."

"And she wants her back," Darla flatly stated while Robert stared in silent disbelief. "Didn't you tell Bonnie that they want to sell off Roma to a puppy mill breeder?"

"As a matter of fact, I had that conversation last night with Bonnie when she first informed me that the dog was chipped. I let her know in the strongest possible terms that such a situation was likely. Bonnie understood, but she was legally obliged to make contact with Dr. Tomlinson, anyhow. And Dr. Tomlinson called her back this morning claiming that she has been distraught over the dog's loss and very anxious to recover her."

James paused and gave Robert a sympathetic look.

"Bonnie assured me that she emphasized to the doctor that she had a waiting list of people who would be happy to adopt Roma," he went on. "Beyond that, she made certain that Dr. Tomlinson understood the fate of any dog turned over to a puppy mill breeder. I do not know if Dr. Tomlinson found that unexpected proselytizing suspicious, but she claimed that she had no such plans. She said that she wanted to keep Roma as a reminder of her late husband. And so Bonnie will be meeting her in the next few hours to return Roma to her rightful owner."

"No!" Robert gave his head a vigorous shake, swiping tears from his cheeks. "I can't let her take Roma. I can't!"

"I fear you have no choice," James gently reminded him. "And perhaps the doctor had a change of heart and truly does intend to keep her as a cherished pet."

"She won't! She'll sell her, just wait and see. All of them hate Roma. I'm the only one who cares!"

With that, he turned and rushed to the front door, flinging it open and letting it slam behind him as he raced from the store. Darla made a move to run after him, but James put a restraining hand on her arm.

"Let the boy go. I agree it is a hard lesson, but it is better for him to accept the situation and move on than for him to keep hoping for something that will not happen."

"Well, you can't blame him for being upset," Darla replied, wiping a suspicious bit of moisture from her own eyes. "He really loves that little dog."

"I understand fully. And that is why, in a few days, I will also suggest that he do a bit of volunteer work with the Fuzzy Berets. He will find many pets that need a loving home, and perhaps Mary Ann will even let him foster a small dog or two in his apartment."

Darla gave him a grateful look. "That's a wonderful idea. It won't make up for losing Roma, but I'm sure he'll feel better if he sees he can help other animals like her." Then, turning a worried eye on the door, she added, "Are you sure I should let him run off like that? What if he does something drastic?"

"Robert is a responsible young man. I am certain after he has an opportunity to compose himself that he will return to his duties."

And James proved right, as usual. A quarter of an hour later, a subdued if red-eyed Robert crept back into the store.

"My bad, Ms. P.," he muttered, giving her a shame-faced look. "I shouldn't have, you know, run off like that. Maybe that can count as my break or something."

"Don't worry, we all understand," she assured him with a smile. "Now, see if you can break down all those shipping cartons for the recycle bin."

The remainder of the afternoon proceeded without incident, the only other excitement occurring when Reese dropped by to update Darla on the Grace Valentine situation.

"The broad's got some heavy hitters behind her," he said with a sour look. "Turns out her mouthpiece, Jerry Titcombe, is the same sleazeball attorney who just got that doctor in the pill mill case acquitted for lack of evidence. He got the Valentine woman bailed out in a couple of hours yesterday, which is almost impossible to get done. Chances are he'll get the assault charge against her dismissed, too."

"What about murder?" Darla wanted to know. "You're not planning to arrest her for that, too, are you?"

"Why? You developing a soft spot for the broad, or something?"

"She might be a first-class B-word," Darla replied, keeping it G-rated in case a customer was in earshot, "but let's just say I'm pretty sure she didn't do it."

Despite her earlier vow to "butt out," she added, "I'll admit, she was my original suspect, especially after she went after Mark Poole with a knife, but I've crossed her off my list. Why would she have wanted to kill her son's father? She was probably getting some sort of support from him, so it was in her best interest for him to stay healthy. And she's stuck around all this time, so maybe she still had hopes of prying him away from his wife."

"Yeah, that's one way to look at it." Reese sounded less than convinced. "On the other hand, maybe she was tired of getting the short end of the stick, he told her to take a hike, and she decided to show him who's boss."

"But no way could she have dragged someone the sensei's size up onto that hook even after shooting him up with the Botox," Darla countered. "She might be training for her black belt, but she's not any bigger than me. I could barely carry his legs when Robert and I dragged him out of the changing room."

"So she had that lawyer guy give her a hand."

Darla shook her head. How could she convince him to focus on Dr. Tomlinson without confessing that it was Hamlet's bit of word juggling that was behind her theory? As for the matter of being strong enough . . . well, the good doctor had two burly sons. Maybe despite their protestations of filial devotion it was time to put them back on the suspect list, too.

"I'm not sure, Reese," she cautiously offered. "What about another look at Jan Tomlinson? What do they say on the cop shows? She's got means, motive, and opportunity."

"Yeah, I'm familiar with the concept. So what's the motive according to Darla?"

Ignoring Reese's patronizing tone, she replied, "I'm betting she just found out that her husband had an affair that resulted in a child, and I'm betting she wasn't too happy about it. Besides, isn't the spouse always the prime suspect?"

"You did notice that she's not any bigger than Ms. Valentine, right?"

"So she had one of her sons give her a hand."

He raised his brows at that last before shooting a look over at Hamlet, who was snoozing again beside the register.

"Whatever floats your boat, Red, just as long as this is your theory, and not the cat's. But if it will make you feel better, no one—except maybe you and Robert—has been crossed off my list. I'm going to be keeping an eye on everyone at that tournament."

 **TWENTY**

"MAYBELLE'S WAITING OUT FRONT," DARLA TOLD REESE VIA the intercom as she buzzed him into the building a few minutes before eight thirty on Saturday morning. "Come on up. I'll call Robert and let him know that you're here, and then we can grab my stuff and get on the road."

She propped the apartment door open for Reese and then dialed the teen. By the time she had hung up with Robert, the detective was already inside and pouring himself a quick cup of coffee into a to-go mug he carried.

"Ready?" he asked.

"I think so," she said, zipping up her overstuffed duffel bag, which had been sitting on the kitchen table. "I've got my uniform and gear, and I've printed up directions to the gym where the tournament is being held."

"Nervous?"

"A little . . . well, yes, a lot," she confessed, putting an anxious hand to her hair, which she'd braided into a neat, tight French braid to keep it out of the way. "It's silly, I know, but it would be nice to win."

"Nothing silly about wanting to be the best in your class. Don't worry, Red," he added with a slow grin that abruptly set the butterflies in her stomach flapping even harder. "No matter how you do today, you're a winner in my book."

"Thanks," she managed, feeling herself blush bright as her hair. It didn't help that the man was dressed for the weekend in a tight black sweater under his black leather bomber, which topped an equally tight-fitting pair of jeans. Distracting, to say the least!

Grabbing up her keys and the directions, she changed the subject and gestured toward her bag. "Remember, you volunteered to be official luggage bearer if I let you come along. So, time to start bearing."

Obediently, he hoisted the bag, only to grunt in surprise. "What the heck do you have in there, bricks?" he demanded as he settled it on his shoulder.

Darla turned at the door and gave him a pitying look.

"It's just my uniform and a towel, and some sparring gear I bought from one of the women in my class. Oh, yeah, and my wallet and phone. Really, Reese, I didn't know you were such a wimp. I haul that same bag with me to class a couple of times a week."

"Remind me not to ever tangle with you, then. C'mon, let's get out of here."

By the time they made it downstairs, Robert was already pacing nervously by the Mercedes, his own bag in hand. "We're gonna be, like, late," he exclaimed. "Hurry!"

"We've got plenty of time," Darla assured him, opening the rear door so they could pile in the gear on one side, and Robert could sit on the other.

Reese, meanwhile, gave the youth a friendly clap on the shoulder that almost sent him reeling. "Don't worry, Robert,

a little case of nerves is good for you. Keeps you from getting overconfident, know what I mean?"

"Yeah, but I'm not overconfident," he confided as he
slipped into his seat. Once Darla and Reese were in the
car with him, he added, "What if I, you know, lose or
something?"

Reese had put on his sunglasses, the black wraparound
ones that neatly hid his expression. Now, looking like the
younger brother of Ah-nold from one of those Terminator
movies, he shot the youth a look via the rearview mirror. But
instead of a poker-faced *Ah'll be bahck*, he said, "You got
the guts to go out there and compete, you're not a loser, no
matter where you place."

The sentiment seemed to resonate with Robert, for he
smiled and appeared to relax a bit. "Yeah, I guess you're
right. The only loser is the one who's afraid to fight."

Traffic on the Brooklyn-Queens Expressway was its
usual weekend snarl, but they still arrived in plenty of time
at the small college gymnasium where the tournament was
taking place. Darla was amazed and a bit daunted to see
that the parking lot was already half full. Between competitors and spectators, it was going to be a respectable crowd.
The same unsettling thought must have occurred to Robert,
for he glanced nervously through the window as they trolled
for a parking place.

Reese pulled into a slot near the gym's main door that,
if not technically illegal, wasn't exactly authorized parking.
Reaching into his jacket pocket, he pulled out one of his
business cards with the NYPD logo and tossed it, face up,
onto the driver's side dashboard.

"There's a reason you ride with me," he deadpanned as
he threw the Mercedes into "Park." "C'mon, let's get going
before I'm any older. My back's starting to ache at the thought
of carrying your bag again."

They piled out of the car, Robert carrying his own gear
bag and Reese carrying Darla's. "You know, I could get used

to this," she told him with a smile as, shifting the bag, he pulled open one of the gym's double doors for her.

He raised a brow. "Yeah? Well, don't," he cheerfully warned her.

A couple of dozen other competitors, mostly teens, were milling about in the long foyer next to a refreshment stand serving drinks, hot dogs, and chips. Small, arrowed signs taped to the walls pointed in the direction of the registration table, which was set up near open double doors leading to the main gym. The noise level coming from there was already high enough that Darla had to repeat her and Robert's names twice to the karate moms checking off incoming registrants.

In return, they both received programs listing their divisions, small tournament patches, and blue paper wristbands to show they were registered as competitors. Reese paid his spectator fee, and then caused a moment of amused consternation with the karate moms as he held out his arm for a yellow guest wristband.

"Here's another one it won't fit, Suze." The middle-aged, bleached blonde giggled to her fellow mom as she held up a paper band that obviously was too small for Reese's wrist. Giving him a coy wink, she added in a cutesy voice, "Guess we're going to have to do like we did with the other big boys earlier and put two of these together for you."

The brunette snorted, and murmured to her friend just loud enough for Darla to hear. "I wouldn't mind putting two together with him, you know what I mean?" she said, jabbing her friend with a sharp elbow as she blatantly ogled Reese. "You know, this is lots better than working another high school golf tournament."

"I'll take those," Darla smoothly interrupted. Snatching the paper bands from the first woman, she quickly made them into a single strip which she wrapped around Reese's wrist.

"There you go, honey, all set," she told him, giving his

arm a familiar pat. She turned and favored the women with a bright smile. "Now, would you ladies mind telling us where the changing rooms are?'

"Through there and to the left," the brunette answered, indicating the main door behind them, and pouting a little as she settled back in her folding chair. Obviously, she knew a tossed gauntlet when she saw one.

Her friend chimed in. "Yeah, and make sure you listen for your division. You know how it goes. The times on the program are pretty much suggestions only. They call your group, and you're not there for the start, you're out," she explained, jerking her thumb over her shoulder like a baseball umpire.

Darla gave them another fake smile and then turned to Robert and Reese. "Let's go, boys. We've got trophies to win."

"Wow, reverse sexual harassment much?" Robert exclaimed as they entered the auditorium, looking a bit shell-shocked from the obvious sexual banter.

Reese, who'd maintained a poker face throughout the incident, now shoved his sunglasses up onto his head with his free hand and grinned. "Hey, kid, don't knock it until you've tried it."

"Don't listen to him, Robert," Darla countered. "Detective Reese is not exactly the poster boy for equal rights."

She didn't hear Reese's sputtered protest to her dismissal, however, for her attention was abruptly fixed on the scene before her. The broad wooden court below where basketball or another indoor sport would normally be played had been converted into six large areas of colored mats, each flagged with a number. Tables and chairs that she assumed were for the tournament officials were set up between them, with the spectators sitting in the surrounding bleachers. At the court's far end, a raised stage complete with TAMA bunting had been set up. Before it sat a long, cloth-covered table covered with the trophies that would be handed out over the course of the day.

At a second table set up to one side of the stage, teenaged girls in short shorts and TAMA tees appeared to be doing a brisk business selling similar shirts to admiring young men. Overhead, sponsorship banners from a well-known sports drink company and several martial arts supply houses hung in colorful rows and added a festive air to the event. This was, indeed, a professionally run event, she saw in approval. She wondered where Hank and Hal were, and what role they had played in coordinating it all.

"Look, someone's putting on a demonstration," Robert said, pointing to the stage and raising his voice to be heard over the echoing hubbub.

Two men—the taller in a white gi, the shorter wearing dark blue—faced each other, the fighter in white acting as the aggressor. Nonstop, he charged his partner with a series of weapons. Though at a definite height disadvantage, the shorter man managed to disarm his attacker every time, drawing applause from the surrounding spectators as he used throws and chokeholds and takedowns.

"The program says they're doing Sambo," Robert explained. "It's some kind of cool Russian martial art."

"Pretty impressive," Darla agreed, wondering if she could learn a technique like that. Of course, as easy as the demonstrators made it look, she knew both men must have studied the art for years.

The teen, meanwhile, was consulting the program again. "And look," he added, pointing, "that's where we're going to be, areas five and six. Maybe we should, like, get seats over there."

There was, of course, at the opposite end of the court from the main stage. Doubtless the higher-ranking competitors fought in the more prestigious rings, which suited Darla just fine. Now that they were actually here at the tournament, she could feel the butterflies in her stomach taking flight again.

"Good idea," she agreed. "Let's find a spot, and then we can go get changed."

A few minutes later, they were settled on bleacher seats a few rows back from the floor, close enough to see, but high enough that their view was better. Reese set down her bag on the bench and promptly rubbed his shoulder.

"Next time, hire a pack horse," he complained.

Darla grinned. "So much for being one of the big boys."

She unzipped the bag and pulled her gi jacket, pants, and belt from the very top, and then zipped the bag back up and added, "Do me a favor and watch my stuff for a minute? I'm going to put on my uniform. I'll be right back."

"Sure, but hurry. I want to wander around the place and see what's what. You two might be here to have fun, but I'm on the clock."

Darla nodded. She'd almost forgotten in the excitement that Reese really was there for something other than luggage-bearer duty.

She and Robert parted company at the restrooms, Darla ducking into the women's side and Robert into the men's. She quickly swapped out her jeans for gi pants and, peeling off the sweatshirt she wore, fastened the gi jacket on over her tank top and sports bra. The last touch was her crisp new yellow belt, which she wrapped twice around her and carefully knotted so that both ends of the belt hung even. Then, with a final look in the mirror, she took her folded clothes and headed out into the auditorium again.

Robert was already waiting outside the door for her, his own new yellow belt tied every bit as carefully as hers. His smile looked a bit shaky, however, and so she raised her clenched fist, knuckles out.

"Fist bump for luck?"

He grinned now and touched knuckles with her. Then, as they headed back toward their seats, he pointed toward the main floor and waved at a middle-aged woman from their class who was warming up along the sidelines with a pair of kamas: short, handheld scythes that Darla knew were used as traditional Japanese weapons. With stylized moves, the woman blocked and then attacked an invisible opponent, wielding with deadly precision what were, for all intents and purposes, humble gardening tools.

Darla watched, impressed . . . and equally relieved that the woman didn't wave back at them. She'd already heard stories in the dojo of careless students putting out an eye or slicing a neck with even the blunted practice weapons!

"Probably half the school is here today," Darla noted, scanning the crowd for more familiar faces. And then she saw a familiar face she *least* wanted to see, hanging out near the closest timekeeping table, earnestly chatting with one of the officials.

"Oh, great, there's Mark Poole," she warned Robert, not daring to point lest she draw attention to them. "Quick, pretend we're looking at the schedule in case he notices us."

Her plan didn't work, however, for Mark turned around and promptly caught her gaze before she could focus on the list. As for Robert, in a voice that sounded deliberately casual, he asked, "You think Chris will be here, and Grace? I mean, after the other night?"

"Chris, maybe. But Grace?" Darla shrugged. "If I were running the tournament, no way. Let's just hope Hank and Hal put her on the Do Not Admit list."

By then, they'd reached their seats again. While the bleachers had filled even more during their brief absence, most of the spectators were along the two main sides of the court, the better to see the more advanced competitors. Only a handful of people were sitting near where they'd left Reese, and most of those were in the first two rows.

The detective rose as they approached.

"They should be getting this show on the road in a few minutes, so I'm going to wander around for a little bit. But don't worry," he added at Darla's questioning look. "I'll be sure to get back here in time to see you two compete."

As Reese headed off, Darla settled down and unzipped her gear bag. Glancing over in the direction Reese had gone, she turned to Robert and said, "So, want to bet the first place he checks out is the T-shirt girls?"

Robert flashed a grin. "That's where I'd go."

Darla grinned back at him as she tucked her street clothes into the bag. But just as she pulled her hand out again, something sharp inside the bag scratched her.

"Eek!"

With a quick little scream that promptly was lost in the sound of the growing crowd, Darla leaped to her feet and stared at the bag. Robert scuttled a safe distance away and gave her a wide-eyed stare. "What's wrong?"

"Something in the bag scratched me!"

She looked down at her hand, which now sported four tiny red spots. All at once suspicious, she gingerly reached for the duffel's strap and lifted it.

"Ugh, this thing weighs a ton!" Then, remembering how Reese had unexpectedly struggled with it, she gasped and set down the bag again. "Either someone stuck a few bricks in there . . . or else someone stowed away inside it."

Robert's eyes opened even wider. "You mean—"

Looking around to make sure that no one was watching, Darla carefully unzipped the bag again and gingerly lifted out her clothes. Her towel was piled in there next, and she pulled it out, as well. Now, she spied two wide green eyes staring up at her . . . green eyes that were, of course, attached to a very large black cat curled up in the bottom of her bag.

"Hamlet!"

Gasping, she quickly sat down and zipped the bag shut again. "I don't believe it! What is he doing in there? Is this some sort of a joke?" she asked Robert.

"No way, not me," Robert exclaimed, raising both hands in protest. "Maybe he, you know, crawled in there after you packed everything up?"

Frowning, Darla thought back to earlier that morning. Her bag *had* been open until Reese came up to the apartment, meaning that the feline had most of the morning to slip inside it without her noticing. But she often left her gear bag open so that it could air out, and he'd never jumped inside before. What had made Hamlet turn kitty stowaway today, of all days?

"I guess it doesn't matter why he's here," she answered her own question aloud. "But what do we do with him? If I leave him out in the car, who knows what he'll do?"

Actually, she had a pretty good idea of what would happen. Picturing the Mercedes's butter-soft leather liberally raked with cat claw marks—not to mention some even more unpleasant damage—she shook her head. "He can't stay loose in the car, but there's no time to take him home, either. Not without missing my division."

"So leave him in the bag," was Robert's prompt response. Then, at Darla's questioning look, he shrugged. "He, you know, seems to like being in it, and there's air holes and stuff so he won't suffocate."

In fact, the bag did sport a number of grommeted holes designed to keep sweaty gym clothes a bit fresher. Hamlet wasn't in any danger of smothering, she agreed. And he'd made the drive out to the tournament without uttering a single mew. But what if he decided he was tired of the bag and started yowling to get out? Darla glanced around again. The clamor in the gym was even louder now. A screaming panther inside that bag probably wouldn't be heard.

Not any worse than a soft-sided cat carrier. She gave a firm nod, even as a small voice inside her told her that she was a bad kitty owner. "Okay, he stays in the bag. Look, the tournament is about to start."

Indeed, a group of black belts—both male and female—was milling about the stage now. A microphone on a tall stand squawked out a bit of earsplitting feedback as someone at ground level wrestled it up onto the stage. The crowd, which Darla estimated to now number several hundred, settled to a murmur. Then everyone hushed as Hank and Hal, both in their usual black gis—though with sleeves per tournament regulations—mounted the stage steps.

But the twins were not alone. They shifted position slightly as they moved toward center stage, and Darla realized that a third, smaller figure, also in a black gi, walked with them. The trio paused at the microphone, and Darla saw two things simultaneously.

The small figure in the center was female, and under one arm she carried a small gray and white hound.

While Hank and Hal looked on, the woman reached with her free arm to adjust the microphone. Then a cool, amplified voice echoed through the gymnasium, saying, "Good morning. I'm Dr. Jan Tomlinson, and I welcome you to the seventeenth annual Tomlinson Academy of the Martial Arts Regional Tournament."

![cat] TWENTY-ONE

"IT'S ROMA!" ROBERT EXCLAIMED, REFERRING, OF COURSE, to the small hound in Dr. Tomlinson's arms. Clutching Darla's gi sleeve, he persisted, "Look, it's her."

"She," Darla corrected automatically; then, as he took a step forward, she added, "and remember, Roma is Dr. Tomlinson's dog now. If you're thinking about running up to see her, don't. It will only confuse the poor little thing. Really, Robert, it's best if you let her go."

He set his jaw and nodded. "I know. I just wish I could say good-bye. I didn't do that before. I-I thought she'd be coming back."

She barely heard this last, however, for all around them, people were rising to their feet and applauding. Not for Dr. Tomlinson, but in memory of the sensei. And so, along with Robert, Darla got to her feet and began applauding, too. Now was not the time to take a moral stand, she told herself. She was there at the tournament as Hank and Hal's guest. She'd not disrespect their father's memory, no matter what less than gracious things she might suspect about the man or his wife.

As the applause finally faded, everyone sat again, and Darla took the opportunity to glance about for Reese. He wasn't with the T-shirt girls, so he had to have settled in the bleachers somewhere.

"Thank you, everyone," Dr. Tomlinson said, her smooth voice washing over the crowd. "Thank you for coming today. My late husband would be humbled to see such a show of love. And now, if you will indulge us, my sons and I, with the help of a few friends"—she paused and gracefully gestured at the black belts standing beside the stage—"have put together a small tribute to Tom."

At those words, the sound of a familiar trumpet fanfare began: *da-DA-da-da-DA-da-da-DA-DA-DA*. The audience started to cheer as the overhead lights dimmed, and a projector flashed the image of the TAMA fist onto the large screen behind the stage. Then the fist dissolved into the familiar face of a young Master Tomlinson while the gymnasium was filled with the pulsing horns and screaming strings of the *Rocky* theme song.

As the music played on, pictures flashed by on the screen. Some, Darla recognized from the sensei's studio wall; most, however, were new to her. Some of the shots were taken during one competition or another, others were with various celebrities, while still more photos were of him and his family. The images flipped past like a time line, with the sensei a bit older in each, but still flashing his familiar warm smile.

It was cliché.

It was corny.

But by the time the final trumpet blare had died way, Darla found herself again on her feet, cheering and applauding with the rest of the roaring crowd.

"That was, like, awesome!" Robert shouted beside her as the lights came up again. Looking up toward the gymnasium ceiling, he added, "I can't wait for him to see me out there."

"Yeah, me, too," Darla admitted, discreetly wiping away a few tears.

And then, as the roar began to die and the crowd resumed their seats, Jan spoke again.

"Thank you for your warm outpouring of love for Tom. So you know, all proceeds from today's event will be going to the Pretty Faces Foundation. That's a small charity that Tom and I founded to assist underprivileged children whose families cannot afford plastic surgery to repair the physical damages from birth defects, accidents, or abuse. We have a jar at the T-shirt stand should you care to make additional donations. And now, I will turn the tournament over to my son."

Hal took the microphone from his mother and yelled, "Thank you, everyone. And now, let the competition begin!"

He handed off the mike to one of the officials standing in front of the stage, who began calling off the beginner divisions. Tiny competitors, some appearing no older than six years old, began pouring onto the tournament floor.

Darla, however, was still staring in the direction of Jan Tomlinson. The doctor did charity surgery on little kids? Could this be the same wicked witch who'd snatched Toto— or, rather, Roma—from Robert's arms a few days earlier? The same woman whom she suspected had murdered her husband in cold blood? Giving herself a mental shake, she turned to Robert.

"We're up soon," she told him. "Better get your gear out."

He nodded and reached into his bag for his sparring gear: dipped foam gloves, boots, and headgear, along with one of those molded mouth guards. He pulled on the first items, leaving the headgear unfastened, and then tucked the mouth guard in his belt.

"Ready," he said. Then, with a glance over at Darla's bag, he asked, "Is you-know-who okay?"

Darla put an ear to her bag, listening. "I think he's purring," she said after a moment, smiling. "Maybe he'll be a good cat, after all. Let's wait until you and I have finished, and then I'll take him out to the car for a bit and give him some water, maybe stretch his legs. Speaking of which, I probably should warm up a little."

Leaving Robert to keep protective watch over the bag, she moved down toward the main floor and picked a spot to one side where a few other competitors had gathered. She did a few jumping jacks and a bit of running in place to warm up, and then finished with a couple of abbreviated rounds of the stretching routine they normally did in class.

As she finished the final stretch, managing almost to bring her head to her knees, she looked up to see Mark again. He was standing near the T-shirt table this time, apparently waiting for someone. Darla promptly bent for another stretch while praying he wouldn't notice her and feel obliged to explain how she was doing her warm-up wrong.

When she straightened again, however, he was gone. Satisfied the coast was clear, she made her way up to the bleachers again. There, she spent the next several minutes with Robert, watching the junior group performing their katas.

Darla took special note of the way they bowed onto the mat, and how they addressed the judges by shouting their names and their schools, and asking permission before beginning their routines. Would she remember to do all that, on top of remembering her forms? Once again, the butterflies in her stomach began their dance, and she reminded herself of what Reese had said.

You got the guts to go out there and compete, you're not a loser, no matter where you place.

And then, all too soon, she heard the announcer call her division.

"That's me," she told Robert, aware that suddenly her hands were shaking. Glancing around, she added, "Since

Reese is still MIA, you want to come down and give me a little moral support?"

"Sure, Ms. P! Let's go."

She pulled her wallet and phone from the outside pocket of her duffel—even with her secret feline weapon guarding her gear, she wasn't going to tempt fate—and handed both items to Robert. Then she hurried down the bleacher steps to the floor toward the sign marked *Two*.

Some of her fellow competitors were there already, though as Hal and Reese had both pointed out, at her age and rank it would likely be a limited field, restricted as well to females. In fact, by the time she'd bowed onto the mat and lined up with the others, there were only three other women besides her.

The next few minutes went by in a blur as the other competitors performed the designated kata. By the luck of the draw, Darla found herself in the final slot; good, in that she could watch and learn from the others, and bad, in that her butterflies had time to organize and perform complicated routines of their own. Finally, the third woman finished her form with a dramatic *kiai*, and it was Darla's turn to step up.

As she moved to the center of the mat, she shot a fleeting glance toward the spectators. Robert was there, giving her a thumbs-up, and Reese had reappeared and was standing beside him. The sight of the two gave her a small boost of confidence. She made her bow to the judges and then assumed her stance, her weight balanced on both feet and her fisted hands in approved position before her. Taking a deep breath, she called out, "Judges, my name is Darla Pettistone."

The rest of the words seemed to pour from her reflexively. She waited for the head judge's nod to begin, and then she made the preliminary block. Swiftly and surely, she completed the next move, and then the next. It was going to be okay, she told herself. Her childhood teacher, Mrs. Morgan, wouldn't be disappointed in her.

And then, all at once, she heard an unmistakable burst of laughter from the spectators.

What had she done? Panic shot through her, but she remembered Reese's advice and forged on, making each move crisper. And still the laughter grew, so that she frantically wondered what had gone wrong. Spinach in her teeth? Maybe a big grease spot on her rear end where she'd accidentally sat in someone's discarded French fries? It made no difference. What mattered was that this competition had become a repeat of her third grade *Evangeline* fiasco, only a hundred times worse! She never should have signed up!

In a fog, she continued her kata until, with a final punch and kick, the nightmare was thankfully over.

Snapping to attention again, Darla made her bow to the judges only to hear cheers and more laughter, along with a round of applause from the spectators that none of the other competitors had earned. Now, her confusion turned to outright anger.

What in the heck is going on?

Catching Reese's gaze, she saw him mouth something and point behind her. Forgetting competition protocol, she spun around.

"Hamlet!"

The black feline sat at the edge of the mat, green eyes blinking innocently up at her. Somehow, he'd made his way out of the bag and had wandered out onto the floor. But that didn't explain the laughter. She glared at her three competitors. Minutes earlier, the women had been holding themselves in rigid silence. Now, however, they were guffawing so hard they were crying. She swung back around again to see that even the judges were grinning.

Well, at least, two of them were.

The head judge, with a sour expression, gestured her to rejoin the other competitors on the sidelines. She did as requested, only to have Hamlet pad over and take a seat beside her, which drew still more laughter from the crowd. The judges conferred for a few moments before motioning Darla and the rest back onto the mat.

"We've made our decision," the head judge announced. "Darla Pettistone, step forward. Unfortunately, Ms. Pettistone, you are hereby disqualified from the competition for bringing an unauthorized animal onto the mat."

The announcement drew a chorus of boos, but the judge ignored the disturbance. "Step back, please. The remaining competitors rank as follows. First place, Thompson; second place, Selinger; third place, Merrill."

Disbelief swept Darla as the other names were called. Now, her outrage was directed at Hamlet. *This* was what the cat had come all the way to the competition to do? Bowing her way off the mat, she snatched him up, grunting only a little under the burden, and stalked over to where Reese and Robert waited.

"Tough break, Red," Reese said with a shake of his head, appearing sincerely disappointed on her behalf. "But you looked really good out there."

"Ms. P, it was great!" Robert crowed. "I mean, I'm real sorry that Hamlet, you know, got you kicked out and stuff, but you should have seen him."

He held up her cell phone, which he'd been holding onto for her. Pressing the camera app, he scrolled to a video clip and hit the "Play" button. "I got it all on video. I thought you'd want to see how you did. Look, Hamlet was doing the kata right along with you."

As Darla watched, her initial reaction of horror morphed into resigned amusement. There she was, looking like a serious student of the martial arts, while behind her—and most definitely unbeknownst to her!—Hamlet wandered onto the edge of the mat, weaving and bobbing and putting out the occasional paw. The contrast of her determined moves and Hamlet's shadow routine was priceless, she had to admit. Had the same thing happened to anyone else, she probably would have been rolling on the floor laughing with the rest of them.

"All right, it's funny," she conceded. She took back her phone and wallet, reaching beneath her loose jacket to tuck both items into the broad elastic band of her gi trousers for safekeeping. "But, Robert, if you post this on YouTube, I'll kill you!"

Then, hefting the cat's weight so that she could hold him more comfortably, she turned to Reese and said, "At least we solved the mystery of why my bag was so heavy."

"Yeah, Robert told me how you found him in there," Reese said. "Smart cat. I guess he was able to unzip himself from the inside and crawl out. Sorry he got you disqualified, but you're lucky he didn't go wandering off in the gymnasium, instead. We might never have found him in a place this size."

"You're right." Torn between relief and frustration, Darla sighed and hugged the feline a little tighter. "Okay, let me get him back into the bag, and maybe I can find something to tie the zipper pulls together so he can't do it again."

But barely had she said that when another announcement came over the loudspeaker. "Beginning sparring, ages sixteen and up, report to mat three."

"Hey, that's me," Robert exclaimed in excitement. "I gotta go fight now."

"Reese, go ahead with him," Darla told him. "I'll take care of Hamlet, and be down there in a minute."

While the two men made their way to the designated spot, Darla started back up the bleacher steps, wishing Hamlet had thought to stow his harness in the bag with him. That way, maybe she could have walked him around the gym pretending he was a service animal. The feline didn't seem at all distressed by the noise and the crowd, she realized in surprise. To the contrary, he seemed quite content to lounge in her arms and watch the goings-on. With any luck, maybe he would snooze in the bag until they were ready to return home.

Halfway to her seat, she saw Chris Valentine bending over to talk to someone in the next row. *Good for him,* she thought. The teen would surely know that rumors would be making their way around the dojo grapevine about what had happened at the TAMA studios. He had guts to show up under such circumstances, and she fervently hoped that he'd bring home a win for his efforts. As for Grace, Darla hoped with equal fervency that she'd had the good sense to stay away.

Chris glanced up, and Darla gave him a friendly nod. He seemed to hesitate, and then he hurried over to her. "Hey, I saw your cat," he told her with a fleeting smile. "He was pretty good."

"He *was* pretty good," she agreed. "Too bad he decided to compete in the wrong age category. He got disqualified, just like me."

"Yeah, kinda stinks," he said, the smile returning. Then, glancing around he said, "I don't suppose you've seen my mom anywhere, have you?"

"No, I don't think I have." Hoping he hadn't heard the surprise in her tone, she added, "But I'll let her know you're looking for her if I see her."

"Guess she's out for a smoke or something." He nodded and wandered off again, and she felt a little outrage on his behalf. Couldn't the woman have stayed home just once, and spared her son some embarrassment?

But she forgot about Grace as soon as she reached her seat. Her duffel, now gaping open, still lay where she'd left it. Sitting down beside the ersatz cat carrier, she gave Hamlet a scratch behind the ears.

"You might be smarter than the average cat, Hamlet, but it's not safe to let you run loose," she told him as she lowered him back into the bag. "I hate to do this to you, but you have to snuggle in there until we're ready to go home again."

For a moment, Hamlet appeared willing to cooperate . . . that was, until the duffel's zipper stuck. Then, as Darla struggled to free it, the cat bounded out of the bag and headed down toward the main floor again.

"Hamlet, no!" she cried, leaping up to rush after him.

The feline, however, was faster. Before Darla could catch up, he gave a quick zigzag, which took him to one of the smaller exits. But rather than running through it, he turned again. Then, with a flick of his black tail, he disappeared beneath a section of bleachers.

Darla gave a cry of dismay and dropped to her knees, peering into the gap behind that section of seating. "Hamlet!" she cried. "Come here, kitty!"

No green eyes stared back at her. Frantic now, she tried to squeeze into the gap, but she didn't have Hamlet's size advantage. Still, she could see that, slightly farther down behind the bleachers, there was an open area. Maybe he was hiding back there and laughing into his cat paws at her.

"What are you looking for, Darla?" a familiar nasal voice behind her suddenly asked.

Darla jumped at the unexpected sound, bumping her head on the bleacher's edge.

"Ouch!" Rubbing the back of her head, she scuttled out from the gap again and glared at Mark Poole, who was dressed in his white gi, the familiar headband with the rising sun tied around his forehead.

"I'm kind of busy now, Mark," she told him, rubbing her tender head again and wondering if this was going to become a habit, experiencing pain every time she saw the man. "So if you'll excuse me, I'll—"

"Yeah, but you didn't tell me what you were looking for."

Darla gave an exasperated sigh and sat back on her heels. "Fine. If you must know, I'm looking for my cat. He got loose out of my duffel bag and ran back there. I really need to find him, so I'll have to talk to you later."

"Your cat?" Mark's eyes behind his glasses blinked rapidly. "That's a good one, Darla. What are you really looking for?"

She gave him a doubtful look. He was blocking her way, and crouched as she was at an awkward angle, she wasn't easily getting past him. "I already told you. You remember Hamlet, the black cat from my store. He's hiding somewhere back here."

His expression cleared. "Oh, yeah, Hamlet. I think maybe I just saw him."

"You did?"

He nodded. "I've been here before, for other tournaments. There's all these little rooms and crawlspaces all through the building. It's kind of fun to go walking around them when it gets boring out on the floor."

"I get it," she told him, cutting him short lest he launch into a thirty-minute discourse on college gyms. "So, what about Hamlet?"

"He's all black, right? Now that I know it's your cat, I'm pretty sure he's the one I saw go into one of those. The crawlspaces, I mean."

He paused and snickered. "I call them creepy crawly spaces . . . you know, because there's always creepy crawlers in them. But, anyhow, you can get to the one he ran into from the back hall, if you want me to show you."

Darla allowed herself a small glimmer of hope. She was certain that Hamlet wouldn't take up residence in the gymnasium for good—he liked his routine far too much to rough it for long—but she wouldn't put it past him to take his sweet time about showing himself again. If she didn't find him right away, she'd have to notify someone that he was hiding there somewhere . . . a fuzzy black needle in a very large concrete and steel-girdered haystack.

"You're sure you don't mind?"

"I said I'd do it," Mark replied, sounding irritated now.

"You better hurry and make up your mind. I've got to go spar in a little while, and it will probably be too late to find him when I'm done."

"Come on, then," she decided with a nod. "Let's go, before he runs off again."

Mark smiled now and stuck out his hand. Seeing no choice for it, she took his sweaty palm and let him help her up. All the martial arts classes had clearly worked for him, since he had no trouble lifting her to her feet.

"This way," he said, still holding her hand as he made his way to the exit.

■ || TWENTY-TWO

UNLIKE THE OTHER DOORWAYS, WHICH LED BACK TO THE main halls or the restrooms, this exit went in a separate direction toward what Darla assumed was the utilities portion of the building. Quickly the sounds from the ongoing competition grew faint, reminding her that she was missing out on Robert's match. And as they moved at something closer to a trot than a walk down the hallway, she wondered why Mark was still hanging on to her like she was a naughty child prone to running away.

"Uh, my hand," she prompted him, trying to tug her fingers from his grasp.

Mark stopped so swiftly that she almost smacked into him. He all but flung her hand away and then shot her a peeved look.

"There, I'm not touching you anymore. Happy?" Not waiting for her answer, he continued, "I was just trying to make sure you didn't get lost. You women are always complaining about something. *Don't touch me. Don't look at me.*"

He said those last words in a mocking falsetto. *Talk about creepy crawlers!* Surreptitiously, she rubbed her palm against her gi trousers and wished she had her bottle of hand sanitizer. Then, abruptly, Mark's expression crumpled a little, and he shoved his slipping glasses higher on his nose.

"Sorry, Darla. I know I was being a real jackass to you, but I didn't mean it. I'm just nervous about my sparring competition. We need to hurry and find your cat so we can get back out on the floor. Maybe you'll even watch me when it's my turn," he added with a hopeful look.

Darla suppressed a snort. Mark had no idea how much she wanted to see him get his "jackass" kicked a little. In fact, she'd pay extra to see it.

"Of course," she assured him as they started walking again. "But let's worry about Hamlet first. Are you sure we're going in the right direction?"

He didn't answer but halted once more, this time in front of a door with the stenciled words *Campus Facilities Personnel Only* emblazoned in chipped black paint. She was about to point out that they weren't said personnel, when he twisted the knob.

The door opened inward with a rusty squeal into a low-ceilinged, concrete brick corridor that was almost totally devoid of light. Not a problem for Hamlet with his super cat vision, she wryly told herself, but probably not the safest place for a blind-in-the-dark human to go traipsing through. No way was she setting foot in there. But then Mark reached in beside the doorframe and apparently found a light switch, for a moment later a series of single-tube fluorescent fixtures feebly flickered to life.

Looking more than a little pleased with himself, he told her, "This way is a shortcut."

But was it?

Darla hesitated, staring down the length of the utilitarian

passageway which, even when lit, looked distinctly uninviting. Mark had said they could reach the storage crawlspace from the back hall, but surely that would have been right around the corner from the exit they'd taken. And already they had walked past several closed service doors that might also have led to the area under the bleachers. Right?

Assuming that her mental map of the gym's layout was correct, they were a good distance now from the spot where Hamlet had vanished. And that realization was beginning to make her feel uneasy. "Hang on, Mark," she spoke up. "I know you're trying to help, but I don't think Hamlet would have gone this far. Why don't we head back to the bleachers, and I'll look there again."

"But we're almost back there, anyhow," he protested. "I told you, I've been all through this building a bunch of times before. It's like a maze. The halls go like this"—he raised a finger and traced a long, narrow U in the air—"so even though it feels like we've walked a long way, we're pretty much back where we started. We're just on a different side of the wall."

"Are you sure?"

Mark nodded vigorously. "Here, I'll show you." He gestured her to follow and started down the passage. Darla strode impatiently after him. If they didn't get to the bleachers in the next minute, she told herself, she was going to abandon him and find her own way back to the gymnasium court.

They'd gone maybe halfway down the corridor when she saw a metal door painted the same utilitarian gray as the walls. An electric light switch in the identical drab color was mounted nearby. This time, the black stenciled letters on the door read *Electrical Room Authorized Personnel Only.*

"This is it," Mark said in satisfaction as he pulled opened the door and simultaneously flipped on the light switch in the corridor.

A series of bare bulbs came to life, their pallid glow bouncing off the metal electrical boxes mounted on both main walls of the room. Metal conduits snaked from them and ran like kudzu along the ceiling. In the room's center, what she guessed was a generator of some sort stretched to the low ceiling and took up a good quarter of the floor space. She could hear it humming, the sound reminding her of a bee swarm in summer. Not a bad comparison, she thought, wondering what it would feel like to get zapped with that much electricity.

Stepping back into the corridor so she could get a better look, Mark pointed directly ahead. "You cut through right here. Just keep walking straight until you run into another door like this one. Open it, and you'll be under the bleachers right about where your cat should be."

"Wonderful," Darla exclaimed with a smile, deciding that perhaps Mark wasn't such a creepoid, after all. "Hopefully Hamlet will be waiting right there for me."

Relieved that she'd gotten all angsty over the situation for nothing, she stepped past him and headed into the room. Turning back for a moment, she added, "Don't worry, I'm not going to ask you to stick around. I know you've got your sparring match in a bit. But let me make sure I have my bearings before you go. Once I find Hamlet, I think all I need to do is—"

She hadn't even finished her sentence when Mark smiled broadly. In a heartbeat, she realized what he intended to do just before he slammed the door on her. And before she could draw breath to protest that, the light flashed off, as well, leaving her in cave-like darkness.

"Mark! You jerk! Turn the light back on this instant," she shrieked in the direction of the door.

Or rather, where she guessed the door might be. For the sudden blackness around her was impenetrable, the door he'd closed upon her fitting so tightly that not even a sliver of light seeped beneath it. Heart pounding faster, Darla could feel herself swaying . . . or maybe she just imagined that she was. Something about the total darkness left her gripped by sudden vertigo, as if she were balancing on the edge of an unlit precipice.

Trying not to panic, she shouted again, "Okay, you've had your joke. Now turn the light back on right now. I mean it, Mark!"

"I mean it, Mark!" came the man's faint mocking falsetto from the other side of the door. Then, resuming his usual nasal tones, he went on, "I don't know, maybe if you ask me reeeeal nice, I'll think about it."

"Open. The. Door," she clipped out. "Now!"

She heard a snigger from him.

"Not going to happen, Darla," he called back in a singsong voice. "I've got to keep you in there until I figure out what to do with you. Don't you think I saw you spying on me? And then you pretended to have a cat with you so you had an excuse to stick your nose into everything. How stupid do you think I am?"

"Do you really want me to answer that?" she shouted back at him, even as she frowned in confusion. Spying? What the heck was he talking about?

But by now she was regaining her equilibrium a bit, as well as a bit of night vision. The various panels had small indicator lights on them . . . not enough to light her way, but sufficient to orient her. Gingerly, she slid one foot forward, and then the other, arms out in a parody of an old mummy movie.

"Mark!" she called again, needing the sound of his voice to guide her, "I don't know what you think I was doing, but you're wrong. I was just trying to find Hamlet."

"No, you weren't," he yelled back, and she found she was nearer to the door than she'd realized. "I thought you were nice. We were friends and everything when we were playing word games on the computer, but you're just like the rest of them."

"What are you talking about, Mark?" she demanded. "I never played against you."

"You did, too, little Ms. *Pettibooks123*. I saw your game open on your store computer once, and I sent you a request to play. We chatted and everything, lots of times. You know me. I'm *Fightingwords*."

Darla sucked in a quick breath, feeling as if she'd just walked into a sparring partner's punch. Never would she have guessed that her unknown opponent was actually Mark. She'd had fun playing against him, had exchanged funny little messages with him. Then a second punch followed in swift succession as she abruptly recalled Hamlet's foray across her keyboard a couple of days earlier.

It hadn't been *Jan* that the cat had tried to spell out to her. The word he'd left in the rack for her to see had been *words* . . . as in the username, *Fightingwords*.

Hamlet had been trying to tell her that Mark Poole was the one who had murdered Master Tomlinson!

Once again, she felt herself swaying, but this time the darkness had no part in that unsettling sensation. But she didn't have time for further reaction, for Mark was saying, "And now that you know what's going on, I have to do something about it."

"I don't know anything!" she lied, even as she was certain her insistence would do no good. For some reason, he thought she knew what he'd done, even though she hadn't made the connection until this very moment. But her racing thoughts were momentarily derailed when her extended hands contacted something hard.

Cautiously, she ran her fingers against the rough surface. Concrete brick, not metal. She'd found the wall. Now, where was the blasted door?

"You might as well make yourself comfy," she heard his voice again, this time much closer and seemingly to her right. Taking a more aggressive tack in her blind search, she scooted sideways in quick little steps, fingers searching. She heard him add, "I'll be back after my match, and then we'll figure out the best way to do it," just as her hands connected with a large expanse of painted metal.

She'd found the door! And there was the knob. Gripping it, Darla positioned her shoulder against the door, gave the knob a twist, and shoved.

It didn't budge.

Frantic now, she rattled the knob. And then she heard another snigger, and the faint mocking jingle of a key ring as he said, "Guess I forgot to tell you that I locked you in, and you need a key to get out. See you later. Don't let the creepy crawlers get you."

Fear and fury gripped her, sending her heart racing even faster as she pounded on the door. "This is kidnapping," she screamed back at him. "If you don't let me out this instant, I'm calling the cops."

He didn't answer, and she realized he must have gone for good this time. Even so, she kept pounding on the door, shouting a few expletives for good measure. Finally, breathless and hands bruised, she turned, her back against the unyielding door. And then she remembered what she'd just threatened to do.

"Call the cops," she repeated, slapping at the waistband of her gi trousers.

She almost sobbed in relief as she felt the familiar slim rectangular shape and realized that she still had her cell phone with her. She pulled it free and, fumbling a moment in the darkness, pressed the "On" button.

A sudden haze of white illumination almost blinded her. Checking the icon, she saw she had at least half a charge. *Good.* She swiped past the wallpaper photo of Hamlet and, pulling up her contact list, quickly pressed Reese's number.

She realized after a moment of no ring tone that the call hadn't gone through. Fingers shaking, she tried again, only to get dead silence once more. Puzzled, she checked the screen to see her signal strength. Where there should have been five bars showing—or, at least, two or three—there were none. Whether it was the room's block concrete construction, or else all the electrical equipment, bottom line was that she had no phone reception at all.

Which meant she was trapped, and with no way to let anyone know where she was.

She tamped down another moment of panic. Maybe a text would go through even if a call wouldn't. Quickly, she started typing.

Need help, no joke. Mark Poole crazy, killed Master T., holding me hostage in electric room behind gymnasium. She hesitated and then added, *Hamlet missing 2.*

She clicked on both Reese and Robert's names; then, hoping for a bit of divine intervention, she pressed the "Send" key.

The message went!

Or did it? Either way, her absence would eventually be noticed. Reese would wonder when she didn't join him to watch Robert's sparring. He probably wouldn't worry, though, until more time had passed, and she still hadn't returned.

She pictured him finding her empty gear bag in the bleachers, knew he'd correctly guess that the cat had escaped again, and that she'd gone in search of him. He would also see that her phone and wallet were not in the bag. No doubt he would try to call her, and maybe then he'd see the text. But if the message never reached him, if he never got an answer when he called her, what then? Where would he and Robert even begin to look for her and Hamlet?

Knees suddenly weak, she slid down the length of the door until she landed with a plop on the cold concrete floor. The metal door was equally chilly through the thin cotton of her uniform jacket, and she began to shiver. It was apparent now that Mark had deliberately led her away from the competition floor and taken her here into the recesses of the gymnasium. He'd said from the start that he didn't believe her cat explanation, and she realized that likely was the truth. But why had Mark done this to her? What made him think she was onto him?

And, more important, what was going to happen when he came back?

"He's going to find an empty room, that's what," she said aloud with more determination than she really felt.

The light on her phone dimmed, leaving her in darkness once more. Hurriedly, she pressed the key again. Though the phone's glow did little to dispel the overall darkness, it still gave off a light substantial enough for her to see a couple of feet in front of her. Almost as good as a flashlight, she told herself, taking a bit of comfort in the illumination. She might not be able to call anyone, but at least she wouldn't be totally in the dark as long as she still had battery power.

Rallying, she got to her feet again.

First things first, she told herself. Just because there had been a light switch in the corridor didn't mean there wasn't a second switch inside the room. Mark wouldn't know she had her cell on her, and thus would be counting on her to be stymied by the dark. If she could shed some literal light on the subject, she'd have a better chance of figuring a way out of her trap.

Using her phone as a makeshift torch, she methodically scanned the area around the doorway. She didn't see another switch, just more metal conduits and panels. And her phone light bounced off any number of red or yellow signs bearing such warnings as *Danger* and *High Voltage* along with trusty pictorials of electrical bolts. Not the safest place to be wandering in the dark.

And then, beneath the constant electric hum, she heard something else behind her . . . a soft scrape, as if something was moving stealthily about near the generator.

She froze. *Watch out for the creepy crawlers,* Mark had snidely warned her. She had assumed the words were a juvenile attempt to frighten her, but maybe he hadn't been joking. Rats, giant cockroaches, snakes . . . ghosts. She shivered a little at that last possibility, though the other three were distinctly unpleasant, too.

Steeling herself, she whipped about and pointed her phone in the direction of the sound, using its light to search the shadows. Too high, she realized and lowered her arm. And then she gasped when a pair of unblinking green eyes reflected back at her.

"Hamlet?"

The cat gave a little *meowrmph* by way of answer and trotted to her. With a cry of relief, Darla dropped to her knees and gathered him in her arms, laughing a little as she heard his rumble of a purr.

"You little so-and-so, why did you run off like that?" she scolded him. "Oh, never mind, I'm sure you had a reason, but now I'm the one in trouble. I was stupid enough to think that our creepoid friend Mark Poole was trying to help me find you. Instead, he's pulling some sort of *Silence of the Lambs* thing on me, locking me in here in the dark. We've got to get out of here, before he comes back."

Hamlet gave a sharp *meow* and struggled free of her grasp. But instead of running off again, he gave another *meow*, this one even more insistent, and then trotted a few steps into the shadows.

"What, you want me to follow you?" Suddenly, Darla realized that if Hamlet was in the electrical room with her, there was obviously another way out besides the now-locked door by which she'd entered. Mark had talked about a second door. Maybe he hadn't been lying about that part.

"All right, let's go," she urged the cat. "I'm right behind you."

Hamlet took off at a trot again, his sleek black fur blending so closely with the shadows that she could barely make him out. He whipped around the generator, and Darla did the same, hoping there were no low-lying pipes to conk her in the head. The room was far larger than she'd initially guessed. In fact, as she made her way farther in, she could see a shadowed area to her left that appeared to be a connecting room.

And in front of her lay the Holy Grail: a reflective sign marked *Exit* attached to another door.

"Thank goodness," she whooshed out and rushed toward it. Now, she could hear the cheers drifting from the tournament floor again, sounding muffled but definitely nearby. Maybe she *was* under the bleachers, after all! But, of course, when she tried the doorknob it rattled uselessly under her grasp.

Locked.

Trying not to give in to despair, she held up her phone to get a better look. One difference she immediately noted was that this door was wood. Even better, the knob appeared to be a simple keyed style, and not a deadbolt as on the corridor door. She recalled how Hal had easily kicked open his father's office door a few days earlier. She might not be a black belt, but she had a mean front kick all the same. All she had to do was position herself properly and do the movie cop thing, and she'd be free.

"Stand back, Hamlet," she told him, shining her makeshift flashlight around to make sure he wasn't somewhere he'd be stepped on.

To her surprise, she found him staring with cat-like intensity into the room beside them. His concentration on that opening gave her pause. Maybe somewhere in that space was where he'd found his way in, and he stubbornly wanted to exit the very same way.

"Okay, we'll try it your way," she told him, "but I doubt someone my size could squeeze through wherever you found an opening."

Raising the phone lantern-style again, she made her cautious way into the room. From what little she could see, the space had been designated as a storage area. Movable racks of folding chairs and stacks of collapsible tables had been stashed there, leaving a single narrow aisle along one side. At the end of the room, she could see light seeping in from a knee-high gap.

Maybe this was what she'd seen when she had first tried to crawl under the bleachers, she realized as she headed toward the light.

Hamlet had padded into the room along with her. Now, she almost tripped over him as he halted right in front of her and started sniffing one of the chair racks.

"No time for that, Hamlet," she sternly told him. "We need to get out of here before Mark comes back with lotion or something."

But when she bent to pick him up, he hissed. Then, to Darla's even greater surprise, he began pawing at the metal tubing as if trying to move the rack. Something back there had piqued his feline interest, and he wasn't leaving until he got a better look at it. Sighing, she shoved her phone back into her waistband.

"Fine, you've got two seconds. If there's a rat back there, you're going to be in my bad book even though you did rescue me. Now, scoot, and let me see what you've found."

Though the rack was heavy, she was able to roll it a few feet, enough so that she'd be able to see behind it. Steeling herself for mouse guts or giant leaping spiders, Darla gingerly leaned forward to take a look.

The first thing she spied, however, was a leopard-print pump. Puzzled, she leaned closer. And then, with a reflexive shriek, she jumped back.

For the leopard-print pump was connected to a woman's long, pale leg . . . a leg that belonged to none other than Grace Valentine.

TWENTY-THREE

NOT ANOTHER ONE, WAS DARLA'S FIRST FRANTIC THOUGHT.
Try as she might, however, she couldn't pull her gaze away from the leopard-print shoe, and the woman attached to it.

Grace lay on her side, knees slightly bent, as if she'd simply settled down for a quick nap. Save for her flashy heels, the outfit was—for Grace—almost conservative. In the low light, Darla could see she was wearing a tight black leather skirt topped by a ruffled white blouse that had come untucked on one side. How the woman had come to be hidden behind a stack of metal chairs, Darla could not guess.

All she knew was that it was no accident.

Then she shuddered. Maybe Mark had pulled his *Silence of the Lambs* routine on Grace, too . . . except that Grace hadn't managed to get away before the final scene. And this must have been what Mark had feared that Darla had seen while searching under the bleachers.

Yeee-ow!

Hamlet's sudden, ear-raking cry was like a dash of water to her face. Darla shook herself. What if Grace was simply unconscious? Why was she staring down at the woman as if she were nothing more than a mannequin, instead of trying to help her?

"Grace!" Seizing the chair rack again, Darla yanked the heavy fixture back so that there was room now for her to squeeze behind it. "Grace!" she cried again, dropping to her knees beside the woman and shaking her by the shoulder. "It's me, Darla. Can you hear me?"

When she got no response, Darla carefully rolled the woman onto her back and laid her ear against Grace's ruffled bust. Her chest didn't seem to be moving, but Darla thought she heard a faint heartbeat. Grace was alive, but perhaps just barely.

Snatching her phone from her waistband again, Darla jumped to her feet and pressed the "On" button. The battery icon had dropped to just a sliver, she saw in dismay. But maybe now, away from the electrical interference, she could get a signal and make a final call. She held her breath and waited. And then, three full bars appeared on the tiny screen.

Almost sobbing in relief, she hit redial. She heard the sound of the call connecting, and then heard the words she'd been praying for.

"Where in the hell are you, Red?" Reese demanded over the echoing sound of the cheering spectators. "I just got this crazy text, and—"

"I'm here," she cut him short, half-yelling so that he could be sure to hear her. "I'm somewhere behind the bleachers near where we were sitting, I think. Quick, call an ambulance!"

"An ambulance?" The outraged tone became clipped, professional. "What's wrong? Are you hurt?"

"Not me, Grace Valentine. Hamlet and I found her. I'm not sure what happened, but she's in pretty bad shape."

She heard a quick, muffled conversation on his end, and

then he was back on the line almost instantly. "Ambulance is being called, and we've got a doctor—hell, two or three of them—in the house. Can you find your way back to the floor so you can guide us to where she is?"

"Yes . . . I mean, I guess so, but I don't know if I should leave her. She's not breathing right."

"Then stay on the line and try to guide us your way."

"Okay, but I'm about to run out of—"

The call dropped, abruptly leaving her talking to herself.

"Battery," she finished in dismay, pulling the phone from her ear and watching its small screen go black. Apparently using the cell as a flashlight had drained the battery faster than she'd expected. Sticking the phone back in her waist-band, she leaned over Grace again. The woman was looking even worse now.

"Help! 9-1-1!" Darla frantically screamed, hoping against hope that she might be heard over the din of the competition. If she'd been directly under the seats, chances were her plan would have worked. As it was, a wall separated her from the main gymnasium. With the crowd and the acoustics being what they were, it would be only by the purest chance if someone heard her cries.

She dropped to her knees again beside Grace. There wasn't time to wait on a doctor or an ambulance, wasn't even time to try to crawl her way out through the gap she'd seen a few minutes ago to find help. She had to start artificial respiration on the woman, and now, and pray that Reese found *her*.

"Can't . . . breathe."

The words were so faint that Darla almost didn't hear them, but then she saw Grace stir, eyelids fluttering.

"Grace, it's Darla. What happened?" she demanded, clutching the woman's hand. "Where are you hurt?"

"Shot . . . me."

"Someone shot you?" Darla asked in astonishment. Then, with a gasp, she added, "Do you mean Mark?"

Eyes still closed, Grace mouthed the word, *Yes*. Frantic, Darla searched the woman's body for a wound, but found nothing worse than dirt and grease marring the white blouse.

"Grace, are you sure? I don't see any blood. Where did he shoot you?"

Weakly, Grace raised a shaking hand, fingers clenched as if she held an invisible pencil. "Shot," she whispered again and pressed her fingers to the crook of her opposite elbow before letting her arm fall onto her chest.

It took an instant for the pantomime to register. "Shot? You mean, he gave you a shot of something?"

Then realization dawned, and everything began to fall into place. Darla had heard and seen enough. Botox would explain why Grace couldn't breathe. The toxin would have paralyzed her chest muscles, just as it had with Master Tomlinson. The fact that Grace was still alive, when a much larger man had died, perhaps meant her dose had been far smaller. Maybe she still had a chance, but surely there was no time to spare. She didn't have time to worry about motives and explanations. For the moment, all that mattered was keeping Grace alive.

Swiftly, Darla tilted the woman's head back in preparation to start rescue breaths. But before she could begin, she heard a sound, like a footstep, directly behind her, and smelled a faint whiff of stale cigarette smoke. Barely had the import of that registered when something abruptly tightened like a noose around her throat.

Instinctively, she clutched at the narrow strip of thick cloth that was pressing into her flesh. Had she been standing, she could have tried the self-defense techniques she'd learned: stomp to the instep, elbow to the solar plexus, head into the nose. But in her crouched position, she was at a disadvantage. All she could attempt was the last one.

She whipped her head backward, praying that from that angle she could cause enough pain that she'd be released.

But her attacker must have been expecting such a move, for she instead hit something hard that she assumed must have been a shoulder. The blow made her head spin, and she sagged toward the floor, her fingers loosening their grip on the karate belt around her throat.

"You're not very good at this, are you, Darla?"

Mark Poole sniggered as he tightened the loop just enough to keep her from sliding farther. "I mean, you were smart to figure out how to get out of that room in the dark, but you're pretty bad at self-defense. Now stand up and make yourself useful, unless you want to end up like Master Tomlinson, hanging from a hook somewhere."

The mocking words stirred her to action. Gasping, Darla dizzily got to her feet, still clutching at the belt as he dragged her backward and out of the gap behind the chair rack. As long as she didn't struggle, she could suck in enough air to keep breathing. But keeping still meant that she was pressed into Mark's bony form in a disgustingly intimate fashion.

When I get loose, she frantically vowed, *this creepoid is going to need surgery to reattach his man parts!* But first, she needed to talk him down.

"Mark," she gasped out, "let me go. I need to help Grace. She's still alive."

"Not for long. I think I'll hang her, too, just like they did with Tess in that stupid book."

The nasal voice was harsh and excited as he pulled the belt fractionally tighter around Darla's throat, so that she clawed at it again. "She deserves to be punished. I took care of her boyfriend, first. Now it's her turn. Don't mess this up for me, Darla."

"I-I'm not. Seriously, y-you're really hurting me," she managed. "Let me go so we can talk about this."

"Talk, talk, talk," he echoed in the now familiar mocking falsetto, though to her relief he loosened the belt again. "You women, you think you can get away with anything you want,

just because you're females. Well, I'm tired of your crap! Hers, too," he added, and scuttled forward to give the unconscious woman a vicious kick in the side.

Darla gave a cry of protest that was abruptly cut off when Mark yanked on the belt.

"I should have done that to her when I found out she was pregnant," he told Darla, his words coming in ragged gasps now. "She was supposed to be *my* girlfriend, and then she went and got herself knocked up by . . . by *him*. And I was all nice about it. I told her I forgave her, and that I'd even marry her, but she just laughed at me and went off and had the kid on her own. She was a slut, just like Tess. But I'm no Angel."

"So you killed Master Tomlinson and tried to frame Grace for his murder?" Darla choked out while desperately wondering why in the hell Reese hadn't yet torn the bleachers apart to find her.

She felt rather than saw Mark's nod.

"I figured they'd think she killed him, but the stupid cops never arrested her, not even after I shredded her class registration and left it in the trash for them to find. Since that didn't work, I left that picture in the file drawer for them to find, and they still never went after her. And then she attacked me in class"—his voice now held a note of injured surprise—"and all they did was put her in handcuffs. So it's all up to me now. I have to execute her myself if the police won't."

Darla was stunned. *Execute her?* The man wasn't just off his meds; he was a whole other country away from them! She'd seen for herself that the book club discussion about *Tess of the D'Urbervilles* had put him into a small frenzy. From what Mark was saying, it seemed he'd known Grace before she'd gotten pregnant with Chris, and had had the idea back then that he and Grace were an item . . . more likely on par with how he'd seemingly decided that *Darla* was his good friend simply because she'd unwittingly been playing word games with him in cyberspace. Whatever the situation, it seemed that his literary revenge fantasy had spun out of control.

"Mark," she managed, deciding to humor him, "I don't blame you for being angry, but there are better ways to get back at Grace than this."

"Like what?" he demanded, while from the tournament floor Darla heard a sudden distant cheer from the spectators. Frantically, she struggled to propose an alternative to murder that would satisfy the man, but drew a blank. Mark, meanwhile, abruptly loosened the belt from around her neck and gave her a shove in Grace's direction.

"Yeah, I didn't think you could come up with anything."

Rubbing her throat, she whipped about to face him. He was twisting the belt he'd been choking her with in his hands now. With a shock of recognition she saw in the dim light the five red stripes and tiny embroidered dragon at one end. This, then, was what had happened to the sensei's missing black belt . . . and, as much as any confession, its presence tied Mark to that murder.

The man noticed the direction of her gaze, and he gave a nervous smile.

"Yeah, this makes it all perfect," he declared, giving the belt another twist. "I've got a great plan for this belt, but we've got to hurry. Now, grab Grace and drag her up onto her feet."

Darla hesitated, recalling Master Tomlinson's credo.

Run when you can.

Mark was still blocking her way, but at least now she had some room to move. Assuming, of course, that he hadn't locked the main door after him. If she could fight her way past him and reach the electrical room again, she might be able to escape that way. Or, she could finally try for the gap underneath the bleachers. If she moved fast enough, she might be able to squeeze her way out onto the competition floor. But could she pull that off?

Mark must have seen the fleeting indecision in her face.

He gave an exaggerated sigh and looped Master Tomlinson's belt like a scarf over his neck before reaching inside his gi jacket.

"I didn't want to have to do this, but since you're not cooperating, I don't have a choice," he said, and pulled out a plastic cylinder from which protruded a short, pointed orange cap.

He popped off the cap, and Darla caught her breath as light momentarily glinted from the shining needle he'd exposed. As syringes went, this one wasn't very large. But she could see that the plunger was pulled back on it, meaning it was partially filled. And she had no doubt as to what was in it.

"You know, I always did like you, Darla," he told her. "I thought maybe we could go out on a date or something. We had lots of fun playing word games together. But I don't think you like me that way, after all. So here's the deal. You do what I say, or I'm going to give you a little shot, just like I did Grace. I think I've got just enough left to do the job."

She had no doubt that Mark meant what he'd just said. Slowly, Darla raised her hands in a gesture that was part surrender, part *let's slow down*. For the moment, her only option was to cooperate.

"All right, you're the boss," she agreed, trying to keep her voice from shaking. "I'll try to get Grace on her feet, but she's in pretty bad shape."

"Then carry her," he shot back, a trickle of sweat sliding from beneath the rising sun headband. "And hurry it up. I don't have all day to spend in here."

Seeing no other choice, Darla knelt beside Grace again. Carefully, she pulled off the woman's spike-heeled pumps and put them to one side. Then she manually bent Grace's slim legs, one at a time, and slid each bare foot closer to the woman's body. When she was done, both the woman's knees now pointed skyward.

She spared a quick look at Grace's face. The flesh had

gone frighteningly slack, and her eyelids didn't even twitch as Darla moved her about. She was rapidly dying . . . would likely be dead before Mark could carry out whatever plan he had to re-create Tess's unfortunate end.

Fight if you must.

Swiftly, Darla caught Grace by the shoulders and, with an effort, pulled her limp body into a seated position. Then, maneuvering behind her, Darla slid her forearms beneath Grace's armpits and tried to lift her. To her relief, she heard a faint moan in return. *Hang in there,* she silently implored the woman. With luck, Darla had a few more minutes to somehow get her some help before it really was too late.

But first, she needed to disarm Mark.

"She's heavier than she looks," Darla told him as she continued to struggle with the limp form. "It's a two-person job. I need your help."

"Nice try, Darla, but you're not fooling me. Get her on her feet, or you're going to get a taste of Mr. Needle," he said with a nasal sneer and waved the syringe threateningly.

Darla shot him an outraged look, feeling her redhead's temper soar past her fear for herself. "You're not listening. It's not working," she clipped out. "She's unconscious, so it's like trying to lift a hundred-pound bag of Jell-O. If you want her moved, you have to do it yourself."

So saying, she let Grace slip down again, so that the woman was once again lying on her back.

Mark's eyes bugged behind his glasses, and his face flushed. "Keep trying!"

"No can do, Mark," she replied in a preternaturally calm voice from her spot on the floor beside Grace. "She's too heavy. You've got two choices. Either help me, or move her yourself."

"Yeah, well, I've . . . I've got a third choice," he sputtered. "I'm going to start counting, and if you don't have her moving by the time I reach ten, this"—he waved the syringe again—"is going to take care of things. One, two . . ."

Three, four . . .

Darla silently counted with him, never taking her eyes from him. Her reaction seemed to unnerve him, for his voice grew steadily more high pitched with each number. What he actually planned to do—leap at her with syringe drawn? flee back into the electrical room?—she wasn't certain, but she planned to be ready for him.

Never give up.

"Five, six, seven . . ." he continued to count.

Darla began edging away from Grace's supine form, giving herself space now as she stealthily reached for the only weapon at hand.

Mark's voice grew higher, more agitated. "Eight, nine . . ."

"Ten!" Darla shouted with all her might as she surged to her feet and charged him, one of Grace's spike-heeled pumps gripped in each hand like leopard-print kamas.

Her sudden attack accompanied by the slash of stiletto heels in the direction of his face made him stumble back, mouth and eyes wide with shock. Darla took speedy advantage of his surprise and managed a quick swipe with one shoe, knocking his glasses askew and drawing a streak of blood down one cheek.

The attack ended just as swiftly as it began. Mark shrieked in pain and flung his arms up to protect himself—and managed in the process to plunge the needle of the syringe directly into his lip.

"Aaargh!"

Mark's scream filled the storage room as he frantically plucked the syringe from his face and flung it away. By then, Darla had whipped around him and was well out of range, leopard-print pumps still tightly clutched in both hands and held at the ready in case he attacked. But the fight had already gone out of the man. He sank to his knees, sobbing and clutching his face.

"Dead!" he shrieked . . . or, rather, tried to. The Botox was already taking effect, paralyzing his mouth. He followed that cry with a mumble of sounds that Darla, with an effort, made out to be, "You killed me, you bitch!"

"Never let injustice go unpunished," Darla coolly told him, though she was already beginning to shake in delayed reaction to what had just gone down.

Behind her now, she could hear the sound of scraping wood and metal, heard Reese's voice over the sounds of the tournament calling, "Darla, where are you? Answer me!"

"Here, I'm back here!" she managed to shout as, giving the hysterical Mark wide berth, she hurried to check on Grace. Kneeling beside the still form, she dropped the leopard heels and swiftly began rescue breaths on her, praying that it wasn't too late. And then someone—Reese, she realized—was lifting her away from Grace. He was not alone, she saw. Hank and Hal, along with a security guard and another man wearing a workman's uniform, had crowded into the space. Pushing past them all, a smaller figure in a black gi rushed to take the spot that Darla had vacated at Grace's side.

Then the newcomer looked up from where she knelt to meet Darla's gaze, and Darla saw in surprise that it was Dr. Tomlinson.

"Quickly, tell me what happened," the doctor clipped out before returning her attention to the motionless woman before her.

Darla caught a steadying breath. "She—Grace—said Mark gave her a shot. I think it was Botox, like with Master Tomlinson."

"Botox?" Dr. Tomlinson had been running her hands with expert speed down the injured woman's body. Now, she whipped her gaze back up to meet Darla's. "You're sure?"

Darla nodded. "That's what Mark"—she gestured in the weeping man's direction—"said he injected her with."

The woman turned to Hank. "Pick her up, and carry her to the main door, now. We'll meet the ambulance there. We can't wait on them to roll a gurney in."

"We can go out this way, ma'am," the facilities worker chimed in. He pointed in the direction of the electrical room and then took off at an awkward lope, a key ring as big as his fist jangling from his belt. Hank, with Grace cradled in his arms, rushed after him.

"I'll go find Chris and bring him to the hospital," the doctor told Hal. Then, with a cold look in Mark's direction, she added, "You stay and take care of things here."

Hal nodded, his expression thunderous as he strode over to where Reese already had Mark flipped over on his stomach and was in the process of handcuffing the man.

"You'd probably better take him to the hospital, too," Darla shakily told Reese. "He was trying to threaten me with another syringe of Botox, and when I went after him, he managed to stick himself in the face with it."

"This one?" the security guard asked as, using a handkerchief to preserve any prints, he gingerly held up the syringe that Mark had flung away.

Dr. Tomlinson hurried over to where the guard stood and squinted at the syringe. "Half full," she declared. "Darla, did you happen to see how much was in it to start with?"

"I'm not sure. But I don't think it was all the way. He told me that the vial had been almost empty."

Her expression thunderous as her son's, the woman stalked over to where Mark lay. "Please roll him over, Detective."

When Reese obliged, the doctor knelt beside Mark and swiftly examined his face. Then, with a cold little smile, she said, "It wouldn't hurt to have him looked at, but I think this one is going to live. He'll just be drooling out of one side of his mouth for a couple of months."

"Get up," Reese growled at the man and dragged him upright by one arm. To the security guard, he said, "Follow us out, but block the way until my guys get here."

"Wait," Darla cried, "what about Hamlet? He was the

one who found Grace, but I haven't seen him since Mark attacked me."

"He's right as rain," Reese answered with a quick nod. "In fact, he's the one who led us to you. He was pacing up and down the bleachers trying to get our attention. Robert's babysitting him and the dog now. C'mon, let's get you out of here, too."

A few minutes later, all of them had squeezed through the makeshift opening under the bleachers and were back on the main gymnasium floor again. As Darla blinked against the flood of overhead lights, she noticed that the tournament activity had ceased. The only sound now was the echo of footsteps as a dozen uniformed officers came storming into the gym. Dr. Tomlinson had raced ahead to where Chris was standing, and Darla saw the youth's expression change from shocked to frantic as the woman apparently explained the situation to him before hustling him off the floor, presumably for the ride to the hospital.

Hal, meanwhile, strode in front of their small procession, clearing a path by gesturing competitors and spectators aside. Darla saw Robert and hurried to join him. He was clutching Roma in one arm and petting Hamlet with the other. She grabbed up the unprotesting cat and momentarily buried her face in his soft black fur. As she did so, she could hear Reese reading his prisoner his rights.

"Mark Poole," she heard him address the man in a cold tone, "you are under arrest for the murder of Tom Tomlinson, the kidnapping and attempted murder of Grace Valentine, and the kidnapping of Darla Pettistone."

As Reese went on to recite the familiar Miranda litany, Darla looked up in time to see Hal turn again and stride back to where a handful of the cops now surrounded the man, the rest having dispersed to presumably begin securing the crime scene.

Reese gave a fleeting nod to the officers, who stepped

back so that Hal and Mark were now face to face. The terror on the latter's face was apparent, while the tattooed tiger on Hal's neck quivered as if ready to spring. His beefy hand whipped out, and for an instant Darla thought he was going to flatten the smaller man.

Instead, Hal caught hold of Master Tomlinson's black belt still draped around Mark's neck and whipped it away from him. Then, carefully folding the belt, he took a few steps away from the man and deliberately turned his back on him.

Darla felt a faint rumble move through the silent crowd. And then, almost in unison, the spectators and competitors all followed suit, simultaneously shaming and shunning the man in handcuffs. Darla saw Reese release Mark to the uniformed officers before she and Robert also turned away. And as the police led the handcuffed man through the silent crowd, Darla could have sworn she heard the sensei's voice in her ear saying, *Good job.*

TWENTY-FOUR

"YOU KNOW WHAT REALLY TICKS ME OFF?" JAKE DECLARED as she reached for a second jelly donut. "Not only did I miss seeing you and Robert competing yesterday, but everything was already over by the time I got to the tournament."

Darla and Jake were doing a modified version of Sunday brunch, courtesy of the latter; Darla had volunteered to cook, but Jake had told her not to bother. This meant coffee, juice, and pastries instead of the usual omelets with all the trimmings. Darla had asked Robert to join them, but he'd politely declined, explaining that he'd already told Sylvie from the rescue group that he'd help clean cages at the no-kill shelter that morning before joining Darla at work at noon.

Wiping a bit of wayward jelly from her chin, Jake added, "I mean, if Alex hadn't told me what happened, I never would have known that I basically missed"—she picked up that morning's sports page and pointed to the lead article— "'the most dramatic denouement to any martial arts event since Steve Lopez's 2008 Olympic tae kwon do sudden-death upset.' Quote, unquote."

"Well, I guess I'd have thought it was pretty dramatic if it had happened to someone else," Darla wryly conceded. Then, registering what her friend had said, she added, "Wait, rewind that. Did you say Alex? As in Alex Putin?"

"Yeah, remember, he's one of the tournament's top sponsors each year. He was there yesterday. He even did a Russian Sambo demonstration that morning."

"He did? Was he the guy in the dark blue gi?"

"The same."

"I can't believe I missed another chance to see the man up close and personal," Darla groaned in good-natured dismay. "So how did he react when you told him about finding his mother on the lam in Atlantic City . . . and as a newly-wed, to boot?"

Jake winced.

"Let's just say his reaction could qualify as the *second* most dramatic martial arts denouement since 2008. He had to write a check before he left to cover repairing the window that he broke when he played javelin with somebody's bo . . . you know, those long wooden staffs. But I'm pretty sure by the time the happy couple gets back from their honeymoon, he'll be over the worst of it."

The PI bit into her donut, adding through a mouthful of jelly, "Oh, and I didn't even tell you who the old geezer is. Remember that article in the paper the other week about the city council guy and his father duking it out in public? Turns out they were fighting over Mrs. Putin."

"Seriously?"

Jake nodded. "They both knew her through the same online singles organization, believe it or not. Sonny boy apparently thought he was a shoo-in for the role of the next Mister Mrs. Putin, but it turned out that it was Pop who had all the right moves."

"I don't want to hear anymore," Darla replied, putting her hands over her ears. "I'm just glad you solved your case."

"Yeah, well, I'd say the same about you and Hamlet, but it sounds like the whole thing is a pretty sad mess."

"You can say that again. And don't give me any credit. Hamlet's the only one who solved anything." Darla paused and gave the feline, who was perched in his usual spot on the couch, a fond look. "I was pretty sure up until Mark locked me in that utility room that Dr. Tomlinson was the one who killed her husband. Hamlet knew better. He even gave me the whole *Tess of the d'Urbervilles*'s theory to work with, and then typed out part of Mark's username."

When Jake shot her a disbelieving look at that last, Darla gave her a quick explanation of the cat's walking-on-keyboard technique, and then added, "It wasn't Hamlet's fault I went the wrong way with it."

"So this Mark Poole guy confessed?"

"Well, with his mouth all Botoxed, he hasn't been doing much talking, from what Reese told me last night. But he pretty well confessed to me, plus he had the sensei's missing black belt. Oh, and the cops found another used syringe and an empty vial of Botox in his gear bag. Apparently, he actually stole the vial from Grace in the first place."

This was another bit of interesting information that Reese had shared. Darla hadn't known that Grace was an aesthetician, but she'd not been surprised to learn that the woman was the sort who did carp pedicures and gave cheap if illegal Botox injections in hotel rooms. But she guessed that the woman might give up those events in the future, assuming she recovered from her own Botox experience.

Then Darla shook her head. "I hate to say it, but it almost seems like reading that novel was what set Mark off. I wonder if the reading group had chosen something else—maybe *Pride and Prejudice*—if none of this would have ever happened."

"Don't even go there, kid." Jake set down her donut and gave Darla a stern look. "That's like blaming the victim. It wasn't the book's fault—your buddy Mark had issues. Unless he took himself off to a shrink and got help for his obsession, he was a ticking time bomb. And there's more of them walking around with us than anyone wants to admit. The best we can do is hope someone hears them ticking in time to get them into treatment before they hurt themselves or someone else."

"I guess you're right."

Darla was ready, however, to change the subject to something far less heart wrenching—say, something like gossiping about the burgeoning romance between James and Martha. But before she could steer the conversation that way, Jake's cell phone went off.

"Guess who?" Jake asked with a lift of one brow.

Darla didn't have to guess. She knew the only person on Jake's phone whose ring tone was the Bee Gee's "Stayin' Alive" was Reese.

"Uh, huh. Yeah. Uh, huh," was Jake's end of the conversation before she handed the phone to Darla. "He actually wanted to talk to you," she explained, "but your phone kept going straight to voice mail."

Darla took the phone, not sure what to expect. She'd already given Reese her statement yesterday and preferred not to rehash it all again. Though, on the bright side, she had glowed more than a little when he'd praised her counterassault on Mark.

Good job, Red, he had told her. *Not many people would have the presence of mind to go all kung fu with a pair of ladies' shoes. Looks like you've got your mojo back.*

And so she had, she realized. Despite the events of the previous day, she had slept a contentedly dreamless sleep that night and awakened more refreshed than she had been in weeks.

And Hamlet seemingly had *his* mojo back, too. In fact,

the feline had spent much of the morning grumping about before complaining vocally about the amount of water in his bowl (not enough) and the extra blanket (too scratchy) that Darla accidentally had left on the sofa back. Apparently, solving Master Tomlinson's murder and finding Grace before she met a similar fate—not to mention leading Reese to where Darla had been trapped behind the bleachers—had proved the official atonement that Brody had said was Hamlet's goal. She'd have to give the cat whisperer, er, feline behavioral empath, a call later that day and let him know Hamlet was officially back to his ornery self again.

"Hi," she said into the cell. "Sorry, after my phone died yesterday I forgot to charge it back up again."

"That's okay, Red. And, actually, I'm not calling for me," he admitted. "I'm bringing Dr. Tomlinson down to the precinct to give a formal statement, and she wanted to know if I could bring her by to talk to you for a minute."

"Uh, sure. How long until you get here?"

"Depending on how long it takes for you to buzz us in, I'd say about thirty seconds."

Darla hung up the phone and handed it back to Jake. "Reese and Dr. Tomlinson are here," she explained as she hit the buzzer. "Feel free to stick around. I'm not sure why she's here, and I think I might need the moral support."

"Consider yourself supported, kid," Jake cheerfully replied, helping herself to donut number three.

Darla, meanwhile, opened the door and waited while Reese and the doctor made their way up the two flights. But as the pair walked in, Darla saw that she actually had three visitors. Roma the Italian greyhound, wearing her familiar mauve sweater, had come along for the ride. The little dog let out an excited yap, and Darla was immediately grateful that Robert had gone off with Sylvie that morning instead of having breakfast with her and Jake.

"Ms. Pettistone, very nice to see you again," Dr. Tomlinson said, coolly offering her hand. No matter that the woman had seen her husband's killer apprehended in dramatic fashion only a day before, and attended to a critically injured patient for however many hours after that. The woman was dressed, as usual, as if she had stepped from the pages of a high-end magazine: black skirted suit, blown-out hair, and makeup with that airbrushed look that Darla could never duplicate on her own.

"Thank you for agreeing to meet with me on such short notice," she added, her words jogging Darla to her hostessing obligations.

"Not at all, and please have a seat. Oh, and this is my friend, Jake Martelli," she added. "Jake, Dr. Jan Tomlinson."

Jake nodded and gave a friendly wave. "We're having donuts," she explained unnecessarily, considering the open box before her. "Care to join us?"

The doctor gave Darla a hesitant look and then smiled just a little. "Actually, that sounds rather nice. I haven't eaten donuts in years."

A few moments later, seated at the dining table with Roma on her lap, the doctor nibbled on a plain glazed donut. Reese settled for coffee only, which he tactfully took with him to the sofa. Hamlet apparently decided to wash his paws of all of them, for he slipped off the sofa back and stalked toward the kitchen.

Darla stirred her own coffee and awkwardly waited for the woman to say something. When she did not, Darla ventured, "I hope Grace is doing better."

"We are guardedly optimistic for her full recovery," Dr. Tomlinson assured her. "It appears that her dose was only a fraction of what my husband was given, so the toxin didn't kill her outright. But if you hadn't found her when you did, there's a good chance that she wouldn't have survived."

And at that, the woman abruptly broke down into a flurry of sobs that startled Darla, and sent her rushing for a box of tissues, while Jake reached for donut number four. Reese did his part by holding on to Roma while the doctor attempted to compose herself. Finally, the woman sat back against her chair and took a calming sip of coffee.

"I am so sorry," she said, dabbing at her eyes with another tissue and looking a bit surprised at what had just happened. Her makeup, however, had remained flawless, much to Darla's unwilling admiration. "As you might guess, this has been a trying week, and tomorrow we'll be holding the memorial service for Tom. It's for family and close friends only. I thought perhaps that you and that young man, Robert, would like to attend."

"We'd be honored," Darla assured the woman.

Dr. Tomlinson smiled. "It's at two p.m. at the dojo. He wanted to be cremated and then put into his trophy case with all the other awards, so that is what we will do."

"Unusual," Darla said, "but I think that's very appropriate."

"Well, I'm still not quite sure I approve, but it's what Tom wanted." And then she shook her head. "Poor Grace. She'll be heartbroken to miss the service, but Chris has promised to make a little video for her so she can see it later."

"That's, uh, nice," Darla managed, confused. While it was commendable that Dr. Tomlinson could be charitable to the woman who'd borne her husband's illegitimate child, this seemed taking tolerance to extremes.

"That reminds me, Dr. Tomlinson," Reese spoke up from his post in the living room. Leaving Roma curled up on Darla's sofa, snoozing away, he set down his coffee and reached into his jacket. "You'll remember we had a warrant to search your husband's office. We found a photo in his file cabinet that we thought might be evidence, but we've already made a copy to use in our case against Mr. Poole. I'm sure you'll want it back."

As he handed the photo to the woman, Darla caught a glimpse of the image and bit back a gasp. It was the incriminating photo of the sensei and Grace together! How could Reese be so insensitive? Not only was he giving a recent widow a picture of her dead husband and his mistress, but said mistress in that photo was obviously within weeks of giving birth.

Darla exchanged quick looks with Jake. She, too, had apparently recognized the photo, if only from Darla's description, for her black brows rose sky high in disbelief. But all Darla could do short of snatching the picture from Reese's hand was to shoot him a warning look.

Unfortunately, it was too late. Dr. Tomlinson had already accepted the snapshot from him and was curiously studying it.

"I can't believe it," she exclaimed. "You found this in his file cabinet?"

Reese nodded, and now Darla's warning look became an all out red alert. *Lie! Make up something!* But to Darla's shock, the doctor burst into a merry little laugh.

"I wondered what had happened to this picture. I thought it was lost years ago!"

"Actually, Ms. Valentine had the photo in her possession. From her statement, she suspected that someone had broken into her house a few weeks ago while she was at work, and she was pretty sure it was Mr. Poole. That's what they were arguing about at the dojo the other day. Anyhow, our guess at this point is that Mr. Poole got hold of the picture at the same time he stole the Botox from her. He put it in Mr. Tomlinson's file cabinet, thinking it would throw suspicion on her for the sensei's murder."

"What an odd thing for him to do. Why would anyone think this snapshot would be a reason for Grace to kill Tom?" Dr. Tomlinson said.

"I'm sure whatever shrink the court appoints to him will come up with an answer," Reese said, not bothering to hide his disgust.

The woman nodded. "As a board-certified plastic surgeon, diagnosing mental illness is rather beyond my scope of expertise, but I do try to keep up with all the journals. In my highly unofficial opinion, Mark Poole is displaying symptoms of borderline personality disorder."

"Yeah, that's it!" Jake spoke up with a snap of sugar-covered fingers. "He's got the symptoms in spades. The mood swings, the physical aggression, the self-destructive behavior, and unrealistic expectations in relationships, like putting people up on pedestals and then hating them when they fall. Textbook case, if you ask me."

When the rest of them stared at her, she shrugged. "What? I read an article on BDP in *Cosmo* while I was getting my carp pedicure last week."

The doctor sighed. "It certainly would explain why Mark went after Tom as well as Grace. Hank and Hal told me once that Mark seemed to have a serious case of hero-worship for Tom. Obviously the photo of him and Grace led him to believe that his hero was sadly mortal."

Though that still didn't answer another question that was foremost in Darla's mind at the moment: Why did Dr. Tomlinson want to keep a picture of the sensei and Grace after all that had happened? Darla made plans to pin down Reese about this subject later as the detective told her, "Thanks for the hospitality, Darla, but Dr. Tomlinson and I need to head out now."

"Wait!"

The exclamation came from Jake, who had lapsed back into silence after her brief turn in the shrink's chair. But now, perhaps fueled by four donuts' worth of sugar, she forged on. "Since Darla is a nice Texas girl and too polite to ask, I will: Why in the world would you want to keep a picture of your husband and his pregnant mistress?"

"His *what*?" The doctor stared openmouthed at her for a moment, only to break into another merry laugh. "Oh, my dear, that is too funny," she went on when she finally stopped laughing. "Grace was never Tom's *mistress*. She was just an unfortunate young woman whom we took into our home when she had nowhere to go. She'd been a student at the dojo and looked up to Tom as a second father, so when her family refused to help her when she got pregnant, we helped her get back on her feet. Tom treated her like a daughter, as did I. In fact, I was the one who took that picture of them together. I always regretted not keeping a copy for myself."

Then, with a genteel snort, she added, "And Chris is certainly not Tom's child, though Tom did think of him as a grandson." Her smile grew mistier. "You have to understand, family was everything to Tom. That's why he insisted on adopting my boys, since their biological father was dead. And he considered all his students to be his family. Nothing gave him greater happiness than their successes. Grace was quite the project for him, and she did not always make the right choices. But he never gave up on her. Given the chance, I'm afraid he would have done the same thing again here, no matter that in the end it turned out badly for him."

She glanced over at Reese and then returned her attention back to Jake and Darla.

"I already told Detective Reese that Tom suspected something wasn't right about the way Mark Poole acted around Grace a few weeks before he"—she paused, seemingly to control herself—"well, a few weeks ago, but Grace claimed everything was fine. And so Tom gave the man the benefit of the doubt. Unfortunately, we had no clue that Grace knew Mark from back in her high school days, and that this whole obsession had started long ago. Why she didn't tell us what was happening, I'll never understand, but I suppose she wanted to prove she was capable of handling issues on her own. She wanted Tom to be proud of her."

She smiled a little and then added, "So do not doubt that, for all his flaws—and he did have his share—Tom was a very good man. And *I* was proud of *him*."

Then, briskly, the doctor got to her feet. "As Detective Reese said, we must be going. Oh, but I do have one last favor to request." She walked over to the couch where Roma napped and put a neatly manicured hand upon the dog's narrow head.

"Tom loved this little creature dearly, but I'm afraid she requires far more attention than I can give her. Even though I'm in private practice, my hours can be long. And, I must admit, I've never been much for pets. I was hoping, Darla, that you might know someone—perhaps a young man?— who could give Roma a good home for me."

Darla stared at her in surprise. First, the icy doctor turned out to do charity work for children; then she gave back the dog she had commandeered a few days earlier? Apparently, Mary Ann's lecture about loss a few days earlier had been spot on, Darla thought in no little shame. No matter, it was a welcome announcement, indeed!

Darla gave her a delighted smile. "As a matter of fact, I think I do know just the right person."

The woman reached into her handbag, withdrawing a sheaf of papers. "Then why don't I leave Roma here with you? It so happens I'm listed on these papers as her owner, so I've already signed in the appropriate spaces. The dog will be Robert's, free and clear. And he is welcome to bring her to the service tomorrow, if he likes."

Snapping her handbag closed, she gave Reese an imperious nod and headed out the door. With a final grin for Darla and Jake, the detective followed after her.

"Well, that was heartwarming," Jake said as the door closed behind them. To Darla's surprise, she saw her friend brush away an actual tear. Then, with a glance at the sleeping pup, the PI added, "How do you think Hamlet is going to react to his new neighbor?"

"Actually, as long as Roma shows him the proper respect, they seem to get along fine," Darla told her with a shrug. "Which reminds me, I still need to call Brody and let him know that Hamlet is cured. He's supposed to do a follow-up visit, so he might as well—"

Darla's front door buzzer sounded abruptly, making her jump and cutting short her suggestion that she invite the feline behavioral empath to drop by that afternoon. "I wonder if Reese left something behind," she exclaimed as she hurried over to the intercom. Pressing the button, she said, "Hello?"

"Darla?" came a tinny voice that sounded vaguely familiar. "It's, uh, Brody. The feline behavioral empath. I believe you feel that Hamlet is now cured?"

She and Jake exchanged looks. Had Brody extended his empathic talents to the human species, as well? Then, recalling that the man was standing out there in the cold, doubtless wearing only the usual thin denim jacket, she hurriedly pressed the button again. "Brody, let me buzz you in so we can chat where it's warm," she urged him and hit the buzzer.

"Oh, no need," the man replied, and she pictured his gentle smile. "Hamlet has let me know that he has regained what he lost, and that he now feels worthy again of his role as your store mascot. I simply wanted to stop by and make certain that you knew that."

"I do. In fact, I think Hamlet and I both are fine now," Darla told him. Though how much of their recovery was attributable to Brody's mind-meld therapy, she wasn't certain.

"I shall consider my work here done, then. Good-bye, Darla. Perhaps we'll meet again down the road."

"Uh, okay," she answered, feeling surprisingly sad to say good-bye to this strange young man. "I'll tell Hamlet you said good-bye, too."

"No need," he repeated. "We've already said our farewells."

Darla released the button and rushed over to the window to see Brody's thin form retreating down the sidewalk. But rather than continue walking, he paused at the curb, and a sleek white limo pulled up alongside him.

Limo? Darla stared in surprise as Brody hopped in—next to the driver, rather than in the back. Apparently, what the man didn't spend on his wardrobe, he spent on his wheels, she thought as she watched the car slip away into traffic.

"Doo-doo-DOO-doo. Doo-doo-DOO-doo."

This approximation of the *Twilight Zone* theme came from Jake standing behind her. Darla smiled and shook her head. "I'm not even going to try to wrap my head around this one. But I can't wait for Robert to get back and see Roma is home for good. And now that Hamlet knows how to walk on a harness, maybe Robert can take them out together every day—"

"Speaking of which," Jake interrupted her with a devious little grin, "do you know that you're already at over ten thousand hits?"

"What in the world are you talking about?"

"Your and Hamlet's YouTube video. They call it 'The Karate Cat.'"

Darla stared at her in shock. "Please tell me you're joking."

"Nope. Scout's honor." She held up two fingers, and then three, and then finally threw up her hands. "Whatever. Anyhow, it looks like you and Hamlet are poised to go viral."

"Darn that Robert, I told him I'd kill him if he posted that!" Darla exclaimed, only to see Jake shaking her head.

"Sorry, kid, it wasn't Robert. I counted at least fourteen different versions last night—eight of them set to music, by the way—and each one was uploaded by a different user. Face it, you and Hamlet are famous."

Hamlet chose that moment to stalk back into the room again. He leaped onto the back of the sofa, only to narrow his eyes at the small dog sleeping in his domain.

Darla waited for the hiss and the growl, but to her surprise the feline blinked, and then settled himself comfortably in his usual spot.

"See," Jake pointed out, "even Hamlet knows he has fans now, and a reputation to uphold. Next thing you know, he'll be wearing wraparound shades and signing paw-tographs."

"Sure, and we'll send him on tour, too," Darla replied, beginning to see the humor—and the possibilities—in the situation. "Hamlet, what do you say? You feel like hitting a few conventions this spring?"

Hamlet opened one green eye again, and Darla didn't have to be Brody the Cat Whisperer to read his mind.

"Start making reservations, Jake," Darla told her friend. "It looks like we're going on a road trip."

From *New York Times* Bestselling Author

Jenn McKinlay

CLOCHE AND DAGGER

THE FIRST IN THE BRAND-NEW HAT SHOP MYSTERIES

Not only is Scarlett Parker's love life in the loo—as her British cousin Vivian Tremont would say—it's also gone viral with an embarrassing video. So when Viv suggests Scarlett leave Florida to lay low in London, she hops on the next plane across the pond to work at Viv's ladies' hat shop, Mim's Whims, and forget her troubles.

But a few surprises await Scarlett in London. First, she is met at the airport not by Viv, but by her handsome business manager, Harrison Wentworth. Second, Viv seems to be missing. No one is too concerned about it until one of her posh clients is found dead wearing the cloche hat Viv made for her—and nothing else. Is Scarlett's cousin in trouble? Or is she in hiding?

"A delightful new heroine!"
—Deborah Crombie, *New York Times* bestselling author

jennmckinlay.com
facebook.com/TheCrimeSceneBooks
penguin.com

M1340T0613

Betty Hechtman

BEHIND THE SEAMS

The crochet group's informal leader, actress CeeCee Collins, has a movie out, and thanks to the building Oscar buzz, she's scheduled to appear o̶... ̶n show. Molly and the g̶... but when one of the H̶... thanks to her wacky b̶... with her.

It's no fun being stuck ̶... producer who remove̶... poisoned sweetener, th̶... worse, CeeCee's niece ̶... sistant on the show—is the one who handed the producer the spiked drink.

As rumors swell, Molly and the Hookers must set aside their crochet projects to clear Nell's name. Because unless they weave together the clues before the killer strikes again, someone else will become the next Hollywood headline . . .

PRAISE FOR THE CROCHET MYSTERIES

"Who can resist a sleuth named Pink, a slew of interesting minor characters and a fun fringe-of-Hollywood setting?"   —Monica Ferris, *USA Today* bestselling author

penguin.com